PHARIM WAR

VOLUME ONE

By Gama Ray Martinez

Oracles of Kurnugi

Delphi

Stepmother's Mirror

Mimir's Well

Pharim War

Shadowguard

Veilspeaker

Beastwalker

Lightgiver

Darkmask

Lifebringer

Shadeslayer

Nylean Chronicles

Under the Moon

Child of the Wilde

Under the Sun

Child of the Stars

*Child of the Moon**

Goblin Star

Nova Dragon

Runestone Fleet

* *Forthcoming*

PHARIM WAR

VOLUME ONE

GAMA RAY MARTINEZ

Pharim War is a work of fiction. All incidents and dialog, and all characters are products of the author's imagination and any resemblance to actual events or locales or persons, living or dead, is entirely coincidental.

ISBN: 1-944091-12-2

ISBN-13: 978-1-944091-12-5

CONTENTS

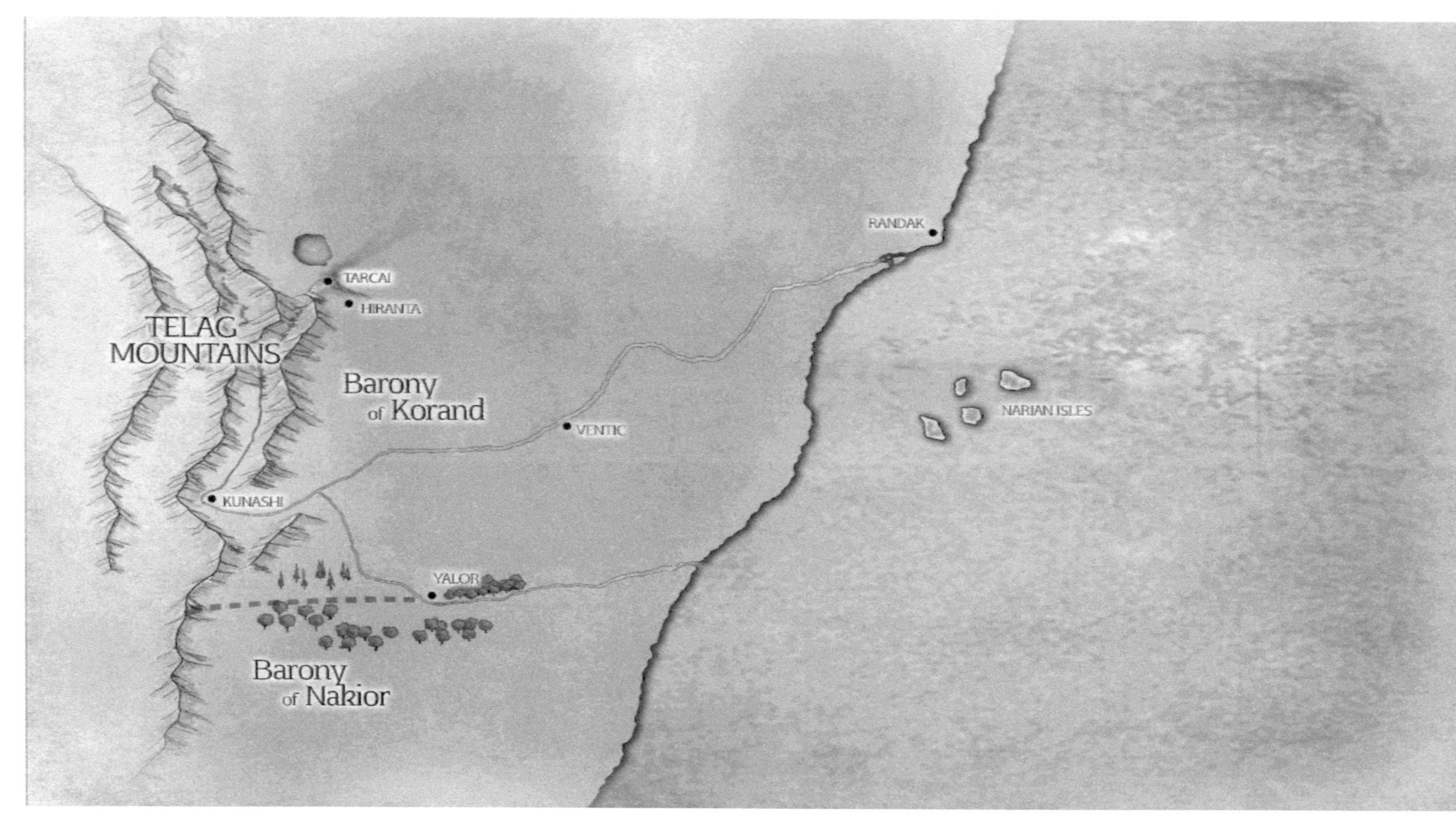
TELAG MOUNTAINS
TARCAI
HIRANTA
RANDAK
Barony of Korand
VENTIC
NARIAN ISLES
KUNASHI
YALOR
Barony of Nakior

SHADOWGUARD

CHAPTER 1

Jez yelped as the azure flames washed over the half-clothed figure. For a moment, a thick cloud of smoke flooded the lower level of the arena. The upper levels, the ones inhabited by those who couldn't afford premium seats, erupted in cheers. The acrid scent almost made Jez gag, but a second later, wind stirred and dispersed the smoke. One of the combatants stood with her hands outstretched, her eyes glowing blue, but the other was surrounded by a bubble of scarlet energy, incandescent and completely opaque. The packed sand around the sphere cooled, forming shards of glass.

The bubble flickered and vanished, revealing a warrior who was already running. He leapt through the air, and for the first time, Jez noticed a youthful face on the fighter. In spite of a height of nearly seven feet, the gladiator couldn't be more than sixteen years old. His opponent, a petite woman with a mousy face, lifted her hand and the sky rumbled. Dark clouds materialized out of nowhere and spewed a bolt of lightning. Electricity filled the air and made the hairs on the back of Jez's arms stand on end. The warrior tried to dodge, but he couldn't move fast enough, and a bolt struck his right shoulder, sending him to the ground. The smell of ozone permeated the air, mixing with the acrid scent of burning hair. The crowd erupted in cheers, half chanting Criera's name, and half cheering for her opponent, the giant Osmund.

Jez's heart pounded so hard that he felt like it would beat out of his chest as Osmund picked himself off the ground. The crowd went silent. He'd had hair a second ago, but it had been burned away. His clothes had been reduced to charred cloth and barely served to preserve modesty. Osmund seemed relatively unharmed, though. He stood up and took a step toward Criera. Her eyes widened and she threw her hands toward her opponent. A beam of emerald energy shot forward. Osmund lifted his arm and caught it in his right hand. White light surrounded it and grew so bright Jez had to turn away. The image of the warrior was burned into his sight, and it took several seconds to fade. By then, the crowd cheered so loud that they drowned out the sounds of the battle. When Jez's vision cleared, Osmund's hand had closed around Criera's throat.

"Disgraceful," Baron Dusan spat.

"My Lord?" Jez asked, tearing his eyes away from the battle.

Dusan's steel gray eyes were as cold as ice. He ran his fingers through his salt and pepper beard. He looked down his nose at the battle ground. "In a proper duel, Jezreel, the combatants never lay a hand on each other. It's supposed to be an elegant dance of power." He waved his hand at the pair. "That brute should be thrown from the arena."

Judging by the cheers of the crowd, most people didn't agree, but Jez simply smiled. He turned his attention back to the combat. Criera's eyes were wide with fear. She was clawing at Osmund's arm, but the larger warrior seemed not to notice. Sweat gleamed on Osmund's forehead. No, it wasn't sweat. Osmund's forehead was glowing. In fact, his entire body had begun emitting light and was growing steadily brighter. Some of the cheering died and whispers rippled through the crowd. Criera was already beaten. There was no need for him to summon more power. A man in the scarlet robes of an arena judge stepped onto the battle ground. He raised a hand in a gesture that would've ended the duel, but just before he completed it, Osmund dropped his opponent, a look of panic on his face. His glow vanished. As soon as Criera's feet hit the ground, she dove at him, sending both of them crashing to the ground.

The crowd erupted again. Criera's hands glowed with power, but Osmund didn't seem to be fighting at all. He just stood there. Her fist connected with his chin so hard that even from twenty feet away, Jez felt the air vibrating with the force of the blow. It lifted Osmund off the ground and sent him up at least a dozen feet before he came crashing back down. He groaned and tried to get up, but his arms gave out, and he fell again. This time, he didn't move. The judge stepped forward and examined the fallen boy. Jez held his breath. If the judge placed a black cloth over the fighter's face, it would mean he was dead. From what Jez had heard, it did happen sometimes, though rarely. It would be a dark way to end the first duel he'd ever seen. Fortunately, the judge simply stood up and raised a hand. He bowed in Criera's direction, declaring her the winner. The crowd cheered, but Baron Dusan just gave a slow clap. Some of those seated nearby gave Dusan sidelong glances and stopped cheering. They looked uneasy, but the baron seemed not to notice. Jez wanted to ask him what was wrong, but the people around them were cheering too loud for them to have any meaningful conversation.

It was several minutes before they were able to get out of the arena. Dusan's guards, led by a bear of a man named Jabur, formed a circle around them that kept the greater part of the crowd away. Every once in a while, though, Dusan would signal, and they would allow a wealthy merchant or minor noble into their perimeter to speak to the baron. These exchanges lasted only a few minutes, but there were a lot of them, and they added up. With the late afternoon sun beating down on

Jez, he just wished they would hurry. The formal clothes the baron had provided looked nice, but they were hot, and Jez was sweating profusely. On the streets outside, coins changed hands and people paid off the bets they'd made. Baron Dusan hadn't allowed Jez to place a wager, saying a boy of thirteen was too young to gamble. Jez was grateful for that. Like many people, he hadn't thought Criera had stood much of a chance against the larger and more powerful Osmund, so Jez would've lost everything he'd bet.

"Thank you for bringing me here," Jez said once they'd finally boarded their carriage. "I'd never seen a battlemage duel. My father never brought me to one."

Dusan grunted. "Well, I doubt your father could afford to bring you here if he saved for a year. What have you learned?"

Jez started to speak, but almost bit his tongue as the carriage started bouncing along. Even after six months, he still wasn't used to how it jostled him about.

"They are very brave," he said finally.

Dusan snorted. "What bravery does it take to fight in such battles? That boy attends the Carceri Academy, and he was a disgrace. They should kick him out for his performance."

"Just because he lost?"

"Because of how he fought," Dusan said. "This is no tavern brawl. When I attended, the Academy meant something. Only the best of society could attend, none of this lower tier nonsense. The chancellor in my day would turn over in his grave if he knew the depths to which this new breed has fallen."

Jez shifted in his chair, trying to find a comfortable position, but it was no use. He'd wanted to tell the baron that the seats were too hard, but since the nobleman had been kind enough to take Jez on as a ward, he never felt right complaining.

"I was thinking about studying battle magic at the Academy."

Some of the color drained from Dusan's face, but it only lasted a second. With visible effort, the baron forced himself to calm down. He straightened his back and looked down his nose at Jez the same way a hawk might look at a mouse. "Absolutely not."

"But…"

"Battle magic is for the lower class, soldiers and such. As my ward you'll be representing me, and I won't have my name sullied by your studying of baser subjects." Jez let out a breath and nodded. Dusan's expression softened. "Look, Jezreel, I don't mean to be harsh, but you're a member of my household now. That has a lot of privileges, but it also comes with responsibilities." Jez sighed and nodded, and the baron let out a long breath. "Would you like it if I took you to see your father?"

"Oh yes, my lord," he said. "If that's ok, I mean."

Dusan raised an eyebrow. "How many times do I have to tell you? Call me Dusan, in private, anyway." Jez nodded and Dusan banged his cane on the roof of the carriage. The wooden slot slid open, and a man with a pointed nose looked inside.

"Take us to Goodman Bartin's home," Dusan said. "Be quick about it."

Jez uttered a thanks, but Dusan waved it aside. They talked idly of what Jez could expect at the Carceri Academy, the premier center of learning in the kingdom of Ashtar. Dusan had attended nearly fifty years before, and he didn't care for some of the changes the current chancellor, a healer named Balud, was making. A quarter hour later, the carriage came to a stop. The smell of salt water hung thick in the air along with the pronounced scent of fish. Dusan wrinkled his nose and nodded at Jez, who slipped out of the carriage.

The sun was nearing the western horizon when he stepped onto the street. He'd barely taken a few steps when the driver urged the horses forward and the carriage disappeared around a corner, kicking up dust as it moved. Jez stared at the plain wooden door of the small house. A plank with a blue starfish painted on it hung over the door, the same symbol his father had painted on his fishing boat. The building was a shack compared to the opulent manor he'd lived in since the baron had taken him as a ward. Jez still didn't know why that had happened. King Haziel had named Dusan as the Baron of Korand six months before. Immediately, Dusan had ordered all the boys in Randak to be brought before him, and for reasons no one could identify, he'd taken on Jez as a ward. Jez had felt out of place ever since. There were plenty of other, higher born boys in town who could benefit the baron's patronage and who wouldn't be a stranger to how highborn boys were supposed to behave. Even so, Jez's father had said to not examine the gift too closely. It would open doors for Jez that would've otherwise remain closed and would provide opportunities neither one of them had ever imagined. Still, they hadn't expected how much it would separate them. They only had the opportunity to visit a handful of times in the past six months. Jez took a deep breath and knocked on the door of the father he had not seen in over a month.

CHAPTER 2

The door creaked open, revealing a man with thin wispy hair. He claimed his hair had been as black as Jez's once, and Jez couldn't help but wonder if his would end up as gray as his father's. Bartin had the sunbaked skin of someone who'd spent his life outdoors, and his weathered face had endured both sun and storm. The smell of fish and saltwater hung heavily around him. For a second, confusion twisted his features. Then, his face lit up and he threw his arms around Jez, who practically fell into his embrace.

"Jez." Jez could practically hear the tears in that voice. "It's so good to see you."

A lump formed in Jez's throat and for a moment, he was unable to speak. When he finally did find his words, his voice cracked. "I'm glad to be here, father."

"Come in, please. It's a cool evening, and I don't want you catching a chill."

In fact, the evening was rather warm, but Jez didn't contradict him. His father scurried out of the doorway. The house had one main room with a stone hearth in the center. A net hung on the wall alongside a pair of fishing lines. Wooden planks groaned underfoot as Jez stepped inside, and he found himself relaxing at the familiar sound. A cauldron boiled on the fire, giving off the aroma fish stew. Jez's mouth watered. It had been too long. Baron Dusan provided him with elaborate meals from all over the world, but none of them could compare with his father's fish stew. None of them tasted so much like home. As he followed his father to the table on the other side of the room, he noticed Bartin favored his left leg.

"What happened?"

For a moment, confusion dance across his father's face, but Jez looked at Bartin's legs and his father shrugged. "This? It's nothing. I had a good catch and had just sold it to the fishmongers. I had a purse full of silver and my head held high. Too high, actually. I tripped over a twice cursed cat and fell on my rump. I think the entire market laughed at me." He grinned. "Can't say that I blame them, but by the seven, did that hurt. Let that go to show you. Don't get too puffed up with pride or the Creator will find a way to bring you down again."

He motioned to the table sitting against one wall. Wrapped bundles of what was probably dried fish sat on one end. Jez took one of the two seats, and his father sat across the table from him.

"Have you eaten?"

Jez's mouth watered, but he nodded. Unfortunately, his stomach betrayed him with a growl. His father wrinkled his brow.

"You weren't expecting me," Jez said. "You only prepared enough for one."

"Bah," his father said, waving off his concern.

He stood up and went outside. He came back a few minutes later with a cod that he'd doubtlessly hung up to dry, though the process hadn't finished yet. It would be fresher than the wrapped bundles on the table. He placed it on a stone slab on top of the hearth. With the practiced hand of one who had done it more times that he could count, Bartin reduced the fish to small pieces which he set by the fire while he cut up vegetables. Once that was done, he put everything into the pot and dipped his hands into a bucket of water to wash off. He shook them dry before going back to join Jez.

"There," he said. "It should be ready in about an hour."

"Baron Dusan's chef says you can't add to a dish while it's cooking."

His father snorted. "Maybe he can't. So tell me. What brings you here tonight?"

"I'm leaving for the Academy tomorrow," Jez said. "I wanted to see you before I left. Baron Dusan dropped me off on the way home from the duel."

"The duel?" his father asked. "You mean that spectacle they put on in the arena? A twelve-year-old boy is too young to be watching such things. It'll put ideas into your head."

Jez rolled his eyes. "I'll be thirteen next month, father. Anyway, Baron Dusan doesn't want me to use battle magic either."

"Maybe if the nobility would concern themselves with things that actually matter, conditions might improve. Did you hear about Kashur?"

"No." Jez leaned forward. Kashur lived next door and Jez had grown up with him. They'd often played before the baron had taken him as a ward.

"He fell asleep two days ago and hasn't woken up. If something isn't done, we'll have a full scale epidemic on our hands."

Jez shook his head. "Father, I've heard of this sleeping sickness. The healers are working on a cure. Baron Dusan says the lower class is making too much of it. It's not like anyone has actually died of it."

Too late, Jez realized his mistake and wished he could take back those words. A hurt look flashed across his father's face, but he banished it with obvious effort.

"I'm sorry," his father said. "I didn't mean to bother you with the concerns of the common man."

"Father, that's not what I meant."

"Yes, I'm sure it's not. Just remember what I said about getting too puffed up with pride."

"Father…"

"Forget about it. Tell me about your life in the past couple of months. I hope you haven't been so caught up in learning how to dress like a peacock that you've forgotten all the useful things I've taught you."

Jez looked down at the silk and velvet doublet he wore and felt his face heat up. The jacket was bright red with gold lining. Jeweled buttons ran down the center, and a ruby pin in the shape of a closed fist, Master Dusan's sigil, sat on the left side of his chest. He wished he'd had the opportunity to change before coming here.

"I don't dress like this every day," he said, his voice a little pained. "It was a gift from Baron Dusan. He wanted me to dress up for the duel."

His father snorted. "Dressing up to see two men throw magic at each other."

"One was a woman."

His father rolled his eyes and threw his hands in the air. "Oh, if one was a woman, that makes it much better. If you don't be careful, you'll become one of them, ready to trade your soul for money and power." He looked at Jez and his face softened. "I'm sorry boy. I've tried to provide what I could for you. It just bothers me that Dusan swoops in here and takes you from me, and without even trying, he gives you all the things I never could."

"I didn't want to go with him," Jez reminded him. "You told me to."

He smiled, though it was obviously forced. "That I did. I don't truly hold anything against the man. I'm glad for all he's provided you with, and I know you'll go far with it. Just don't forget about your old father when you go out into the world."

"I won't. I promise."

They talked of their memories together, avoiding any mention of the baron. Minutes flew by, and eventually, Bartin got up and served Jez soup in a wooden bowl. It tasted as wondrous as Jez remembered. The fish almost seemed to melt in his mouth, and it was spiced just right, adding the slightest bit of zest to the cod without covering the flavor. He'd tried to get Dusan's cook to make him soup like this, and while it never tasted bad, the attempts had never measured up to his father's cooking. After dinner, they spoke for another half hour. The fire in the hearth had been reduced to embers when a loud knock came at the door. His father opened it and a large man in a chain shirt stood in the doorway. He wore a tabard with a closed fist on it. Bartin's eyes flickered to the heavy dagger at his belt, and his eyes narrowed on the closed fist sigil on the hilt.

"Hello Jabur," Jez said. "It's time to go?"

The burly man smiled at Jez's father before nodding. Jez embraced his father before following Jabur back out to the carriage. The full moon had just started to rise and looked like it was emerging from the sea. Jez wondered how long it would be before he saw his father again. As they started down the road, Jez resisted the urge to look back. He worried his father would see the tears in his eyes.

CHAPTER 3

"Will Baron Dusan be joining us?" Jez asked as he popped a slice of apple into his mouth.

It seemed like his voice should echo in the cavernous room, but it didn't. He always felt a little ridiculous eating alone here, but he'd never had the nerve to ask to be served somewhere else. The long table could seat a dozen people. It often did at the dinners the baron hosted, but in the mornings it was nearly always deserted, and Jez sat alone at one end. He'd briefly toyed with the idea of sitting at the head, the spot reserved for the baron, but just the thought of Jabur's scowl deterred him. He looked up at the guard standing near the doorway.

"I'm afraid not," Jabur said. "He's busy in his counting room. He received a fresh batch of reports this morning, and he's likely to be busy with them for some time. Korand doesn't run itself you know."

"He's always busy in his counting room." Jez dragged a biscuit across his plate, soaking up the juices left from the fruit he'd just eaten. The mix of berries, apples, and oranges blended with the buttery flavor of the bread, and he smiled as he chewed it. "Maybe I can go in there to say goodbye."

Jabur gave him a smile. "You know you're not allowed in there."

"It doesn't feel right to just leave after all he's done. I should at least thank him."

Jabur thought for a second. "Oh, very well. If you're done with your breakfast, we'll stop by."

Jez pushed aside his plate and got to his feet. The burly man nodded to a nearby servant who set about clearing the table. Jez and Jabur walked down the tiled hall. Jez grinned at the memory of the first time he'd walked through this passage. The tapestries adorning the walls had seemed so amazing. One depicted the Rumar Keep, the home of King Haziel. The setting sun colored the landscape orange. Jez had studied that one for hours. Master Dusan had promised to take him to meet King Haziel once his first term at the Academy was complete, and Jez was looking forward to that more than he had let on. Other tapestries showed great battles and legendary creatures. A few showed people or animals with strange proportions against backgrounds of eye-jarring colors. Jez thought they were ugly, but Dusan had called them dream tapestries, supposedly from a style far to the east. Apparently, they were modeled after what their creators had seen in their dreams. Jez had told him they didn't look much like any dreams he'd ever had. The baron had looked down his nose at Jez who had eventually murmured an apology. Dusan had half a dozen dream tapestries, and Jez suspected each was worth more than his father's home.

"He sure does like red." Jez spoke more to fill the silence than out of any real desire for conversation with Jabur.

"What?" he looked up at an image of a ship sailing on rough seas. The sun hung near the horizon. Its reflection was distorted by the waves as it tinged everything with red, making the sea look more like blood than water. "Oh, those are just his house colors. After spending so much time here, I'd have thought you would've realized that by now."

"I did," Jez said. "There's just so much of it."

The edges of Jabur's lips tightened as he tried to hold in a laugh. "Well, I suppose he is overly fond of that color. Don't you tell him I said that." Jabur jabbed at Jez's shoulder with a heavy finger, and Jez nodded as he held in a laugh.

Near the end of the hall, they turned a corner and went through a small side passage that Jez had rarely gone down. Here, the walls were bare and unadorned, and their footsteps sounded oddly empty. A single door stood at the end of the hall. Jabur knocked twice. The silence stretched on for several seconds. Jabur was about to knock again, when the door opened just wide enough for the baron to poke his head out. His hair was disheveled, and he had dark circles under his eyes. His body blocked the doorway so Jez couldn't see the room beyond, but he did catch a flash of green light. The hair on the back of his neck stood on end.

"What was that?" Jez asked.

Dusan looked over his shoulder before shrugging at Jez. "Yes, was there something you wanted?"

"Forgive the interruption, Baron," Jabur said, his head bobbing. "Master Jezreel wanted to see you before he left for the Academy."

Dusan's eyes widened. "Oh yes. Of course." He opened the door wider and stepped out, closing it behind him before Jez could get a look inside. "I'm glad you came by, or I would've forgotten until you were already gone. You wouldn't believe the problems I have to deal with." He glanced at Jabur. "I'll need half a dozen messengers at noon."

"I'll see to it."

"Good." He turned to Jez. "I have some gifts for you. I would've given them to you last night, but I was already busy with the reports when you got back in."

"But Jabur said you just got them in this morning."

The baron glanced at Jabur, and the large man took a step back, but then Dusan shrugged. "Those were yesterday's reports. Still, I should've taken the time to see you."

"I understand," Jez said.

"Of course you understand," Dusan said. "I wouldn't be proper otherwise. Still it's no excuse. I am a gentleman after all, and I should be held to some standards."

Jez knew Master Dusan was trying to be funny and he forced a laugh. Dusan turned and gave him a hurt look. This time, Jez's laugh was genuine, and the baron joined in. He reached into his pocket and pulled out a gold ring with a red stone. An open hand had been carved in. He offered it to Jez who took it and turned it in his hands.

"If you're going to represent my house, you'll need a signet ring."

Jez slipped in on his finger and stared at it for a few seconds before looking at Dusan. "Thank you."

Dusan nodded and motioned for Jez to follow. They walked in silence, turning down a series of halls until they entered a wide corridor with its walls covered with various forms of art. They stopped before a large gilded door with mystic shapes carved into it, Baron Dusan's quarters. Dusan asked Jez to wait while he went in. He left the door cracked open, and Jez peered inside, though he couldn't see much aside from an ebony table with a fist sized crystal atop it, Baron Dusan's speaking stone. The baron came out after a few seconds carrying a wrapped bundle, which he handed to Jez. It felt heavy, and he waited for Dusan to nod before unwrapping it. He almost gasped when the leather hilt came into view.

It was a sword.

He shook it until the wrapping came free. The blade was long and thin, not like the heavy weapons he'd seen soldiers carrying. The sheath was made of some dark wood and the image of a man with bat wings had been carved into it. The pommel bore the symbol of the closed fist. Jez drew the weapon; the blade's silvery metal shone so brightly it almost glowed. He swung it a few times, it felt lighter than he'd expected.

"A duelist's weapon," Master Dusan said. He wore the biggest smile Jez had ever seen on him.

"But Baron," Dusan raised an eyebrow. "Dusan, I mean. I don't know how to use a weapon like this."

Dusan chuckled. "Few boys your age do. I've arranged for a private tutor once you reach the Academy. Mind you, this is a gentleman's blade. I don't want to hear you've gotten into fights in back alleys. Proper duels happen by the light of day and with witnesses."

"Oh, of course not," Jez said.

"Do what you have to do, though."

"Baron?"

"This is a lesson they won't teach you in the Academy. Fools concern themselves with matters of right and wrong, but real life is never as simple as that, and you'll find right and wrong are mere illusions. Things aren't black and white, and many of us have to exist in the shades of gray. If you must get in back alley fights for whatever reason, handle your business quietly." He narrowed his eyes. "I don't want to hear about it. Do you understand?"

Jez's throat went dry and for a moment, he couldn't find his words, so he nodded. Dusan smiled.

"You really are a terrible liar." Jez's face heat up, and he was on the verge of saying he was proud of that, but the baron laughed. "Don't worry. Once you spend enough time among the right kind of people, you'll learn. I've taken the liberty of arranging your classes for your first term. You'll study art, history, and philosophy. I know you have an interest in magic so I've signed you up for an illusion class."

"Illusion?"

"It's the only area of magic people of our class study. Oh, there are some that dabble in other areas, but almost everyone has some training in illusion." Dusan smiled and his eyes glowed red for a second. "It's like art and will give you something in common with your peers."

"What about battle magic?" Jez asked.

Dusan snorted. "You saw the combatants last night. Oh, they're entertaining enough, and we certainly need their kind in the army, but those aren't exactly the kind of people we want to associate with on a daily basis."

Jez lowered his eyes. "Oh."

"Don't get me wrong. You're free to make friends with them. They're useful to have around." He nodded at Jabur. "Jabur himself is quite skilled at battle magic, but you come from different worlds, and there's a wide chasm between your relative positions in society."

Jez looked at the ground. "Like there is between me and my father, you mean."

Dusan put a hand on his shoulder, and Jez looked up. The smile on the baron's face had faded.

"Jezreel, I know you love your father very much, and you always will. You'll be able to provide for him in a way you never could if you'd followed in his footsteps and become a simple fisherman. You could very easily end up with an appointment to King Haziel's court, but you need to remember that you and your father are now from different worlds."

"I know."

"If it'll make you feel better, I promise I'll see he's taken care of while you're away."

"Thank you, Dusan."

Jez only stumbled a little when saying the name. Dusan smiled and drew him into an embrace. It only lasted a second, and Jez found himself looking into the baron's eyes. He thought he saw tears there, but they had to be his imagination. The baron never cried.

"Jezreel, my life has been enriched by your presence more than you could believe. I think of you almost as a son, and I would love to spend the morning talking with you. Unfortunately, the business of the barony will not wait." He gave Jez a small smile. "I'm afraid it's another one of those matters where responsibility takes precedence over privilege. Why don't we go make sure all your things have been carried into the coach, and I'll see you off?"

Jez, left speechless by the uncharacteristic show of emotion, only nodded. They went outside. The coach Dusan had hired was waiting. One of the servants Jez didn't know was overseeing a group of men as they loaded the heavy trunk containing Jez's belongings, though most of those had been a gift from the baron. Jabur extend his hand to Jez. They shook, with Jez's hand almost disappearing in the man's meaty fist. When Jez tried to shake Dusan's hand, the baron drew him into an embrace again.

"Be well, Jezreel, son of Bartin. Remember, you go bearing the honor of Korand."

CHAPTER 4

The Korandish grasslands seemed to go on forever. The wind created waves in the sea of grass, and Jez imagined bandits charging out at them. He pictured fending them off with his new sword. He was honest enough to admit that he wouldn't be able to do very much, but in his imagination, he fought off a dozen men on his own.

His coach was one of six on a road that cut through the grass. A dozen armed men rode around them, and if there were any bandits nearby, the sight of such a heavily armed party scared them away. They ate smoked meat and bread that was stale more often than not. Once, one of the guards shot a rabbit. There wasn't enough to go around, but the caravan leader, a stout woman with red hair, made sure Jez got some and made Jez promise to tell the baron she'd treated him well.

At night, their wagons would make a circle and they had a fire. The adults talked, but Jez didn't feel very welcome among them. They kept giving him sidelong glances and he had the feeling they were guarding their words. On the third night, he just began eating his food apart from them and lay down as soon as he was finished. He was filled with a sense of perpetual emptiness, and it took him four days to realize it was because he missed the smell of the sea.

After two weeks of uneventful travel, the Telag Mountains appeared on the horizon. One peak stood out and seemed to have a flat top. The caravan headed in that direction. Three days later, they reached the city of Hiranta at the base of the flat mountain. It was a bleak city made of black stone, the buildings were square and there weren't any that rose higher than two floors. They arrived in the middle of the day. It was perhaps twice as big as Randak and as soon as they reached the town square, they were surrounded by people eager to buy supplies off the wagons. Jez waited for his coach to stop, but it broke away from the others and stopped in front of an inn. Unlike the ones in Randak, this one had a single floor but took up the space of three buildings. As soon as Jez stepped off, he was greeted by a man in a blue robe. He was short man, no taller than Jez himself, but looked solidly built. If not for the robes, Jez might have thought he was a blacksmith or a stonemason.

"You are Jezreel Bartinson?"

"I am."

He extended a hand. Jez shook it and realized his hands were covered in callouses, but he didn't intentionally try to hurt Jez as some of the nobles he'd met recently did.

"I am Besis, protection master of the Carceri Academy. I will see you the rest of the way to the Academy in the morning."

"Why wait?"

"It takes most of the day to get up Mount Carcer."

"Up the mountain?" Jez glanced upward. Far wider than it was tall, the flat topped peak dominated the sky. Spots of white, where he assumed the snow hadn't melted yet, dotted the areas near the top. It was like some great beast slumbering on the edge of wakefulness. Jez had trouble believing anything could be that big. "We're going up there?"

"Of course. The Academy is a place of power, and few places offer as much power as a fire mountain."

The stew the inn provided had neither the savory taste of his father's fish soup nor the overly spiced tasted of the more exotic food Dusan had provided. By comparison, it was bland and tasteless. Chunks of meat Jez couldn't identify floated in a broth that tasted more like dirty water than anything else. He decided he didn't really want to know what it was. Still, it was better than most of what he'd had on the road, so he suffered through it. The innkeeper apologized to Master Besis for the quality of the meal by saying that he'd been running low on supplies before the caravan had arrived, and offered them a free room as compensation. Jez couldn't help but notice he didn't do that to anyone else, though.

"The Academy carries a lot of prestige," Besis said when Jez asked.

The inn itself was filled with wood smoke. Big men, most with black smudges on their faces, occupied nearly all of the tables. Besis said they were miners who searched the mountains for gems. They looked like rough men, but as soon as it became apparent that an Academy master was looking for a table, two men who were only slightly smaller than mountains vacated theirs.

"Aren't you worried that the fire mountain will explode?" Jez asked

Master Besis chuckled. "Everyone asks that. No, the Academy uses potent magic to keep it dormant."

"I still think it would be safer to have it in the city."

This time, Besis erupted in laughter, drawing uneasy looks from other patrons. "If the fire mountain exploded, the base of the mountain would be no safer than the top."

"That doesn't exactly make me feel better."

Besis's face grew serious. "The Academy has stood for a thousand years. In that time, Mount Carcer has tried to erupt twice without success. The first time, the Academy's terramages redirected that power and used it to build the central spire that now houses some of the quarters of the Academy. A two-hundred-foot tower arose overnight. The second time, they constructed the subterranean levels where some of the most dangerous artifacts are stored, and they created permanent wards there. If the mountain tries to erupt again, we'll use its power for some other beneficial purpose."

"Can I learn to do that?"

"Terra magic?" Besis shrugged. "It depends on whether or not you have the talent for it, but terra magic is a down-to-earth sort of power." The master chuckled at his own joke. "Most people have an affinity for one dominion, and terra magic is part of mine, but it's not something the nobility usually concern themselves with."

"I'm not really part of the nobility," Jez said.

"True, but you are in the upper tier, and with Baron Dusan as your patron, many will treat you as if you are. More to the point, the baron pays for your tuition, and he has final approval over your classes. He's given us a list of approved areas of study. It gives you considerable leeway, but terra magic wasn't on it."

"He's telling me what I can study?"

"You can request approval for other areas if you wish, but given what he's told us about what he wants for you, I doubt he'd agree to any meaningful study of terra magic."

Jez thought back to his father and an idea took form. How often had he complained about the weather? "What about water magic? Or maybe air."

"Aqua magic," Besis corrected him, "and venta magic. They're in the dominions of protection and destruction, respectively. Few people have an aptitude for both, but it has happened before. They weren't on the list either, but you might have better luck with them. There are some who use them for art. He'd never consent to you being a stormmage though, if that's what you're thinking."

Jez shrugged. The limitless possibilities of the Academy seemed to be vanishing rapidly. "Then what can I study?"

"You'll forgive me if I don't have the entire list memorized." Besis wrinkled his brow and thought for a second. "History, illusion, philosophy, and art, obviously. There was also literature, economics, diplomacy, music. A smattering of other subjects as well."

Jez suppressed the urge to sigh. Those were all subjects his father would consider useless, but his father generally considered anyone who wasn't working with their hands to be wasting their time. Given the callouses on the protection master's hands, Jez wondered how his father would feel about Master Besis.

"I don't guess it will matter until I finish my first term anyway."

"Most students do two or three years before they settle on an area of study. I myself jumped from one to another for six years before I settled on binding. I spread out into other areas of protection as well. I'm sure you'll find an area you're gifted in that the baron approves of."

"What if it's fishing?" Jez asked under his breath.

"What was that?"

"Nothing. I'm really excited about starting tomorrow."

"Good. You should get some rest. We'll be departing before first light."

CHAPTER 5

The world had been born from fire. It had spun as a ball of molten rock for a time so long humans couldn't comprehend it. Creatures wandered the fiery wastelands, the greatest of which were monstrous beings that even the worst nightmares of man would fear. The world was theirs, and they embodied fear and hatred long before there had been humans to feel such emotions, but these demons weren't alone. Others, equally powerful, inhabited the skies, but these were beings of hope, joy, and of the anger that could not allow evil to prevail. Pure light did battle against fire and darkness. They fought for untold eons until, finally, the light overcame, banishing the fires to the deep places far beneath the surface of the world, and light was set to guard over them. After ages beyond measure, the world cooled, and the Creator brought forth water and plants. Mountains rose up from the ground, and rivers gave it life. Animals walked the surface of the earth. They flew above it, and they swam in the seas. Last of all, from earth and stone the Creator brought forth man, but as man grew and knew fear and hatred, the dark creatures began to stir.

Jez awoke in a cold sweat. The sun shone through the windows, and he was surprised he hadn't woken up earlier. His father had always made him wake up before dawn, and even in the six months he'd spent with the baron, he had never broken the habit. Someone was knocking at his door, and he slipped into a shirt before answering. Besis was at the door, with a pack slung over one shoulder. He had exchanged his blue robes for a plain shirt and trousers. He looked Jez up and down and frowned.

"Well, I admit I told you to dress light, but I was expecting a little more than a shirt and undergarments."

Jez's face heated up. "Sorry. You woke me up."

"We should've left two hours ago. Get dressed. The trail will be hard enough with the sun already beating down on us."

"Sorry," Jez said again. He waved his hand at the ceiling. "That thing is giving me nightmares. I didn't sleep well."

"What thing?"

"The mountain." Jez didn't know where that answer had come from, but as soon as he said it, he knew it was true. There was something wrong about the peak.

"Your room has no windows. You can't even see it."

"No, but I know it's there."

Jez took a deep breath. There was the faintest scent of sulfur in the air. He hadn't noticed it in the dream, but thinking back, the smell had been there. The fiery creatures had reeked of it. They had been so strong, but the light beings didn't have a choice. Such creatures didn't belong in this world, and they had to be banished. Jez shook his head to clear away the image. Master Besis was staring at him.

"I'm sorry. I'll be ready in a few minutes."

"I'll be downstairs. I'll send someone for your things. Grab some food on the way out. It'll be a long day." He tossed Jez a waterskin. "You'll need this."

After four hours, Jez was convinced mules were thoroughly unpleasant creatures. Stepper, the animal Jez rode, seemed to take almost childlike glee in struggling against Jez's instructions. Master Besis was trying not to laugh, but he wasn't doing a very good job of it. Two other mules trailed behind them carrying supplies for the Academy. A third pulled a small cart that carried Jez's chest. According to Besis, Tarcai, the city in the caldera of Mount Carcer, had crops and livestock of their own, but they still occasionally needed items from the outside, and Besis had agreed to pick up some things. For all their faults, the mules seemed to be doing better than Jez was. The gravel crunched underfoot and they plodded on, but the sun beat against his skin with relentless fury. The air around them shimmered with heat, and his lips cracked in the arid climate. Jez squeezed his waterskin trying to find any drop, but it was as dry as the stone. He could practically feel his insides shriveling away in the heat.

"It's not just the sun," Besis said as they reigned in to take a midday meal. "You're used to the air at sea level. It's a lot thinner here. You'll find yourself getting tired until you get accustomed to that. On top of that, fire flows through the veins of this mountain. It gives off warmth even in the dead of winter."

The master pulled out a chunk of bread and some of the salted beef he'd picked up in the town. He lay a pot on the ground and cut thin slices of meat. He placed them in the pot without even bothering to light a fire. It started to smoke a few seconds later. He tossed Jez an apple and pulled another waterskin out of the packs to water the mules. Jez gaped at him.

"How many of those do you have?"

"Quite a few." He grinned at Jez. "We wouldn't want the animals to dehydrate on the way up, would we?"

"I've been practically dying of thirst for the past couple of hours, and you've had water this entire time?"

Besis snorted and tossed Jez a skin. "You never asked, and you were hardly dying. Besides, at the rate you drank the first one, you would've emptied two others before the first hour was done, and it's not good to drink so much so fast."

The water was warm and tasted faintly of leather, but it felt amazing going down his throat. Some of it spilled and steamed as it hit the ground. It took a concentrated effort of will for Jez to stop drinking before it was entirely empty.

"Well, that's fine," Jez said, "but did you have to let me go all morning with only one?"

"Probably not." He tossed Jez another waterskin. "Don't drink it too quickly, and let me know if you need any more."

They made small talk as they ate, but Jez's heart wasn't in it. The heat was making him feel sick, and he didn't want to eat much. His eyes kept getting drawn to the flat top of the mountain. They were closer to it than they were to the bottom now. It might've been his imagination, but he could've sworn he saw a curl of smoke rising up, and for a moment, he thought the ground trembled. Besis, however, seemed not to notice, and after a few minutes, they climbed back onto their mules and continued up the path.

Three hours and four waterskins later, they climbed up on to the rim of Mount Carcer. Jez stared down into the fire mountain with wide-eyed shock. The mountain dipped down like the inside of a sphere. He could just make out the rim of Carcer on the other side. When Besis had told him about Tarcai, he'd expected a small collection of buildings with a tower in the center.

The only thing he'd been right about was the tower.

An obsidian spire rose up over its surroundings, but it was too far to tell for certain how big it was. Far from a small cluster of buildings, the surrounding city was a sprawling metropolis. People filled the streets, and buildings ranged from the size of small houses to large manors. Beyond the city was a large swath of green, presumably where the farmland was. There were a few patches of plant life in Tarcai itself.

Other than that, the city was uniform black, but it shimmered in the light of the setting sun.

"What makes it do that?"

"Most of the buildings are overlaid with obsidian. People here don't have very many options to make their homes look nice, so they do whatever they can."

"You mean people actually live here?" Jez asked. "I mean I thought it was just the Academy."

"The Academy has some two hundred students. A good portion of them are wealthy. In fact, it's one of the greatest concentrations of wealth for a hundred leagues in any direction. Enterprising merchants take advantage of that to provide the luxuries these youths are used to."

"But it's inside a fire mountain."

Besis smirked. "That never stopped a merchant from trying to make a few coins."

"How big is all this?" Jez waved his hand at the city below.

"The caldera is four miles across."

"Where is the Academy?"

"At the base of the tower. Shall we go?"

CHAPTER 6

The day had started to cool by the time they went down into the city. People crowded the streets going from one shop to another. Some sold foods, cloth, or other mundane items. Others, however displayed crystals or dried herbs. Once Jez saw books with strange runes on them like those Baron Dusan had displayed. Even more than in Hiranta, the people of Tarcai made way for Master Besis. It was a stark contrast to how the people of Randak reacted to Dusan. The baron had called the looks the people gave him signs of respect, but to Jez, many had seemed more like fear. Here, people stared openly, and pointed, their faces showing their obvious pleasure at seeing him. One little boy, heedless of the important figure, ran out from the crowd. He bumped into Master Besis, and fell back. The boy, no older than three, looked up at the master and whimpered. A few seconds later, his mother came running after him. Besis picked him up and handed him to the woman with a smile. The woman thanked him for several long moments before Besis put a hand on her shoulder. She looked at him with wide eyes, but there was no fear on her face. She was beaming. Besis nodded at her and continued to walk.

The street led to an open gate in a wall surrounding the Academy grounds. The buildings inside seemed to shimmer a little more. They were the same blocky style as those in the city, unlike the single storied ones outside though, these each had at least two floors, and when he looked closely, he saw a faint rune carved on a large building to his left. People of all ages, some as young as Jez and others with wrinkled faces and stooped postures, moved through the streets. Most on the left wore green robes. On the right, they wore blue, though there were plenty of other robes as well.

"The main streets mark district boundaries," Besis said when Jez asked. "There are seven districts, each devoted to a different dominion, beasts on the left and protection on the right. The next term won't start for another three weeks, so you'll have time to settle in. Has the baron had you awakened?"

"Awakened?"

"You're going to study illusion and presumably other schools of magic. You need to be awakened before you can do that." Jez shook his head, and Besis shrugged. "Well, we can get that taken care of before the start of the term."

"It doesn't look like anyone else here is just waiting for the term to start," Jez said, glancing at all the robed students hustling about. One girl in blue saw Master Besis and approached to speak, but Besis shook his head. The student frowned and turned away.

"We're at the end of a term right now, and exams are keeping everyone busy. A few, like Cinatra," he nodded at the departing student, "always try to make excuses for not being ready."

"You think she'll fail then?"

Besis shook his head. "Actually, she's rather gifted. If she would only realize that, she'd have an easier time of it."

"And you give all these people their exams?"

Besis shrugged. "I'm the protection master, but I let my adjutants issue all but the advanced binding tests, and even those are relatively straightforward. I summon a spirit and unleash it on the student. If they bind it, they pass. If they don't, well…"

He let it hang for a second, and it was only when Jez gaped at him that a grin split his face.

"Only joking, my young friend. My tests are a bit more complex than that, but my preparations were done days ago. If you ever study binding, I'll show you."

"If Master Dusan approves, you mean."

Besis inclined his head. "Yes, there is that."

Before Jez could say anything else, his nostrils flared to the overpowering scent of sulfur. His eyes locked on the nearest building. Besis went silent and followed his gaze. He said something, but it seemed far away, and Jez's attention was locked on the building. He took a step toward it, and Besis put a hand on his shoulder. Jez looked at him. He seemed to be saying something about the purpose of the building, but the exact words escaped him. All of Jez's attention was focused beyond the wall. There was something inside, something that didn't belong. Its presence spoke into the depth of Jez's soul, and it spoke the language of fear. Jez shook himself free of the master's grasp. Besis tried to reach for him, but then, the screaming started.

The main door of the building was flung open, and three people practically tripped over each other trying to get out. A crack ran up the wall, glowing fiery orange. One of the students spotted Master Besis and ran toward him, but before he was halfway there, the wall exploded outward. A shower of dust and stone rushed out from the hole, covering everyone within twenty yards and forming a cloud of blackness. People screamed. One boy in green turned into a bird and flew away. A pang of terror ran through Jez, but it was a distant thing, more like a memory or a dream than an actual emotion. The student running toward them fell to the ground, shouting in terror.

The cloud roared so loud the ground shook. Some people nearby screamed that the mountain was erupting, but somehow, Jez knew that wasn't the case. A second later, his suspicions were confirmed as the smoke congealed into a winged figure wreathed in flame. It stood at least ten feet tall. Bone spikes jutted from its arms and legs. Its face was covered in scales and a pair of curved horns came from its head. Fire billowed from its nostrils with every breath, and a forked tongue flickered from its mouth. Its skin looked like the same black stone as the rest of the city. Burning cracks ran up and down its body which constantly spurted fire and smoke. Twin flames burned where its eyes should be. It took a step forward and began bringing a flaming foot down on the fallen student. The boy, perhaps two years older than Jez himself, shrieked in terror.

Jez didn't think. He just threw his arms forward. Energy surged through him. Raw force rushed at the creature, distorting the air. It crashed into the beast's leg and the creature came down hard on the ground several feet away from the fallen student. Cracks spread out from the point of impact. One made its way under the student who yelped and rolled out of the way. Master Besis gaped at Jez and lowered his arms. Some distant part of Jez's mind recognized that the master had been about to do the same thing Jez did. Jez had simply been quicker. He had known this creature was coming.

The creature, the phobos, though he didn't know how he knew the name, had already gotten to its feet. It took a step toward them. Jez made two quick circular motions with his left hand and one with his right. Lights rushed at the creature, splashing against the middle of its chest. It spread out and formed a wide circle. The fear in Jez vanished, and others around him began to regain their composure. They were still afraid, but it was no longer the supernatural fear the monster had been giving off.

The phobos turned its gaze to Jez. It reached for him, but his fingers danced in complex patterns his eyes couldn't follow. A thin strand of light shot forward from his hand, expanding as it moved toward the creature. It wrapped itself around the demon's claws and forced its hand to the side of its body. Another did the same to the other claw. Strand after strand shot from Jez's hand as he wove incomprehensible patterns in the air. A few seconds later, the phobos was covered in web-like strands of power, as a fly caught by a spider. It tried to move, but the bindings held it fast. It toppled forward, shrinking as it did. By the time it reached the ground, it was the size of a doll that fit in the palm of his hand. Jez let out a breath, and his legs collapsed out from under him. Instantly, Master Besis was at his side. He helped Jez to his feet and scooped up the imprisoned phobos.

"How did you…" Besis began, but he looked around. A crowd had formed and was pointing at them. "Never mind. Let's discuss this in my office." He turned to one of the nearby students and waved at the broken building. "Get Liandra to fix this. Tell her if she can have it done before moonrise, she'll have a perfect mark on her exam. I want to see whoever is responsible for that thing escaping in two hours. Can you walk, Jezreel?"

Jez had to lean heavily on Besis, but he nodded. They started toward the building the demon had come from, but Master Besis sighed and shook his head.

"No, I don't suppose that will work. I really should maintain an office outside of the practice house. Come, some of the classrooms should be available."

They made their way through the protection district to a long, one story building. The story of what had happened apparently rushed out in front of them because everywhere, people stared at Jez in wide-eyed shock. They all stopped at the master's glare, however. Besis pulled open a door. The building was dark, but Besis waved a hand and uttered a word and lanterns all along the hall sprang to life. Unlike the exterior, the hall was white stone and was polished to the point of gleaming in the lantern light. They entered the first room they came to, which had half a dozen wooden chairs arranged in a circle with a small window looking out into the street. Besis helped Jez into one of the chairs and sat in the one next to him.

"Tell me what happened."

"I don't know."

"You chose an emotional binding followed by a physical one. Why?"

"I did?"

"That was a fear demon, a phobos." Jez nodded slowly. Master Besis didn't look surprised he knew the name. "If you hadn't done the emotional binding, it would've still been radiating fear even from the prison you put it in, but why not bind it physically first to deal with the immediate threat?"

"The gossamer web locks the creature away entirely, but it also prevents any conscious magic from penetrating it. The emotional binding wouldn't have been able to get through."

Jez's jaw dropped. He had no idea where the words had come from. He wasn't even entirely sure what they meant. Master Besis, however, nodded.

"Why did you choose that binding? There are others that would've been quicker, though admittedly not as effective."

Jez shook his head and his hand went to his forehead. His head was pounding, and it was a struggle to think straight. Master Besis put a hand on his shoulder. He seemed to be fond of that particular gesture.

"You knew it was there before it came out of the building, didn't you?" Jez hesitated for a second before nodding. Besis let out a low whistle. "If I hadn't seen it, I wouldn't have believed it. I've never seen instinctual magic of this level."

"Instinctual magic?"

"Magic is just what we call the primal forces of the universe. It's a living, breathing thing. Certain people have a natural gift in one area or another, but to a blessed few, magic…" he paused for a second as if looking for the right word. He began tapping his foot on the ground, and the sound made Jez's headache throb. Besis met his gaze, and apparently realizing what he was doing, stopped. "Speaks to them. We don't entirely understand it, and it hasn't happened on this level for almost a hundred years. You performed a mid-level binding by instinct. You obviously haven't trained for it or it wouldn't have taken so much out of you."

"A mid-level?" Jez said. "You mean that thing wasn't…"

"Oh it was powerful," Besis said, "but a few well-placed arrows could've taken it down. Most of the big ones are like that. They seem worse than they actually are. The truly dangerous ones don't need to be so flashy."

Jez nodded. It all seemed so familiar. He'd known all of this, and he felt that if he concentrated, he could come up with a lot more information, but it was like trying to remember a dream. The knowledge was there, but it kept slipping through his grasp. He tried to stand up, but his legs shook and he fell back into his seat, groaning at the hard wood. He looked at Besis. "How long will I be like this?"

"You should be better by the end of the day. You didn't lose consciousness, so you're not in any danger. Jezreel, I want you to study binding." Jez glanced at him, but Besis smiled. "Your natural talent is nothing short of extraordinary. If you could develop that, you might be the greatest binder the Carceri Academy has ever seen."

"But Baron Dusan has already picked my first term classes."

"The term hasn't started yet. Those classes can still be changed, provided the baron approves, of course. We'll contact him right now if you're willing."

"It's not exactly a noble's area of study, is it?"

"It's not generally considered such, no, but practically every noble has dipped their fingers in one improper area of study or another. Even Dusan did that."

"He did?"

"Oh yes. He was quite gifted at binding, from what I've been told. There was even talk of him becoming protection master. Of course, they also said the same about destruction, secrets, and knowledge. He could've easily been chancellor if he hadn't decided to commit himself to King Haziel's court. He was gifted in almost every branch of magic he studied. He's one of the few who could easily grasp magics in multiple dominions. Didn't you know?" Jez shook his head. "Well, what do you say? Do you want to ask him? Given what I saw, I wouldn't be surprised if you surpassed your patron, in binding at least."

Jez thought back to his confrontation with the phobos. That creature had not belonged in this world. It had been alien and wrong. Such things had no place among mortals. His eyes wandered down to the prison in Master Besis's hand. What had he called it? A gossamer web. Somehow, he knew that the demon wasn't truly contained in the doll. Rather, the doll was a doorway to some dark and terrible realm, the only place where such creatures belonged. Such creatures couldn't be killed, at least not while in the mortal world. It felt right that he had bound it away, even if the effort had left him so weak from exhaustion he could barely stand.

"All right," he said. "I'll do it."

CHAPTER 7

They entered the bottom level of the central spire, a single room with a vaulted ceiling. Colored light shone through the stained-glass windows casting rainbow patterns on the marble ground. Two guards stood at the entrance to a corridor. Besis instructed him to wait while he deposited the phobos's prison in a secure location. The protection master was only gone for a few minutes before returning and leading Jez up the stairs on the opposite side of the room.

The Academy's speaking stone was in a room at the top of the central spire, and Besis started up, but Jez hesitated. After spending all day climbing the mountain and being drained by his efforts against the phobos, Jez looked at the stairs with an almost primal dread. Besis looked over his shoulder and cleared his throat. Jez sighed and started following. The stairs wound up on the inside of the spire's outer wall, and he and Besis climbed the stairs slowly, stopping often for Jez to catch his breath. Every once in a while, they would pass a door on one side and a window on the other. The black city below almost seemed to swallow the light of the setting sun. The first time he looked down on the protection district, the damage caused by his confrontation with the phobos had been obvious, but every time they circled around, the damage had lessened. By the time they reached the top, his legs felt like jelly, and he was covered in sweat. The city had been completely repaired.

Besis said the Academy preferred its students to keep their concentration on their studies, so access to the speaking stone was restricted and deliberately made difficult. Master Besis spoke to the two men standing guard for a few seconds before they stepped aside. Unlike the stone in Dusan's manor, this one was deep blue, and if Jez stared into it, he could almost hear the sounds of waves crashing against the shore. Besis nodded at Jez who felt his face redden. He shifted his weight from one foot to another and didn't look up.

"What is it?" Besis asked.

"I've never actually used one of those things."

Besis raised an eyebrow. "Oh come on. Everyone has used…" His features softened. "Oh, I see. I suppose that would make sense, wouldn't it?"

"I only lived with Baron Dusan for six months. The only person I really talked to was my father and the other people I grew up with. None of them have speaking stones."

One of the guards snorted, but Master Besis shot him a glare that could've cut stone. The guard paled and suddenly found the wall to be most interesting as he studied it. Besis turned to Jez and gave him a smile that melted away his embarrassment.

"Well, that's a problem that's easily enough resolved. Do you have a stone keyed to it?" Jez shrugged, and Besis frowned. "Likely, the baron thought you'd taken an impression of it."

Jez stared at the master, the meaning of the words lost on him. Besis opened a drawer and pulled out a milky white stone on a gold chain. He pressed it against the speaking stone for a second and closed his eyes. Both stones flickered for an instant, and Besis handed the smaller one to Jez.

"This is now sender-keyed to the school's stone so you'll be able to contact it more easily. All you need to do is touch it to another stone in range and think of the Academy. It won't help connect to the Baron's though, so put it away. Now, I assume you've seen the baron's stone."

"Yes, a couple of times."

"Good, what color is it?"

"Clear."

"Really? Those are incredibly rare and have nearly limitless range. I don't suppose you've touched it." Jez shook his head. "Well, no matter. Picture the stone in your mind."

"I don't really remember exactly what it looks like. I never saw it for more than a few seconds."

"That doesn't matter. Just imagine it, and be sure you associate it with the baron in your mind. When that's done, touch the stone."

Jez concentrated until he could see the stone in his head. The crystal in front of him hummed, and the image in his mind began to change. It wasn't just a stone. It was *Dusan's* stone. Lights in the speaking stone began to swirl, and Jez could almost see figures inside. He reached out and lay a finger on it. It gave him a small shock and he drew back. The stone was pulsing, intermittently giving off blue and white light. He looked at Besis.

"The baron's stone is doing the same thing right now as is any stone that's receiver-keyed to it, if it's close enough. If he's able, he'll answer soon."

Sure enough, after a few minutes, the pulsing vanished, and the swirling resolved into the image of a face. Distorted by the crystal, at first, Jez thought it was his own reflection, but the face was more wrinkled, and the nose more pointed, just like Baron Dusan's.

"Jezreel," he said. "This is a pleasant surprise. Most boys don't call home nearly so soon after leaving it."

The way he said 'home' made it sound like Jez belonged with him instead of with his father. Jez glanced at Besis who nodded. "Master Besis thought I should call."

"Besis?" The face in the stone glanced at the master. "Besis, I don't believe I know you."

"I've never had the pleasure, Baron," Besis said, inclining his head. "I'm the Academy's protection master."

Dusan's lip twitched, though Jez couldn't be sure if it had actually happened or if it was just some trick of the light. "Ah yes. That would explain it. I didn't concern myself much with that field after I graduated." He turned back to Jez. "So to what do I owe this pleasure?"

Besis cleared his throat, and the baron gave him an annoyed look, but his attention quickly returned to Jez. Jez looked at Besis for support, and the protection master shrugged and motioned for him to go on. Slowly, Jez recounted the story of the phobos coming out of the building and how he'd bound it. He left out the part about how the effort had exhausted him, but even so, when he was done, Dusan's eyes narrowed at the story, and he glared at Besis.

"Security around the Academy has become rather lax since I attended. Isn't taking care of a minor fear demon something better suited for the protection master than a student who hasn't even begun his studies yet?"

"Normally yes," Besis said, "but the boy reacted before I did. He's amazingly fast. Once I saw he had the situation under control, I decided to let it play out. I was prepared in case he faltered. Rest assured, Baron, he was in no danger."

"You'll excuse me if I don't take your word for it," he said. "I'll be wanting to speak with the chancellor as soon as he is able."

"Of course," Besis said, though is expression said he was anything but happy about it. "There is one other thing I wanted to discuss with you. As the situation demonstrated, young Jezreel has a rare gift for binding. I would like your permission to replace one of his classes with binding, or I could arrange to tutor him privately, if you prefer."

"Absolutely not," Dusan said. "The classes I enrolled him in are essential for his education, though I am beginning to wonder if the Academy is the proper place for him. I'm not sure you're capable of dealing with instinctual magic on this level. I think that perhaps I should handle that."

Besis raised his hands toward the crystal. "There's no need to be hasty."

"Jezreel was not on campus for an hour before he was attacked by one of your demons."

"Please, at least speak with the chancellor first. Jezreel has a great deal of potential, and it would be a shame for that to go to waste."

Besis nodded. "I will speak with him, but I won't promise I'll change my mind. No binding, though."

"But Baron Dusan," Jez said.

The image in the crystal turned to him, and for a moment, it seemed to glow brighter as the baron's brow wrinkled in barely controlled anger. Jez had only seen that expression once, when the king's tax collector had demanded to see Dusan's books. At the time, Jez had wondered if Dusan was hiding something from the king, but nothing had ever come of it.

"No, Jezreel," the baron said. "The world is dangerous enough without you meddling with binding, especially without proper supervision. I don't want you to have anything to do with it."

Jez barely noticed Besis scowling at the insult. "But…"

"I've made my decision. Now, Master Besis, I'll expect to be hearing from the chancellor before the end of the day. I'll make sure he keeps you away from Jezreel."

"That's not necessary. I'll abide by your wishes."

"So you say." His voice was flat and emotionless. He turned back to

Jez and his features softened. He showed none of the anger that had been present a moment ago. "It's good to hear from you. I hope the rest of your term is more pleasant than your first day. I'll talk to you soon."

The image of the baron faded before Jez had a chance to reply. The stone went still, but Jez stared at it until Master Besis cleared his throat. Jez looked up.

"Well he didn't take that very well, did he?"

Jez looked from the crystal to Master Besis and back again. He opened his mouth to speak but closed it before he said anything. He opened it again, but no words came out.

"Out with it."

"Master Besis, it just felt so right. Maybe I could…"

"No."

"You don't even know what I was going to say."

"You were going to suggest studying binding without the baron knowing. No."

"Why not?"

"Aside from the fact that your patron has forbidden it, binding isn't something you can study in backrooms hidden away from everyone, not if you want to live long. We have an entire building devoted to it covered in protective magic. Even that's not always enough as you well know."

Jez glanced out the window. Though from this height, he couldn't tell one building from another, he imagined the building the phobos had come out of. He nodded.

"It's too dangerous to study away from those protections," Besis said, "and the building is too public for me to teach you in secret."

"But…"

"Don't worry. I'm not about to give up on you. The baron may change his mind once he calms down, but for now the matter is closed."

CHAPTER 8

Jez was assigned quarters on the second level of the central spire. His rooms were bigger than his father's house, nearly as big as the rooms he'd had in Baron Dusan's manor. The bed was soft and every time Jez lay down in it, he thought it was going to swallow him. In a drawer by the bed, he found several silver buttons, the sign of the upper tier at the Academy. Additionally, a number of brown acolyte robes had been added to his clothing chest. He wouldn't be issued colored robes until was promoted to adept and picked an area of study. A dream tapestry hung on one wall, though one of the servants promised to remove it if Jez wished. He also had a sitting room containing two cushioned chairs and a small table. A fireplace big enough for him to stand in sat in one wall. It all seemed so wasteful, and he thought the idea would keep him awake, but as soon as he got into bed, the exhaustion from the day settled on him, and he fell asleep.

Early the first morning, there was a heavy knock. Jez rolled out of bed and threw on the same shirt from the day before. He stumbled into his sitting room and opened the door to find a tall man with dark skin. He wore a blade on his belt.

"Jezreel Bartinson?" Jez nodded. "I am Murus. Baron Dusan has hired me to teach you the blade."

Jez glanced out the window. The sky had just begun to redden in the light of the rising sun, and Jez's eyelids felt heavy.

"Do we have to do it so early?"

Murus rolled his eyes. "What else were you going to do with the beginning of the day? Come. Change into some fighting clothes. Leave your weapon. You won't be needing it today."

Jez had no idea what "fighting clothes" were so he put on some of the clothes the baron had given him. As soon as he came out of his room, Murus sent him back in and told him that his clothes, a silk shirt and trousers, were too fine and likely to be ruined by their training. Jez changed into a homespun shirt with plain brown pants, one of the few outfits he still had from living with his father. Murus approved of this.

In spite of the early hour, Jez was excited about the prospect of learning to fight, and he took the stairs two at a time. There was a plot of land near the Academy grounds. A few soldiers were there engaged in mock sword fights. One nodded at Murus as the teacher led Jez to one end of the practice ground. Jez's excitement of learning the sword quickly faded, as Murus spent the entire morning teaching him how to stand.

"When am I going to learn how to use the sword?" Jez asked.

"You're learning now."

"No I'm not," Jez said. "You're just telling me how I'm standing wrong."

Murus reached out and shoved Jez who stumbled a few feet back. When he looked up, the swordsman had a finger pointed at Jez's throat. Murus took a step forward and jabbed his finger into flesh so hard Jez coughed a few times.

"You see? If this had been a sword, you'd be in trouble now, all because you weren't standing properly. Now, let's start again."

It went on like that for hours. No matter how hard Jez tried, Murus always found some minute problem with his stance. By lunchtime, Jez had cramps in muscles he hadn't even known he had, and his arms felt like lead weights. Under Murus's harsh gaze, Jez found himself wondering if he would ever actually get to hold his weapon.

Near the middle of the day, Murus dismissed him. Rather than going to the eating hall near the base of the spire, Jez went to the Quarter Horse, a nearby inn that he'd heard some of the other students talking about. Most of the tables were occupied by people pouring over books. A thin man with wispy hair was wiping down a table. When he saw Jez, his eyes brightened, and he walked over to him and shook his hand.

"You're him, aren't you?"

"Him?"

"The one who saved Kilos from that thing. I'm Lufka, Kilos's father."

Jez looked at him blankly, but the innkeeper seemed not to notice. He practically dragged Jez to the table he'd been cleaning and called for a bowl of beef stew before sitting down across from Jez.

"Kilos told me he lost control of that monster. It would've killed him, if not for you."

"You mean the phobos," Jez said.

Lufka touched two fingers to his forehead and bowed his head in a warding gesture before meeting Jez's eyes. "Most people wouldn't do that, especially not for a student of the lower tier."

"Sir, it wasn't…" Jez hesitated. Wasn't what? He couldn't very well tell this man that he'd saved Kilos by accident. Jez turned away. "I only did what I could."

Lufka stood and patted Jez's back. "Well, if you ever get tired of those rooms at the Academy, you'll always have a place here. I can't offer the luxury that you upper tiers are used to, but I'll do what I can."

A serving girl brought food, and Lufka left to attend others. Jez just stared at him as he bustled around the common room. He didn't even notice the man who'd sat across from him until he spoke.

"That'll get cold if you don't eat it."

Jez jumped. The man across from him was tall and had olive skin. A well-trimmed beard covered his face, and he had dark eyes. He extended a hand.

"I am Master Kerag, master of shadows."

Jez shook his hand. The man's skin felt cold, and Jez found himself snatching his hand back as soon as the master had released it. Kerag grinned. "You don't know why I'm here, do you?"

Jez shook his head. "Sorry."

Kerag waved off the apology. "I'm here to awaken you. We'll get started once you're done with lunch."

"But the Baron…"

"The chancellor has spoken to him. Once he pointed out that withdrawing you so suddenly would draw a lot of attention, he conceded and allowed you to remain." Master Kerag smiled. "Every noble has some secrets after all, and Baron Dusan is no different."

Jez nodded. "I thought I would get time to rest until the term started."

Kerag's brow furled. "Where would you get that idea?"

CHAPTER 9

It went on that way for the next three weeks. The mornings were spent with Murus learning the sword. After three days, Murus actually let him handle his own weapon, and he began seeing some progress, though his muscles still ached almost constantly. Kerag controlled his afternoons, which mainly consisted of sitting in silence in a small room while the shadow master wove power over him. That part was even more frustrating than his first day with Murus had been. At least in that lesson, Jez's failures were his fault, but with Master Kerag, he had no idea if there was something he could be doing better.

With what little time Jez had left over, he tried to find Master Besis, but the protection master seemed to be avoiding him. Jez tried to go into the building the phobos had come out of, but Master Besis had warned the adepts guarding the building, and they refused to let him in. Instead, Jez just stayed near it. Every once in a while, he'd catch the scent of sulfur and he knew someone had called a particularly powerful demon, but there was no repeat of the incident with the phobos.

Three days before the start of the term, Kerag nodded.

"There, it's done."

"I'm awakened? Shouldn't there be lights or sounds or something?"

Kerag laughed. "There's a lot of nonsense about magic in stories.

Some of it is loud and flashy, but the vast majority of it, including an awakening, is subtle and easy to miss, but you are awakened."

Jez cupped his hand in front his face and concentered, trying to create a ball of light, but nothing came. He looked at Kerag.

"You didn't expect it to be that easy, did you? You have the ability." Kerag smiled. "You have a lot of ability, in fact. You still have to learn to use it, though. It's close to the surface now, and you should be able to access it easier. It shouldn't leave you feeling as drained either."

"Does it always take that long?"

Kerag pursed his lips. "No, in fact, it generally happens within a day or two."

Jez lowered his eyes. "Oh."

Kerag laughed. "Don't concern yourself with that. It's not unusual for those with instinctual magic to resist awakening. With you being as strong as you are, I'm a little surprised it didn't take longer. Take the rest of the day off." He grinned. "Try to avoid binding any demons."

The next day, Murus, apparently having been informed that Jez had his afternoon free, called him back for a session after lunch. It left him feeling exhausted, and what little time he had left, he spent the time wandering the city. The story of the phobos had spread through the town quickly, but it had died off just as suddenly, dismissed as just another of the strange things that happened in a place that taught magic, and he was able to lose himself in the crowd.

On the first day of the term, Murus didn't call him for lesson. Instead, Jez joined with a dozen other new students in a large room at the base of a central spire. Food of every type was laid on tables scattered throughout the room. Soft music filled the hall, though it had no obvious source. Paintings adorned the wall and a crystal chandelier sent colored lights dancing across the wall. Silver buttons decorated each robe marking the wearer as a member of the upper tier, children of nobles or influential merchants. Many, including Jez himself, wore swords at their waist, though the weapon still made Jez feel uncomfortable. The lower tier, those coming from common families who had been allowed into the Academy on the recommendation of one of the masters, hadn't been invited. These people had spent all their lives in luxury. He felt like an imposter.

The other attendees seemed perfectly at ease in these lavish surroundings, and they spoke easily with each other. Jez tried to involve himself in their conversations, but they all seemed to be talking about how much money or influence their families had. It was as if they were trying to outdo each other, so whenever someone turned to him, he'd politely withdrew from the conversation. He felt like they were laughing behind his back, but he never caught anyone actually doing it.

Finally, after what felt like an eternity, a door swung open at the end of the hall. A short woman in a yellow robe stepped through it, followed by Besis, who wore blue. Five others, each in difference colors filed into the hall. A hush fell over the gathered people as they lined up near the door. The man in orange stepped forward. His long pointed face reminded Jez of an eagle, and he found himself flinching when the man looked in his direction. He cleared his throat as if to quiet the room, though no one was actually speaking.

"Greetings all," he said in a loud, booming voice. "I am Chancellor Balud, master of healing, and head of the Carceri Academy. You have all been accepted as acolytes into the most prestigious institute of learning in the world. As part of the upper tier, you make up the elite of those attending this Academy."

Jez wondered what Dusan could've said about him to get him into the upper tier. He had been the baron's ward for less than a year, and though Dusan had hired tutors, Jez couldn't imagine his education was anywhere near those who had grown up in noble houses, and who'd had access to such resources all their lives.

"Your first term will be something of a probationary period," the chancellor continued. "We will determine whether or not you are fit to study here. Don't worry. As members of the upper tier, I'm sure none of you have anything to worry about. These," he indicated the men and women beside him, "are masters in every major area of study. Master Linala of knowledge, Master Horgar of beasts, Master Besis of protection, Master Rael of secrets, Master Kerag of shadows, and Master Fina of destruction." Each person inclined their heads as the chancellor said their name. "For most of the term, you'll work with their adjutants, advanced students who've studied a given subject for several terms, but the tests at the end of the term will be administered by the masters themselves. You've each been assigned a master to serve as guide, though I understand some changes," his eyes flickered to Besis, "have been requested. These guides will serve to help you work through any difficulties the first term. Go to them with any questions. For now, enjoy the reception, and get to know the masters and fellow students."

He inclined his head and the masters began moving through the crowd. Besis pulled Jez aside which set off a torrent of whispers nearby. The chancellor glared at them, but Besis ignored it.

"I'm sorry I've been ignoring you. The other masters spend a lot of time preparing for examinations, but their actual workload during the tests is actually rather light. I'm somewhat the opposite. Many of the strongest demons are summoned during this time, and they keep me busy. I am still your guide, for now at any rate."

"But why?" Jez asked. "I mean, I thought the baron would've insisted you get removed."

"Oh he did," Besis said, "but there's been a peculiar sickness in Hiranta. It's resisted Balud's efforts to heal it. Most of his time has been spent in the city trying to find a cure, and he hasn't had time to pick a replacement."

"What kind of disease?"

"Oh, I don't know the details. Something about people falling asleep and not waking up again. He says he's never seen anything like it."

The hairs on the back of Jez's neck stood on end, and the blood drained from his face. Besis noticed and waved off his concern.

"Don't give it any mind. It seems confined to the city below. It hasn't made its way up the mountain. At any rate, it doesn't appear to be contagious. It was probably just something they ate."

"But it's not just in Hiranta. Some people have it in Randak."

Besis lifted an eyebrow. "Really? I'll let the chancellor know. Perhaps there's a common cause."

"You're the duke's boy," a boy said.

The speaker was short but stout with soft brown hair and brown eyes. He wore a smile that looked natural, as if smiling were all he did. Besis inclined his head and moved away.

"Actually, I'm Baron Dusan's ward."

Some of the boys around laughed and the pudgy boys face went red. He bowed to Jez. More because he didn't know what else to do than for any other reason, Jez bowed back.

"Don't pay him any mind," a rail thin girl with blond hair said. "His father is a knight. He has a granted title." She the world 'granted' as if it should mean something to Jez. "He's not true nobility. I'm Lina."

She extended a hand, and Jez looked her up and down. She had pale skin and deep green eyes, and he didn't think her gown would look out of place at King Haziel's court. Simply put, she was lovely, but she was also willing to dismiss others as being of lesser worth than she was, and he'd had enough of that over the past couple of months. With a flash of insight, he realized this was what his father feared he would become.

"Neither am I," he said.

The room went silent and Jez looked around, somewhat surprised. About half the students were staring at him. Besis grinned at him but didn't say anything. Lina's eyes went wide and her mouth opened a little. He relished the shocked look on her face. He might not actually be nobility, but he was savvy enough to know that Master Dusan was an important man. He was also childless. Rumors had been circulation around Randak that the baron would eventually adopt him. Dusan had never mentioned it to him, but he'd hoped the rumors had spread to other parts of the kingdom as well. Lina looked back to a pair of students standing nearby, but they seemed just as shocked as she was. Lina was sputtering, and Jez considered saying something, but he had no idea what. Instead, he just nodded at the pudgy boy and walked out of the room. He was halfway up the stairs to the second floor when he realized he hadn't actually gotten the boy's name.

CHAPTER 10

All in all, Jez felt satisfied with his performance. He definitely didn't want to associate with people like Lina. His only real mistake had been going up to his room from the reception. There was no way to leave the central spire without being seen by those downstairs, and he had no idea how to react if he was confronted again. As a result, he spent the next several hours, trapped in his own room. Finally, three hours later a knock came at his door. He opened it to find Master Besis.

"Well, you certainly know how to make friends," Besis said.

Jez's face reddened, and he stepped aside. Besis went in and sat in one of Jez's chairs. Jez took the other one. Besis took in the room.

"You keep a clean room."

Jez tried to keep a straight face, though the words made him feel a little ashamed. He glanced at the trunk that held all his worldly belongings. "I just don't have that many things."

Besis nodded once. "Ah, my apologies. It's so easy to forget you weren't born to this life. You do it so naturally."

Jez stared at him for a second. "What?"

"You handled Lina expertly. She won't be quick to cross words with you again." Jez shook his head and tried to understand what Besis was staying, but it escaped him. Besis's eyes widened slightly. "Are you saying you don't know what you did?"

"I was actually wondering if I should find her to apologize."

Besis let out a bark of laughter. "Don't be ridiculous. Lina Varindatter is a spoiled little girl who spends most of her time figuring out her exact rank among the nobility, which isn't anywhere near yours, by the way."

"But I'm not noble."

Besis shrugged. "It's a little complicated, and to tell you the truth, it's not something I generally concern myself with. For all her talk of true nobility, her grandfather was elevated to the rank of Lord only fifty years ago, and her family has done nothing of significance since then. Their fief is composed of about half a dozen families."

"That's more than I can say," Jez said.

Besis huffed and looked pointedly at the ring on Jez's finger. Jez blushed and covered it with one hand. Besis raised an eyebrow, but Jez didn't explain. Finally, Besis shrugged.

"The general belief is that Dusan will formally adopt you within the next year. Even if he doesn't, you'll likely get an appointment in his barony, if not one in the court of King Haziel himself. Either would put you far above Lord Varin. On top of that, once you master binding, you'll be one of the most respected mages in the kingdom, and master mages have a hierarchy of their own."

"But Baron Dusan doesn't want me to study binding."

Besis shrugged. "Not yet, but he's too intelligent to let this opportunity pass him by. A master mage of any sort will bring much prestige and influence to his house. He'll come around. You just have to bide your time."

"Assuming I don't get kicked out, you mean."

"Why would you be worried about that?"

"Up until six months ago, I was just a fisherman's son. I didn't even know how to read. I'm still not that good at it. These people have all had private tutors and books and things like that all their lives."

"Oh, I wouldn't worry about that. It takes a lot for one of the upper tier to be expelled. The chancellor wouldn't dream of putting you out, not after he went to the trouble of keeping you here. He'll force the other masters to give you private lessons to help you catch up if that's what it takes."

"Why would he do that?"

Besis waved his hand at the room, and Jez looked around. The dream tapestry had been taken down, replaced by one of a wolf howling at the full moon. The wolf's eyes seemed to be made of woven gold. For the first time, he realized the handle for the lantern hanging from the wall was made of silver, and he wondered when he'd become so used to that sort of thing that he stopped noticing it. Even the table had intricate carvings along the side. They were needlessly decadent, but the truth was that he enjoyed them.

"Do you think we provide a room like this for everyone?" Besis asked. "Your patron is Baron Dusan of Korand and he had half a dozen other titles before he was named to the barony. Balud would never dream of offending someone that important. On top of that, if you become baron one day, he'll want you as the Academy's ally. He'll tolerate faults in you that would get anyone else kicked out. As long as you don't commit murder, you won't be expelled."

"It doesn't seem terribly fair, does it?"

Besis raised an eyebrow. "A ward of Baron Dusan worried about fairness? From what I've heard of the man, that's not a quality he cultivates."

Jez shrugged. "I don't really know him that well. I just lived in his house, but he's always been nice to me."

"Yes, I imagine so. Come, it's almost time for your philosophy class."

"You came up here to walk me to class?"

Besis rose and walked to the door. "I came up here to tell you that not everyone is as far below you as Lina. I assumed you were used to outranking everyone around you. I didn't realize the opposite was true."

"I'll be careful," Jez said and followed the master down the tower stairs.

Like the town, most people at the Academy seemed to have forgotten about Jez's involvement with the phobos. Those that did remember downplayed what he'd done. No one wanted to believe an untrained boy could do what one who'd studied for years could not. He'd even heard one rumor saying that Master Besis had actually done the binding. That suited him just fine. He'd seen enough of the students to know that he wanted little to do with them. Still, a few gave him sidelong glances as he walked through the courtyard.

Philosophy was under the dominion of secrets, and Besis led him to a two-story building that might've been an inn in any other place. Like every other building, it was made of black stone. The interior had runes and symbols carved on the wall. Besis pointed to a stairway before leaving to see to his own business. Jez made his way to a room on the second floor. It had a single window. A group of students sat in a circle of chairs. They ranged in age from twelve to sixteen. Most wore brown robes, but a few had the colored robes of adepts. A man of about twenty nodded at him as he came in. He wore deep purple robes with a gold sash marking him as an adjutant. His buttons proclaimed him as one of the upper tier.

"Jezreel Bartinson?" Jez nodded. "Good. That would be everyone then. Have a seat." He looked around the room. "I am Adjutant Lajen. I will be instructing you in your introduction to philosophy. The first thing you need to understand is that you will not find absolute truth here. For the enlightened, absolutes do not exist. Abandon any ideas of good and evil. Those are constructs used by the ignorant masses.

Everything is a shade of gray."

He'd only spoken for a few minutes before Jez's mind started to wander. Lajen's voice stayed completely monotone, never wavering. He sounded like he was reciting a speech he'd given several times. Jez wasn't the only one having trouble paying attention. A few people's heads bobbed as they struggled to stay awake. Lajen seemed not to notice, however. He was too preoccupied with the sound of his own voice. He droned on for what felt like an entire day but was really only an hour judging by the sun. He was in the middle of talking about the difference between good and right, apparently heedless of his previous assertion that good didn't exist, when someone knocked on the door. Lajen looked up with an annoyed look.

"Yes?"

The door swung inward and a purple robed master stood in the doorway, though Jez couldn't remember her name. Lajen inclined his head and smiled.

"Master Rael."

"You've kept them a quarter hour late, Lajen."

"Oh did I?"

"I've warned you about that." The master looked at the students. "You may go."

CHAPTER 11

Jez almost ran out of the building. He was already going to be late for his next class because of Lajen's babbling. He barreled into a giant of a person, and the two tumbled to the ground. The larger person got to his feet first and he helped Jez up. For a moment, Jez could only stare. He had to be at least seven feet tall. A large nose dominated his face, and his left eye looked bigger than his right. His sandy hair was cut short. He wore the same brown robes as Jez, though he lacked the silver buttons of the upper tier.

"Sorry about that." He spoke slowly, and some of the students nearby snickered.

"It was my fault," Jez said. "Sorry, I have to go. I'm late for art." He paused. "Where exactly do they teach art?"

The other student laughed. "Art is in the dominion of shadows. Are you going to the introduction class?" Jez nodded and the other boy extended his hand. "I'm going there myself. I'm Osmund."

The name rang a bell in Jez's mind. He searched his memory until he found it. "You fought in Randak a few weeks ago. I see your hair grew back."

Osmund actually blushed. "I lost."

"But you didn't have to," Jez said. "I mean you hesitated right at the end."

"Look, I'm late for class."

"Sorry, so am I." He shook Osmund's hand. "Jez."

Osmund started walking, and Jez practically had to jog to keep up with his long strides.

"Pleasure to meet you," Osmund said. He missed a step, and for a moment, Jez envisioned the massive form falling on him, but Osmund regained his balance a second later. "Jez? Of Randak? Jezreel? The one who bound the phobos?"

Jez groaned. So much for people forgetting that story. "You heard about that?"

"First that and then being late to Barna's class? You sure like to make an impression."

"Philosophy went long."

Osmund grinned. "Let me guess, Lajen?"

"You've taken the class then?"

"Taken it and gotten kicked out. On the first day, in fact."

"Kicked out? Why?"

"I disagreed when he said good and evil don't exist."

"That's it?"

"Well, I disagreed rather vocally. In fact, we spent half the class in a shouting match."

Jez tried to imagine that stuffy adjutant shouting at Osmund and laughed at the thought. Some of the students near them glanced at him, but they turned away once they saw he was with Osmund.

"So I take it that's not a view you agree with?"

"Oh don't get me wrong. In morality, there are shades of gray, but don't fall into the trap of believing there are only shades of gray. There is absolute good in this world, and there is absolute evil."

Unlike the philosophy adjutant, Osmund spoke with fire and conviction. He wasn't just reciting something. It sounded personal as if

Osmund had experienced both.

"So which is fighting in the arena? Good or evil?"

Osmund shrugged. "That's one of those shades of gray. I need money to pay for my tuition. I make sure no one gets hurt."

"Is that why you hesitated?"

"Here's the shadows district," Osmund said as he pushed open the door to a building the size of a large house. Jez waited for him to answer the question, but he just rushed in and took a seat.

The house was a single room. About twenty students were seated in front of canvases with paintbrushes in their hands. A woman with gray hair down her shoulder and spectacles that sat on a long nose sniffed at them as they came in.

"Good of you to join us, Mister Jecklson. I take it you are Jezreel Bartinson?"

Jez nodded. "Sorry, my last class…"

"It was Lajen," Osmund broke in.

The teacher frowned. "You'd think a philosopher would have a better understanding of time. Or is that another of his absolutes that don't exist?"

A round of laughter told Jez that many people shared Osmund's low opinion of the philosophy teacher. At first, he wondered why someone like that would be allowed to teach a class, but then he remembered what Master Besis had said about how the chancellor wouldn't allow Jez to be kicked out. Lajen likely belonged to a rich and powerful family. Jez was beginning to realize the Academy was not the bastion of learning he'd imagined it to be.

CHAPTER 12

Jez sat next to Osmund as Barna began explaining the techniques a beginning painter would use. Before each student, there were a handful of paintbrushes of different sizes and a palette holding ten colors. A wooden cup filled with water also stood nearby to clean his brushes. He could see paint stains inside indicating it had been used for this purpose for a long time. Barna pointed to a bowl of fruit in the center of the room and instructed them to paint it.

"Don't worry if it doesn't look too real," she said. "At this stage, I just want to assess each of your skills."

Without thinking, Jez picked up the thickest brush and dipped it in white paint and slathered it across the canvas.

"That's an interesting choice," Osmund said. "You want a white background?"

Jez shrugged and dipped the brush in the white again and started evening out the paint on the canvas.

"Did you really bind the phobos or was it Master Besis?" Osmund asked.

"Why did you hold back in your battle?"

Osmund's eyes flickered at Jez before he returned his attention to his painting. The larger boy seemed to be painting the apple though Jez only guessed that because of the color. The red blob was at least four times the size of the actual fruit, and Osmund had slathered on the paint so thick that it was running down the canvas and dripping onto the floor. Absently, Jez switched brushes and dipped it in black.

"I don't fight anymore," Osmund said.

"Why not? You're good at it."

"If I tell you, will you tell me about binding the phobos?"

"You can ask anyone about that. A lot of people saw it."

"A lot of people were running away from it. I want to hear what you have to say."

Jez switched to purple. He considered for a second before nodding. "All right, but not here."

Some of the students were already throwing glances their way while try to pretend they weren't listening. Osmund looked around, apparently seeing the others for the first time and nodded. He went back to his painting and seemed to be trying to add an orange next to his apple, but he wasn't having any success.

"They don't want me to fight anymore," he said after a minute of silence. "That's the third time I've almost won but stopped at the last minute. The gamblers thought I was throwing the fights."

"But you weren't."

Osmund shook his head. "Battle magic does something to me. It makes me want to hurt some people."

There was pain in his voice, and he reached up to wipe a tear from his eye. He hadn't realized there was paint on his fingers, so he left a blue streak on his face. Jez put a large glob of purple near the center of his palate and added a little red and white to it. He didn't have anything to stir the mixture with so he used the back of the largest brush. He wouldn't be using that one anymore anyway.

"That girl you were fighting at Randak…"

"I would've killed her. I wanted to. She's a skilled fighter, but outside of the arena, she uses threats to get what she wants. She's little more than a bully."

For a second, it looked like Osmund's eyes glowed, but he blinked. When he opened them again, they were back to steel gray.

"Did she hurt someone you care about?"

"No, I'd never seen her before that day in the arena."

"Then how did you know?" Jez went back to white.

"That's just it," Osmund said. "There's no way I could know, but I'm sure. I wanted to kill her based on a feeling."

The white needed just a touch of yellow.

"So you stopped and let her beat you."

"I just stopped," he said. "The beating, she managed on her own. Anyway, like I said, that was the third time. The arena masters don't want to see me anymore. I'm not sure how I'll pay for my next term."

Red now. Then orange and yellow. Green and blue. Then a mixture of blue, black, and purple. Then purple by itself.

"Mister Bartinson, what are you doing?"

Jez blinked. Barna was standing over him, staring at his canvas. He looked at it and gasped. Instead of the fruit, he'd painted something else. He didn't even know what to call it. A pillar of cloud dominated the center of the picture, deep purple at the edges and lightening toward the center. They blended together, giving it shadow and texture. It looked so real, almost seeming to pop out of the canvas.

Inside the cloud, he could make out spheres and dots of light. The cloud was set along a black background filled with stars. One star, closer than the others, was emerging from the cloud. He realized he was looking at a star being born. In fact, many of the stars had wisps of cloud, barely visible, that trailed back to the central mass. Toward the top, the cloud gave way to the torso, neck, and head of a human. The face was outlined in yellow, but it was so faint no details of the being could be determined. At the edges of the canvas stood seven figures, each only a few inches tall and clothed in a robe of a different color, red, orange, yellow, green, blue, indigo, and violet. Their faces were the only spots on the entire canvas that had no color. Jez looked down and saw that he'd been mixing yellow, white, and orange to create the skin tone of a light skinned person. He knew that, given time, he would've mixed other colors that together would represent a wide swath of humanity. Even knowing that, he had no idea what he'd painted.

"I'm sorry," he said. "I don't know."

Barna barely noticed his response. "This detail is amazing. It's more intricate than I would've thought someone capable of with these brushes. The stars. How did you do them?" She picked up the smallest brush, which was still perfectly clean. "They're too fine for this, even if you had used it."

Jez stared at her. He searched his memory but came up empty.

"He painted around them," Osmund said. "I thought it was odd that he'd picked a white background. He painted most of the canvas white and then went over it with other colors, leaving small dots everywhere. I thought he was just creating a strange background."

They both looked as Osmund, but the other boy was staring at the painting. Barna shrugged.

"Yes, I suppose that makes sense." She waved her hand over the center of the cloud. "This color. How did you make it?" What were the proportions?"

"I really don't know," Jez said. "The whole thing was instinct."

There were murmurs from the class and Barna looked around. She blinked, realizing they had become the center of attention.

"Well, as impressive as it may be, it wasn't the assignment." She glanced at Osmund's painting, which was little more than a couple of blobs of color of indeterminate shape. "And what exactly is this?"

Osmund cleared his throat. "It's the bowl of fruit."

Barna started and looked closer. "Oh yes. I see it now. There's the apple. Well, we'll need to work on that. I'll be speaking to the master about you, Mister Bartinson. I don't think you belong in a beginner class. That's enough everyone. Wash up, and you can go."

She went back to the center of the room and started writing on a sheet of paper. The rest of the students started washing off their brushes. For a moment, Jez just stared at his painting.

"I don't even know what this is."

"It's the creation," Osmund said, his voice barely above a whisper.

"The creation of what?"

"Everything." He pointed at the figure at the top. Somehow, it gave the impression of being enormous. "You see? There's the Creator presiding over the birth of the universe. There are the seven pharim lords who stand guard." He pointed at one in red. "Manakel." His finger moved down to the one in orange. "Apalel." He went on, touching each as he spoke their name. "Gayel, Aniel, Sariel, Leziel, and Daziel, each presiding over a different dominion and look." He pointed at the cloud and Jez realized there was a vaguely human shaped figure inside of it. In fact, it was one of many. "It's the pharim placing everything in its proper place. This is the most detailed depiction of the creation I've ever seen, and you did it in under an hour."

It took Jez several seconds to find his words. He scanned the painting, his eyes lingering briefly on the blue-robed figure, the one Osmund had called Sariel. Osmund's words resonated true. "How did I do this?"

"You're asking me?"

Jez shrugged and shook his head. "Sorry, but ever since I arrived here, my life has been strange."

"I'll say. Do you have another class today?" Jez shook his head. "Good. Let's go. You promised to tell me about the phobos."

Jez nodded once. As they left the room, he turned back and gave the painting one last look. The whole scene seemed entirely too familiar, and that thought sent chills down his spine.

CHAPTER 13

"It just came to you?" Osmund asked.

They had gone to Osmund's room on the fourth floor of the tower. It was much smaller than the space Jez had and was little more than a bed and a table with a single chair. Osmund gave Jez the chair, which, unlike the ones in his room, lacked a cushion, and the larger boy sat on the bed. Jez wished they'd gone to his room, but he hadn't wanted to offend Osmund by suggesting it.

Jez nodded. "I'd never even seen a demon before that day, but I knew exactly how to bind it."

"You're a limaph," Osmund said.

"A what?"

"A limaph." Seeing the blank look on Jez's face, he quirked his head. "Didn't you attend temple services in Randak?"

Jez shrugged. "I was a fisherman most of my life. We had to rise early in the morning. I went with my mother before she died, but I don't really remember. Ever since I was old enough, I went out with my father to go fishing. He didn't really have a lot of time for anything else."

"What about when you lived with Baron Dusan?"

"It never really came up."

Osmund looked incredulous, but finally, he let out a breath. "You know about the rebellion of the pharim, right?"

Jez rolled his eyes. "Of course."

"Well, after some of the pharim rebelled against the Creator, he cursed them to wander the earth. He called them the afur, those who were brought low. Some of them had children with mortal women and…"

"I've heard this story before," Jez said. "Why only women?"

"What?"

"You said they had children with mortal women. Why only women? Why not men?"

"Ah. No one really knows. Some theorize there are only male pharim, but they're a minority. I don't think pharim actually have genders. Even their shape is more a reflection of their will than anything else. Most scholars think that a pharim is a creative being, and as such, it is capable of providing the spark needed to start a new life, but not being alive themselves, they are incapable of nurturing a life within them the way a human woman can."

Jez's eyes glazed over for a second. "You study theology, don't you?"

Osmund grinned. "Is it that obvious?" Jez nodded, and Osmund continued. "Anyway, these children were the limaph. Being closer to pure creation than ordinary humans, many of the limaph were powerful mages, and sometimes, they had insights into the secret knowledge of the pharim."

"That's what you think I am?"

"Not a first generation, obviously," Osmund said. "The afur vanished from history so long ago only the oldest records mention them at all, but some of the most powerful magicians in history have claimed to be descended from them. If you really banished a phobos by instinct…It makes sense."

"An interesting theory, Osmund," a voice said from the doorway.

Jez turned to see a woman in an indigo robe. She was carrying a leather satchel with a rolled up paper sticking out of it. She was the same one who'd stopped Lajen's class, and he searched his mind for the name. Osmund rose and inclined his head.

"Master Rael."

"I'm surprised to find you here. I would've thought you'd go to Jezreel's room."

"I didn't want to just invite myself in there," Osmund said.

Jez looked at him. "Is that why we came here?"

Rael cleared her throat, and both of the boys looked at her. "I would speak with your young friend, Osmund," she said. "If you will give us a minute."

"Of course," he said, walking toward the door. "I'll go for a walk."

"We won't be long," she said. "Perhaps a quarter hour."

Osmund nodded again and left, closing the door behind him. Jez stood up to offer her the chair, but she waved him off and plopped down on the bed. She pursed her lips and pressed down on it.

"You know, these really are dreadful. I understand wanting to offer more to the upper tier, but we should at least give the lower beds without lumps in them, wouldn't you say?"

Jez nodded. "I guess so."

"I suppose you've experienced both poverty and wealth. That's not something many can say."

Jez felt his face heat up. "We weren't really poor."

Rael bowed her head. "Forgive me. I meant no offense. You've certainly made a splash in our quiet corner of the world."

"It wasn't really by choice, Master."

Jez almost said more but thought better of it. Master Rael, however, sensed the unspoken words and cocked her head.

"What aren't you saying?"

"It's just that I doubt this place is ever quiet. I mean that phobos would've escaped even if I wasn't here, and Master Besis would've stopped it."

Giving up any hope of finding a comfortable sitting position, she got up and walked to the window. Osmund's room overlooked the protection district, so he guessed she was looking at the building the demon had come out of.

"True enough," she said without turning around, "but an escaped spirit isn't really a rare thing. As you say, Besis would've handled it. Most of his adjutants could take care of a phobos without too much difficulty as well. A boy without any training binding it, however, *that* is a rare thing. That's not really why I'm here, though. Tell me, have you ever studied theology?" The question caught Jez off guard, and he hesitated. She turned to him and he shook his head. "Are you sure?"

"Master, I haven't studied anything." He turned away from her, but with the small room, there wasn't really anything else to look at. "I can barely read. I didn't even know who the limaph were until Osmund told me. Why?"

She took the paper out of her satchel and unrolled it on the table revealing the picture Jez had painted. She placed a finger on the pharim lord dressed in red. Then she tapped on a nearby dot. For the first time, Jez realized all the stars weren't white. They each had a slight coloring.

"You placed Manakel with his head near a blue star, just below the place where the creative storm changed to the Creator." She moved her hand to the figure in blue, and Jez was filled with a sense of familiarity. "He was opposite to Sariel who you put between a red star and an indigo one."

"I did?"

She nodded. "Manakel is the pharim lord over destruction, so his dominion overlaps protection. Sariel rules over protection, which includes an aspect of destruction as well as secrets. There are at least fifty other details in that painting associated with obscure details found only in the most ancient sacred texts. At least half that many other ones deal with areas that have been debated for several centuries."

"I don't know what to say, Master," Jez said. "I wasn't paying attention to what I was doing. It just happened."

"First a binding, and then this. You are a most interesting person, Jezreel Bartinson. May I have your permission to ask your patron if you can study theology? I have a feeling you would excel in that area. A few nobles take that as an area of study, though it would be for next term, of course."

Jez muttered a response, but he was so surprise even he didn't know what he'd said. Jez's mind was drawn back to the fiery dream he'd had the night before he'd arrived at the Academy. His nostrils flared at the scent of sulfur, but it only lasted a second. Master Rael raised an eyebrow, and Jez shook his head.

"I'm sorry, Master Rael. I need to get to my next class. I don't want to be late."

He scurried out the door before she had a chance to call him on the lie. He practically ran down the hall and through the door leading to the stairs. Osmund's quarters were on the fourth floor, but Jez flew down the steps and burst into the first floor chamber. The painting had been unnerving enough without knowing just how much information had gone into creating it. He wasn't sure what was going on with him or where all this knowledge was coming from, but it terrified him.

CHAPTER 14

Once again, Jez rushed out the door, and once again, he barreled into Osmund. The two tumbled to the ground. Jez bit his lip and tasted blood. They spent several seconds untangling themselves. For an irrational second, Jez wanted to blame Osmund for everything that had happened. If the other boy hadn't distracted him with all the talk about the phobos, Jez would've been focused on painting the bowl of fruit, and he would've never attracted the attention of Master Rael. That was foolish, of course. The incident with the phobos had happened before he'd met Osmund, and Jez knew his hidden knowledge would've come out eventually. He mumbled an apology. He caught a few people staring at them, so he motioned to Osmund, and they moved away from the tower entrance and into a side street on the edge of the beast district.

"What happened?" Osmund asked.

"It's just too much," Jez cried out. "How do I know the things I know? How can I do the things I can do? Am I some sort of freak?"

Osmund shook his head. "No, not a freak. A limaph."

"It sounds like the same thing."

"Jez." The tone of his voice caught Jez's attention. He looked up, but Osmund was staring at the ground and wouldn't lift his gaze. "I am a limaph."

For a moment, Jez just stared at him. He was the biggest person he'd ever seen, and his face had never looked quite right. Was that because he wasn't really a person? But no, that was an unworthy thought. Osmund was the only student who hadn't tried to get on Jez's good side because of the baron. He realized he was staring and turned away, but that was equally conspicuous.

"Sorry," he said finally. "I didn't mean to insult you."

Osmund shrugged, but he still wouldn't meet Jez's eyes. He spoke softly almost as if he should be the one apologizing to Jez. "It's no more than others have called me. Look, I'll understand if you'd rather not be seen with me. I don't exactly belong to a powerful family or anything."

"No, Osmund, I really am sorry. I shouldn't have said that."

"Forget it," Osmund said. "How did your meeting with Master Rael go?"

"She wants me to study theology."

"That makes sense, especially if you really are a limaph. Are you going to do it?"

"It's not really my choice."

"Why not? You get to decide what classes you take."

"No, *you* get to decide what classes to take," Jez said. "I have to get approval from Baron Dusan. I already asked him if I could study binding, and I thought he was going to pull me out of the Academy for asking."

"Really? Why?"

"He says it's too dangerous."

"Well, you can't really argue with him on that point."

Jez paused as a hawk landed a few feet away. It shimmered and became a green robed adept. The girl looked at them before scurrying away, though she looked over her shoulder at Osmund several times, obviously afraid of him. She turned a corner and Jez raised an eyebrow at Osmund.

"Says the person who studied battle magic."

Osmund shrugged. "I told you. I have to pay for my tuition. Besides, it's not as dangerous."

Jez's jaw dropped. "What do you mean it's not as dangerous? It uses the dominion of destruction. The whole point is to be dangerous."

Osmund shrugged. "When I'm practicing battle magic, I have a human opponent, and they think the way a human does. If something goes wrong, they stop and are declared the winner. If something goes wrong when you're trying to bind something, you still have a spirit doing its best to kill you. The baron shouldn't have a problem with theology, though. I've gotten a few paper cuts, but that's as dangerous as it's ever been."

"I don't know. The baron just wants me studying things a noble should learn."

Osmund rolled his eyes. "I've heard some of the upper tier go on for hours about their family and lineage. For you, theology is almost the same thing. Don't you want to learn about your heritage?"

"I guess." He sounded as unsure as he felt, and he couldn't shake the feeling that some secrets were better left unknown. "We should probably go talk to Master Rael. I just sort of ran out on her."

Osmund nodded, and they headed back for the tower. They were about to open the door when Lina came out of the door leading a group of students. Though they weren't in their student's robes, Jez recognized them as first term students in the upper tier. Lina herself wore a violet dress, obviously intended to impersonate the robes of an adept of shadows, though there was no way she'd advanced enough to be allowed to choose an area of focus. She looked at them and turned up her nose.

"Jezreel," she said.

"Lina," he said with just as much contempt in his voice. He was speaking before he knew what he was saying. "I was hoping you could help me with something. I was looking at a map of Ashtar, and I couldn't tell where your father's lands were. I found Baron Dusan's easily enough. They're so big, after all, but I couldn't find Lord Varin's."

She clenched her teeth and her face went scarlet. Some of her friends looked at each other in surprise, though a few tried to hide smile. Behind him, Osmund snickered. Jez was doing his best to keep from smiling, but he wasn't doing a very good job of it.

It took Lina almost a full minute to regain her composure. "You're new to this life, so I'm going to explain some things to you. The tiers are separate for a reason. It won't do you any good to associate with people like that."

"Thanks," Jez said flatly. "I'm sure your grandfather would agree."

Lina went even redder than before. She was about to say something, but Osmund broke in.

"I don't think he needs advice from someone like you about what kind of people to associate with."

"What was that, freak?"

A pale skinned blond boy stepped forward with balled fists. His friends cheered him on. Emboldened by their support, he stood right in front of the larger boy. A crowd had started to gather, shouting jeers at them. Osmund stood up straight and towered over the other boy by at least two feet. He tensed his muscles, and the boy took a step back and scowled.

"Someone needs to teach you to respect your betters."

Osmund smirked. "I've met some who I think were better people than me, Regis. You're not one of them."

Regis's sputtered and started to say something, but Osmund grinned. His eyes glowed with orange fire, and a thin wisp of smoke rose from each. A yelp escaped Regis's throat, and most of the others took a step back, but Lina remained where she was. She closed her eyes and began to whimper, but she didn't move. Jez was impressed, in spite of himself. A second later, the fire in Osmund's eyes died, and his shoulders slumped.

"Just leave me alone," Osmund said and started to walk through them, headed for the entrance to the tower.

They parted for him, but as he stepped onto the stairs leading up, Regis clasped his hands together and reached up to slam them into the back of Osmund's head. Osmund was so much taller than him, however, that the angle was awkward, so he didn't get a solid hit. Osmund stumbled and turned to face his attacker. Regis didn't hesitate. He stepped onto the stairs and slammed his fist into Osmund's face. Just before it impacted, Jez saw his friend's eyes glowing, though not with fire they'd had a few moments ago. No, they glowed with pure white light, the light that he'd seen in Osmund's eyes in the battle at Randak, when Osmund said he'd almost killed his opponent. Osmund's head jerked in response to the impact, and Regis drew back to strike again.

"Regis, stop!"

Jez reached for him, but one of the other boys tackled him, and held him to the ground. One put a hand on Jez's sword, though it hadn't even occurred to him to draw it. Regis glared at him.

"You're no better than he is." He delivered a hard punch into Osmund's stomach, and the larger boy fell over. In spite of their difference in size, Regis showed no fear. He kept his fists raised, and Jez kept worrying he'd draw the sword he wore at his belt, but he just sneered. "Peasants without an ounce of noble blood in your veins."

"I have noble blood," Osmund said from the floor. He rolled onto his stomach and stood on hands and knees, though he kept is head down. His voice was deeper, and there was the unmistakable tinge of anger. It seemed to echo forever. "It is a nobility you know nothing about."

Regis launched a kick, but before it connected, a wing of pure light emerged from Osmund's back and blocked the blow. It swept the bully's legs out from under him. Another wing grew from Osmund. Lina screamed and those with her huddled together, shaking with fear. All around them, people cried out in shock, and many in the crowd fled including those who had been holding Jez down.

"Osmund?" Jez asked as he got to his feet.

Light crept out from the wings and crawled along Osmund's skin until his entire body glowed. His arms thickened, and his student robes melted together and formed a brilliant red robe that seemed to be on fire, yet did not burn. His skin became the sunbaked tan of someone who spent their entire life outside, and his hair elongated and became jet black. He got to his feet, and then kept on rising until he stood a several inches off the ground. Muscles covered every inch of him and he grew a foot taller. He reached for his belt and closed his hand around the hilt of a sword that hadn't been there a moment before. Thunder crashed as he drew it, and a wind that threatened to lift Jez off his feet blew through the crowd.

"Osmund is a weak fool." He glared at Lina and her friends. The pure white of his eyes grew too bright for Jez to look at, and his wings shone with the brightness of the noonday sun, then they grew brighter still. Even the sword seemed more light than metal. "These evil ones will face my sword."

Regis scrambled to his feet and tried to run, but Osmund's wings shot out, tripping the student. He tried to draw his weapon, but Osmund kicked it away. Others with him started backing away, but Osmund spread his wings, dispelling every shadow, and they froze in their tracks. Steam rose from their skin as it started to blister. Lina began to weep, and tried to run, but Osmund swung his sword, cutting a shallow gash on her face. The flaming sword cauterized the wound before it had a chance to bleed, and Lina screamed.

"I would have you know my name before I kill you," the shining being said. "I am Ziary, sword of justice, and destroyer of all that is evil."

He pointed his sword at Regis, and it rippled as if made of fire. Regis yelped and tried to back up, but Ziary roared out a sound that could never have come from a human throat. Regis froze, his eyes wide in terror.

"Osmund, don't!" Jez cried out.

"I am not Osmund!" Ziary shouted.

His sword pulsed with every word. Dark clouds swirled above them. Jez tried to get between them, but Ziary flapped his wings once, and the force of the wind sent Jez to his knees. In desperation, he searched inside himself for some hint of how to bind this thing, but there was nothing. Ziary didn't exude that sense of wrongness that had prompted his previous actions. Jez tried to remember what he had done to the phobos, how he'd created the gossamer web, but he came up empty. Finally, he threw his hands forward and tried to summon power, to do anything, but nothing happened. Ziary, however, seemed to notice his efforts and turned to him.

"You would defend them from me? Why?"

There was genuine confusion in his voice as if this being couldn't understand why it shouldn't just kill the students cowering before him. Before Jez could respond, Ziary spoke again.

"No."

Though the word came from Ziary own lips, it was higher pitched and lacked the unnerving echo of Ziary's voice. Ziary blinked, and the light in his eyes went out, revealing the gray of Osmund's eyes.

"No," Ziary's voice said. "I won't let you!"

"You don't have a choice. This is my body. I won't let you use it to commit murder."

"Murder is a crime," Ziary said. "An execution is justice."

"No," Osmund said. "It isn't."

The wings had become translucent and the sword vanished altogether. The winds calmed, and the clouds dispersed. The light around Ziary faded, and he floated to the ground, returning to normal proportions as his feet came to rest on the stone. The robes disappeared, replaced by Osmund's student ones.

"You'll pay for this, freak," Regis cried out.

Osmund's eyes glowed, but it faded after a moment, and Osmund looked away. Regis was blubbering. His face was red and covered in blisters. Jez couldn't understand what he was saying. Many of the others had been similarly burned. Lina was crying as she ran her hand across the wound on her face. Her touch seemed to make it hurt more, and she fell to her knees cried out in anguish.

Someone must have gone to get the chancellor because Balud arrived a second later. He took one look at the burned bullies and called for an adept to take them to the healing district. Several students offered the injured shoulders to lean on and helped them walk. Lina wouldn't get up, and they called for a stretcher. It arrived a few minutes later, and she was carried off. Balud glared at Jez and Osmund.

"Does anyone want to tell me what happened or shall I guess?"

"It was an accident, Chancellor," Osmund said.

"You promised there wouldn't be any more of these accidents."

Jez stared at his friend. Osmund only nodded, obviously not intending to say anything more.

"They attacked him," Jez said. "They hit him in the back of the head."

"Yes, those boys will be punished too. I can ignore a fist fight in some back alley, but this wasn't even a duel. You could have killed them. Osmund, you'll be imprisoned beneath the tower. If there are complications with their healing, you will be held personally responsible." He pointed at a nearby adjutant in a blue robe. "Go get Master Besis. I need Osmund's power bound."

CHAPTER 15

"What just happened?" Jez asked.

Osmund stared at him through the bars of the cell in the basement of the tower. It was in a bleak corridor. Although the walls and floor were made from the same black stone as the rest of the city, it seemed somehow muted, and lacked the shimmering quality of the stone outside. Even the lanterns barely seemed to dent the darkness. Osmund was sitting in a stone bench built into the wall. He kept his eyes down and his shoulders slumped. Master Besis had been apologetic as he locked him up, but Regis was the nephew of a powerful lord, and with Osmund having no connections at all, the chancellor had decided to deal with him harshly until the situation was sorted out. Besis had placed bindings around the cell that would keep Osmund from accessing his power, though he hadn't been sure if those would keep Osmund from transforming.

"Ziary came out," Osmund said.

"I saw that," Jez said. "Who is Ziary?"

"It's just like he said. He's the sword of justice. He's…" Osmund scanned the ceiling. "The afur passed down something to the limaph. It's something grafted to our souls. Some call it a scion of the pharim. I thought I had him under control. It's been a long time since he came out."

"You can do it because you're a limaph?" Osmund nodded. "You think I can transform into something like that?"

Osmund shrugged. "Maybe you can't. It depends on how much of you is pharim. Master Rael thinks my line is the culmination of several different lines of limaph. Ziary can manifest himself if I'm not careful, but only about one in a thousand limaph have a scion powerful enough to do that."

"That didn't seem much like the pharim I've heard of."

Osmund chuckled and leaned back into the darkness. "The pharim you've heard of are the watered down versions used in children's tales. True pharim are creatures of absolutes, and the scions are only slightly less so. They are terrible if they think you're opposed to their purpose. Ziary has no room for mercy."

They both went silent at the sound of footsteps coming down the stairs. The chancellor's hair was frazzled and his robe hung loose. He was breathing heavily and when he saw them, he let out a long breath and looked at Osmund.

"I don't suppose you can tell me what exactly you did to them."

"It wasn't really me. I don't have any control when Ziary comes out."

"Fine. What did that thing you become do?"

"Ziary used the fires of justice to burn them with their own evil."

"No dramatics, please. I need specifics. I'll grant you they're bullies, but I wouldn't call them evil."

"Chancellor I don't know exactly how it works. I do know that if they didn't have at least some evil, the light wouldn't have burned them."

"No matter what I try, I can't heal their burns. I don't suppose you know how to help them."

Osmund shook his head. "It's pharim power. I'm not sure it can be healed magically. It should heal naturally, though."

Balud nodded. "What about Lina?"

"He hit her with a sword."

"Obviously. In the others, I could at least dull their pain. I can't even do that much for her. She screamed until her voice went hoarse."

"Chancellor, I just don't know. If Ziary's sword isn't a pharim's weapon, then it's at least close."

Jez shook his head, but stopped himself before he actually spoke. Ziary's sword was nothing like those wielded by the pharim. Lina would never have survived a pharim's blade. He just had no idea how he knew that.

"The pain seems to be subsiding on its own," the chancellor said. She won't die, but she'll bear an ugly scar for the rest of her life. Her family won't soon forgive you for that."

"But her family isn't that important, right?" Jez asked.

Balud raised an eyebrow. "Not important compared to Baron Dusan, but compared to a boy with no family? She may as well be a queen. Add that to the testimony of Regis and the others and things aren't looking well for you, Osmund. Master Rael has asked for lenience, but I'm limited in what I can do. I have no choice but to banish you from the Carceri Academy."

"What?" Jez cried out, but he took a step back when the chancellor's eyes fell on him. He clenched his fists and stepped forward. "Chancellor, they started it."

"A few punches and kicks don't compare with throwing deadly magic against someone."

"What if I vouch for him?" Jez asked. "Master Dusan is more important than Lina's family, right?"

"If you were the baron's son, and if he added his word to yours, then maybe, but as it is? No, I'm sorry. It wouldn't be enough."

"But…"

"I understand," Osmund cut him off. "How long do I have before I need to be gone?"

"You'll leave first thing in the morning. Master Besis will go with you while you prepare your belongings. You'll come back here to sleep, and he'll escort you to the edge of the city."

Osmund managed a weak grin. "The protection master himself. I guess I'm honored."

The chancellor chuckled. "Regis objected most severely. He wanted you to go alone as a way to shame you. I think he might've insisted on your execution if he could've found a way to justify it. I convinced him by saying that if you got it in your head to do harm, Master Besis would be there to stop you."

"Do you really think I'd go after him?"

"Vengeance can do strange things to a person." Balud shrugged. "Particularly to someone with a spirit of vengeance inside of them."

Osmund looked down. "Ziary is a spirit of justice, not vengeance."

"Say that to the half dozen children in my sick ward. No, I don't think you'd go after him, but Ziary might. I'm sorry to see you go, Osmund, but I'm not sorry to have that thing out of my school. I'll be right back. Besis is waiting upstairs."

CHAPTER 16

Osmund didn't have much, just a few changes of clothes and some sheets of paper. There were a couple of books in his room, but they belonged to the Academy. Jez gave him a handful of gold coins. Osmund tried to refuse, but Jez wouldn't take them back. For his part, Master Besis just watched as Osmund packed all his belongings into a small travel sack. He slung it over his shoulder and looked at the protection master.

"Do I really have to go back to the cell?"

"I'm the only one the chancellor will trust to keep your powers in check, and I can't watch over you all night. Even if it can't suppress your transformation, the cell is specially prepared to dampen access to magic. Even Ziary would have trouble there. Aside from that, you are a skilled battlemage."

"What if I just leave now?"

"The sun will set in a few hours. You won't have time to make it all the way down. That trail is dangerous in the dark."

"I can take care of myself."

"What if you fall?"

Osmund shrugged. "Ziary can fly."

Besis sighed. "The chancellor won't like it, but since you've been expelled, he'll have no real authority over you once you leave Tarcai. I'll walk you to the edge of town."

"Are you sure?" Jez asked. "Maybe I can talk to Baron Dusan. If he steps in…"

Osmund shook his head. "I've heard of the baron. I don't think I'd like to be indebted to him."

"He's not such a bad guy."

"Didn't you say you barely know him?"

"Well, yes."

Osmund stood up and walked to his window. He stared out over the city for several seconds. Jez walked up next to him, though he felt like a child next to a giant.

"And you're from his lands, where it's probably a crime to speak out against him."

"I've never heard anyone say anything, but that doesn't mean…"

"How many times have you heard people complaining about the masters?"

Jez threw a sidelong glance at Besis, but the master simply smiled. "Do you think we don't know?"

Jez nodded. "All the time."

"Exactly. People always complain about their leaders. They usually don't mean anything by it, but they always do. If they don't, you have to wonder why. Baron Dusan is not a man whose attention I want to grab."

"But you're going through Randak, aren't you?" Besis asked.

Osmund nodded, and Jez looked at him quizzically.

"You are?"

"I'm from the Narian Isles, and Randak is the closest port."

"Can you wait a little while? I want to write a letter to my father."

"You could speak to him through the speaking stone," Besis said.

Jez shook his head. "He doesn't have a stone, and he never really trusted Master Dusan. I would send a letter with one of the normal messengers, but he can't read, and even if I paid the messenger to do it…"

Osmund nodded. "He might charge your father to read it anyway. Go ahead. I'll wait here."

Jez uttered a thanks and ran down the two flights of stairs to his room. He pulled a sheet of paper out of his desk and scribbled a letter mentioning everything that had happened to him, though he left out the part about Osmund thinking he was a limaph. When he looked over it, he frowned. It was barely legible, so he pulled out another sheet of paper and forced himself to write slowly. Satisfied that Osmund would, at least, be able to read it, he folded it up and stuffed it in an envelope. He dripped wax from a candle onto it, but didn't bother to seal it. The ring Dusan had given him would only serve to upset his father.

He ran back up and almost crashed into Master Rael. She was coming out of Osmund's room and nodded at him. She didn't bring up his study of theology, but he had a feeling she wasn't one to give up. He found Osmund and Besis waiting for him. He handed the letter to Osmund and told him where to deliver it. Then, he walked with him to the edge of the city. The plains beneath them seemed to stretch out forever. There was an odd peace in the air, but Osmund was looking in the opposite direction and couldn't seem to turn away from Tarcai.

"After you step off the caldera, you won't be permitted to return," Besis said. "The city's wards will alert us if you try. Are you sure you wouldn't rather spend one more night here and say goodbye to your friends?"

"I don't really have any friends here, aside from Jez that is. Master Rael is the closest I've come, and I've already said all that needs to be said to her."

Besis nodded and extended a hand. Osmund looked at it, somewhat surprised before clasping it. "Live well, Osmund Jecklson. I regret that you never studied under me. I would've been interested to see what someone with your talents could've done with the study of binding."

Osmund inclined his head. "Thank you, Master Besis. Maybe in time, I'll be able to come back."

"Perhaps," the master said, though Jez could tell neither of them believed it.

Osmund turned to Jez, and they clasped hands. "Thank you for your friendship. I wish I could've gotten to know you better."

"So do I," Jez said. "Live well, Osmund Jecklson."

"Live well, Jezreel Bartinson. You are a good person. Don't let them change you."

"You know, we do try to improve people, Mister Jecklson."

"And I try to keep Ziary under control. We both failed. Half a dozen students are in the sick ward. One is disfigured, and I am expelled. Guard yourself, Jez. There are few enough good men in places of power. The world could use someone like you."

"I'll do my best."

Osmund nodded to each of them and headed down the mountain.

CHAPTER 17

Jez cried out as the practice sword whacked his thigh. A second later, another blow knocked his own weapon from his hand. Murus held the point of his weapon to Jez's throat and sighed.

"I think you may be even worse than when you started."

"I'm sorry. I'm having trouble concentrating."

Murus sneered. "That's no excuse. More than one swordsman has lost his head because he couldn't be bothered to keep his mind on what he was doing. If you get in a duel, you must be able to fight at the top of your ability. Put everything else away. Your opponent won't wait around for you to have a good day."

Jez inclined his head. "Yes, Murus."

"Go. Clean yourself up. You should have just enough time before your first class."

Jez nodded and ran to his rooms. Servants in the tower had standing orders to have his bathtub filled whenever he returned from his training sessions. He didn't have time to enjoy it though and barely spent any time in the water before getting out and throwing on his robes. He rushed to the building in the shadows district where his illusion class was held and took a seat. It was only then that he realized he was actually a few minutes early.

Jez's thoughts were still on Osmund as the other students trickled in. No one sat beside him, and Jez realized that a myth had already started building around him. The binding and the painting were bad enough, but people had started associating him with Ziary's attack.

Curiously enough, this class was not taught by an adjutant, but rather by Kerag, master of shadows himself. From the way the other students looked at each other, it was obvious he didn't normally do this. His eyes roamed the crowd, pausing briefly on one boy who wore bright clothes instead of proper robes. The boy gave a sheepish grin, and Kerag sighed and continued looking over the class until his gaze settled on Jez. After a moment, Jez felt his face go red. Kerag only stared at Jez for a second but enough others noticed that they began throwing him sidelong glances and whispering to each other. Kerag cleared his throat and the class went silent.

"To the masses, illusion is the art of creating false images, and indeed, that's what the street tricksters who perform in village inns do. A master illusionist, however, can use his abilities to deceive all twelve senses."

"Twelve?" a boy in the front row asked.

"The five primary senses and the seven dealing with the different dominions. Those are much harder to deceive and are beyond the scope of this class, but keep that in mind. There are even people who specialize in the dominion of shadow who can make an illusion seem real even to an illusionist. Has anyone ever actually done illusions before?"

Three people raised their hands and Master Kerag pointed at a pudgy boy with a round face. It took Jez a second to recognize him as the boy from the reception who'd confused him with a duke's son.

"Atrius, was it?" Some of the others snickered, but the boy nodded. "Come on up here."

He pointed at the spot next to him. Atrius went red in the face and shrank back into his chair, but Master Kerag glared at him. He broke out in a sweat, but got up and walked next to the master.

"Show us what you can do."

Atrius looked around. For a second, panic painted his features. Then, he took a few deep breaths and turned back to Master Kerag. "Can you have the class clap?"

Kerag wrinkled his brow. "Why? You haven't done anything yet."

A few in the class started laughing. Atrius went even redder but he lifted a shaky hand and held it before his face, horizontally. It gleamed with sweat and though he obviously tried, Atrius couldn't keep it steady. Finally, he sighed and lowered his hand. The laughing grew quieter, though not because the students were laughing any softer. The two boys who were laughing stopped and looked at each other. They started to say something, but their voices came out too softly to hear. Atrius grinned and waved a hand, bringing their voices came back to full volume.

"An auditory illusion." Kerag had a faint smile on his face. "A good one too."

Atrius shrugged. "Sometimes, I needed to calm the horses. Loud noises startle them."

"You mean when you were mucking out the stables?" a tall boy with dark hair said. He was the same one who hadn't worn his robe.

The class erupted in laughter, and Atrius turned away. The master lifted a closed fist. Instantly, everyone went silent. He leveled his eyes at the perpetrator, and the boy looked for all the world, like he wanted to turn invisible. "Misco, come up here please. Atrius, you may sit."

The two boys exchanged places. Misco's doublet was bright yellow, so much so that it almost hurt to look at. His pants were red and equally bright. He held his chin high, but flinched when Master Kerag cleared his throat. He squeaked and the sound echoed throughout the room. Most people were obviously trying to hold in laughs.

"An auditory illusion that can change a voice as it is being spoken is extremely difficult." Kerag's voice sounded like it was coming from everywhere at once. "Few can manage it, and most of them can only do it badly. I would advise you not to get on the bad side of someone who will very likely be a master of illusion one day." His eyes roamed over the students until he was looking right at Jez. "Or any school of magic, for that matter. Such people are highly regarded, and their influence is often unsurpassed by any save the king himself."

His voice was so loud Jez could feel it vibrating on his skin. Jez wasn't sure if it was an auditory illusion or a tactile one. Misco nodded furiously, but Kerag's gaze stayed locked on Jez. He nodded once and the master motioned for Misco to sit down.

"Oh, Misco? Please dress properly next time."

The boy's face reddened, but he nodded. Kerag asked the other two to demonstrate what they knew. A tall girl with green eyes could make a flame appear on her finger, but it didn't seem to actually be giving off any light. A lanky boy with hair down to his shoulders could make his eyes go black, but the illusion would dissipate if he moved too quickly. Kerag nodded at each but didn't remark on them.

"The key to illusion is holding an image of what is not true in your head. Focus on that image and cast your power into it. Optical illusions that are stationary are the easiest, though most people have trouble with tactile, olfactory, and gustatory illusions." A short boy with close cropped hair raised his hand, and Master Kerag sighed. "That's touch, smell, and taste illusions." The boy gave a sheepish grin and lowered his hand. "We're going to try something simple. Look at the floor. Try to change a portion of it to a different color."

"How big," Atrius asked.

"I leave the size and shape up to you. Once you succeed call me over. Anyone who can call me and maintain their illusion at the same time can leave early."

He waved a hand. The students looked at each other for a second before turning their eyes to the floor. The three who'd had previous experience with illusions completed their tasks almost instantly. Each called Master Kerag in turn. He examined their work and dismissed them with a warning that future classes would not be so easy. He then went from student to student, spending a minute with each so he could offer advice. He left their side without giving them a chance to try again. A few called after him, and he returned, but in each case, calling him made the student lose their concentration and their illusion faltered. He smiled and shook his head.

Jez focused on the wooden floor, but it stubbornly refused to change. Its grain remained the same brown. No matter how hard he tried, he just couldn't imagine it as blue. It was brown. It couldn't be any other color. In desperation, he tried to make it a darker shade of brown, but it did no good. He tried to force power into the wood, but nothing happened. After a few minutes, his head began to throb.

"You're just throwing power at the ground. You're not giving it any shape." Kerag's voice came from behind him, making him jump. He spun around. "If you're not careful…"

The wood beneath Jez groaned, interrupting him. He looked down just as a crack formed in the wooden plank he'd been trying to change. Kerag sighed.

"That will happen. I'll call one of Balud's students to come fix that later. Your problem, Jezreel, is that you're not imposing your idea of the wood being another color."

Jez opened his mouth to speak but closed it without saying anything.

"What is it?" Kerag asked.

"It just…" he fumbled for words for a second. "It's not another color. It's brown. I don't know how to picture it any other way."

"You painted an amazing piece earlier this week. You can't tell me you didn't picture that before you painted it."

The entire room went silent at the mention at the painting, and Jez shivered as ten pairs of eyes turned to him. Master Kerag also noticed and looked around the room. He cleared his throat, and suddenly, everyone found the floor interesting again. He nodded at Jez and started his cycle around the room again. Jez tried a different tactic. He imagined his father's floor, perpetually covered with dust. He closed his eyes until he could picture it. He opened his eyes and tried to throw the image onto the floor. For a moment, the wood flickered and lightened, but Jez was hit with a profound sense of wrongness, and the illusion vanished.

After two hours, only Jez and a petite girl name Nelama remained, and Nelama could, at least, maintain the illusion as long as she didn't call to Master Kerag. The brief flicker had been the greatest success Jez had had. Finally, Master Kerag dismissed them. As Jez walked by him on the way out, the master grinned.

"It's good to know there's something you're not instantly a master of."

CHAPTER 18

Lajen didn't show up for philosophy. Some of the students started talking about how if the teacher didn't show up after a quarter hour, it meant everyone could leave. Even so, no one left when the time came. After twenty minutes, Master Rael came and said Lajen wouldn't be coming in. A few people cheered, but a stern look from the master silenced them.

"So we can go?" Liandra asked.

"Not all at once," she said. He pointed at Jez. "You first."

"Why me?" Jez asked.

"Because I am the master of this dominion, and I told you to."

Her cold blue eyes left no room for argument. Jez nodded and stood up. Commotion broke out before he'd even left the room, and he heard Rael raise her voice just as the door closed behind him. Jez walked down the hall and found the chancellor along with a pair of green robed adjutants waiting for him in front of the door leading outside. He looked Jez up and down and stepped aside as he spoke to one of the adjutants, who ran back down the hall to the class.

"You may go," Balud said.

"What's going on?" Jez asked.

"That's not something you need to concern yourself with."

"It's the sleeping sickness, isn't it? Lajen has it." Jez felt his eyes go wide as the unexpected words left his lips. The chancellor looked almost as surprised as Jez himself. "I'm right, aren't I?"

"How could you know that, child?"

Jez shook his head. "I don't know. How many people have it?"

"Only one in the caldera." He looked at the adjutant and held his hand to forestall the other student who was coming down the hall. He motioned Jez closer. "Three dozen down in Hiranta. You've surprised us all with your knowledge before. Can you do so again? Do you know anything about this plague?"

Jez thought for a few seconds before shaking his head. "I'm sorry. I just don't know. It's like trying to remember a dream."

The chancellor nodded. He looked at the adjutant. "Can you handle checking the students?"

The adjutant nodded and the chancellor went into the class and came out with Master Rael. He motioned for Jez to follow, and they left the building and headed to the other side of the district. Jez could practically feel the eyes watching him as he walked with a master on either side. They went into the small house that served as the office for the master of secrets. Paintings and sculptures decorated the main room, and Jez found himself drawn to an image of a gray-haired man with tanned skin and blue eyes. He jumped when the chancellor touched him on the shoulder. Both of the masters were staring at him, and he shrugged. Rael motioned for them to follow, and she led them to a small room with a heavy oaken desk. There were half a dozen chairs in front of the desk, and they each took one.

"It seems Mister Bartinson has secrets locked away in his mind," the chancellor said. "I would like you to try to pry them free."

"But chancellor…" Rael began, but Balud raised a hand.

"With his permission, of course."

The both turned to Jez who looked back and forth between them. "I don't understand."

"Master Rael can go into your mind. If there's something hidden there, she can find it, but searching a mind like that is generally forbidden unless the person consents."

"Will it hurt?"

"It depends on how deeply the secrets are hidden," Master Rael said. "I can pull back before that happens."

"And you think this will help?"

"Jezreel, I have no idea," Balud said. "This sickness appeared nearly fifteen years ago, and it was just as resistant to magic then as it is now. That time it just died off, but we can't count on that happening again. I've tried everything I know to cure this disease, but nothing works. Someone died of it two days ago. We've been trying to shelter the Academy from the news, but we can only keep that going for so long. I'm desperate, and I'm willing to try almost anything."

"What do I do?" Jez asked.

"Simply try to remember," Rael said.

Jez nodded, but Rael didn't seem to be paying attention. She had her eyes closed and was humming softly. Jez looked at Balud who nodded. He thought about the sleeping sickness, about how his father had been worried, but Dusan had dismissed it. Dusan with the closed fist. For some reason, that image hung in Jez's mind. He found himself focusing on Rael's humming. It lulled him to listlessness. Suddenly, Rael took in a sharp breath, and a stake was driven through Jez's head. His vision went red and pain wracked every inch of his body. He screamed and it took him a while to realize he wasn't the only one. Master Rael had her head clutched in her hands and was rocking back and forth, murmuring. Balud was instantly by her side and held two fingers to Rael's forehead. He let out a breath and nodded before turning to Jez and repeating the gesture.

"There's nothing physically wrong with either of you," he said.

"What happened?"

Jez tried to speak, but his words came out garbled. He tried again, but all he managed to say was "hurt."

It took several minutes for Master Rael to regain her composure. She walked to the other side of her desk and reached into a drawer to pull out a tin cup. She took some dried herbs out of an ivory container and poured them in before filling the cup with water from a flask. She stared at it for a second and it began to steam. Then, she handed it to Jez.

"Drink this," she said. "It'll help."

"What…you?" Jez asked. It was so hard to form words.

"Don't worry about me. I've gone through that enough that I recover fairly quickly." She smiled. "A hazard of my profession, I suppose. Besides, I only have one cup." Rael turned to Balud. "There's something hidden there, but I can't say what. There are barriers in his mind like I've never seen. They reacted violently before I even knew they were there. I think I've shaken some things loose, but it'll take time before they come up to his conscious mind. Even so, there's far more hidden than I could've revealed."

"How would a fishermen's son end up with barriers locking away secrets in his mind?" Balud asked.

They both looked at Jez. The tea was still steaming in his hands, and he took a drink, though it was more to break eye contact than out of any real desire to drink. It tasted faintly of mint. Warmth spread through his body; he felt strength creeping back into his limbs, and the fog cleared from his mind. Master Rael smiled.

"We should let him rest. That tea will help, but it's no substitute for sleep. I doubt we'll get anything more out of him today at any rate."

"Are you sure?" Jez asked as panic gripped him. "I mean, what if I don't wake up?"

He let it hang, but Balud shook his head. "That's why we were examining Lajen's students. You don't have the sleeping sickness as far as we can tell."

"As far as you can tell?"

"The disease doesn't seem to be contagious to those who are awake. I think you can only catch it while asleep. We're keeping the sick separate, so you should be safe."

"But that doesn't make sense," Jez said. "I mean if that's all it took, the disease would never have reached the caldera, right? It's not like people can sleep on their way up here."

Balud lifted an eyebrow at Rael. "He's a smart one. We don't entirely understand this disease, though we think people who are awake can carry it. In any case, it only seems to affect those who lack a certain strength of will. Most who come to the Academy would already be immune, and I don't think anyone like you has anything to worry about. Mastery of things like binding requires strength of mind. You're in no greater danger than anyone. You're probably a fair bit less, in fact."

The room had finally stopped spinning, and Jez was able to meet their eyes. His head was still pounding, but it was at a more manageable level.

"But sir, I'm hardly a master."

"No, but you very easily could be. Trust me, Jezreel, you're safe."

Jez nodded and the chancellor dismissed him. As he reached the door, he turned around.

"If only the sleeping can catch this disease, why were you checking the students? None of them are asleep."

Balud sighed. He'd obviously hoped Jez wouldn't ask that question. "Because I've been wrong before."

CHAPTER 19

It was wrong.

No matter what else was happening that one truth filled Jez. This thing was wrong. The thing had been locked away for a reason. There was no place in the world for the likes of it. The man had no business trying to free it. He had to be stopped.

Jez made himself known. "You must not do this, Mortal."

The man's face was clouded in shadow, and a gem hanging around his neck glowed orange. His entire body blurred, hiding any details, though Jez found his eyes drawn to a small red splotch on his chest. He drew runes of light in the air.

"I've long ago lost track of the things I've done that must not be done, Shadowguard."

"Those do not concern me. Only this place, this time concerns me, and here and now, you must not be allowed to succeed."

"You can't stop me."

Jez drew his sword. The crystal blade burned blue, its light dispelling all shadows. The man flinched but didn't stop. He was in the middle of a powerful ritual, and he could not stop without risking tragedy. There was too much power flowing through him. The fear flickering on his face said he hadn't anticipated Jez's arrival. Jez swung, but the blade collided against a shield of green power. He tried again, and the shield weakened. Given enough time, he would be able to break through, but the summoning was almost complete. The man's precautions had kept Jez away for too long. Jez scanned the runes burning in the air. One stuck out, that of the closed eye. Jez lifted his sword again. The man's face paled. He knew. Jez's blade was no mortal weapon, and it could strike at things untouchable by ordinary means.

He began to swing, and the man's eyes went wide, and a sense of triumph suffused Jez. The mage hadn't considered this possibility. The sword whistled as it tore through the air. The man cried out as the blade sliced through the closed eye. For a second, it looked like the eye split in two. Then, it began to steam. The green light was consumed by blue flames, and it vanished in a puff of smoke. The air around them rippled with power as runes around the place where the eye had been vanished in an ever expanding circle. Unbound by the runes, the magic the man had gathered coursed through the room. The orange crystal exploded, and the mage cried out as power surged through his body. Men dealt with magic of this magnitude at their own peril. A disrupted ritual of this size could destroy everything within half a mile. Many mortals would die, and Jez felt regret at that, but his only task was stopping this spell. Nothing else mattered.

The man's face became as still as a statue, though Jez could still sense the spark of life within him. Then, light shone from his eyes and mouth. He lifted his arms and the power of the ritual swirled around them and congealed between his hands. Too late, Jez realized what was happening. The man had reigned in the magic. It pulsed within him, threatening to consume him. He couldn't last long like that. Mortal flesh couldn't contain that much energy, but for that moment, the mage had control of the power. Jez slammed his sword against the shield again and again. Cracks began to form, but it wouldn't be soon enough.

The man threw the power at Jez. Pain like he had never felt lanced through him. He had no true physical form, but he had remained in the image of a human for so long, he had no memory of being anything else. Even the minor effort of will needed to retain that shape was disrupted by the pain, and he dissolved into formless energy. The magic remained though, threatening to overwhelm him. Jez held fast. To be doing so much pain to him, the mage had to be using a lot of power, and even with all that was gathered for the ritual, he couldn't sustain this for long. Jez just had to hold out a little longer.

Bands of power constricted around his formless body in ways only a master binder could manage. He could feel them trying to destroy him, but Jez had been created by a being far older and more powerful than the mage, and he could only be destroyed in a place where his power resided. The mage realized it, and once again, redirected his power. It forced Jez back into the shape of a human. His sword formed at his waist, and he tried to lift it, but the bands of power held him fast. Darkness surrounded Jez, a darkness so absolute it consumed the light of his sword. He struggled against his bindings, but strength had left his limbs.

Suddenly, a light appeared in front of him, and Jez was forced forward. Voices came from it, deep and incomprehensible. It wouldn't destroy him, but it might well do something far worse, and for the first time in more years than mortal minds could comprehend, Jez felt fear.

CHAPTER 20

Jez woke in a cold sweat, breathing heavily. A fear that he was still asleep seized him, and he pinched himself several times to try to wake himself up, but if this was a dream, that didn't work. As the next several seconds passed, Jez's heart slowed, and he sorted through his thoughts. The sun shone outside, and he made a mental note to request quarters that faced west so that he wouldn't have the morning sun in his eyes when he woke. He'd had the same dream nearly every night in the months since Osmund had been kicked out. He'd pushed himself in his lessons and training with the sword in an effort to exhaust himself, hoping he'd be too tired to dream, but it never worked. He'd even go to temple services once in an attempt to find peace, but that night, his dream had been worse, so he'd never returned.

Jez tried to push the memory of the dream out of his mind as he rolled out of bed. He started putting his clothes on when someone knocked on the door. He threw on his student's robes and shambled into his sitting room to open the door. A short boy stood there, looking from side to side. When he saw Jez, he squeaked.

"Are you the boy wizard Jezreel?"

"Boy wizard? Who told you that?"

The boy paled and stumbled back a few steps. "Oh, I'm sorry, sir. Please don't hurt me. I didn't mean anything by it."

Jez sighed. This was obviously a boy from Tarcai. It seemed his reputation beyond the walls of the Academy hadn't quite died off yet. 'Boy wizard' was a new one, though.

"It's just Jez. Who told you to come and find me?"

"It was a giant, sir."

"A giant?"

"Oh yes sir. He was at least ten feet tall. I was afraid he would eat me or something. He said he knew you."

"Stop calling me sir. Who was this giant?"

"He said his name was Osmund."

"Osmund? Where is he?"

"He's waiting for you at the edge of the mountain."

Jez nodded. It made sense that Osmund wouldn't come into the city. Master Besis had warned them about the wards. Jez didn't think they would actually hurt Osmund, but he wouldn't have wanted to take that chance either. Still, why would Osmund come here in the first place?

"Lead the way," he said to the boy.

At this hour, Tarcai was just beginning to come alive as people started to trickle onto the streets. Jez followed the boy through the city. It only took them a quarter hour to reach the edge. As they neared the rim of Mount Carcer Osmund came into view. The larger boy threw the messenger a silver coin. It slipped between his fingers and the boy scrambled to pick it up before disappearing back into town. Osmund looked at his friend.

"Boy wizard?"

Osmund shrugged. "I needed to make sure the message would reach you. I told him you would know if he just ran off and that you'd hunt him down."

Jez sighed. "I've been trying to avoid that kind of reputation. What do you want?" Osmund looked away, and Jez's blood went cold. "My father?"

"I'm sorry, Jez. He has the sleeping sickness."

For a moment, his reason deserted him, and he just stared at his friend. It was impossible. His father was the strongest man he knew. The sleeping sickness was a thing that happened to other people, not to those Jez cared about. His father couldn't have it, but when he saw the look in Osmund's face, he knew it was true.

"How long?" His voice cracked as he spoke and he felt something wet running down his cheek.

"What?"

"How long has he been asleep?"

"I read him your message when I got into town. He made me promise to come back for lunch the following day. When I got there, he was asleep. That was almost a month ago."

"Why didn't you tell Master Dusan?" Jez asked. "He could've used his speaking stone to tell me."

"Jez, I tried. He had me waiting three days to speak to him. Finally, I gave up and left a message with one of his servants. They promised to deliver it, but I didn't have high hopes. Then, I found a caravan headed to Hiranta and came back here. I see I was right to do it."

"I need to go back home," Jez said.

"You'll have to speak to the masters."

"I don't care what the masters say. My father could be dying."

"Jez, they've awakened you. They'll be able to track you down. Go speak to them. It won't be the first time they've granted permission to leave because of a family member. They might even help you get there faster. It's why I risked making the trip up the mountain at night. I wanted to tell you as soon as possible. If they give permission, we can leave right away."

"You're going with me?"

Osmund nodded. "Do you know how many people have been kind to me since I got to the Academy? The tier of nobles considers me a freak, and the tier of commoners is afraid of me. Even back home, most people stayed away from me because of," he waved his hand in front of his face. Jez had almost gotten used to his mismatched eyes and overly large nose, but others hadn't. "People who have been kind to me are few and far between. I don't easily abandon them."

"Will you come with me to speak with the masters?"

Osmund looked into the city for several seconds. Finally, he nodded. "Let's go."

CHAPTER 21

They had only gone a hundred yards into the city before guards ran down the street with spears leveled. The two boys froze as the men surrounded them. One held a glowing diamond in his left hand and bore the insignia of a captain on his chest. When he pointed the gem at Osmund, it brightened and some of the guards pressed their spears forward.

"You were banished from Tarcai. You will leave now."

"We need to see the masters," Jez said.

"You are free to," the captain said. "He must leave."

Osmund looked to Jez, and he realized the larger boy would do whatever he asked. One of the guards grunted at the captain.

"Sir, that's a battlemage. I saw him in the arena."

"I saw that fight too," another said. "He lost."

"He lost to another battlemage," the first said. "We don't have one of those with us. We should send to the Academy for help."

"Lovely," Osmund said. "We'll go with you."

The captain looked like he was about to refuse but thought better of it. The other guards exchanged glances but they lowered their weapons at the captain's gesture. He had a resigned look on his face. Normal city guards just weren't equipped to deal with a battlemage of Osmund's caliber, and he knew it. The only place in the city that had people who could was the Academy, and he motioned for them to follow.

"Don't try anything," the captain said

Jez suppressed a laugh, but Osmund put a hand on his shoulder and nodded. They fell into step behind the guards. Their armed escort attracted the attention of the townspeople, but crowds parted for them, so they made it through the town quickly. Master Besis was waiting for them at the edge of the Academy grounds. The captain bowed to him.

"I take it these two behaved themselves?"

"Yes, Master, aside from refusing to leave that is."

"Thank you. I'll take it from here."

The captain nodded and gave Osmund a hard look before departing. Besis rolled his eyes and watched them disappear around the corner.

"I take it I don't have to bind you, Osmund?"

"No, Master Besis. I won't be staying long."

They briefly related the information about Jez's father. Besis nodded and sent a student with a message for Chancellor Balud to meet them at the speaking stone. Ordinarily, they would've released Jez to go to his father without any sort of formality, but since his presence at the Academy was sponsored, they had to get permission from his patron. They climbed the stairs of the central spire and activated the stone. By the time Baron Dusan's image appeared in the crystal, Balud had come into the room as well. Dusan scowled at the binding master, but listened to what Jez had to say.

"I'm sorry," the baron said. "I never got the message. You can be assured the servant who received it will be severely punished."

"You don't really need to do that, sir," Jez said. "I just want to know if I can come home."

"Of course. Chancellor, I presume he'll be allowed back next term." Balud nodded. "Good. I'll handle his education until then. Please provide him with the best horse you can get ahold of. I'll pay whatever is needed."

Jez cleared his throat. "Sir, I don't know how to ride."

"You don't?" The image cocked its head. "No, I suppose you wouldn't. Chancellor, please see that a riding teacher is hired for him next term. In the meantime, get him a coach and send guards with him. I want him on his way within the hour." The chancellor nodded and the baron's image vanished.

"I'll see to the arrangements," Balud said. "We'll forgive your intrusion into the city, Osmund, provided you leave now."

"Chancellor, I want him to go with me," Jez said.

"Out of the question. He's been banished."

"I wouldn't be so hasty, Chancellor," Besis said. "It makes a lot of sense."

"How so?"

"The baron wanted Jezreel protected. Osmund is his friend, and he's enough of a battlemage to provide better protection than half a dozen guards. We can send a few with him to help, but a small party would travel quicker than a large one."

Balud thought for a second before nodding. "Pack your things. We'll send some of our guards with you along with a writ giving you access to our stables in Hiranta. You'll have our fastest horses. You should be back in Randak in a matter of days."

Osmund waited outside while Jez changed out of his student robes and into a sturdy shirt and pants better suited for travel. They were plain but still much finer than anything he'd had before moving in with Dusan. He packed a few things. At the last moment, he belted his sword and headed down. Their escort was waiting for them when Jez came out of the tower with his things. Going down the mountain took about half the time it took to go up it. It was still early afternoon when they reached the city. The guards with them wasted no time in retrieving their transportation and supplies for the journey. They left the city before the sun had set in the direction of home.

CHAPTER 22

The trip to Randak lacked the comfort of the trip to the Academy. The only requirement here was speed. The coach thundered across the plain, slowing only as it was necessary to rest the horses. Osmund rode in the coach with him, but they spoke little. Each day, they traveled long after the sun had set. Even from inside the coach, the trip was draining, and often, Jez had fallen asleep before they made camp, and more than once, he didn't wake up until after they had left so the trip seemed like one long continuous journey. He wasn't even sure if they took him out of the coach on those days. Judging from the way his muscled ached when he woke, he suspected not.

After a week, Jez caught the smell of the sea. He hadn't realized how much he'd missed it. The scent revitalized him, and he kept poking his head out the window, hoping to catch sight of it. He squealed in delight when he first saw the sun reflecting off the water in the distance. Before long, every dip and rise on the plains seemed familiar. The tops of buildings poked over the horizon as his hometown came into sight. The sun had nearly vanished beneath the western horizon when they pulled into Randak. The coach headed for Dusan's manor.

"Not that way," he said to the driver through the sliding window at the front.

"We have our orders, sir," he said. "We're to take you directly to the baron."

Jez rolled his eyes and tried to open the door, but it was locked. Osmund motioned for him to stand back. His eyes glowed red and Jez pressed himself against his seat. Osmund threw his hand forward, and a gust of wind as strong as a hurricane rushed past Jez and crashed into the door. The wood groaned in resistance for a few seconds. Then, there was a loud crack, and the door exploded outward in a shower of splinters. There were cries of surprise from the guards as the unexpected sound startled the horses. Osmund grabbed Jez, and they leapt out of the coach. They hadn't been going very fast and Osmund was able to hit the ground running. People all around gasped and cried out as Osmund barreled through them. They turned down a series of streets before diving into a crowd.

"Did you really have to do that?" Jez asked as he struggled to catch his breath. His heart was racing.

"You said you wanted to see your father."

"I didn't mean to break out of the coach. Baron Dusan would've let me see him."

"Are you so sure?"

"Yes. I don't understand why you're so suspicious of him."

Osmund shrugged. "I don't either. Maybe I'm having one of those limaph flashes of knowledge that you seem to get so often. Look, it won't take them long to find us. Your father's house is this way, right?"

Half an hour later, they'd seen no sign of the baron's guards. They arrived at the house to find it empty. There were no wrapped bundles of fish, and the hearth was cold. Dust covered the floor, and the only footprints were Jez's own. He walked out feeling dejected and having no idea what to do next.

"Jezreel?"

Jez looked up. Mistress Tuvon was coming out of the house next to Bartin's. She was a tall woman whose raven black hair was sprinkled with a few strands of white. She looked tired and seemed much older than the last time Jez had seen her. He almost asked her how Kashur was, but he caught himself at the last moment. Kashur had caught the sleeping sickness just before Jez had left for the Academy. She seemed to know what he was thinking. She smiled, but it looked forced.

"You're looking for your father."

"Yes."

"He's with Master Clont." Her eyes gleamed with unshed tears. "I used to hate that old man. He has a foul manner and an even fouler tongue, but he changed his inn into a sick house and cares for those poor souls who won't wake up. Even Kashur…" she turned away.

Jez motioned for Osmund to remain. He walked over to her house and put a hand on her shoulder. She looked up and tears streamed down her cheek. She nodded once but didn't say anything more. He squeezed her shoulder and returned to Osmund.

"I didn't realize there were enough of the sick to fill an entire inn," Jez said as they walked through the city.

"There weren't when I was here last time. It's gotten a lot worse."

The common room of the inn was empty. Clont hustled over to them and gave Osmund an uneasy look. "I'm sorry, young masters, we're closed." His eyes wandered over Jez and stopped on his face. His nose wrinkled in surprise and his voice took on a kindly tone. "Oh, I see. I didn't recognize you in those clothes, Jez. I suppose you want to see your father?"

Jez tried to speak, but a lump formed in his throat. He looked down at himself and felt like a traitor. He should've at least changed clothes before he came here. Of course he hadn't really had an opportunity. He sighed and nodded. Master Clont motioned for him to follow, and the husky man led them up the stairs and down the hall.

"He was the first to get sick with no one to look after him." Clont said it with no accusation in his voice, but it still made tears well in Jez's eyes. "I couldn't just let him die, so I brought him here. People didn't want to sleep in the same building as someone who has the disease, so they left. Eventually, others started bringing the sick to me. I'm almost out of room."

"It's good of you to sacrifice your livelihood like this Master Clont," Osmund said.

"People give me what coin they can. Some of them may seem coarse, but no one really wants to see the people here abandoned. They're not hard to care for, and it's enough to let me get by."

He opened a door at the end of the hall, and Jez asked Osmund to wait outside. He went in and, for a second, he couldn't believe what he saw. His father was a mere shadow of what he had been. His face was gaunt, and his limbs looked like little more than bones wrapped in skin. His chest was moving with the regular rhythm of breath, but even that was barely detectable. This looked nothing like the irritable fisherman who had little patience for the foolishness of nobility. The room smelled musty, and Jez tried to open the window, but it was jammed. He gazed down at his father, and a wave of sorrow washed over him. Jez knelt down by the bed and wept.

"I'm sorry," he said through tears. "I should've been here."

Jez wasn't sure how long he stayed there weeping. Eventually, he felt a hand on his shoulder, and he looked up. Osmund stood over him. He wore a somber expression. Jez looked out the window and saw stars twinkling in the sky. He must've been there for hours.

"We should go see the baron."

"He knows where I am."

"Probably," Osmund said, "but I'd prefer not to have him more irritated than he already is."

Jez stood up and followed his friend. At the doorway, he turned and took one last look at his father. He had been such a strong man. He shouldn't be like this.

It wasn't right.

The smell of sulfur flared in Jez's nostrils. He didn't remember moving across the room. He was just there, standing over his father. The past was screaming at him, drowning out everything else. He splayed his fingers and ran them from the top of Bartin's head to the left side of his chest, where his heart beat all too weakly. Power rushed out of Jez and his father groaned. Behind him, Osmund gasped. Slowly, his father opened his eyes and tried to focus.

"Jez?"

The voice was so soft it could hardly have been called a whisper. Bartin tried to lift his head, but the strength to do that had long ago left his body, and he fell back into his pillow.

"I'm here, Father."

"Have you come home?"

"Yes, Father." Tears were streaming down his cheeks. "I'll stay with you as long as you need me to."

For a moment, Bartin's eyes focused on Jez, and the edges of his lips turned up in a smile. Jez began to believe everything would be all right.

"That's good." He closed his eyes. When he opened them again, he was squinting. "You're glowing. Did you know that? Why are you doing that?"

Jez looked down at his hands but didn't see any light. When he looked up, his father had a blank look on his face, and his chest had stopped the gentle rising and falling of breath. He stared at the bed for almost a full minute before the realization hit him.

His father was dead.

The room blurred and it took Jez a second to realize he was crying again. Powerful arms encircled him as Osmund drew him into an embrace.

"I'm so sorry."

CHAPTER 23

Clont gave them warm soup and bread, and offered them beds for the night. There were still a couple that weren't occupied by the sick, but Jez refused. They went outside and found Dusan's guards waiting for him. Jabur inclined his head.

"It's good to see you Jezreel. The baron instructed us to wait until you came out. He offers his apologies for trying to bring you to the manor first. He wishes to see you."

"Why was my father here?" Jez's voice cracked as he spoke. "The baron promised to look after him. Why was he in a sick house for people who had no one?"

"I'm afraid I don't know the answer to that. You'll have to ask the baron."

"What if I don't want to go?"

"We'll escort you to your father's house if that's what you wish. Baron Dusan arranged for food to be sent there. If you don't want to see him, you'll be left alone. Whatever you wish." He looked at Osmund. "Of course your friend is welcome to come with us if you do."

Briefly, Jez considered telling them to go away, but he rejected the idea. It wouldn't do any good, and he would have to see the baron eventually. He nodded at the guards and they led him through town. The streets were empty. Few people went out after dark, but Jez had never seen the city so devoid of life. Lights could be seen through the windows, but even they seemed dim. Even the manor was almost as still as the city.

"Where are the guards?" he asked.

"These are hard times," Jabur said. "The baron didn't want his home to seem foreboding so he removed them from the grounds. They're still inside."

"That's not like him," Jez said. "At least, I don't think it is."

They came in through the front door. As expected, men patrolled the halls inside. Jabur spoke to one who ran down the hall in the direction of the baron's counting room. Jez and Osmund were led to a small dining room. This one had only half a dozen chairs around a table and was used when the baron wanted to conduct negotiations in a more private setting. They sat down, but Jez couldn't bring himself to speak. Jabur had only been gone for a few minutes when Dusan walked in the room. He went to Jez and embraced him.

"Oh, Jezreel. I'm so sorry."

Jez's suspicion wavered, and he started sobbing into Dusan's shirt. He looked up when Osmund cleared his throat. Jez wiped away his tears.

"Sorry." His voice wavered. "Baron Dusan, this is my friend Osmund. Osmund, Baron Dusan of Korand."

Osmund gave a graceful bow, but the Baron smirked.

"I've heard of you. Didn't you get exiled from the Academy?"

Osmund's face reddened, but Jez spoke up. "Baron…"

"You're right. This isn't the time for that. I've been told you've eaten." Jez nodded. "I'll send for some chilled juice then." He called orders to a servant standing in the doorway that Jez hadn't seen. The girl's head bobbed and she turned and ran. "I've prepared your room.

I'll have someone arrange quarters for your friend and the men who came with you. They were very annoyed with you for leaving." When he saw Jez's expression, he waved him off. "Don't give it a second thought. I've already spoken to the Academy and taken responsibility. I should've told them to take you right to your father."

"Why was he there, in some inn, dying alone?" Jez didn't even try to hide the accusation in his voice.

"Jezreel, I didn't know."

"I left you a message," Osmund accused, but he backed away when the baron glared at him.

Dusan sighed at Jez. "You have to understand, a boy with no rank and stinking of the road showed up and asked to speak with me. My chamberlain thought he was a vagrant. He nearly called the guards and had him thrown out. They never thought to give me the message."

"But he gave them my name," Jez said.

"Everyone in town knows I took you as a ward. He could've gotten your name from anyone. I'm sorry, Jezreel. I offered to take your father into my household, but he refused. He was too proud to accept help when it was offered."

Jez realized he was nodding and stopped. "That does sound like him."

"I decided to respect his wishes. I told him to let me know if he needed anything, figuring he'd tell me if he got desperate enough, but other than that, I left him alone. I regret that I didn't have someone watching him."

Jez almost acknowledged that it made sense when a thought struck him. "But I called you over a week ago. Why did you leave him there all this time?"

"You saw how weak he was. I sent healers, but they didn't think it was safe to move him. I provided the innkeeper with gold to take care of his patients. I didn't know what else to do."

Jez's mind cast about, looking desperately for some way to blame him. This had to be someone's fault. Jez's father couldn't just die. Someone had to be responsible, but everything the baron had said sounded true.

"I've spoken to King Haziel," the baron said, breaking Jez out of his thoughts. "He's given his approval for your adoption. The official document is already on its way."

"What?"

"Your father was your only family. You have no one left, and I need an heir. I intend for you to follow me as Baron of Korand."

CHAPTER 24

"Are you all right?" Osmund asked.

They were in Jez's quarters. Even after the ostentatious rooms the Academy had given him, these seemed gaudy. His bed was too soft, and the tapestries hanging from the walls hurt his eyes. He and Osmund were seated in ornate chairs around a heavy stone table.

"There's just been so much. I don't even know what to think anymore." He noticed Osmund glancing around as if afraid to meet Jez's eyes. "What is it?"

"It's just that now that you're the heir instead of a ward…"

"You want me to speak to the Academy masters."

"I don't want to impose on you," Osmund said, "but the Academy has the most complete theological library in the world. There's nowhere else I can study about the limaph."

"Of course," Jez said, patting his pocket where the key stone was. "The baron's speaking stone is in his quarters. I'll go speak to them now."

"There's no rush. We won't be leaving for a few days, right?"

Jez nodded. "There's no reason to wait though. It would make me feel better to do something."

He got up and walked into the hall. The guard glared at Jez as he came out of his room. Jez sighed and went back in to belt his sword before coming out again. This time, the guard nodded and let him out. He went down the hall to Dusan's quarters. They were locked, and there no guard at the door, so he knew Dusan had to be in his counting room. He considered sending a servant but decided against it. If he was to be baron one day, he needed to know the business of the barony. He led Osmund to the central hall and down the small passage. This door was locked as well. He was about to knock when his nostrils flared at the smell of sulfur. There was something on the other side that didn't belong.

"Osmund, the door," Jez said.

"What?"

"Break down the door. Do it now!"

Osmund hesitated only a second before throwing his arms forward. Fire and wind erupted from his fingers. They crashed against the door. For a second, Jez thought he saw the magic impact against a green energy shield. The flames roared and spread out against the shield. It only lasted for a moment before shattering. The fire consumed the door, reducing it to ash and molten iron.

The air was still thick with smoke, but Jez didn't care. He coughed as he leapt through the doorway, but the floor wasn't where he expected, and he tumbled down a set of stairs he hadn't known were there. He slammed against the ground, his body throbbing with pain. Osmund's heavy footsteps sounded on the stairs behind him. Jez forced himself to his feet and looked around. Glowing runes covered the walls casting an unearthly light. Everything radiated the smell of another world. A circle of entwined silver and gold sat embedded in the floor at the center of the room. Jez could practically see energy flowing out from it and passing through the walls. Dusan stood inside of the circle with his arms raised just like last time.

"Last time?" Jez said to the room.

Suddenly, the room shifted. The walls and floor became indistinct. Osmund dissolved and glowing runes popped into existence in the air around him. His skin fell away, leaving a glowing body that was more spirit than flesh. Some dim part of his mind realized this wasn't really happening. It was just like his dream had been, but it wasn't a dream. Master Rael said she'd shaken some things free in his mind, and one of those pieces had contained this memory.

The blurred figure from before came together. The red splotch resolved itself to the form of a closed fist, Dusan's sigil. Jez looked around taking all the runes in. They pulsed with the power that the mortal mage, that Baron Dusan, had gathered. He channeled it against wards Jezreel himself had set long before mortal kind had walked the earth. The magician could no more stand against Jez's power than a splash of water could stand against a mountain, but just as, over time, water could wear down a mountain to dust, the magician was systematically tearing down Jezreel's wards, the wards meant to keep the sleeping demon locked away.

"You must not do this, Mortal."

The mortal drew in more power, and Jezreel saw connections he hadn't noticed before, feeding Dusan power. There were thousands of them. Each was individually so small they would've provided next to nothing, but together they enhanced this magician's power tenfold. His body couldn't maintain that power for long. Eventually, mortal flesh would burn out. The mage had to know that, but he didn't seem to care.

They spoke, but the mage would not abandon his course. Jezreel struck, but his attacked was rebuffed by the green energy shield, one of the same type that had protected the door to this chamber only much stronger. Jezreel examined the room. Everything converged on closed eye. Jezreel's sword tore through it, and for a moment the rune seemed to be cut in two. Then, it vanished. The crystal the mage wore at his neck shattered. The thousands of link snapped, cutting him off from his source of power, from the dreams of the minds held by the sleeping sickness.

The shock of the realization drew Jez back to the real world. His eyes locked onto Dusan's face.

"It was you." He looked at the circle in horror. The power emanating from it was slowly infecting those in Randak. "It was you all along. You created the sleeping sickness."

"Yes," he said simply.

"You killed my father."

"That part was not intentional. It takes some people quicker than others. By the time I found out about him, he was already too far gone for me to help. I would've preferred to spare you that pain for now."

"For now?"

"Jezreel, you are so much more than he was. I can help you reach your full potential. You can't imagine what you have the ability to do."

"Because I'm a limaph?"

"A limaph?" Dusan glared at Osmund. "Is that what this thing has told you? That you're some half-blood with a few enhanced abilities? No, Jezreel, you're no limaph. You're what all limaph wish they could be. You're a full pharim."

Osmund gaped at Jez. "He's one of the afur?"

Even before Dusan shook his head, Jez knew that wasn't right. Before, when he had confronted Dusan, it hadn't been as an exiled being doomed to wander the earth. It had been as one with a singular purpose, one that had to be fulfilled at all costs. He'd succeeded, but not without paying a price.

"You did this to me. You made me…" Jez stumbled over the word. "Mortal."

"You left me little choice," Dusan said, "but look at what I've done since then. I gave you everything. I made it possible for you to experience life in a way no pharim ever had, and it doesn't have to end. Don't you understand? Marrowit can give us immortality." Jez shivered at the name of the demon, but Dusan went on. "With his power, and yours, added to my own, we could overthrow King Haziel. We could take the world. I know you Jezreel. You have a keen sense of justice. The world is a cold, dark place. You've seen the Academy. The rich and powerful rule there at the expense of good and decent people. Join me and you could change that."

"But you've killed so many people."

"With Marrowit's blessing, there's no limit to what I can do. What are a few lives next to that?"

"I thought you wanted justice."

"You want justice. I want power. Marrowit is the way to both."

"No!"

Ziary's voice was practically torn from Osmund's lips. There was a flash of light, and the giant was gone. Ziary stood there, his wings blazing and his sword drawn, burning with white hot flame. Regis had been a bully. All evil needed to be destroyed, but Regis's had been small, and so the manifestation of Ziary had been minor. What Dusan was doing was vile. It was a perversion against the universe itself, and Ziary came forth in his full power, radiating energy. Jez looked at Dusan, half expecting him to burst into flames under that light, but the baron simply smiled.

"Ever since I saw you in the arena, I've wondered if you would make yourself known. You might have actually succeeded if I hadn't been expecting this."

Ziary lurched at him, but his sword crashed against a wall of green energy. He struck twice more in quick succession, but Dusan laughed.

"I've held back pharim boy, and you're a far cry from one of them." Suddenly, the shield expanded and wrapped itself around Osmund, holding him prone. Dusan looked at Jez. "He would've killed me, you know. Should I have just stood by and allow that to happen?"

"You're a murderer!"

"You would've been too, if I hadn't stopped you. You disrupted my ritual and destroyed my focusing crystal. The power would've torn the entire city apart, and you didn't care. I had to redirect it, and turn it toward you, to bind you to human flesh so that you could learn what it means to be one of us. Tell me, Jezreel, was saving all those lives evil?"

Jez stared at him, speechless. He had a point, but he refused to let himself dwell on it. "I don't know if that's evil, but I know what you're doing now is."

His fingers moved so quickly he didn't know what he was doing. Power went out of him and into the energy holding Osmund. It glowed briefly but remained in place.

"I spent weeks building that trap. Even you won't be able to disarm it quickly. I'm giving you one more chance. Join me."

Jez's head was shaking before he even realized he was doing it. He threw his hands forward, searching his mind for something, anything he could use to bind Dusan, but the baron was quicker. He uttered a word, and Jez fell to the ground, completely unable to move. He'd failed. Again. Dusan stood over him, scowling. Power burned in Jez, demanding to be released, but with his arms unresponsive, there was nothing he could do.

"Don't worry" Dusan said. "I won't kill you. I'll just hold you and hope you eventually change your mind. Him, on the other hand…"

He drew a curved dagger from his robes. It gleamed in the light of the runes and he walked over to Ziary. The scion struggled against his bonds, but to no avail. Dusan would kill him, and it was all Jez's fault.

Rage mixed with power and threw itself at the magic holding Jez prone, but just as a physical blow delivered from an awkward angle would lack power, magic without word or gesture to release it was devoid of much of its strength. The paralyzing magic weakened slightly, but it wasn't enough. It wasn't nearly enough.

Jez's lower lip quivered, and he seized on the motion. His magic was all but spent, but he still had his will, a will fueled by anger at the man who had killed his father. Dusan was right about corruption in the world, but that didn't excuse the steps he took. What he'd done was evil.

Jez's mouth opened and closed. He could feel Dusan's magic writhing across his skin, threatening to freeze him again. He had mere seconds.

"Stop!"

He poured every ounce of his remaining power into that word. He could practically see its power rippling through the air and envelop Dusan. It did nothing. The runes pulsed with power. Dusan looked at him and sighed. He shook his head.

"I'm sorry, Jezreel. You never really had a chance. Not against me."

"He didn't, but I do."

If Ziary's voice sounded like a storm, this voice was a hurricane that could destroy cities and not leave one stone standing on another. It was vast and terrible. It was gentle and kind. The mage's eyes widened as a point of light appeared on the other side of the room as though it had come through the wall. It floated forward. Then, in a flash of light, it expanded. The figure stood ten feet tall. It had three pairs of wings, the first reached up through the stone of the ceiling. The second stretched out and covered almost the entire wall. The third sank down beneath the ground. It had ivory skin that seemed to burn with cleansing fire. Its robe was the purest blue Jez had ever seen. At the same time, it reminded him of a cloudless sky and the sapphire of the ocean under a noonday sun. They rustled in wind that wasn't there, and Jez caught the faint scent of the sea. The being's eyes were flawless sapphires, and though he didn't know how he knew, Jez could see anger in those eyes.

The name came unbidden into his head. Sariel, prince among the pharim and High Lord of the Shadowguard.

Dusan took a step back as Sariel floated forward. When the pharim drew his sword, thunder filled the room. The sword itself seemed to be made of a crystal that glowed with its own inner light. Dusan recoiled at the sight of it, but with visible effort, he refrained from taking another step back.

"I know you, pharim," he said. "You cannot interfere in mortal matters."

"True." The voice echoed through the room. "The one at your feet, however, is not a mortal. He is one of mine, and you will not touch him."

"I have bound him," Dusan cried out. "I have claimed him. He is mine."

Sariel's laughter set the room shaking. Even the runes flickered. "Little man, you may be powerful for one of your kind, but you cannot claim pharim, and Luntayary is a pharim no matter the skin he wears."

"The other is mine then," Dusan said. "You have no claim on him."

"You appear to think this is a negotiation. I do not negotiate with your kind. I will take these two, and I will go. Try to stop me at your peril." Sariel's massive form loomed over Jez. "Release him, or I will."

Panic painted the baron's features. He waved a hand and Jez could move again. He scrambled to his feet. The pharim prince glanced at Osmund and then at Dusan. Dusan waved a hand and the green energy surrounding Osmund disappeared. Sariel took Jez in one hand and Osmund in another. There was a flash of light, and the room vanished.

CHAPTER 25

The place they appeared wasn't really a place. Jez had been there before, but he couldn't quite remember. Their feet vanished into a layer of fog. The ground was soft, like they were standing on grass. The sky was a white so pure Jez doubted it had ever existed in the mortal world. Sariel stood in front of him, but he'd shrunk to human size, or maybe Jez and Osmund had grown. He shook his head. No, that wasn't right. Size didn't exist, not in this place.

"Where are we?" Osmund asked.

"We are Between." Sariel said.

"Between what?"

"Between here and there. Between then and now and waking and sleeping. We are between moments, between possibilities. Few mortals, even those descended from us, have ever seen this place."

"Thank you," Osmund said.

"I am glad I was able to get you out."

"What do you mean?" Jez asked. "He was afraid of you. You could've destroyed him."

Sariel shook his head. "Dusan was right about one thing. We may not interfere in mortal matters unless they interfere in ours."

"But you said if he didn't release Osmund, you would."

"No, I said if he didn't release you, I would. That was in my power to do. I said nothing about your friend."

Jez thought back to the confrontation. "You were bluffing."

"I permitted him to come to his own conclusion."

"Aren't pharim supposed to be honest?"

"I spoke no untrue words, but I'm no Lightgiver. My order guards, and you had set in your mind to guard your friend. I only did what I could."

"You're really Sariel then," Jez said.

The pharim nodded and Osmund yelped. He bowed deeply. Instantly, Sariel was at his side, helping him to stand.

"Rise, Osmund Jecklson. I am neither king nor Creator. I do not desire your subservience."

"Forgive me, Lord Sariel."

"Nor do I grant forgiveness."

"Why did you save us?" Jez asked.

"I've been looking for you for fourteen years, Luntayary. Impossible though it may be to believe, I was beginning to think you'd been destroyed. It was only a few weeks ago that I realized you still existed."

"A few weeks ago?"

"You used your powers."

"I bound the phobos. I didn't know how I'd done it."

"You are Shadowguard, Luntayary. Your purpose is to bind and to watch over those who are bound, and that cannot be taken from you, not even in your current form."

"Why do you keep calling me Luntayary?"

"Did you think your mortal name was the same one the Creator gave you?"

Jez staggered back a step. He thought he was going to fall, but the fog solidified and kept him up. "What did Dusan do to me?"

"I didn't know until I'd seen you, but now the binding is open to me. When he found he couldn't destroy you, he forced your spirit into the body of a stillborn child. The child passed to what lies beyond mortal life, and you became the body's soul, giving it life."

"But why?"

"He wants to free the demon Marrowit, the demon you are charged to guard. Mortal flesh cannot channel the full powers of a pharim, and you would be much easier to defeat as a mortal."

"But he provided for me."

"He couldn't destroy you."

"What does that have to do with anything?"

"Flesh can contain your powers, but it is a poor vessel. Once it is destroyed, you will once again be Luntayary and can stand against him in the fullness of who you are."

"Once the vessel is destroyed?"

"Once you die."

Jez gaped at him. "You want me to die?"

"It's why I rescued you. He would not have killed you."

"Well, I'm not going to kill myself."

"Why?"

"What do you mean why?"

"You are not a human. This life is a single breath, one heartbeat next to the eons you have existed. What is mortal existence next to that?"

What was mortal existence? Jez had experienced so much since being born. He thought about the sea breeze in his face. He remembered looking down at Tarcai from the top floor of the tower and the taste of his father's fish soup. He'd never eat it again, but that just made the memory that much more priceless. Even his grief made him hesitate. His father had raised him with love. He deserved Jez's tears, tears that he would no longer be able to shed if he died. He'd been through so much that a being like Sariel would never be able to comprehend, and he still had a life to live. He shook his head.

"Are you certain?" Sariel asked. "Be warned, I won't be able to help you again. Before, you didn't know what you were, but now you're making a choice as a mortal, and that is the one thing all pharim must respect. I will have no power to protect you from what comes after."

"I understand. Will you set another pharim to guard over Marrowit?"

Sariel shook his head. "I could if you had been destroyed. So long as you exist, Marrowit is your charge. If he is to be stopped, it must be by you."

"But you saw what Dusan just did to me. I don't stand a chance."

Sariel looked down at him. For moment, Jez felt an odd kinship with this being. The thought was almost laughable. The pharim lord nodded and extended his wings, showering Jez and Osmund in light.

"You don't always fight evil because you think you can defeat it," he said. "You fight it because evil needs to be fought. That is what it means to be one of us."

"You'll let us go, then?"

"The choice is yours. Where would you like to go?"

Jez thought for a second. "Tarcai."

Jez thought he saw a hint of a smile on the pharim's face. "As you wish."

The wings brightened until Jez could see no more.

CHAPTER 26

The central spire seemed to split the setting sun in two. Sariel had deposited them just inside the city. No one seemed to have noticed their mysterious appearance, and they made their way toward the Academy grounds. With examinations so close, the students were scrambling. They ran in and out of the various libraries, many carrying armloads of books. A few people glanced at Jez and Osmund as they made their way through Tarcai, but no one said anything. Jez kept expecting guards to come arrest them, but they passed through the Academy gates without incident. They circled the outer edge of the grounds until they reached the healing district. Earthen smells permeated the air, and most buildings had plants hanging from the windows. They made their way to a large building that served at chancellor Balud's house. Vines covered one wall and a tree seemed to be growing out of the building. Jez lifted his hand to knock but glanced at Osmund.

"Are you sure you want to do this? You're still banished."

"If we're going to stop Dusan, we need more information. There's no better place in the world to get that from than here. If that annoys the chancellor, then so be it."

Jez nodded and knocked on the door. After a few seconds, it

creaked open. An adjutant poked his head out and his eyes went wide when he saw the pair.

"Who is it, Jakar?" The chancellor drew up behind Jakar. He met the gaze of each of the two boys and nodded. "See to your studies, Jakar. I'll handle this. Mister Bartinson, Mister Jecklson, please follow me."

Jakar ran out of the house and ducked into one of the healing district's libraries. Balud motioned for them to come in. The house was practically a garden. Plants of every shape and size filled every open space. The tree that Jez had noticed from outside dominated the center of the room and was at least three feet wide. It had a face on its trunk, though Jez couldn't tell if it had been carved or grown. Balud led them to a room in the back. There were no plants in the room. Instead, a human skeleton hung in one corner and a drawing of what seemed to be a person lacking any skin had been affixed to the wall behind the chancellor's desk. Balud waved at a couple of chairs in front of his desk and he sat opposite to them.

"You are no longer a student of the Carceri Academy, Jezreel. Osmund, you have been banished entirely. How did you get past the detection spells around the city anyway?"

"I'm not sure," Osmund admitted.

"Hmm." The chancellor glanced at Jez. "I have to say I'll regret losing you. We haven't had such a promising student in a long time."

"I only left for the term, Chancellor. I intend to come back."

"I'm afraid not. I spoke to Baron Dusan less than an hour ago. He has withdrawn you permanently in spite of my objections. Strictly speaking, I should've sent word to him as soon as I saw you." Jez looked around, but Balud raised a hand. "Calm yourself. I have no intention of doing so."

Jez and Osmund exchanged glances. "We're grateful for that, Chancellor." Jez spoke slowly. "Why not?"

Balud closed his eyes and took a deep breath before looking at Jez again. "Have you learned anything about this sleeping sickness?"

Jez nodded. "It's Baron Dusan. He started it. He did it fourteen years ago too." Jez hesitated, unsure of how much to tell Balud. "He was stopped, but he's trying again. He's using it to draw power from those who are sleeping."

Balud sat up straight in his chair. "What? How?"

Briefly, Jez and Osmund related what they knew about the disease, which wasn't much. They left out the part about Jez being pharim and how Sariel had saved them. Instead, they made it seem like they had gotten away on their own, but Balud didn't seem to care about the omission. The chancellor asked them a few questions, none of which they could answer. Finally, he drew back and let out a sigh.

"That's a lot you're asking me to believe," he said.

"It's the truth."

"You word against one of the most powerful nobles in the kingdom," he said, "and you can't even tell me how to cure the disease. No, I'm sorry. If it were up to me, I'd allow you into the Academy, even if it was only as one of the lower tier, but the baron has forbidden it. I'm afraid that without proof of your accusations, I can't readmit you."

"But chancellor, we don't know anything about this Marrowit. If we're going to have any chance of stopping him, we need access to the information in the libraries."

"And we're in the middle of examinations. Do you think I can just allow you trounce around without Baron Dusan finding out?"

"I thought you were chancellor of this Academy," Osmund said.

"A chancellor who is subject to the rules of the kingdom, and I cannot just ignore a baron's command."

"We're not asking you to take me on as a student. Just let us look at the libraries."

"I'm sorry. It's out of the question. I don't know what you did to him, but I thought he would order me to seize you if you came here again. I won't openly ally myself with you."

"But…"

"I will investigate your claims. For now, you may stay in the city. Try to stay out of sight. If I find any truth to what you say, I'll send for you."

Jez almost argued, but thought better of it. It was the most he could reasonably expect, so he nodded.

CHAPTER 27

They spent the day at the Quarter Horse. The innkeeper constantly stopped by their table to thank Jez for saving his son, which wouldn't have been so bad if the place wasn't so crowded. The common room was full of students pouring over books, and Lufka's attentions made Jez's presence obvious. A few people glanced uncomfortably at Jez and Osmund, but no one actually said anything. As the sun had set, they each retired to the rooms Lufka had provided. Jez's room was small and the bed was hard. His pillow felt only slightly softer than a rock, and he was tossing and turning trying to find a comfortable spot when someone knocked. He rolled out of bed and opened the door to find Osmund, fully dressed and carrying a lantern.

"Aren't you ready?"

"Ready for what?"

"To sneak into the libraries."

Jez searched his friend's face looking for any hint of a joke, but there was none. "I didn't know we were doing that."

"Chancellor Balud told us to."

"No, he didn't. He said he would speak to us in a few days."

Osmund rolled his eyes. "He said he couldn't help us openly. He didn't say anything about helping us in secret."

"And you think that means he wants us to break in?"

"What else could it mean?"

"Maybe he meant he wants us to wait in town for a few days while he confirmed our story," Jez suggested. "Just like he said."

"You were never in the lower tier," Osmund said.

"I'm a fisherman's son," Jez pointed out.

"Yes, but you were always among fishermen or other people of your standing. Then the baron took you in, and you instantly became associated with one of the most powerful men in the kingdom. You were never a commoner among nobles. Men like the baron can do almost anything without consequence. Without proof, Balud won't move against him, but he's giving us the opportunity to get it."

"But we already have proof."

"Where?"

Jez thought for a second. "In the baron's counting room."

"Do you expect him to just let us in there?"

"What about the sleeping sickness? It's magical."

"And they might be able to prove that, but they'll never link it to the baron. We have no way to prove he's the cause, at least nothing Balud will accept, but he's seen you remember things you have no way of knowing. If he thinks there's even a chance you can help, he won't stand in your way, at least he won't if you don't make it obvious what you're doing. That leaves breaking in."

"I guess this is another one of those shades of gray, isn't it?"

"So are you coming?"

Jez sighed and nodded. He went back into the room and changed. Then, he stepped into the hall and closed the door behind him. The floorboards creaked underfoot, but no one awakened. The door was locked, but Lufka had left a key hanging by the door, and they slipped out of the inn.

"Do we start in the district of knowledge?"

Osmund shook his head. "Secrets. Knowledge about demons was never meant to be widely distributed."

The streets of Tarcai were quiet at night. Osmund held his lantern low to avoid drawing attention, but there was no need. They reached the gates of the Academy which seemed closed at first glance, but they swung open at Osmund's touch. The larger boy glanced at Jez and smiled.

The Academy was as quiet as the rest of the city. All but the most basic magics were forbidden to students outside of the practice houses. There was too great a chance of something going wrong, so activity on the Academy grounds was reduced to almost nothing. They circled the library of secrets two times trying to find a way in before settling on a window on the second floor near the back of the house. Osmund lifted Jez up, and he reached forward to push the window open when a voice came out of the shadows.

"I wouldn't do that if I were you."

Osmund jumped and lost his grip on Jez who slammed into the ground, knocking the lantern out of Osmund's hand. It shattered and the oil spilled on the ground. Jez tasted blood and reached up to find his lip bleeding. A fire appeared in Osmund's hand, illuminating the area. He took in a sharp breath and looked around. Besis laughed as he came out of a shaded corner. The protection master wore all black, and only his face was showing. Jez scowled when he saw the grin.

"Forgive me." He was obviously trying to hold in a laugh. "I should've made myself known when you first arrived."

"You were here all along?"

"Just because I'm the protection master doesn't mean I'm completely useless at illusions. I can hide in shadows, provided it's dark, and I don't move. Balud sent me to help you."

"See," Osmund said. "I told you he wanted us to break in."

"You're looking in the wrong place, though." Besis said.

"We are?"

"Oh, the library of secrets had general knowledge about demons and such, but to get information of specific demons, such as Marrowit, you need to research knowledge. Summoners are the ones who most need that information. Them and binders, that is."

"Do you know anything about Marrowit?"

Besis shook his head. "He's never been unleashed so far as I know. We have no knowledge of him."

Jez glared at Osmund. "Someone told me there wouldn't be any information on specific demons in the library of knowledge."

The larger boy shrugged. Besis waved at him, and the fire in Osmund's hand puffed out of existence. Jez blinked several times while his vision adjusted to the darkness.

"It's not in the main library. It's in the secret one beneath the practice house."

"I didn't know the knowledge district had a secret library." Jez said. "Doesn't that go against the philosophy of the dominion of knowledge? They want to be open about sharing information, don't they?"

Besis shook his head. "The dominion of secrets hides information and believes that anyone who can learn it deserves to know it. The dominion of knowledge knows that some information must be earned by learning what comes before it. Knowledge of individual demons is one of those things."

"But you can get it?"

"I can get it. I'm not supposed to, not without Master Linala's permission. That won't stop me, though."

Jez was surprised, but Osmund simply nodded. "Shades of gray, remember?"

They moved through the city trying to stay out of sight. Every time

Jez stepped too hard or kicked a stray pebble, he thought the noise would wake half the Academy. He found himself wishing he had Atrius's ability to reduce noise. It didn't take them long to reach the district of knowledge. Unlike the district of secrets, this one had lanterns hanging every few feet, and Jez couldn't help but feel like they were being watched. To his surprise, Besis walked right up to the front door of the practice house. He pulled an iron key ring out is robe and opened the door. He smiled at their surprised faces.

"You have a key?" Jez asked.

"Why wouldn't I? It's not like there's anything in here that needs to be locked away."

"Besides a secret library, you mean."

"Yes, well, there are other more potent safeguards against unauthorized entry to that."

"Were you going to tell us about that?"

"I didn't find it particularly relevant."

"You didn't?"

Besis laughed. "I'm the protection master. I'm the one that placed all the wards on the most sensitive areas of the Academy."

He turned the key and pushed the door open. As soon as they stepped inside, lanterns around the room came alight. There were several circles similar the one Dusan had used and runes had been carved into the walls. Jez yelped and looked around, but the room was empty. Besis cursed and waved a hand, plunging the room into darkness. Only the moon shining through the windows provided any illumination at all.

"I forgot about that. The dominion of knowledge tries to welcome all. I just wish it wouldn't be so obvious about it. The secret library is this way."

Having never studied any magic in the dominion of knowledge, Jez had never been in the building. As they passed by one of the circles in the floor, Jez felt a profound sense of wrongness. He shook his head and continued after the protection master. Besis led them to a small office opposite the door, presumably where Master Linala would sit. The door was locked, but this time, Besis closed his eyes and mumbled a word. The lock clicked and the door swung open.

"How…" Jez began.

Besis cut him off with a wave of his hand. His fingernail clinked on the door handle. "Iron," he whispered. He wiggled his fingers. "Terra magic."

They stepped into the office and Besis strode across the room. He ran his fingers along the back wall until he found something. He pressed in, and the wall clicked. The ground rumbled and pair of wooden planks parted, revealing stairs down. Besis waved a hand and said a few words. A wall of blue energy shimmered into existence before vanishing. He nodded at them and they started down the stairs. As with the chamber above, lanterns came to life as they approached, though this time, Besis left them alone.

The library was not what Jez had expected. The stairs came out into a hall lined with half a dozen bookshelves, though only two of them had actual books. Two others held scroll containers made of wood or ivory. The rest contained clay tablets and carved wooden disks along with a number of other writing mediums. Besis led them to the end of the hall and into a large room, nearly as big as the practice house above. A large circle encompassing the entire room had been carved into the ground. Besis walked over it and into a small room lined with books and tablets. He pulled a book out and handed one to Osmund. Then, he turned to Jez.

"Do you read any ancient languages?"

Jez started to shake his head, but then paused. "I don't know."

Besis raised an eyebrow. He handed Jez a set of wooden slates tied together with a white chord. Strange writing was painted on them. It had faded, but he could still make out the characters. Even so, they were incomprehensible. Jez shook his head and handed it back.

"That would've been too much to hope for. Even I can't read that one." Besis gave him a leather bound tome. "Look in this one."

After three hours of searching, they'd still found nothing. Osmund had fallen asleep, and Jez was finding it difficult to keep his eyes open. He stared into a book and realized he hadn't turned the page in several minutes. He closed it and put it back on the shelf. He looked up at Master Besis who was running his fingers over a flat piece of wood covered in lumps. Besis stopped his examination.

"Tired?" Jez nodded. "Well, Master Linala will open the practice house in a few hours. We shouldn't let her find us here."

Jez nodded again and shook Osmund. The other boy groaned and opened his eyes. He blinked several times.

"Sorry," he said. "What happened to the lantern?"

"What?" Jez looked up at the lantern hanging from the ceiling. It was as bright as ever, but shadows swirled around it.

"Master Besis?"

"Yes?" Besis followed Jez's gaze. "Oh. How is your binding?"

"My binding?"

"Yes, you haven't had someone teach you, have you?"

"No, you said that was too dangerous. Why?"

"Those are living shadows." His voice was completely flat. "They're about to try to kill us."

CHAPTER 28

Jez didn't have time to respond. The shadows broke apart. Each piece grew darker and expanded until they were the size and shape of a small dog. There had to be at least thirty of them. They growled, and Jez could feel their combined sound vibrating against his skin. Besis waved his hand and bands of energy shot out, wrapping one of the shadows. It squealed, but the others leapt forward. Jez screamed and punched at the air. The area rippled as energy rushed out of him, and the three shadows closest to him screamed and faded as if someone had suddenly shone a bright light on them.

One of the shadows bit into his arm, but rather than hurting, all sensation beneath his elbow ceased. He looked down and tried to shake the shadow free. Suddenly, fire enveloped it, though the flames didn't touch his skin.

The shadow screamed for just a second before it dissolved. Another jumped at Jez, but a glowing sword sliced it in two. Ziary stepped between Jez and the shadows. His sword moved through the air with inhuman grace, cutting shadow dogs from the air. When more than one creature approached him at once, he threw out his hand, engulfing them in fire or lightning. With every move he made, a shadow died. Jez could only look on in awe as Ziary mowed his way through them in a deadly dance. Even those who tried to come at Jez or Besis fell before they came anywhere close. In just a few heartbeats, the living shadows had been destroyed.

Ziary turned to look at Jez, his features twisted in anger, and Jez took a step back as he realized what the scion was thinking. Osmund had said Ziary was a creature of absolutes. He couldn't comprehend shades of gray. All he knew was that they had broken into a place where they did not belong. He cared nothing for the why.

"Take control, Osmund." Besis had his arms raised. "Don't let him do something you'll regret."

"I am not Osmund!" The flames around Ziary's sword pulsed as he cried out. "You will suffer for your crimes."

"No."

Osmund's voice cut him off. Ziary closed his eyes, but when he opened them, they were still the twin points of fire. He lifted his sword and took a step toward Jez. Then, the air around him rippled. His eyes brightened as he tried to take another step forward but couldn't.

"You are Osmund." Besis's voice was calm and steady. He held his hand up, and Jez could see muscles straining against the binding that held Ziary. "You determine how to use your power, not him."

"Evil must be destroyed!"

Besis grunted as Ziary took another step forward. Jez heard a sound like glass breaking in his mind, and Besis gasped and fell forward. Ziary stood over the binding master and prepared to strike. His sword was halfway down when it vanished. Osmund fell to the ground next to Besis, gasping.

"I'm sorry," he said between heavy breaths. "I tried to stop him."

Besis stood up and offered Osmund a hand. "No lasting harm was done. Without your help, I doubt we would've survived."

"What were those things?" Jez asked

"Living shadows," he said. "They're not really demons. They're creatures born from the nightmares of man. Which of you were sleeping?"

They both looked at Osmund who looked away. "I was dreaming about the time I was attacked by a stray dog. I'm sorry."

"Don't be," Besis said. "If it hadn't been you, an attack would've come for some other reason. These things don't appear naturally. They have to be sent."

"Dusan?" Jez asked.

Besis nodded. "Very likely. Come, the two of you need to get some rest, and I have to give examinations in a few hours."

"But we didn't find anything."

"I'll keep looking when I have a chance. If I don't find anything by tomorrow night, we'll try again then."

CHAPTER 29

"Can you turn into Ziary whenever you want?" Jez asked.

They had both slept for several hours and were now eating in the common room of the Quarter Horse. They had been fortunate to find an empty table, though it was large enough to seat six. Every once in a while, someone would approach, intending to sit at one of the empty seats as was common at an inn like this. When they saw who was already there, however, they turned and walked in the other direction.

"I've never really tried unless I was in danger," Osmund said. "Why?"

"He's good at battle magic," Jez said.

"He's a Darkhunter," Osmund said, "or at least he's a scion of the Darkhunters."

"I wonder if he can teach me."

Osmund's head snapped toward Jez. "No. It's too dangerous. I could teach you what I know. I'm not exactly weak in that area."

"But you're not as strong as he is. It's not just that. Actual pharim can't interfere with human affairs, but that rule doesn't apply to him, and he has pharim magic. He might be the only person who can teach me to use my power."

"Person?" Osmund asked.

"You know what I mean."

Osmund shook his head. "Jez, I could barely hold him back last time. If you make any mistake, if he sees you be anything less than perfect, he could kill you."

Jez took a bite of chicken and chewed it slowly. He washed it down with a gulp of fruit juice. He looked around to make sure no one was nearby before he answered. Even then, he spoke softly.

"And if he does, I go back to being a pharim." Jez tried to sound like the idea didn't bother him, but he didn't know how well he succeeded. "Then, we don't have anything to worry about, and I can face Dusan while I'm much stronger than he is."

"I'll think about it." The tone of his voice said he'd already made up his mind. "Have you remembered anything else about Marrowit?"

"He's a nightmare demon, high up in their hierarchy." Jez spoke the words before he realized what he was saying. Osmund was gaping at him, and his own response surprised him so much he wasn't able to speak for several seconds. "It was on those wooden slates Master Besis gave me, the ones I couldn't read."

"If you couldn't read them, how do you know what they said?"

Jez sighed. "I'm getting really tired of saying this. I don't know." He glanced at a nearby table. A student had a star chart laid out in front of him. For a second, Jez was enthralled by it. It seemed important. The memory was just beneath the surface. Then, he slammed a fist on the table. "Come on. We need to go find Besis."

"We should wait until night."

"We don't really have a lot of time to waste."

"We don't?"

"I really don't know. You know, Master Rael did a really bad job of giving me back my memories. They all come in patches."

"Maybe we should talk to her."

Jez shook his head. "She said she'd done all she could. We can't leave the city until the morning, right?"

"Why are we leaving the city?"

"To stop Dusan. We need to hurry."

"We can if we have to, but the path down is dangerous in the dark, and you can't fly."

Jez stood up and started walking toward the door. Osmund caught up with him just before he stepped outside.

"Come on. There's something else we can do until Master Besis is ready for us." Jez patted his pockets and smiled when they jingled. He drew out a few coins. They might just be enough to get the supplies he needed.

"What's that?" Osmund asked.

Jez grinned. "I'm going to paint something."

CHAPTER 30

The supplies he was able to buy weren't nearly as extensive as what he'd used in the intermediate painting class he'd been placed in. He could only get a few colors and two brushes. He wouldn't be painting a masterpiece. Hopefully, he wouldn't need to. He sat down in his room at the Quarter Horse and stared at the canvas he had set down on his bed. He held the larger of the two brushes and waited for inspiration to hit him, but nothing happened.

"Say something," he said to Osmund who was standing just inside the door.

"What do you want me to say?"

"I don't know. Anything. The last time, I was too busy talking to you to pay attention to what I was doing."

"What were we talking about?"

"I don't really remember. Just pick something. Tell me about your family."

Osmund turned away. "I'd really rather not."

"Why not?"

"I didn't exactly have a happy childhood. My parents were both limaph, but they didn't understand what that meant. Neither of them could transform, and it wasn't as obvious with them as it is with me.

My father is a small man, and my whole life, people have been asking me if he really is my father. More than once, I had bullies threaten to run me out of town."

"When did you leave?"

"A few years ago. Master Rael came to the Narian Isles. He recognized me for what I was, and offered to fund my first year. With how hard my life was, I jumped at the chance. I didn't realize how much there was to learn until I got here."

"What will you do now?"

"I'm not sure. Now that the baron disowned you, I suppose I'll go back home."

He obviously wasn't looking forward to that. Jez reached over to put a hand on Osmund's shoulder, and the paintbrush in his hand left a black smear on the other boy's face. For a moment, they both stared at the brush before turning to look at the canvas.

The depiction of Dusan was crude, being made of lines that were too thick, but it was obviously him. He had his arms stretched out in an unnerving gesture. Green runes floated in the air above him, and the ground was made of red stone.

"What is it?" Osmund asked.

"It's from when Dusan bound me."

"Didn't he bind you in Randak?"

Jez closed his eyes for a second. Images flashed in his mind, but they were gone before he could get any details. "I thought so, but no, it was somewhere else." He shrugged. "I still don't think this helps us."

"Maybe it does." Osmund put a finger on a rune made of wavy lines. A second later, he pulled back and scowled at the green splotch on his finger. "This one is an air symbol. It can only be used where the air is thin. This is on a mountain somewhere."

"There are a lot of mountains."

"It narrows it down from the entire world."

Jez nodded in concession. Without access to the library, they couldn't look up the rest of the runes, and they spent a nerve-wracking day in the inn. As the sun neared the horizon, they rolled up the painting and headed back into the Academy grounds. As they neared the protection district, Jez found his steps quickening. The smell of sulfur grew so gradually, he didn't notice until it overpowered everything else. By then, he was running. Osmund was right behind him, and other students rushed to get out of their way. Jez's eyes focused on the practice house, and his body pulsed with power. He lowered his shoulder and charged into the door, somehow using his power to strengthen his body. The door shattered into splinters.

Both of Jez's hands flew in complex patterns. Four bursts of energy shot out from him almost simultaneously. A web of darkness engulfed a bat made of fire. A sword of ice impaled a smoke man. A line of blue fire split a floating ice ball, and a spinning disk of yellow light exploded, vaporizing a lion with an iron mane. The room went silent as the four students who'd been working to bind their demons gaped at him. Osmund's jaw dropped and he stared at Jez. At one end of the room, Master Besis cleared his throat. He glared at Jez before glancing at the other students and waving toward the door.

"You may go," he said. "You all get a neutral grade. If you wish to try for something better, you can come back in a week."

"But examinations will be over by then."

"Then, don't come back. It makes no difference to me. Now go."

His voice left no room for interpretation, and the students fled. Once the door closed behind the last one, the master strode across the hall. He looked from Jez to Osmund and shook his head.

"Well, so much for remaining inconspicuous. You just bound three middling spirits and one greater one with as much effort as I would take to bind an imp. Can you tell me why exactly you interrupted my examinations?"

"I'm sorry," Jez stammered. "I didn't mean to. I just knew there were things that didn't belong here, and I had to send them back."

"I don't suppose you'd care to explain what you mean by that." Jez considered for a second before shaking his head. Besis sighed. "You're no limaph."

"What?"

"You've bound five demons without even transforming. That's more power than any untransformed limaph." Jez started to shake his head, but Besis went on. "We all have the right to keep our own secrets, but if you don't tell me the truth, I may not be able to help you."

Jez glanced at Osmund, but the larger boy shook his head. "It's your decision, Jez."

Jez considered for a second. "You're right. I'm no limaph. I'm a pharim."

It didn't take them long to go through all the relevant details. For his part, Besis just sat there quietly. When they were done, Besis was nodding.

"I take it you don't want this known."

"You're not surprised?" Jez asked.

"I am, and I'll want to have a long talk with you once this is all done, but for now, we have work to do. I'll keep your secret. Why did you interrupt my teachings? I would've thought you would want to remain hidden."

Jez gave him a sheepish grin. "We meant to wait until you were done."

"Well, there's no point in dwelling on it. I take it there was something you wanted to tell me."

Jez related what he had remembered about the wooden slates and what he knew about Marrowit. They showed him the painting and he nodded.

"Sleep, fear, earth, darkness, moon, and life," he said. "Those are the other runes. You say there's some sort of urgency?"

"Yes, but I don't know what that is."

"Linala will still be in her practice house, but I think this is important enough. I'll get the document from her officially. My library will have interpretations of these runes." He waved a hand over them. "That will allow you through the wards holding it closed at night. I'll meet you there. Try to not to attract much more attention than you already have. Balud will have his hands full dealing with what you've already done."

Fortunately, the library was close to the practice house, and they made it without anyone seeing. Osmund was more familiar with the organization of the library so he went and retrieved an armload of books, and they sat down at one of the tables near the door. They began flipping through them, and while they found descriptions of each individual rune, neither of the two were familiar enough with the theory to know where to look to find how they fit together. Besis came in after half an hour of frustrated searching. He handed Jez the wooden slate.

"She wasn't happy about it. This is one of the oldest documents in the Academy."

Jez scanned the markings. They seemed almost familiar. One symbol jumped out at him, and suddenly, he was filled with anger. He pointed at it.

"Marrowit."

"Are you sure?"

Jez nodded. With that gesture, the mystery fell away, and he could read the writing as easily as if he had been reading it all his life.

"Marrowit, the lord of nightmares, of the third order of demons." Besis let out a low whistle. Jez looked up, but the protection master motioned for him to continue. "He delights in keeping mortals in the grip of sleep and feeding off their fear as he gives them nightmares."

"Wait," Besis said and went to a nearby office and retrieved a stack of paper and a quill.

Jez read through the section on Marrowit with Besis writing it down. A few times, he had Jez stop and repeat a section, especially when he got to the more complex portion dealing with the demon's attributes. Most of it was over Jez's head, but by the time he'd finished, Besis had gone pale.

"I take it this is bad?"

"I suppose it could be worse," Besis said. "In theory. The third order of demons are basically minor gods. There hasn't been one unleashed in over a thousand years, before even the Academy was founded. Given enough time, this Marrowit could take over the entire kingdom. You'll need at least six major bindings to hold him. He could either come into this world in a form of his own, or he could possess someone. Most of the third order can do either."

"Do you know what bindings?"

"The symbols should help with that. What have you found?"

When they admitted they hadn't found anything, Besis looked at the books they were reading. He shook his head and pushed them aside. He went to one corner and pulled out three volumes. He came back to the table and flipped through them. He pulled out another sheet of paper and started making notes. Ten minutes, and two full pages later, he sighed.

"It'll probably possess someone. It can't exist in this world for more than a few minutes otherwise."

"Dusan?" Jez asked.

Besis shook his head. "I doubt very much that the baron hasn't taken safeguards against that, and Marrowit has a legion of sleeping victims to choose from. Jezreel, do you know how to combine a spirit chain with a dream net?"

Jez looked at him blankly. "Master, I don't even know what those are."

"A dream web keeps a spirit bound to one state of wakefulness."

"State of wakefulness?"

"Certain spirits can exist in this world and the various worlds created by dreamers. Marrowit can exist in multiple of these worlds at the same time. A dream web keeps the spirit in this world, but it was never meant to hold something as powerful as Marrowit. He could rip through it like it was made of paper. A spirit chain is used to keep particularly strong spirits from fleeing into the spirit world. As long as you pour enough power into it, it'll keep getting stronger. It could hold even something like Marrowit, but dream worlds aren't the spirit world. You'd need to combine them. He'd still break out eventually, but it's a start."

"Why can't you do it?" Osmund asked.

"I don't have nearly enough power to make a spirit chain for a demon of the third order. No single binder does."

"Then gather more," Osmund said. "Use a full contingent."

"There's no time."

"A contingent?" Jez asked.

"A circle of multiple mages working together," Besis said. "It's difficult to set up, and we'd never get it done in time, not if we also have to travel anywhere."

"Do you know how much time we have?"

"You painted the runes for darkness and moon. Together, they work best under an eclipsed full moon. The last time that happened was fourteen years ago."

"When the last sleeping sickness ended."

"Exactly. The next time is in eight days. If he's going to be stopped, it has to be by then."

"Eight days?" Jez asked. "But we don't even know where Dusan is going to summon from."

"We know something. Osmund was right. He has to be on a mountain, high enough for the air to be thin, but he can't be so high that he's above the peaks around him, and he has to be standing on stone, not snow or ice. There also has to be an abundance of life. Those conditions together aren't terribly common. More than that, the location has to be close enough for Dusan to make there from Randak in time. That leaves only three possibilities."

"Red stone," Jez said.

"What?"

"In the painting, Dusan was standing on red stone."

Besis thought for a second. "Kunashi. It's an iron mining village in a lush valley. The stones there are red from the iron. If we leave now, we can make it there in six days."

Besis gave them a list of books to gather from the various libraries along with a note with his personal seal that would convince the other masters to give them the items. Besis himself went to prepare supplies and get Master Fina. The other masters wouldn't be a great deal of help in this type of conflict, but he didn't want to go without the destruction master.

They met at the base of the central spire after an hour. Balud was with Besis, but Fina wasn't with them.

"I don't know how Dusan learned you were here, but he gave me new instructions," Balud said. "I'm to have you arrested." Jez took a step back, but Balud shook his head. "You should be glad I don't intend to fulfill that order."

"Chancellor…"

Balud waved him off. "I don't know how you got in the middle of all this, but it's obvious there's more to you than meets the eye. We all have our secrets, and I'll respect your right to keep yours. I suspect you may be able to do what no one else can, so I'll give you what aid I can."

"What about Fina?"

Balud shook his head. "We couldn't wake him. Can you do anything about it?"

"I don't know," Jez asked. "I'll try."

The destruction master lay on his bed, unmoving. Unlike Jez's father, Master Fina's body still retained his strength. He had arms like stone pillars and calloused hands well used to the sword. A man like that looked like he should be able to wake up in an instant and be ready for danger, but he remained unmoving in spite of their efforts to wake him. Jez breathed deeply, looking for that sulfuric scent that had always triggered his uses of the abilities, but there was nothing. He splayed his fingers and ran them from the master's head to his heart as he done with his father, but Fina remained asleep. Jez turned to Besis.

"This is how I woke my father." He repeated the gesture in the air. "Do you know this binding?"

"Besis shook his head. """It looks like the one used to remove a possession, but I've already tried that. At least it tells me I was on the right track. Given enough time, I'm sure I could figure it out, but chancellor, I can't do it in eight days. I wish we could take him with us, but we just don't have time."

Balud nodded. "Very well. You'll leave in the morning. Meanwhile, I'll prepare things in case we have to deal with the cataclysm here."

"What's happening here?" Jez asked.

"I've looked through some of the archives. Dusan may be performing the ritual to free Marrowit from Kunashi, but the demon is imprisoned inside of this mountain. If he's freed, the mountain will erupt."

CHAPTER 31

They left the city an hour before first light. The moved slowly until the sun rose enough for them to walk more quickly. It took a few hours to reach the bottom of the mountain. By then, the packs they were carrying felt like lead weights. At Besis's instruction, Jez and Osmund dawned hooded cloaks before heading into Hiranta. Dusan had contacted the officials of that city as well, and they were on the lookout for them. The heat made it almost unbearable, and after a few minutes he was soaked in sweat. Initially, Jez was sure he'd be discovered, but apparently, no one wanted to interfere with a master at the Academy. The few times anyone approached, one look from Besis turned them away.

They only stayed in the city long enough for Besis to find them horses. There was no road that would take them directly from Hiranta to Kunashi, and the quickest path required them to go cross country for a day. They went to the Academy stables at the edge of town, and Besis wasted no time in picking three of the horses. The stable master bowed several times to Besis and ordered the horses saddled. Osmund mounted the largest creature, but Jez just stared at his. The horse's black coat gleamed in the afternoon sun, and the animal seemed to be made of muscle. Jez stepped forward with a hand extended. The horse snorted, and Jez yelped and jumped back.

"Oh just get on," Besis said. "Shadow is a tame animal."

Jez eyed the horse. "Are you sure? I think it wants to eat me."

Osmund rolled his eyes and hopped off his own brown stallion, though his size made it look more like a pony. He lifted Jez in one arm.

"Let me down," Jez said, kicking at the air.

"I'm about to," Osmund said just as he deposited Jez on the horse. The animal looked back at him. Jez could've sworn it smirked.

"That's not what I meant. Can't we just hire a coach like last time?"

Besis climbed on his horse, a gray animal with a bushy mane. "A coach can't go cross country with any appreciable speed, and there's too great a risk of it being damaged. We don't have time to deal with it."

"We don't have time for me to be picking myself up off the ground every couple of feet either."

"It won't be that bad. We'll take it slowly at first."

Jez worked the reigns trying to make the horse go forward, but instead, it took a few steps back. Nearby, the stable master laughed, and Jez glared at him but turned away before the man recognized him. He threw his arms up frustration.

"If we're going to go slowly anyway, why don't we just walk?"

"We're only going slowly at first, Jezreel," Besis said. "You'll learn as we go. Come on. Follow me."

Fortunately, the horse seemed perfectly willing to follow others, and they walked out of town. The first day was miserable. Jez bounced up and down throughout the journey, though he didn't fall. They walked for a while before bringing the horses to a trot. As increased their speed, Jez maintained a death grip on the horse's reins, and when they slowed again, he was sure Osmund was smirking ahead of him. They ate a dinner of bread and meat while they rode and didn't stop until the sun disappeared behind the mountains. They made camp near the side of the road. The night was warm and with the half-moon shining brightly, they didn't bother with a fire. As the other two fell asleep, Jez worried that they wouldn't wake up. He was afraid to go to sleep, but the trek down the mountain was long and difficult. Added with everything else that had been going on, Jez was utterly exhausted, and before long, he fell into slumber.

He awoke to pain in his legs, and it hurt to walk. Besis laughed and told him it was normal for those unused to riding. He gave Jez a few suggestions on maintaining a better posture, and they moved on. The next couple of days passed without incident. Except for the dreams. Jez's nights were filled with images of fire and sulfur, though he couldn't say for sure if they were memories or more ordinary nightmares. The others tried to draw him into conversation, but Jez felt like he was perpetual daze. Osmund tried to instruct him in battle magic and Besis tried to bring his unconscious abilities under his control, but Jez couldn't focus, and he made little progress. On the third day, they turned off the road and headed into the Korandish plains. The ride wasn't as smooth as on the road, and at every second, Jez worried he'd fall off, though he never did. On the fourth day, the horses didn't wake up.

"It's no use," Besis said after half an hour of shaking the animals.

"I didn't even know horses could catch the sleeping sickness," Jez said.

"This was done deliberately," Besis said

"What do you mean?"

"By now, Dusan has learned we've left the Academy. He's attacking us."

"But why come at the horses. Why not attack us directly?"

"I think it's you," Besis said.

"Me?"

"You are a Shadowguard. You have more ability in the dominion of protection than anyone living. I'd wager you've been worried about us catching the sleeping sickness?"

"Well, yes."

"And you've been distracted ever since we left the Academy. You're probably guarding us without realizing it."

A gust of wind blew across the plain, and one of the horses snorted. They all looked at the animal, but it remained asleep. The slumbering animals made Jez uneasy, and he stepped away and turned his back to them. The others moved in front of him. Osmund raised an eyebrow, but Jez only shrugged.

"Do you really think I can do that?" Jez asked.

Besis shrugged. "It makes sense."

"What do we do now?"

"Can you wake the horses?"

Jez splayed his fingers and dragged them from the horses head to its chest, but nothing happened. He breathed deeply looking for any sign of sulfur, but there was nothing. He tried the gesture again, but the horses remained still. He shook his head. "Can we make it to Kunashi in time without the horses?"

"No. Even if we could run the whole way, we still wouldn't make it by the eclipse."

"What if we went Between?" Osmund asked.

"Between what?" Besis asked.

Osmund looked at Jez. "You know, that place Sariel took us. By going through there, we went from Randak to the Academy in a few seconds."

"Osmund, that wasn't mortal magic."

"You're not exactly a mortal."

"I wouldn't even know where to begin."

Osmund bit his lower lip. "I would."

"Ziary would, you mean."

Osmund nodded. "We're not doing anything wrong right now. It should be safe to summon him."

"Would he even know how to get us there? Sariel said even most scions have never been there."

"Osmund may be right," Besis said. "He's the strongest limaph I've ever heard about. Master Rael thought he might be the purest one in twenty generations. Most scions may not be able to get there, but if there are any who can, it is Ziary."

Jez nodded and Osmund turned to Besis. "Be ready to bind him if you have to."

Besis inclined his head. Osmund closed his eyes, and his breathing slowed. His skin seemed to shimmer.

"Ziary."

Though Osmund whispered the word, the sound overpowered everything else. It echoed through the mountains and resonated in the earth. The way Osmund said it, it was no ordinary word. Jez felt the name inside his mind humming with energy. The shadows lengthened as Osmund began to emit a soft white light. Wings emerged from his back, and he began to float off the ground. The flaming sword appeared at his waist, and when he opened his eyes, they were points of fire. They moved over Besis and settled on Jez.

"There is no evil here to destroy," Ziary said. "Why am I here?"

"Are you a pharim?" Jez asked.

"You know that I am not."

"But you have access to their power."

"Some of it, that which is needed to destroy."

"Can you get Between?"

"Between is denied to my kind."

"But do you know how to get there?"

"Yes."

"How?"

"Why?"

The question caught Jez off guard. "What?"

"Why should I tell you what I know? You are mortal. You could not go there even if you knew how."

"I have a pharim's soul."

Ziary chuckled, and the sound reminded Jez of swords clashing. He backed up until he bumped into a sleeping horse. The scion's smile sent chills down Jez's spine.

"A pleasant appellation."

"It's not an appellation. Do you remember the other times you've been summoned?"

His eyes glowed brighter. "Yes. The last time I was in your presence, you and the binder had entered a place you did not belong. I tried to destroy you."

Jez took in a breath, but the scion didn't seem to want try again. "What about the time before?"

"I was bound by a mortal mage. His evil far exceeded anything you have in you."

"That same mage bound me to this form, but I am a pharim. I just don't remember."

"A mortal pharim." Ziary's eyes went from blue to yellow. Then they dimmed, and he floated to the ground. "You are a Shadowguard."

"And I need to get Between in order to stop that mage from releasing a demon."

Ziary's eyes returned to blue and brightened so much that the light colored everything for a dozen feet in every direction. His muscles tensed, and he lifted his sword. Jez cried out as the blade came down, but it stopped just as it hit his skin. Flames rippled down the blade and surrounded Jez. Pain shot through his body as images flashed through his mind, but they shifted so quickly he couldn't tell what they were. He felt like he was everywhere at once. He could see everything. It was too much. His throat felt raw, and he realized he'd been screaming for several seconds, and he was on his knees. His head felt like it would split open. Everything blurred, and Jez was lost in the pain.

"Jezreel, are you all right?"

He was on his back, and Besis was standing over him. Osmund was back and looked worried. Stars twinkled in the sky.

"What happened?" he asked.

"We were hoping you could tell us," Besis said. "You've been unconscious for two days."

"Two days?" he asked. "That means Dusan will summon Marrowit tonight."

"Yes. Is there anything you can do to get us there?"

Jezreel searched his mind. Strange images and concepts floated around in his thoughts, though they made his head hurt if he dwelled on them too long. It was knowledge never meant for a mortal mind, and though his soul was pharim, his mind was still flesh and was bound by those limits. He wouldn't be able to hold that knowledge for long, but for now, it was his.

"Yes."

Jez closed his eyes, and concentrated. He allowed his thoughts to flow around Besis and Osmund. They were a few feet away, but there was something in the intervening distance. There was something Between. Jez forced his thoughts into that gap, breaking it apart. Osmund and Besis fell into the space Between, but it wasn't truly an existence, and mortal beings had to be sustained by a will of something other than mortal.

Jez's mind cried out under the strain. He couldn't hold them both. If he tired, at least one would be lost. More likely, they all would be. In desperation, he threw one out and surrounded the other with his thoughts, though the strain on his mind was too much for him to differentiate one from the other. The world vanished, and the fogs of Between swirled around them. The form of the one with him writhed in his mind, threatening to slip away. Jez remembered Kunashi. He remembered being there before, when he'd first been bound, and he took them there.

CHAPTER 32

Once again, Jez awoke on his back. Osmund lay next to him, coughing. Jez stood on shaky legs and took in the area. They stood at the edge of a city filled with buildings of red stone. The light of the rising sun made the streets look like rivers of blood. A breeze kicked up a cloud of crimson dust. They had made it, but something wasn't right. The city was completely silent. He looked at a nearby tree and saw a sparrow that had fallen onto the ground, completely still, though Jez had a feeling it wasn't dead.

"Where is Master Besis?"

Jez shook his head. "I couldn't carry you both."

"Can you go back for him?"

Jez closed his eyes, and tried to concentrate, but the images Ziary had given him were gone. "I don't know how anymore."

"Maybe we could get Ziary to show you again."

The thought made Jez feel sick, and his head began to throb. "No, that took two days, and it was almost more than I could bear. There's no way I could survive doing it twice more so soon, and even if I could, I would probably just forget again as soon as I got back to him."

"Where do we go?"

Jez nodded toward the center of the city, and they started walking in that direction. The smell of sulfur emanated from every stone, and he felt his power writhing beneath his skin, looking for a target. He had been here before. He could feel the memory trying to force its way to the forefront of his mind. It nearly drowned out every other thought. Whatever shield Dusan had placed in his mind when he'd been bound was now paper thin. Memories merged with perceptions, and he couldn't tell what he was seeing now from what he had seen fourteen years ago. There was a sense of emptiness as well, and it gnawed at him.

"There is no Between." Even as the words left Jez's lips, he suppressed a shiver.

"What?"

"Somehow, Dusan has hidden this place from Between. That's why we appeared in the outskirts of town. I couldn't bring us any closer. It's just like last time. I had to go through the city then too."

"Have you thought about what we're going to do once we reach Dusan?"

Jez nodded. "We stop him."

"That's what you tried last time," Osmund said. "It didn't really work out well for you."

"It worked well enough." Jez was no longer sure if the words were his or Luntayary's. He wasn't sure there was a difference. "Marrowit remains bound."

"For now," Osmund said.

Jez's brow creased in anger. He closed his hand around the leather hilt at his waist. For a second, he was confused. He concentrated and the metal blade was replaced with one of crystal, but it only lasted a few heartbeats before fading away. It had only been a shadow of his true weapon, the most he could summon while he wore mortal flesh, but it would still be stronger than the sword Ziary wielded. Jez shook his head to try to clear his mind, but the weapon refused to come.

"He's bound, and he will stay bound."

They reached the town square. Through the window of one of the shops, Jez could see the shop owner snoring with his head on a table. A customer had his hand extended with a silver coin held between her fingers. Other buildings had similar scenes, and horses snored in front of buildings. There was even a mouse lying in the middle of the square. This was far worse than the sleeping sickness. That had only come upon those who were already asleep, but this had obviously struck those going about their day to day lives, and even the animals had been affected. Jez pointed to a house that seemed to be the source of the sulfuric scent. Thick curtains covered the windows and a heavy door of black wood stood closed.

Jez approached it and was filled with the desire to go somewhere else. The house radiated fear, and Osmund took a step back. On instinct, Jez reached up and touched his own forehead, shielding himself from the fear ward on the house. The desire to leave vanished. Once he'd done the same for Osmund, he reached out to the door, and it opened at his touch. Osmund lifted his hand, and a ball of fire appeared over it, banishing the darkness in the house. The room immediately inside was empty. A thick layer of dust carpeted a floor made of the same red stone as the rest of the building. A trail of footprints led deeper into the house.

"It's a little obvious," Osmund said.

"The place was warded. Who would come in here?" Jez asked. "Besides, everyone is asleep."

They followed the trail of footprints into the hall, walking slowly and alert for any traps. The trail led to a small chamber that would've been a bedroom in any other house. Here though, it was devoid of any furniture or decoration. The footprints vanished in the center of the room.

"There's a passage under the floor."

"How did you open it last time?"

"Last time I could walk through walls. We should just break through."

"Aren't we worried about Dusan hearing us?"

Jez shook his head. "I'm pretty sure he already knows we're here. He's too good a mage not to."

"Well, in that case…"

Osmund closed his hand, and the ball of fire expanded until it had wreathed his fist in flame. He leaped into the air as wind rushed into the room, propelling him up. He crashed into the ceiling, breaking through and showering Jez with red dust. Osmund went up another few feet. Then, the air whistled as he surged down, slamming his burning fist into the ground. The crack could've been heard from a mile away and set Jez's ears ringing. The entire house shuddered, and a square immediately below Osmund's fist dissolved into powder, revealing a stone staircase descending into darkness.

"Shall we go?" he asked.

No sooner had the words left his lips than the darkness in the passage congealed. It spilled out of the hole like water splashing onto a dock. It swirled and rose up into the form of a massive featureless person, larger even than Osmund. The roof cracked as it stood its full height, nearly twenty feet. Even the sunlight seemed to be consumed by its form, and though it lacked a face, Jez knew it was looking right at them.

"Maybe we should've tried to be stealthy," Jez said.

CHAPTER 33

In a flash of light, Ziary shot forward, his sword blazing. He slashed upward, leaving a trail of fire in the creature's chest. The thing, the nightmare, growled, and the darkness subsumed the flames. It slammed a fist into Ziary, who was once again leaping through the air. The warrior grunted as the blow sent him sailing across the room, but Ziary spread his wings and redirected his body until he was diving, sword first, at the nightmare. The creature thinned until it became transparent. Ziary passed right through it, his sword melting a hole in the wall on the other side of the creature. The nightmare rippled like it was smoke before solidifying. It brought its fist down on Ziary, sending him to the ground and holding him there with a shadowed foot.

Jez slashed downward with his hand and a shackle made of glowing blue metal shot forward and closed around the nightmare's feet. It stumbled, and Ziary rolled out from underfoot. Brilliant cracks began spreading through the metal, but Jez's hands were already moving, crafting a binding that was even more complex and powerful. The shackles shattered, and its pieces vanished in the air.

"Hold it off," Jez cried out. "I need a few seconds."

Ziary leapt back into the combat, slashing and cutting. The fiery trails left by his sword were swallowed by the darkness, but each one took a little longer to disappear. The nightmare struck back, but this time, Ziary was ready and dodged out of the way. His sword lashed out and severed the shadow's hand. The limb evaporated before hitting the ground. The creature gave a silent roar that Jez heard only in his mind.

One link at a time, Jez forged the chain that would hold this monster. It lashed out at Ziary again, but the warrior soared into the air. The nightmare's remaining hand shimmered and became a rope that shot out from its arm and tied itself around Ziary's left wing. The creature pulled hard, and Ziary crashed to the ground. Jez released his binding, though he hadn't completed it yet. The chain wrapped around the nightmare. The creature squirmed and tried to free itself. Beneath them, the smell of sulfur surged, and anger bubbled up inside of Jez. Too much time had already been expended with this thing.

Jez took a step forward and drew his weapon. Mist swirled around it and came together, transmuting the blade into one made of crystal. Jez's personality had been crafted by his thirteen years of life, but the consciousness that came upon him had come into existence at the same time as creation itself, and no mortal could truly stand against it. Ziary inclined his head and took a step back. The nightmare looked at Luntayary with its empty face. Such a creature was not truly capable of fear, but still, it struggled to get away from him. His weapon was no mere scion's sword. Luntayary's sword was nearly as old as the universe, and though he only wielded a poor reflection of that weapon, nothing in existence could easily recover from the wounds he could inflict.

The chains around the nightmare groaned as it struggled to free itself. Luntayary held his sword in both hands and drove it into the creature's head. It screamed in his mind and shriveled as its essence was drawn back into the abyss from which it had come; the place where the core of its power still resided. The light around Ziary faded as he shrank back into the form of the mortal. With nothing to bind, Luntayary retreated into the deepest reaches of Jez's mind.

Jez fell to the ground, breathing hard. His skin tingled and he couldn't make his legs work. Tears streamed down his face, and he clenched his fists as he tried to regain his composure. He looked up at Osmund. His friend seemed to be doing better than he was. He didn't look bothered at all.

"Is it like that every time?"

"Is what like that?"

"Luntayary took me over," Jez said. "I thought I was losing myself."

"I don't think it's quite the same thing," Osmund said. "Ziary is something else. He's a scion attached to my soul. Even when he takes over, there is a difference between me and him, but you…"

"I am Luntayary," Jez said. "He's not really a separate being. Sariel told me I would become Luntayary if I died, but I don't want him to take over while I'm still alive."

"Jez," Osmund hesitated for a second. "What if it's the only way? Even if he's confined by human flesh, Luntayary is stronger than Ziary."

Jez nodded. "I don't want to die, and if I lose myself to Luntayary, that's the same thing."

Osmund put a hand on his shoulder. "We'll make sure it doesn't come to that. Are you ready?"

Jez looked up through the hole in the roof. A shadow had begun to creep across the moon. He shrugged. "It doesn't really matter. Let's go."

CHAPTER 34

Green light pulsed in the room beneath them as they descended the stairs. Dusan's voice chanted harsh syllables. The whole room hummed with power, and Jez almost gagged on the smell of sulfur. His skin tingled. He could feel Luntayary's waiting restlessly just beneath the surface of his mind, and Jez thought he could feel himself slipping away. After they had gone down a dozen steps, they came into a wide chamber. As before, runes glowed in the air around Dusan who held his arms up. His black robe was ornamented only by the symbol of the closed fist embroidered on the front. Instinctively, Jez sought out the symbol of the closed eye which floated directly in front of Dusan. The mage smiled and lowered his hands.

"You're too late this time. I refined the ritual. It's already been set in motion. It just needs time to finish."

"The eye," Jez said to Osmund. "If we can destroy the eye, it'll stop the ritual. I think Ziary's sword can do it."

"I wouldn't." Dusan brought his hand to his chest. "That focusing stone was an extremely rare artifact. I looked, but I couldn't find another. If you disrupt the ritual this time, I won't be able to take control of the power."

"You say that like it's a bad thing."

"I know you, Jezreel. You have a keen sense of justice, keener even than your pharim counterpart. If I can't control the power, it'll be released with terrible force. Everyone in Kunashi will die. I don't think you're ready to have that on your conscience."

"Is he right?" Osmund asked.

Rage filled Jez, and he spoke in a voice not quite his own. "They will die anyway if Marrowit is free."

The crystal sword appeared in his hands, and he dashed across the room, his consciousness falling to Luntayary. Ziary, propelled on wings of light, flew ahead of him. He pulled up several feet from Dusan and swung his sword. The green energy appeared around Dusan and the mage laughed. Ziary attacked again and again, but to no avail. Luntayary reached them and joined his attacks to Ziary's. The shield weakened but not by enough. Luntayary's eyes locked on the symbol of the closed eye. He struck at it, but another green shield appeared around it.

"Did you think I didn't learn my lesson last time? The ritual has no weaknesses anymore."

"Ziary, attack the mortal on my mark. He may be able to defend against one, but not against two."

"By your command, lord pharim."

"Now!"

In the same instant, Ziary's sword slammed against the shield around Dusan, and Luntayary's struck the protections around the rune. Dusan groaned, and Luntayary felt the shield weakening. He drew deeply of his past, accessing what he had once been. His mortal flesh screamed in pain, slowly being consumed by the power coursing through him as Luntayary's presence grew stronger. It was like he was dying and being born at the same time. His sword inched closer to the rune, and Luntayary sent even more power through the blade. The shield around the rune shattered.

"No!"

The word came from both Dusan and Luntayary, but the voice was not that of a pharim. It belonged to the mortal who, even now, was fading.

"This must be done." Luntayary's silent voice spoke to Jez. "Your time in this world is over."

"I'll die if I have to," Jez said. "But I won't kill. Kunashi…"

"Kunashi is already dead!"

Luntayary lifted his sword. His will was too strong. Jez would never be able to stop the attack, not entirely. He threw his will against the pharim's. The sword turned aside, and missed the closed eye as it sliced through an image of a head.

"No! You don't know what you've done!"

Dusan's voice was filled with fear. His fingers danced through the air, trying to recreate the rune that protected him from possession. The room rumbled, and Dusan flinched, losing the power he'd been weaving. He tried again, but he was out of time. He screamed and clawed at his head, but he couldn't stop the horns from emerging. Fiery wings grew from his back, and his face elongated, his mouth growing dagger-like teeth. Ziary took a step back and lifted his weapon. Dusan's flesh twisted and writhed. The screams were no longer human. Marrowit roared as he consumed Dusan's body. Without Dusan to sustain it, the shield around him faded. Ziary surged forward but Marrowit lifted a hand and Ziary stumbled. His wings came free of his body and the light faded, leaving only Osmund to crash to the ground

"Sleep, little scion," the inhuman voice said. It kicked him with a clawed foot. The tattered remains of a boot went flying as Osmund skidded across the ground. Then, it turned its eyes to Luntayary. "You've changed."

Luntayary charged.

CHAPTER 35

Luntayary's sword tore through the air, and Marrowit caught it in his hand. The demon laughed, and Luntayary thought the room would collapse on them. The demon ripped the sword from his hand and tossed it aside. The blade returned to normal steel as it clattered to the ground.

"You are no Shadeslayer," Marrowit said.

"I am a Shadowguard," Luntayary said.

He waved his hands in wide circles. The demon roared and jumped at him, but Luntayary formed a minor binding that redirected the charge and continued with his weaving. Besis had been right about combining the dream web with a spirit chain, but that wasn't all that needed to be done. Even Luntayary didn't have the power to do what was required, not alone. There had to be a hole in his binding, one that only led to one place. Otherwise, the demon would throw his strength against the binding and would eventually break free. Luntayary ducked under Marrowit's attack and thrust his hands upward, entangling the creature in bands of light.

Marrowit roared against the chains as Jez pumped more power into them. He could feel the demon's mind struggling against the bindings, trying to find a way out in this world or any other. With Dusan's death, all his magic had failed, even that which had isolated Kunashi. Luntayary allowed a crack to open, and Marrowit seized on it, opening the way to Between. He tried to flee, Luntayary kept a powerful grip on the chain, and the demon pulled him in. At the last instant, Luntayary grabbed Osmund's unconscious form, and they both disappeared into Between.

There was still too much mortality in Luntayary, and he couldn't shape Between as readily as a full pharim could. Marrowit strained against his bonds, but Between was no place for demons, and his attacks were weakened by the need to maintain himself here. Luntayary summoned the image of the Carceri Academy and went there, holding his grip. The demon screamed as it was dragged back into the physical world.

The ground was shaking, and people were screaming. The sky was filled with birds who Luntayary guessed were mortals skilled enough to change their forms. The moon had gone dark, and only the fire erupting from the ground gave any light. A portion of the central spire broke and fell off barely missing a group of blue robed students. To their credit, they didn't flee but kept channeling their power into the mountain, though it did little good. With neither Master Besis to guide the terramages or Master Fina to guide the pyromages, the Academy was ill suited to deal with the eruption of Mount Carcer.

A contingent of pyromages stood nearby, trying to take hold of the power in the mountain, but they didn't have the skill to do anything useful with it. They simply redirected it upward. Great gouts of flames shot into the sky. They looked surprised when Luntayary appeared in their midst, but these were students of destruction, and they recognized the thing he brought with him as an enemy. As one, they directed their destructive energies at the demon.

"No!" Luntayary cried out, but their attacks were already sailing through the air.

If he'd had his full power, Luntayary could have warded off their attacks, but the battle and his time Between had drained him. He tried to tap into the power of the erupting fire mountain, but he wasn't fast enough. Marrowit screamed in pain, but a second later, it became a laugh as the remainder of Dusan's physical form was consumed. Jez's bindings, lacking a form to hold onto, shattered and the demon fled into the realm of dreams.

"What was that?" One of the pyromages asked.

There was no time to explain. Mount Carcer still rumbled and threatened to explode. Luntayary reached into the earth and took hold of the power he'd hoped to use to seal away Marrowit. Even as a mortal, he'd performed the binding to release a sleeping victim. Now, he did that same binding a thousand times on every person asleep in Tarcai and Hiranta. It wasted a lot of power to do it without being physically near all the victims, but he had a lot of power to waste.

One by one, they woke up, as Luntayary drew out the curse of the sleeping sickness and forced it into a physical form, but there was still too much power in the eruption. Luntayary took hold of it and summoned an image of the mountain in his mind. With Marrowit free, he'd be able to bring the sleeping sickness on anyone he desired, and Luntayary wove a ward that would protect everyone within five miles of Mount Carcer from the demon, pouring the remaining power of the eruption into his weaving. The effort strained his mind, but finally the ward fell into place.

Slowly, the mountain quieted, and Luntayary let out a breath. Then, he collapsed, utterly exhausted.

CHAPTER 36

Jez woke with Master Balud standing over him. The chancellor was humming softly as pain receded from Jez's body. He sat up, and the room started to spin. He took a deep breath, and his vision cleared. He was in a room lined with beds. Several of them were occupied by people with arms or legs in slings or bandages on their bodies. Murus sat unconscious in a nearby bed with a bruise covering half his face. Jez was in the sick ward with those who had been hurt when the mountain nearly erupted, but there were none who seemed to be under the sway of the sleeping sickness.

"It worked," he said, though the effort of speaking exhausted him.

"So it did," the chancellor said. "It very nearly killed you. There's damage I can't repair."

"It was Luntayary. My body couldn't contain him."

"Luntayary?" Balud asked. "Is that your scion?"

Jez hesitated. "Something like that."

"I've never heard of one so strong. He took control of the eruption by himself. I've never seen anything like it. Has Marrowit been destroyed?"

Jez shook his head. "Not destroyed, just driven off. He'll be back once he's had a chance to gather his power."

Balud sighed. "I was afraid it wouldn't be that easy. Where is he?"

"In the dream world, specifically in the dream created by all of those with the sleeping sickness."

"But you woke them up."

Jez shook his head. "I woke up those who were nearby, but the sleeping sickness is in Randak and Kunashi and who knows how many other places. Marrowit will barely even notice the ones who were here."

"Then what do we do?"

Jez looked around and patted his pockets, but they were empty. For a moment, panic seized him, but he forced himself to calm down.

"I should've had a stone with me," Jez said. "What happened to it?"

Balud reached into his pocket and pulled out a smooth pebble the color of the sky. Milky images swirled on its surface. Before Jez realized what he was doing, he'd snatched the stone away.

Balud looked surprised as Jez let out a breath of relief. "I'm sorry. It's very dangerous."

"What is it?"

"It's the sleeping sickness, or at least the part I drew out of the people nearby."

"You think we can use this to cure it permanently?"

Jez shook his head. "It's not exactly a disease. It can't really be cured. It's more like a curse."

"So we can use this to break the curse?"

Again, Jez shook his head. "It's not really that complicated to cure. It just takes a lot of power, more than most here aside from me can manage."

"Then what do you intend to do with that?"

"I'm going to use it to curse myself with the sleeping sickness."

"What? Why?"

"Because with this, I can follow Marrowit into the dream world and fight him there."

For a second, Balud gaped at him. "Jezreel, I won't claim to know as much about this demon as your, but I've done research into nightmare demons since you told me about him. If you go in there, you'll just add your dream to his."

Jez lifted the stone. "The curse did more than force people to sleep. It joined their dreams to form a single whole. This is the very substance of dreams, and if I use its power, I may be able to control my dreams enough to face Marrowit on equal terms. That'll never happen in this world."

"You're getting this information from your scion?" Jez just stared at him. "Remarkable. This is how he was bound the first time, isn't it?"

Jez nodded, though it was a complete lie. When Marrowit had first been bound near the creation of the world, three pharim had been needed to take him down. Sariel had made it clear that wasn't happening this time.

"Very well," Balud said. "What do you need?"

"Just a quiet place to rest."

Balud nodded and Jez clutched the stone in his hand. He could feel the demon's power inside. He didn't tell the chancellor that there would be no retreating if this went wrong. The curse was too strong, even for him. He would never be able to break it. From the moment he took the curse into himself, he would be asleep and no one would be able to wake him as long as Marrowit remained free. He would win or he'd be forever trapped. He closed his eyes and loosened the binding around the stone. The curse leaked out and was absorbed by his skin. He drank it in. As the binding fell, he tried to seize control of the curse and harness its power, but it slipped through his fingers, and the sleeping sickness of a thousand people came to rest on him. Darkness consumed him.

CHAPTER 37

He landed in Tarcai, but the city was empty. The buildings had been torn down, and a massive crack ran through the caldera. Lava flowed through the streets. Jez was on a piece of stone floating on a molten river. He realized his makeshift boat had once been the walls to his quarters. He had failed. Tarcai had been destroyed by the escaping demon. He looked into the lava and considered jumping in. Everyone had depended on him, and he had let them down. He hadn't cared for some of them, but that didn't mean they deserved this. It would be right for him to end his life in the fires that had claimed theirs.

Something tugged at his mind, a memory that he couldn't quite remember. A stone with milky images floating on its surface appeared in his hand for a second before vanishing. This wasn't right. He shook his head to clear his thoughts and tried to remember. Mount Carcer was huge, and Tarcai sat in the middle of it. If the mountain had erupted, it wouldn't have left this ruined shell. The entire city would've been consumed.

He hadn't failed. The power had been redirected, freeing those under Marrowit's curse and protecting anyone who was close enough. The mountain rested again, and the city was safe. He held the power of the curse.

Slowly, like the high tide receding, the lava retreated beneath the earth which closed behind it. He blinked, and the city was restored. He now stood in the courtyard in front of the central spire which once again seemed whole.

"I'm here," he said to no one. "Where are you?"

This was Jez's dream, but it was also part of a much greater whole, one composed of the dreams of all those under Marrowit's sway. Perhaps he just had to walk far enough to find the demon. He looked at the edge of the mountain rising up over the city. It would take the greater part of a day to reach the bottom. At least it would in the real world.

He took a step forward, and the world shifted. He found himself looking down the edge of the caldera. He'd been a mile away, but that didn't make a difference in a place where the mind mattered more than the body. Most of the mountain looked every bit as large as its counterpart in the real world, but at its base, a snowy plain stretched out before him, and beyond that, he could see a patch of desert. Even more terrain waited beyond that. It looked like a bad quilt. Some pieces were long and wide. Others were so small he could barely make them out. Mount Carcer dwarfed them all, though whether its size was due to the strength of the sleeping sickness on him or the power of Jez's own mind, he couldn't be sure.

On impulse, he spread his arms and leapt into the air. He imagined wings carrying him high in the air, and suddenly, the mountain vanished, and Jez was left suspended by wings formed of his own imagination. He was so shocked by the change that his mind went blank. Then, the ground rushed up toward him, and he cried out, forcing the image of the wings back into his mind. At the last instant, they appeared, and he flapped, catching himself before he crashed into the ground. A few seconds later, he was soaring through the sky.

The sensation of flight was exhilarating. It felt like the whole world stretched out before him. It was so familiar. Wind ruffled his sapphire robes, and he looked down, wondering where those had come from. He scanned the landscape, looking for any sign of the demon, but there was nothing aside from the interweaving of thousands of dreams.

"And what does a demon dream about?" he asked the sky.

Marrowit's nightmares had to be of Mount Carcer, where he'd been held since the foundations of the earth were laid, but he obviously hadn't been there. Dusan had followed Marrowit for power. If the demon had spared any thought for the baron, perhaps he'd be in the manor at Randak.

Jez headed east, though he had no real reason to suspect the manor would lie in that direction in the dream world. Still, it was the best idea he had. The landscape changed rapidly beneath him: a patchwork of forests, plains, and mountains. On three separate occasions, he saw the red stones of Kunashi. At first, he thought he was going in circles, but the surrounding area was different, and he understood. With the entire town asleep, it made sense that many people would dream of home.

Time was odd in this place, and Jez had no idea if he had been flying for a minute or an hour before he reached the edge of the dream. The world just stopped. The ground below ended like a cliff over a sea of darkness. Jez's wings continued to flap, but the ground underneath remained still as if the dream would not allow him past its borders.

He landed on a patch of sand that could've been desert or shore. He moved to the edge and tried to force his hand past the edge. He met no resistance, yet his hand wouldn't move forward. Off to one side, a patch of ground materialized, extending the border of the dream slightly. A tree sat in the center of the new ground. Something moved in its branches. He flew in that direction, but found nothing other than the tree growing on a field of grass. It was a good climbing tree with low branches and thick knots of wood that would provide places to grab onto. There had been something in the branches, but it was gone now

"Where are the people?" he asked himself.

Every piece here had come from a sleeping mind. This newest section had to be from a person recently brought under the sway of the sleeping sickness, but he couldn't find any sign of the dreamer. They had to be here somewhere. Jez launched himself into the air, flying along the edge of the dream. Every time a new section was added, he swooped down, but he found nothing. Finally, after a dozen tries, he got lucky.

He landed on a stretch of rocky ground. There was no one there, but just before he lifted off, a street with a building on either side appeared. A young girl, no more than five years old, stood in the center of the street. She saw him and, for a moment, she looked confused. A gust of wind blew her hair into her face. She lifted her hand to move it away, but her finger seemed to turn to sand and blew away. Her jaw dropped as the rest of the hand was carried off. Her arm followed a second later. Before he could do anything, she was gone. He could barely see the specks of dust carried on the wind. Jez spread his wings and took to the air. He lost the trail of dust before he had gone a mile, but he kept going in the same direction.

After another few miles, he stopped, scanning the patchwork landscape. Off to one side, a wisp moved across desert sand, and he went after it, barely catching a glimpse of the specks that must've belonged to some other dreamer. He kept on like that, finding a new gust whenever he lost the one he was following. He went through dozens before he saw where they were going.

He'd only seen Rumar Keep in paintings, but Dusan had possessed several images of it. Jez had dreamed of it often. Its stone looked like gold shining under a morning sun. Its towers rose high enough to survey the land for miles in every direction. A moat of crystalline water surrounded it. Rumar Keep was the jewel of the civilized world, but even in a dream, he could smell the otherworldly nature of the inhabitant.

Jez tucked his wings and dove. He landed in the courtyard. Massive red doors were held closed by a large wooden beam. Jez lifted both hands. The stone of the castle might only have been a dream, but it still responded to the magic of the earth. The doorway twisted, causing the door to crack. A second later, it fell to the ground in pieces. Jez stepped over broken stone and entered the home of the demon.

CHAPTER 38

Though Jez had never seen the inside of Rumar Keep, he was certain it didn't look like this. Pits of fire dotted a hall that looked more like a cave than a palace. Shadows danced among the stalactites, and the ground rumbled constantly. The air was thick with smoke and ash, and it became difficult to breathe until Jez remembered that this was a dream, and he didn't need air in this place. Instantly, his difficulty vanished. Even the heat stopped bothering him, though he was still aware of it.

Small passages snaked off from the main hall. Other lesser nightmare demons inhabited the building, but they shrank away from Jez. Here, he could've destroyed them, but he needed to preserve his strength. He could sense Marrowit further down the hall. Jez summoned his sword as he approached the door at the end of the passage. Here, in the dream, it came easily. The door blocking his way was decorated with mystic runes designed for protection, but it offered no more resistance than the one in the courtyard. With that out of the way, Jez stepped into the throne room.

Marrowit sat on a throne of molten gold that flowed into a fiery pool around him. Images of faces appeared there and vanished a second later. The demon himself looked at Jez with utter contempt. A gust of wind blew past Jez and made the throne ripple. For a second, Jez heard screaming in his mind. A new face emerged from the throne, shrieking and trying to force its way out. Marrowit laughed.

"You couldn't defeat me in your world, Luntayary. Do you really think you can face me here, where I'm at my strongest? Here, where your fears are mine to use?"

Jez wanted to deny the name, to say he was Jezreel, not Luntayary, but the voice that came out of his mouth was much older and more powerful than his own.

"You shouldn't have made it so easy to follow you," Luntayary said. "In your place of power, I don't have to bind you. Here, I can destroy you."

"In my place of power, my strength is greater by a hundredfold!"

Marrowit threw his hand forward, and the room vanished, replaced by utter darkness. Jez felt himself being pulled toward a terrible light. Fear gripped him, and he tried to pull away, but the light came closer and closer until it consumed him. Luntayary screamed again, but then, he was back in the darkness, and the light was approaching again, with all its terror. With all its weakness.

"Is this what you fear?" Marrowit's voice echoed through the darkness. "Becoming mortal and losing who you are?"

The presence of Luntayary retreated in Jez's mind, and the fear vanished with it. The light was life; it was the sight of Jez being born. Everything he was could be traced to this moment.

"I am not Luntayary," he said

The throne room returned. He was several steps closer than he had been, and though Luntayary no longer controlled him, he still held the pharim's sword in his hand. Marrowit's eyes blazed.

"No, it appears you are not. I think this is more to your tastes."

Suddenly, he was back in Kunashi. Dusan was laughing at him, and the sound filled him with rage. His flesh burned away as his mind was pushed aside, leaving him as little more than an observer in his own body. He wouldn't last long. The other him focused on one of the floating runes, the one that would disrupt the ritual and keep the demon bound, the one that would kill so many people. The sword came down, and Jez tried to stop it, to turn it aside, to do anything, but this time, he could only watch. The sword cut through the rune, and he could hear the screams of the dying. All that blood was on his hands, not that it would matter much longer. The pharim was consuming him from the inside. He blinked, and the sword cut the rune again. This time, he saw the image of a sleeping child. She woke just as the energy of the disrupted ritual swept over her. She seemed to age a hundred years in a second. She laid her head down and didn't move again.

Again and again, he cut the rune. Each time, he saw a different face or heard a different voice. Each time added guilt and pain. Each time was a wound against his soul. Finally, when the grief had nearly destroyed him, his sense of self was restored, and he felt renewed. His sword was rushing toward the rune that would start this whole vicious cycle over again.

"This is what you fear," Marrowit's voice said. "How ironic that both mortal and pharim fear the same thing, losing yourself to the other."

At the demon's voice, the presence within Jez stirred. He felt it growing inside, but Marrowit noticed too, and the scene changed back to the darkness and the light, driving Luntayary away until Jez alone remained. Then, it changed back to the sword and the rune. He lost track of how many times the images shifted, holding him in perpetual terror. Before long, he didn't even know which consciousness was dominant. All he knew was fear. He had failed everyone. His father. Besis. Osmund.

Osmund. He'd said Luntayary was different from Ziary. Ziary was a separate entity, something passed down from the afur. He was a piece of them grafted on to his soul, but Luntayary was Jez and Jez was Luntayary. He'd tried to deny it, but it was like trying to deny the sea or the sky. You could not just pretend away reality. He and Luntayary were one.

The light grew before him, until it surrounded him. It didn't destroy him. It had never been able to. Instead, it changed Luntayary. Like Ziary, Luntayary had been a creature of absolutes, but it had lived for years as a mortal, and because that, he saw what no pharim ever had. Shades of gray. That didn't diminish him. It made him more.

Luntayary's presence appeared in his mind, but it didn't push Jez aside as it had done before. It came forward as a deeper part of himself, something greater and truer to his own nature than anything else. It wasn't something other than him. It was his true self, what remained when everything else had been stripped away. Here was a creature incapable of fear, but they had never truly been separate. Luntayary's courage had enabled Jez to stand up against a dark mage infinitely greater than himself. Luntayary could not speak a lie, and that inability made Jez woefully inadequate at illusion. They were the same and always had been.

The fear vision Marrowit had encased him in shattered. The demon actually looked surprised as Jez lifted his sword.

"Impressive," Marrowit said. His throne bubbled and spewed molten metal. Jez jumped back, but it wasn't meant as an attack. The liquid resolved itself into the form of a human. The fiery orange gave way to pale skin and gray hair. A dark robe was embroidered with the image of a closed fist.

"Jezreel?" Dusan said, his face awash with fear.

"Here," Marrowit said. "I give him to you."

Jez stuttered. "What?"

"He died under my power. His soul belongs to me. He has taken everything from you. He is yours to do with as you will. Torture him for eternity if that is what you wish."

"You think this will convince me not to attack you?"

"Jezreel, please," Dusan said in tears. "Take me with you. I can teach you. Together, we can come back. We could destroy him."

"Perhaps he is right," Marrowit said. "I will release you. Take him. I care not. Simply leave me be. Challenge me again when he has taught you all. You are no match for me as you are."

Jez hesitated. He'd known from the beginning that he had a slim chance to defeat Marrowit in his own realm, perhaps given time, with Dusan's help…

No. Dusan may be a master mage, but he was also evil. Learning from him would inevitably taint Jez. He didn't know what that corruption would do to the part of him that was Luntayary, but he doubted it would be a good thing. Marrowit had to know that. A bound pharim was one thing, but a corrupted one would be another thing entirely. Perhaps it would be as great a threat as Marrowit himself. Jez shook his head.

"A pity." Dusan screamed and vanished as his body melted back into the throne. Marrowit lifted his hand again. "Perhaps this."

Again, the seat boiled and spewed out another form. Jez gasped when it came together. It was his father.

CHAPTER 39

Bartin was on hands and knees, weeping, while Marrowit sat on his throne, impassively. Jez reached forward, but snatched his hand back before he touched the crouching figure.

"This isn't possible," Jez took a step back. "My father died while he was awake. You didn't have him."

Marrowit waved off his denial. "What you saw was nothing but a remnant. I had already taken most of his soul. Do you want it? It's yours if you wish."

"Why would you just give him up?"

"He is only one soul. It is nothing to me, but it means a great deal to you. What do you say, Shadowguard? What would you have me do? His body is gone, but it is a simple matter to release his soul into the body of another in my grasp, or if you wish, I will release him to whatever fate awaits mortal souls. I will send you back to your body, and you may live out your life."

"You're afraid I'll succeed."

Marrowit laughed. "You have as much chance to destroy me as a fly has to destroy you."

"Then why?"

"What do I gain by destroying you? I could kill you, but that would only restore you. In this place, I could even cripple your soul so that your full power is never restored, but that would break your charge to guard over me. Sariel," Marrowit cringed at the name, "would only set another to the task. So long as your soul is whole, I am under your charge, and so long as you are mortal, you can choose. If you decide to leave me be…"

"Pharim cannot violate mortal choice," Jez said.

"I would be free."

"The Shadeslayers…"

"The Shadeslayers could not reach me here."

"You'll try to bring the whole world under your sway."

"I will not touch you or your father."

"And have us watch the world crumble around us?"

Marrowit inclined his head. "I give you my oath that if you accept the soul of your father, I will not take another mortal for as long as you live. In fact, I will release all those I currently hold. They will wake, and you will be a hero." Jez gaped at him, but the demon shrugged, a gesture that looked odd with his inhuman form. "I have been bound since the foundation of the earth was laid. What is another hundred years to me?"

Demons had made bargains since mortal kind had first learned of them. If they made an oath, they were bound by it. They were experts in twisting words, but Marrowit had spoken plainly. If Jez took him up on it, he would leave them alone.

"Jez?"

The voice cut through Jez's thoughts. The sword faded from his hand. His father had finally managed to look up. His eyes were red with tears. He crawled to Jez and held on to his leg, and Jez felt himself go weak in the knees. He closed his eyes.

"Is this truly my father?" he asked. "Speak it to me in an oath."

"I give you my oath that this is your father, save for the part of him which passed beyond when you woke him."

He opened his eyes just as his father turned and saw the demon. He yelped and looked up at Jez.

"Jez, what's going on?" his father asked. "What is that? What's been happening? I've been seeing your mother die over and over again."

Jez's breath caught in his throat. His mother had died screaming, drenched in sweat, and unable to control her own body, all because she'd been cut by a rusty fishhook. He'd seen it happen. It had given him nightmares for weeks, and now his father had been tortured by the memory.

"I'm here to get you out of here, Father," Jez said, kneeling and embracing him.

"Then, you accept?"

Jez looked up at the demon on the verge of nodding.

"Where are we?" Bartin asked.

"It's only a nightmare. Don't worry."

Bartin shook his head. "I've never dreamed anything like this."

"That's because it's not your nightmare." Jez pointed at Marrowit. "It's his."

"Do you agree?" Marrowit asked.

"It's a demon, isn't it?"

"Yes."

"Don't do it."

"But Father…"

"I told you before you left, don't become one of those people who trade their souls for money and power."

"I'm not doing this for money or power. I'm doing it for you."

"Some prices are too high."

Tears streamed down his face. Bartin knew exactly what would happen if Jez refused. Marrowit would drag him down into an eternal nightmare, but he was willing to deny Marrowit what he wanted. His father understood what Osmund had told Jez on the first day they'd met. There were shades of gray but not always. There was such a thing as absolute good, and there was absolute evil.

Jez summoned the image of what he'd been into his mind, and the dream shaped itself to his will. His sword reformed in his hand, and shining wings emerged from his back. His clothes transformed into sapphire robes that shone with their own light. He looked up at the demon. Its eyes blazed as it realized what he was going to say.

"No."

His father didn't even cry out as he melted into a pool of liquid gold and was reabsorbed into Marrowit's throne. The demon rose and stepped down, a fiery sword appearing in its hands. Its face showed no emotion, but Jez could feel the hate radiating from him. It started to speak, but Jez didn't wait. He leapt at it, his sword empowered by the strength his father had granted him, and the demon roared and lifted its sword to meet the attack.

CHAPTER 40

The swords clashed with a sound like a hurricane on the open seas. The palace shattered, and the throne crumbled. For just a moment, Jez thought they were evenly matched, but it didn't take long take for Marrowit to dispel that illusion. Immediately, his sword lashed out toward Jez's face. He swung his sword in a wide arc, batting the other weapon away just before it pierced his skull. He could feel the heat radiating off the weapon before Marrowit drew back. The demon moved faster than he would've believed possible. Its sword seemed to be everywhere at once. Jez had to draw on everything he'd learned from both Murus and his memories of his time as a pharim to ward off the attacks.

Every blow sent pain shooting down Jez's arm. He didn't have time to counter. All his efforts were spent in staying alive. One blow drove Jez back a step. At a second, he fell to his knees. He knew a third would rip the weapon from his grasp. Jez rolled out of its way at the last instant, lashing with his own sword at the demon's leg. His weapon bit into the creature, and Marrowit roared. The demon stumbled, and Jez attacked again. Marrowit's sword crashed into Jez's blade, driving it to the ground. Jez brought his wings forward, slamming one into Marrowit. The touch of the demon seared his wings, but it also knocked Marrowit off balance. Jez thrust, but Marrowit had already moved out of the way.

His father screamed in terror, and the sound caught Jez off guard. He turned in that direction, but there was no one there. He turned back to see the demon's sword about to disembowel him. He brought his sword up, but Marrowit twisted its blade, catching Jez's weapon and tearing it from his grip. The sword skidded across the floor. The demon delivered a powerful kick to Jez's chest that sent him into the air. He'd only gone about a foot before Marrowit brought a fist down on him. He slammed into the ground so hard cracks spread across the stone. Marrowit put a foot on his face and held its sword at Jez's throat.

"You never really had a chance. Dusan's curse bound you too well."

"Go ahead. Kill me," Jez said. "I'll come back unbound by human flesh."

"I don't have to kill you." With a swipe of his sword, he cut off Jez's left wing. Jez screamed. "I just have to hold you. I can sustain your body for a few years before it dies and restores you to what you once were." With another flick of his sword, he cut off the other wing. "By then, more of the world will have fallen under my sway, and every mind will be giving me strength. I will surpass what I was the first time you bound me. In the meantime…" Another slash removed Jez's sword arm. "I can have fun."

Jez's blood sprayed from his wound, covering the ground in crimson. It should've been enough to kill him, but it wasn't real blood. It was only a dream, and his body didn't need it. Marrowit lifted its sword to strike again and removed his other arm. Jez's eyes went wide as the sword sheered through flesh and bone. He barely felt the pain as the arm flopped to one side, and Jez's eyes widened as he watched the arm. It wasn't really an arm. It was no more real than the blood.

Dusan had bound him to human flesh for one lifetime, and that flesh restrained his power. A mortal body could not withstand the full power of a pharim flowing through it, but this was a dream, and his body was just a construct of his mind. His soul was still a pharim's soul, and his will was still a pharim's will. In this place, the bindings Dusan had placed on him meant only as much as Jez allowed. In this place, he summoned the full power of Luntayary unbound by human flesh.

Wings erupted from his back, but these weren't the wings formed from the dream. These were true pharim's wings. His wings. His arms grew back, shimmering with power. He grabbed Marrowit's leg. The touch that would've seared his human form was little more than a pinprick to his true hands. He threw the demon off himself and rose until he stood a foot above the ground. His sword materialized in his hand, his true sword, not just the shadow he'd been able to create before. The mortal world was governed by human choice, and pharim could not violate that, thus their power in that world was limited, but here, in a demon's place of power, those limits were removed, and Jez's form blazed with an angry light. Marrowit took a step back before standing to his full height.

"You're fully here," he said.

"So are you."

An evil grin spread across the demon's face. They stared at each other for several seconds before launching themselves forward in a combat that would only end when one was destroyed utterly.

CHAPTER 41

This time, it wasn't sword against sword. It was lightning against fire. Jez was a storm, and Marrowit was a city aflame. Jez's weapon crashed against Marrowit's, sending jolts of energy into the demon. In the same instant, at Jez's command, an iron spike rose from the earth, but Marrowit leapt out of the way before it impaled him. The demon threw his hands forward, and Jez's mind was filled with images of death and destruction, but Jez forced them away as a fountain of fire appeared under him. His wings carried him off to one side, but Marrowit was already moving, its clawed hand reaching for Jez's wing, but he twisted out of the way.

Back and forth they went, neither able to gain the upper hand over the other. After a few strikes, everything for a hundred yards had been reduced to rubble. Jez took to the air in an attempt to get some sort of advantage over Marrowit by attacking from above. As soon as his plans became apparent, however, Marrowit unfurled wings of his own, bat-like appendages wreathed in flames. He leapt into the air, leaving trails of fire behind him. They clashed in the skies over the patchwork of dreams. Storm clouds stirred around them. Marrowit roared and the clouds thundered in response. Too late, Jez realized his mistake. Fire and air were of the dominion of destruction, and Marrowit's control over them was nearly absolute. Up here, the demon had the advantage. Lightning spewed from the clouds, arcing through the air. It struck his chest and pain suffused every inch of him. He was halfway to the ground before he realized he'd started falling. Rather than recovering from his fall, he bent his wings forward and dove into one of the patches, one that was made of water. Marrowit's shadow fell over him. He could feel the fear radiating from the demon, slowly infecting Jez.

They splashed into the water, an element governed by protection. Instantly, the fear vanished, and Jez spun. Marrowit was surrounded in steam as his skin evaporated the water. Jez pointed his sword and sent power into the surrounding sea. Water hardened around the demon, freezing him in place, and Jez rushed forward. At the last instant, however, Marrowit's muscles tensed. Everything turned to steam. It billowed into Jez's face, and he didn't even see the demon's hand until it closed around his throat.

He reached up to try to pull it away, but Marrowit held on with a grip like a vice, and he didn't just hold on to his physical form. Somehow, Marrowit held his power in check as well. The demon dragged him onto shore. They stepped onto a wooden dock, Marrowit's steps leaving blackened footprints on the planks. Nearby was a boat with a blue starfish painted on it, the same one that had been painted on his father's door. His father who had sacrificed himself to deny this demon.

"You did better than I expected," Marrowit said. "But did you really think you could defeat me here? This is my realm. This is my home."

"No," Jez said, his eyes locked on the blue starfish "It's mine."

For a second, Marrowit's face twisted in confusion. Jez's fist crashed against the demon's face with enough force to shatter a mountain. He threw himself at Marrowit, pummeling him with his bare hands, consumed with a rage that was wholly human, just like Osmund when Jez had seen him in the arena. Unlike the limaph, however, Jez had no reason to hold back. Marrowit struck him with his wings, but Jez barely registered the pain. This was the being that held his father.

Marrowit struck with his own sword, but Jez slammed his fist into the demon's arm, sending the sword flying. It steamed as it burned through the dock and fell into the water. Jez lifted his hands and his sword materialized. The demon's eyes grew brighter, and for the first time, the fear Marrowit gave off was his own.

"Do not do this, pharim. With my power and yours, there is nothing we could not do."

"Except good," Jez said and drove his sword into the demon's chest. This was no mere banishment, not here in Marrowit's place of power, the one place he could be destroyed. The demon roared and his entire realm roared with him. One by one, people formed in the patches of ground before vanishing, either to wakefulness or to whatever lies beyond mortal life.

"Jez?"

A lump formed in Jez's throat, and he turned around. His father was stepping out of the boat. No longer the broken shell that Marrowit had shown him in the throne room, Bartin looked strong like he had before Dusan had taken Jez as a ward.

"You're here."

His father smiled and opened his arms. "Where else would I be, son?" He waved his hand to indicate the boat. The blue starfish seemed brighter, and the wood looked brand new. "This is my home."

"This is our home," Jez said as he shed his pharim body and fell into his father's arms.

"So it is, son. So it is."

"I did it, father. I destroyed the demon. You're free. So is everyone else."

"I am proud of you."

The voice was fading. Jez looked up. His father had tears in his eyes, but he was vanishing. For a moment, Jez tried to stop it, but not even a pharim could hold on to a soul whose time had come.

"Goodbye, father."

"Live well, Jezreel."

Then, the world vanished.

CHAPTER 42

The first thing Jez saw when he awoke was fire. For a second, he worried that he was back under Marrowit's sway. He tried to get up, but something held him down. He began to panic, but he realized the fire was small and wasn't spreading. He blinked several times. It was in a fireplace. He looked down at himself. He was in a bed, and the thing holding him down was a blanket that had been tucked in just a little too tight. He squirmed until it came loose. Then he sat up. He was still in the Academy's sick house, though he seemed to be the only one in residence. He swung his legs over the side of the bed and tried to stand up, but his knees buckled. He flailed and knocked over a small table with a teapot on it. The pot clattered to the ground spilling its contents. He hit his elbow on the ground and winced at a jolt of pain.

By the time one of Balud's adjutants had come in to see what was causing all the noise, Jez was bleeding. His sick robes were wet from the tea, and he smelled distinctly of mint. He was also laughing. The adjutant just stared at him for a few seconds before turning and running back into the hall. The chancellor came in a few minutes later. He took one look at Jez before scowling at his adjutant. The boy shrank away.

"Help me get him back into bed," he said, "like you should've done when you first saw him like that."

The boy turned red and moved to Jez's side. Together, the two hefted him up, though they almost dropped him because of his laughter. Then, Balud scolded the adjutant on how he should never leave a patient alone under those conditions. After a minute of that, the adjutant slinked away. At the doorway, he turned and said something to Jez that might've been an apology, but he mumbled so Jez couldn't be sure. Once the door closed, the chancellor turned to him.

"Why in the seven are you laughing?"

It took effort for Jez to regain control of himself. "I'm sorry, Chancellor. It's just so funny."

"What is?"

"This." Jez gestured down at his tea stained robe. "I just destroyed a demon in his own realm and saved the soul of my father and thousands of others. After all that, I hurt myself with a teapot. You have to admit, that's pretty funny."

The edges Balud's lips turned up in a smile. "Yes, I suppose it is. Let's get you into clean robes and I'll bandage that elbow."

He went to a drawer and pulled out a bandage. He wiped at the cut with liquid that stung a little. A few seconds later, the wound was wrapped.

"Can you change on your own? You've been asleep for a week, and your body's not used to walking anymore."

"A week?" Jez asked in shock.

"A week and a day actually. I can help you into clean clothes if you're not up to it."

Jez's face reddened. "I think I can manage it."

Balud nodded and brought a clean robe to him. "I'll be right outside if you change your mind."

It took Jez five minutes to get out of the wet robe. The tea made it cling to his skin, and he almost fell several times. Once, Master Balud poked his head in to check on him. With an obvious effort, he resisted the urge to laugh at Jez seemingly entangled in his own robe. He asked Jez if he needed help, but Jez refused. When he'd finally changed, he called the chancellor back into the room. The adjutant came with him and picked up the old robes. For a moment, he looked at the spilled tea. Then, he shrugged and wiped up the rest of it with the robe. Master Balud sighed as the adjutant left.

"You'll have to forgive Dombar. He really is a gifted healer once he forces himself to slow down and think a little."

"He's fine," Jez said.

Balud nodded. "I take it from your assertion that you destroyed a demon that Marrowit is banished."

Jez shook his head "Not banished. Destroyed. Marrowit doesn't exist anymore."

Balud blinked and let out a short gasp. "I thought demons couldn't be destroyed."

"He was a nightmare demon," Jez said. "The dream world was his place of power. He had nowhere to retreat to when I defeated him."

"Destroyed." Balud said the word in a half whisper. "Has that ever happened before?"

Jez closed his eyes and searched his memory, but it was gone. He still had memories of the past thirteen years, and he remembered knowing other things, but the memories from before his life were gone. He shrugged.

"I don't know," he said through a smile.

Balud raised an eyebrow at that and inclined his head. "If you're feeling strong enough, there are people who'd like to see you."

Jez leaned forward. "Osmund?"

"He woke up a few hours after you went to sleep. Master Besis got back this morning."

Jez nodded and Balud opened the door to call for Dombar. The adjutant came in with his head down. The edges of his sleeves were still wet from the tea. He kept his face lowered and mumbled when Balud told him to go get the guests. Balud sighed as the adjutant ran out.

"He'll learn one of these days. It might not be for another fifty years, but I'm sure he'll learn."

Jez barked a laugh, and very nearly couldn't stop again. Besis and Osmund came in a few seconds later. Osmund scooped Jez into a bear hug before Balud could stop him. The chancellor had to shout three times for him to put Jez down before he listened.

"It's truly over?" Besis asked.

Jez nodded and related the story to them, though with Balud here, he made it sound like he was a limaph, sure that the others would understand. Each of them asked for more details at different points. Balud wanted to know how Marrowit had kept the souls away from their bodies and seemed disappointed when Jez couldn't answer. Besis wondered if Marrowit could've been bound if all the sleepers had been awakened, though from the demon's words, Jez doubted it. Osmund asked about the battle and if Jez remembered how he'd summoned Luntayary's sword, but Jez shook his head.

"You have Ziary's sword," Jez said. He pursed his lips. "You do, don't you? You can still change?"

A smile spread across Osmund's face. "I can control him."

"What? How?"

"I don't know. I think Ziary's mind is still asleep."

"There are few magics that can survive their caster's death, but it does make sense," Besis said. "Marrowit never actually put the sleeping sickness on Ziary. That would've sent him to the dream world, and I doubt he wanted that. Since he didn't hold the soul, Ziary didn't awaken when Marrowit was destroyed."

"I'll take your word for it," Osmund said. "I'm just glad it happened."

"Well, be sure you don't lose control," Balud said. "I would hate to expel you again."

"Again?" Jez asked. "You're letting him back in?"

"Of course. Assuming that's what you want."

"Well, yes, but why does it matter what I want?"

"Didn't Dusan tell you?" Balud asked. "He adopted you with the king's approval."

"Well, yes, but he also tried to have me arrested."

Balud shrugged. "He never rescinded his request for adoption. The king's men found his lair at Kunashi and concluded he'd attempted some dark ritual. Besis confirmed it, and I testified to what I saw when the demon arrived. It was enough to convince King Haziel that he's dead. You are the Baron of Korand now, and that makes you a great deal more important than anyone Osmund offended. Of course you're welcome back, too." His eyes flickered to Besis. "And you may study whatever you wish." Jez was at a loss for words, so he just nodded. "Good. The term starts in a week. It'll be a hard road back to recovery if you're going to be ready on time."

Jez nodded again and Balud ushered everyone out, insisting he needed his rest. Jez tried to point out that he'd had enough rest, but Balud wouldn't hear of it and forced everyone to leave. A few minutes later, a new adjutant returned with a bowl of soup and a crust of bread. His stomach growled. He hadn't realized how hungry he was until that moment, and the food vanished almost before Jez realized he'd started eating.

Strength returned to Jez slowly over the next several days. Master Balud instructed him to take walks every day, and told him to never go alone. At first, Jez chaffed against the restriction, but once, he fell and wouldn't have been able to get up if Osmund hadn't been there. He signed up for classes, including binding, theology, and aqua magic. At

Besis's insistence, he also included literature as something a proper noble would study. With the assistance of Master Linala, he made arrangements to hire a regent to govern Korand while he was at the Academy. On the night before the term started, he found he was looking forward to it.

He awoke to a bright light. At first, he thought the sun had risen, but the light was too bright, too pure. He sat up and saw a pillar of light in one corner. He blinked several times until he made out the face inside.

"Sariel."

"Luntayary."

"Jez."

The pharim lord inclined his head. "Jez." The light receded, and he became a tanned skinned man with gray hair and blue eyes. "You did well. As well as any Shadeslayer might have. You do the Shadowguards great honor."

"What happened to my memories?"

"Dusan put an imperfect binding on you when he confined you to this form. It allowed memories from before to leak through, especially when dealing with the demon under your charge. I simply perfected the binding."

"So I won't remember?" he asked. "I won't be so good at binding?"

"Your memories are locked away, but the power remains. You are a Shadowguard, and I would not change that if I could. I simply allowed you to be mortal as well."

"Then you won't try to get me to kill myself."

Sariel shook his head. "Your charge is destroyed."

"You'll leave me alone, then?"

"Perhaps."

"What's that supposed to mean?"

"You are still pharim, and you are still Shadowguard. There may yet be tasks for a mortal who can claim those titles, but for now, you are free. Live well, Jezreel Bartinson. Luntayary of the Shadowguards."

Sariel inclined his head, and vanished. The next thing Jez knew, the morning sun was streaming through his window. He wondered if the whole thing had been a dream. Somehow, he didn't think so.

Osmund was waiting for him at the base of tower, dressed in brown robes but lacking any silver buttons.

"I thought they were going to let you into the upper tier," Jez said.

Osmund shrugged. "Even you can't just declare someone to be nobility."

Jez rolled his eyes. "You don't have to be nobility to get into the upper tier. I wasn't the first time."

"No, you were just a noble's ward."

"And you're a noble's friend" Jez said. "Come on. Let's go see Master Balud."

Osmund shook his head. "Jez, I was born to a poor family, and I don't want to forget where I came from, so if it's all the same to you, I'll keep these."

He thumbed his plain black buttons, and Jez looked at his own and felt a sudden pang at the loss of his father. Osmund shook his head. "You were always noble, Jez, but if it'll make you feel better…"

Osmund raised a finger and small flame shot to Jez's shoulder. He yelped and jumped back, but the fire didn't burn through the robe. It just singed a little. When it went out, the blackened form of a smiling starfish had been burned there. He smiled.

"Thanks."

Osmund nodded. "We should go. Besis won't be happy if we're late."

Jez nodded, and they headed for their binding class. Jez didn't know how well he could be both mortal and Shadowguard, but the pharim lord had told him there might still be tasks for him to do. He would be ready.

VIELSPEAKER

CHAPTER 1

The waiting room in Rumar Keep was ornate to the point of being gaudy. Jez paced back and forth as he and his companions awaited his audience with King Haziel. Three tapestries covered one wall, each depicting great battles. A gold statue of King Haziel himself stood in the center of the room holding a spear in one hand and a scepter in the other. He seemed to be sneering at Jez. He squirmed in his chair and tugged at the lace at his collar to scratch his neck. Sileon, the squat little man who served as Jez's advisor, cleared his throat, but Jez ignored him. The only reason the man was here was because the masters at the Carceri Academy said the king's court was no place for a boy of thirteen to be unaided. Osmund, the only other person in the room, laughed and Jez glared at the seven foot boy. Osmund grinned, his too large nose wrinkling.

"You really shouldn't do that, Baron," Sileon said.

Jez resisted the urge to look around for Dusan, the man from whom he'd inherited that title. Unknown to most, Dusan had been an evil man who'd meddled with dark forces that had ultimately destroyed him. He had even taken a guardian spirit, a Shadowguard named Luntayary, and bound him to a stillborn child, giving it life and a soul. The secret known only to Osmund and one of the masters of the

Carceri Academy, was that that child had been Jez himself, and though he no longer had memories from the time before his birth, much of his power remained.

"It itches," Jez said. "Couldn't I have just worn my Academy robes?"

Sileon snorted. "You're the Baron of Korand, my lord. You can't go before the king dressed as anything other than who you are."

"But I *am* a student at the Academy," Jez said.

"You're not only that, though. This is your first appearance at court, and you need to make a good impression."

"Assuming the king wasn't working with Dusan," Jez said under his breath.

"What was that?"

"Nothing."

The diplomat glanced down at the ring on Jez's finger which bore the symbol of a blue starfish, the sigil Jez had chosen for himself. Sileon reached into his pocket. "Are you sure you wouldn't prefer the closed fist? As Dusan's adopted son—"

"No." Jez lifted his hand. "Dusan may have adopted me, but this is the sign my real father always painted on his fishing boat. It's what I want to be known by."

"Oh very well. Could you at least wear the sword?"

Jez shrugged. "I left it in my quarters."

Sileon cleared his throat, and Jez looked up at him. The man tugged at his collar and reached into his robes. He pulled out a blade in a scabbard of black wood. The image of a man with bat-like wings had been carved into it. A ruby engraved with the closed fist had been set in the pommel. The sight of the weapon made Jez shiver. Dusan had given it to him before he'd departed for the Academy. Not for the first time, Jez wished he'd just thrown the sword away. He started to shake his head, but Sileon interrupted.

"Dusan was a powerful and influential man when he was at court. He could manipulate the tides of politics with a skill Ashtar has rarely seen. You would do well to have people think of you as his protégé."

"But I wasn't his protégé," Jez said. "I only knew him a few months."

Sileon grinned. "It's what people think that matters."

Jez let out a breath and took the sword. "Fine."

He belted the sword and tried not to grind his teeth as Sileon smiled at him. Once it was done, Jez stood up for Sileon to examine him. The advisor bowed his head.

"Much better. Now, if you would only pick a more…" he looked Osmund up and down, and hesitated. "Appropriate bodyguard. I'm sure I could arrange something."

Osmund stood by the door and was dressed in a loose fitting shirt and trousers. They were wrinkled but seemed mostly clean. He wore a tabard with a blue starfish on it and a sword that Jez probably wouldn't be able to lift in two hands. The other boy grinned at the advisor, and for a second, his steel gray eyes became fiery orange. Sileon yelped, and fell out of his chair. Jez did his best to hold in a chuckle. Osmund didn't bother and erupted in laughter.

"You really shouldn't do that, Sileon," Jez said. "You know how battlemages are."

"Ah, well yes. Of course." He made a point of not looking at Osmund. "Perhaps we should go over proper court procedure."

Jez sighed. "Sileon we hardly talked about anything else in the month it took us to get here. I think I know all I need."

"Well, it never hurts to review."

Jez groaned, but Sileon pretended not to notice. He drilled Jez on how deeply to bow to the king and to other barons. He should only incline his head to minor lords unless he happened to encounter Lord Nalion who was the king's second cousin. It was inappropriate for him to speak to the king unless Haziel spoke first, or at least it was inappropriate in a formal audience. In a formal dinner, however, he could speak as long as he inclined his head to the king, but sometimes it was better to speak to the person seated next to the king and simply speak loud enough for the king to hear.

On and on it went as it had gone in the weeks since they'd left the Academy and headed for Rumar, the capital of the kingdom of Ashtar. Osmund didn't escape Sileon's lectures either. He was to have his sword tied to his sheath with a silk ribbon anytime they were in the keep. He should keep his hand on his hilt whenever Jez was in a meeting with anyone ranked lower than him. He could also do that with someone of equal rank, but only if Jez wanted to deliver an insult. Under no circumstances, save to protect Jez, was he to actually draw his weapon. Osmund's eyes glazed over. Jez couldn't blame him. All the talk of swords was pointless. If it came down to it, Osmund was more likely to fight with fire and wind than with a blade.

Jez didn't know how long they waited. Sileon said it wasn't unexpected. With Jez being both a baron and, potentially, a powerful mage, Haziel was probably making them wait as a way to establish dominance over Jez. Dusan had done things like that when he'd received visitors, and Jez hadn't cared for it then either.

"Have you been able to find out why King Haziel appointed Dusan as the Baron of Korand?"

Sileon shook his head. "I'm afraid not, my lord. I would refrain from asking him, though. He might take that as an accusation."

Jez grunted but didn't reply. A few minutes later, an old man with brown eyes and a hawk-like nose came into the room. Though shorter than Osmund by nearly two feet, he managed to give the appearance of looking down on the boy. He inclined his head to Jez. Jez remembered just enough of Sileon's lessons to know that was a calculated insult, but he didn't let it bother him.

"The king will see you now." He sniffed at Osmund. "You may bring your retainers, if you wish."

Sileon's face reddened. Any noble of Jez's rank was permitted to bring his party before the king unless specifically forbidden. By explicitly granting permission, the king had implied Jez was equal to a minor lordling. Jez nodded to the chamberlain and followed him into the hall. If being insulted was the worst thing that happened to him, he'd be happy. He just hoped it didn't turn out that Haziel, King of all Ashtar and Defender of the Land, was his enemy.

CHAPTER 2

King Haziel's throne room was even more opulent than the waiting room. Marble statues of the past kings of Ashtar lined the walls. The vaulted ceiling had to be at least three stories up. Seven windows, each twenty feet tall, held the stained glass images of the seven pharim high lords. Jez's eyes immediately locked on the image of Sariel, lord of the Shadowguards. It was only by the blue robe that Jez recognized him. He had deep blue eyes and wore a gentle smile. He looked more like a kindly old grandfather than one of the most powerful beings in existence. Whoever had created it had obviously never seen the real Sariel. Jez chuckled under his breath. It was entirely possible that, aside from Osmund and himself, no living being had ever seen the pharim lord.

They approached a pair of thrones made of gold and ivory, though only one throne was occupied. Four guards in mail shirts and steel helmets stood around them, men by the king's throne and women by the one that should've been occupied by the queen. A woman with dark brown skin and black hair that went to her shoulders stood next to the throne. Like the king, she wore deep purple robes, and a word from Sileon identified her as Villia, the king's chief mage. A boy a few years older than Jez himself with short red hair and pale green eyes stood behind her, presumably her apprentice.

King Haziel had a well-trimmed beard. Gray had long ago begun to encroach on his dark hair, which was closer to white than black. Aside from that however, he showed few signs of age. He had wide shoulders and piercing brown eyes. The crown of Ashtar, a single golden band, rested on his head. He wore deep purple robes, and had a pair of swords at his waist, one long and one short, the throne having been built to accommodate the weapons. If the stories were to be believed, though, his wife, Queen Istar was the deadlier of the two. Jez fell to one knee and heard Osmund and Sileon do the same behind him. They were on the ground for at least a minute before the king spoke.

"Rise." Jez obeyed. "We are pleased to finally meet you."

"The honor is mine, Your Majesty. Thank you for inviting me to your court." His eyes flickered to the empty throne. "Is your lady wife not present?"

"She and our son are visiting the Baron of Nakior at the moment. This summons," Haziel let the world hang for a second as he narrowed his eyes and made it clear that the 'invitation' had been a command, "was long overdue. Though we cannot condone the actions that led to his death, we offer our condolences for the loss of your adopted father, our esteemed cousin."

"Cousin?" Jez asked, but as soon as the word had left his lips, he wished he could call it back. The higher nobility all referred to themselves as cousins. He felt his face redden. "Yes, of course, Your Majesty. I'm sorry. I didn't spend a lot of time with Dusan, and I'm sorry I didn't get a chance to learn more from him."

The king raised an eyebrow and the guards shifted their weight. One of them brought a hand to the hilt of his sword. Too late Jez realized what he had said. He opened his mouth to explain, but the king's sharp voice cut him off.

"Be glad you did not. I'm told his lair contained workings used to summon the greatest of evils. Man was never meant to meddle with those forces. I would not like to learn that you have an interest in such things."

Jez's head bobbed. "Yes, Your Majesty. I mean no, I don't. I only meant that I'm sorry he didn't teach me the proper manners of the court."

The king snorted. "Then, you know nothing of what he was trying to do?"

Actually, Jez knew a great deal. Dusan had freed the demon lord Marrowit, and only by accessing the power hidden deep inside himself was Jez able to fight the creature and eventually destroy him. In the end, Balud, the chancellor of the Carceri Academy had decided to suppress knowledge of the incident, even from the king. Haziel may rule Ashtar, but matters of magic and demons were the province of the masters of the Academy.

"No, Your Majesty. I was only his ward for a few months and his son for just over a week before he died. The masters say he had to have been preparing for years."

"Yes, so I've been told. There are many who have asked me to relieve you of your title. They think he intended to take you on as an apprentice."

Behind him, Sileon took in a sharp breath. Jez nodded once. The title didn't really mean much to him, but without it, he doubted he'd be able to afford to attend the Academy. Still, he couldn't really offer an argument. It wasn't like he was qualified to hold the position. The king raised a hand.

"As despicable as what Dusan did was, it's not illegal to summon such creatures. No doubt he intended some treachery once he succeeded, but I will not punish you for what he only intended to do, not when I myself approved your adoption. I've been told you have great potential as a mage, and I would not want to lose you as an ally."

"Thank you, Your Majesty. You are most kind, and I am your faithful servant."

The king nodded. "You will join us tonight for dinner. Lord Varin has also arrived recently, and I would have you acquainted with him."

"Of course, Your Majesty. It would be my pleasure."

Haziel's eyes flickered over Jez's shoulder. "After that, we will talk further. I believe you would benefit if I were to send an advisor with you when you return to Korand." Jez nodded, and the king waved at him. "You may go."

Jez bowed deeply and turned. Sileon's face was red, and he was clenching his teeth, but he didn't say anything as Jez walked past him. He was almost at the door when the king's voice stopped him.

"Baron Jezreel."

Jez looked over his shoulder. "Yes, Your Majesty?"

"It's not necessary to use my title in every sentence."

Jez nodded. "Yes, Your Majesty."

The corners of the king's mouth tightened and Jez felt blood rush to his face. He bowed again and rushed out, Osmund and Sileon on his heels.

CHAPTER 3

As soon as the door to Jez's sitting room closed, Sileon cried out. The act was so uncharacteristic of the normally calm man that both Jez and Osmund stared at him.

"Insult after insult," Sileon said. "I don't know how you can stand it, my lord."

"How did he insult me?" Jez asked as he walked across the room and plopped down in one of the half dozen cushioned chairs. "He actually seemed nice at the end. He invited us to dinner after all."

"He invited us to dinner with Lord Varin." Sileon practically spat the name. "He's one of the lowest ranked nobles in the kingdom. To make matters worse, the king didn't even claim you as an honored guest. He's putting you on the same level as Varin."

"Varin," Osmund spoke slowly, as if tasting the name. "Why does that name sound so familiar?"

Sileon shook his head. "Varin is a minor lordling from…" he hesitated for a second. "I don't even know the barony."

"You don't think we should refuse to go to dinner, do you?"

Sileon paled a little and shook his head so hard it could almost be called violent. "Oh no. That would be an insult to the king. Perhaps you could manage that if you had Dusan's influence, but your position in the court is too precarious to risk insulting anyone."

Jez rolled his eyes. "I thought I was one of the highest nobles in the kingdom."

Sileon let out a long breath. "There is rank, and there is influence. The lowliest knight can affect change if he has the right alliances."

"Rank can help, but it's not enough by itself." Jez completed the thought almost by rote. "I know. You've said that before."

"But you don't *learn*." Jez looked up at him, and Sileon bowed his head. "Forgive me, my lord. I meant no offence."

Jez waved off the apology. "He didn't actually tell us when dinner was, did he?"

Sileon shook his head. "I can find out if you wish, though it may be seen as a sign of weakness to display our ignorance. Still, the alternative is to stay here and wait to be summoned. It may have been intended as another insult. We should be careful in how we proceed."

Jez threw up his arms in frustration. "Oh go ahead and ask. I'm getting so tired of this. We've only been in Rumar a few hours, and I already have a headache. I just want to get this over with."

Sileon's eyes widened. "But sir, if you want to increase your influence, court is the best place—"

"Go Sileon."

The advisor's face went red, but he bowed his head and scurried out. Jez tried to glare as he left, but Sileon looked so ridiculous trying to maintain his dignity that it was impossible. He disappeared through the door. Osmund met Jez's gaze, and they both laughed. It was several seconds before they calmed down enough to speak.

"All this talking about politics almost makes me long for the times we were fighting an evil mage bent on releasing a nightmare demon."

Jez grinned. "Yeah, if only something like that would happen here. It would certainly make things more interesting."

CHAPTER 4

Dinner, as it turned out, was still two hours away, but Sileon insisted they spend that time getting ready. He summoned an army of servants, seemingly from nowhere. When Jez asked about it, the stout man simply said that being a baron had its advantages. Jez took that to mean he was paying them a great deal of money.

The servants helped him out of his clothes and into new ones, something he'd never really gotten used to. They ignored his assertions that the clothes he'd worn before the king were good enough. They even tried to comb his hair, which he'd allowed to grow a little longer in recent weeks. He managed to stop them from doing that, however, and he was glad for that small mercy. Every time Jez tried to speak with Osmund, Sileon cleared his throat, wordlessly instructing him to say nothing in front of the servants, as if Jez had any secrets to keep.

Osmund stood by the door. Every once in a while, he would grumble something to one of the servants, and they would take a step back, stammering and pale faced. Sileon scowled, but Jez could tell his friend's actions more out of boredom than any perceived threat to Jez.

Finally, Sileon settled on a bright blue doublet with gold embroidery, leaving Jez to wonder who would think to weave gold into clothes. Like his previous outfit, it had lace at its neck, and Jez struggled to avoid scratching. Sileon ushered the servants out of the room. Getting dressed had taken almost the full two hours, and Sileon spent the next several minutes drilling Jez on the finer points of etiquette that might come up in a formal dinner. Eventually, a servant in the purple livery of the king came to lead them to the dining hall.

The king was seated at the head of a table made of lacquered wood. The seat to his right was occupied by a tall pale skinned man with yellow hair. A whispered word from Sileon told Jez it was Lord Varin. Many of the other chairs were occupied by men and women wearing the same dark green as their lord. It seemed Varin had brought a dozen people with him. Three of Varin's guards stood against one wall, next to those of the king. Jez motioned for Osmund to join them. Villia and her apprentice were also present, and her eyes kept wandering from Jez to Osmund. Her gaze made the hairs on the back of Jez's neck stand on end.

Only two seats sat empty, one at the king's left, and one next to Varin, though as soon as Jez glanced at it, Varin glared at him. That seat must be reserved for someone else in Varin's party. This time, Jez didn't have to be told that he'd been insulted. He bowed deeply to the king and inclined his head to Varin. Propriety demanded that Varin, ranked much lower than Jez, rise to greet him, but instead, the lord just returned the gesture. Since there was nowhere for Sileon to sit, Jez waved toward the door. For a second, it looked like Sileon would object, but a glare from Jez sent him away. Jez would just have to make it through this dinner unaided.

As soon as Jez sat down, a girl in a flowing green dress stepped into the room followed by a pair of guards. One was a bearded man with a crooked nose and the other was a raven haired woman with ice blue eyes. The noble they were guarding was a tall girl with pale skin and golden hair. Anger flashed in her eyes as she met Jez's gaze, and his blood went cold. He realized why Osmund had thought he'd heard of Lord Varin. He was the father of Lina, a former student of the Academy who had almost gotten Osmund kicked out.

Jez stared at her face, astonished that the supposedly unhealable scar that had once marred her cheek was completely gone. Quite deliberately, she turned away and eyed the guards lined up on the wall. When she saw Osmund, a gasp escaped her throat. Her face wavered, and a red line appeared on her face, running from just beneath her right eye to the bottom of her chin. It had been hidden by an illusion. Tears streamed down her cheeks, and Osmund turned away and mumbled something. Instantly, Lord Varin was at Lina's side asking what was the matter. The king stared. Finally, she lifted her hand and pointed at Osmund.

"It was him. He did this to me."

Lord Varin's face twisted in rage, and he stormed up to Osmund. He looked like a child next to the large boy. "Is this true?"

For a moment, Jez thought his friend would deny it, but Osmund closed his eyes and nodded. His voice was so quiet Jez barely heard it. "I'm sorry."

Varin turned to Haziel, his face red with fury. "I demand you arrest this monster."

Jez shot to his feet, but a glare from the king kept him silent. Haziel looked from Osmund to Jez. Finally, he addressed Jez.

"He is a commoner?"

"Well yes, but—"

"Guards! Take the baron's body servant, and throw him in the dungeon until we can decide how he is to be punished for assaulting a noble."

CHAPTER 5

Jez stared at Osmund through the iron bars in the dungeon under Rumar Keep. The room was almost ridiculously small for his large form, and even sitting on the stone slab carved from the wall, the cell looked tiny. Torches lined the hall though they were spaced so far apart they barely provided any illumination at all. A musty smell hung in the air, and from somewhere in the darkness, Jez heard a scurrying sound accompanied by the squeaking of rats.

"Osmund, why does this always happen to you?" Osmund's eyes narrowed, but he didn't respond. Jez eyed the bars. "Can't you break out of here?"

Osmund shrugged. "It's warded, just like the cells under the Academy. I think I could still change." He ran his fingers along the bars. "Ziary's sword would cut right through these. Somehow, I don't think that would be the best thing."

"No, it wouldn't," a voice said from behind.

Jez spun. For a moment, a ball of water appeared around his closed fist shedding, a soft blue light. The boy, a few years older than Jez himself took a step back, his eyes wide. It took Jez a second to recognize him as Villia's apprentice. He searched his mind for the name, but it didn't come. He lowered his hand and the water dripped to the floor. The boy took a step forward, his eyes locked on Jez's hand.

"Pulling water from there air?" His voice was barely above a whisper. His eyes were so wide Jez thought they would pop out of their sockets. "That's incredible."

Jez shrugged. "I studied aqua magic at the Academy. It's not exactly dry down here. I'm sorry. I don't remember your name."

It looked like his face reddened, though in the darkness, Jez couldn't be sure. The boy went to one knee, accidently wetting his robes in the water from Jez's working.

"Oh, forgive me, my lord. I am Sharim, Mage Villia's apprentice."

"Sharim, please get up." The boy did and started to brush off his robe. Apparently realizing it was useless, he gave up and inclined his head. Jez sighed. "What were you saying?"

"Only that it would not be wise for your guard to try to escape. There are twice as many guards patrolling the dungeon than there normally would be. Out of respect for your position, they're staying out of sight, but they're here, and there are archers stationed at the end of the hall. Is it true that you're both limaph?"

For a few seconds, everything went silent except for the sound of rats scurrying in some unseen corner. Jez and Osmund exchanged glances. Osmund was one of the most powerful limaph in a thousand years. They had circulated the rumor that Jez was one as well as a way to explain the knowledge and power he'd gotten from Luntayary. Jez nodded slowly. Sharim's eyes grew even wider.

"He can transform?" Jez started to shake his head, but Sharim went on. "I overheard you. Ziary is his scion? Did he give Lady Lina that scar?"

Jez glanced at Osmund who shrugged. Jez nodded. "It was an accident. He can't really control Ziary."

That wasn't exactly true anymore, but Sharim nodded in acceptance. "Can you transform too, Baron?"

"No."

"They say that you—"

"I didn't," Jez said. "Please, it's not something I like talking about."

"Oh, I'm sorry, my lord. I didn't mean to offend. If you'll come with me, I'll take you to Mage Villia."

"What?"

"Mage Villia. Oh, I'm sorry. I'm jumping around, aren't I? It's why I came down here. She was going to ask to speak to the two of you after dinner, but…" Sharim waved his hand at Osmund. "She still wants to see you, though, my lord."

"I don't know," Jez said. "I should probably see if Sileon has had any luck negotiating with Lord Varin."

"That's the thing. Lord Varin is furious. I don't think he will change his mind, but Mage Villia can intercede with the king on your behalf."

"And she'll do that if I go talk to her?" Sharim nodded. Jez turned to Osmund and gave his friend a half smile. "Well, Sileon did say I needed to get allies at the court. I guess I could do worse than one of Haziel's mages. I'll be back."

Osmund nodded, and Jez turned to follow Sharim as the boy dashed up the stairs and back into the keep.

CHAPTER 6

Villia's workshop took an entire floor near the top of the south tower. It was a round room twenty feet tall. A quarter of the wall was covered from floor to ceiling with shelves of books. Tapestries and paintings covered the rest. A half-finished sculpture of a dog sat in the middle of the room. Its head had been carved with such detail, Jez half expected it to bark at him. Villia was seated at a nearby table. She was staring upward and didn't look down as Jez and Sharim entered. A picture of the night sky had been painted on the ceiling. Jez stared at it for several seconds before he realized the stars were moving across the image.

"Remarkable, isn't it?"

Jez jumped. Villia was staring at him, and he realized she had violet eyes. She was middle-aged, and her purple robe seemed to shimmer and reflect the stars from above. Jez glanced back at the ceiling. The full moon was just coming into view at the western edge.

"It's an illusion?"

Villia had a musical laugh. "Did you think I had transported the night sky onto my ceiling?"

Jez found himself smiling. "No, I don't guess I do. Sharim said you wanted to see me."

She turned to her apprentice. "You may go. Practice tactile illusions, and come to me in two hours for a lesson."

Sharim looked to Jez. "But…"

"I said go. I need to speak with Mister Dusanson alone."

"Bartinson," Jez said through clenched teeth. "My father's name was Bartin."

"Forgive me." She glared at her apprentice. Sharim bowed his head and disappeared down the stairs, and she looked back to Jez. "Please take a seat."

Jez sat down across from her. She stared at him for several seconds, and he slumped in his chair, uneasy under the weight of her examination. Finally, he broke the silence. "Sharim said you can help Osmund."

"Your bodyguard?"

"Yes."

"I believe I can. Is he truly a limaph? One of a pure enough bloodline to transform?" Jez nodded. "And you?"

"I can't transform."

"You're lying." The frankness of the accusation caught him off guard. He blinked and struggled to find his words, but she raised her hand. "No, don't bother denying it. You're not a good enough liar to deceive me. Your friend's scion is of the Shadeslayers?" Jez gaped at her. "I don't think any of the others could make a wound that wouldn't heal. What about you?"

"I…I don't have a scion." Jez struggled to keep his voice steady.

Villia smiled. "Don't worry. I have no intention of revealing your secret to anyone else. Neither will Sharim. Tell me, when did you first learn you were a limaph?"

Jez's mind was racing. "In painting class."

"Really? I'd heard you bound a fear demon the day you arrived at the Academy."

Jez sputtered for a second. He hadn't been expecting to be questioned like this and hadn't come up with a good lie to give, so he settled on a partial truth. "Well yes, but I didn't know what it meant then. It was only after my paining class that Osmund explained."

She got up and walked to a shelf that held several rolled papers. Jez eyed her as he tried to regain his composure. She pulled out one as long as her arm and brought it back to the table. The bottom fell out of Jez's stomach as she unrolled it. The picture was a masterpiece. Against a background of stars, a purplish cloud had been painted that seemed to be expanding outward. Near the top, the cloud became a vaguely human form, and around its edges, seven robed figures stood garbed in all the colors of the rainbow. Their faces were the only spots in the entire painting that lacked any color. It was the picture Jez himself had painted when he'd first accessed Luntayary's memories, before Sariel had sealed them off.

Jez's mouth had gone dry, and it was several seconds before he moistened his mouth enough to speak. "Where did you get that?"

"Master Kerag sent me a copy. It's remarkable work. Do you know what this is?"

He nodded. "It's the creation of the universe."

"According to Master Kerag, you're a skilled painter, but you haven't created anything nearly on this level since your first day. Why is that?"

Jez was so off balance by the questions that he could only shrug. "I don't know."

Villia raised an eyebrow but didn't accuse him of lying again. He had a feeling she knew though. He looked over his shoulder at the door, but she cleared her throat.

"How much do you remember?"

"Nothing."

Jez spoke almost too quickly, but the mage was looking into his eyes as he spoke. She pursed her lips and nodded. Jez took several deep breaths as he forced himself to calm down. Villia leaned back in her chair. The lights in the room had dimmed at some point, but now they brightened. Villia let out a breath. Jez's thoughts were racing. He thought back and tried remember if he'd felt the characteristic listlessness that would indicate a telepathic intrusion, but Villia shook her head.

"Don't worry. I wasn't in your mind."

"You know when someone says that, it's a pretty good sign they're lying."

Villia chuckled, and the sound did nothing to calm him down. She was right though. Mind reading was complex magic, and very few could manage it. It was also considered a high crime if done without consent. He didn't know if Villia had the ability, but even if she did, in his time at the Academy, he'd learned to build wards around his thoughts. Even if she was strong enough to break through, she wouldn't be able to do it without him knowing. He felt his face heat up.

"I take it I don't have to continue to deny it?" He raised an eyebrow, and she smirked. "I don't need to read your mind when your thoughts are written on your face."

"What do you want from me?" Jez asked.

She waved at the painting. "I've already told you. I want to know how you were able to paint this while remembering nothing."

"It was instinct," he said. "I was distracted and didn't realize what I was painting. It just happened."

"And since then, you've remembered nothing?"

"No."

"You're lying again."

It didn't catch him as much by surprise this time, and he tensed his muscles and nodded. Her eyes widened a little, and she drummed her fingers on the table. He scowled at her.

"Yes, I am, but I don't know you, and I don't know if I should trust you."

Her eyes narrowed. "I'm the only one who can get your friend out of the dungeon."

"Why did the king make Dusan the Baron of Korand?"

"Dusan was a powerful mage. With the Academy just outside the borders of Korand, it made sense to give it to him."

"Then, it was the king's choice, not Dusan's."

Villia gave him a level gaze before letting out a breath and shaking her head. "No, when Ashab died without an heir, Dusan requested the title."

"And the king just gave it to him?"

"Hardly 'just'. Dusan gave up his lands north of Rumar to get it. They had a greater income, but the title was higher as the Baron of Korand. Many others would've made the same trade, given the chance."

"Didn't anyone object?"

"Oh, of course they did, but no one had as much influence, and the income his lands brought the crown was considerable."

Jez nodded. Assuming it was true, then Haziel had only been used by Dusan. If Villia was lying, however, then not only the king, but a powerful mage was his enemy. Still, if it could help…

"If you can get Osmund out, I'll tell you what you want to know."

She looked him in the eye for a long time. Her gaze made shivers run down his spine. The stars swirled above them for a few minutes before fading, leaving a plain stone ceiling. Villia nodded.

"Lord Varin is insisting on a trial. I cannot prevent that."

"You said you could help."

She grinned. "Oh I can. I'm the one who will preside over the trail."

CHAPTER 7

Jez clenched his teeth as Osmund walked into the chamber, flanked by a pair of guards. His hands were shackled, and the chains at his feet grated as he dragged them across the floor. He almost fell into the chair at the center of the room. On one side, a curved platform held a long, semicircular table. Villia was seated at the center, looking down at Osmund. The king sat at her right hand, and Jez at her left. Sileon was seated next to Jez. Lord Varin and his daughter sat next to the king. The illusion once again covered Lina's scar. She looked away as soon as Osmund sat down.

There were other chairs along the wall that held various minor nobles, though they went silent as Osmund sat. A man with a brown robe and a blue sash stood just inside the door, staring intently at the prisoner. Jez could feel the power flowing out of him and around Osmund, binding his power, though it wouldn't be enough to stop Osmund from transforming. Jez wondered if the mage knew that. The king waved a hand at Villia.

"Your Majesty, is this truly necessary? I have spoken to Chancellor Balud, and this boy has already been punished for his crime."

Lord Varin banged his fist on the table and shot to his feet. His face was red. Lina tugged on his sleeve to try to get him to sit back down, but he tore his arm away. "He assaulted my daughter and half a dozen others. For that, he was banished from his school for a few weeks. That's not a punishment. That's a vacation."

The king cleared his throat. Varin blinked. For a second, Jez thought he would actually shout at Haziel, but the lord inclined his head and sat down. He put a hand on Lina's, and she smiled at him before glaring at Osmund, fear and anger mixed on her face.

"He makes a good point, Villia," the king said. "That punishment hardly fits the crime. Proceed."

"As you wish. The accused is Osmund Jecklson, retainer and guard to Baron Jezreel Dusanson," Jez winced, but he let it pass. "His accuser is Lord Varin Durnson of Quintiar. Lord Varin, of what do you accuse him?"

"He assaulted my daughter and her friends, all of them nobility. He wounded her with a magical sword that prevented her from healing."

"Do you have the names of those assaulted?"

Varin looked surprised. "What?"

"The names, Lord Varin. You can't accuse someone of assaulting six nameless nobles. Give me their names or he will be tried as if they were commoners."

Varin looked at Lina. She let out a deep breath and rattled them off. Jez didn't recognize most of them. Like Lina, they had left the Academy after Osmund had been readmitted. With every name, Osmund sank deeper into his chair. Saying them seemed to banish Lina's fear, and with every one, her glare on Osmund intensified. When she was done, Villia nodded.

"What happened?"

"He attacked us," Lina said. "He just turned into that thing and attacked us."

Jez was on his feet before he realized he was moving. "That's not what happened!"

Lina gave him a hard look. Unshed tears welled in her eyes. The illusion covering her scar had fallen away, though she didn't seem to have noticed. Jez hadn't realized how much the experience had affected her. He sat down, but Villia glared at him.

"You will have a chance to speak, Baron. First, I want to hear Lady Lina's story." Jez nodded, and Villia turned back to Lina. "What thing did he transform into?"

"It was this thing with wings and a flaming sword. He burned everyone around and cut me with the sword."

"Everyone? Wasn't the baron there?"

"No," Lina said. "Well, yes, but he wasn't the baron yet."

"Odd that he should choose a bodyguard who had so injured him."

"Well no, he wasn't burned."

"I don't see how any of this is relevant," Lord Varin said.

Villia stared at Varin, not looking away until Varin did. Some of the assembled nobles murmured to each other, though they all went silent when Varin glared at them.

"I am simply trying to establish the facts."

"You know the facts. He assaulted my daughter."

"Why wasn't the baron burned?"

"What difference does that make?"

"Maybe all the difference in the world." The mage looked at Jez. "Well, young Baron?"

"They attacked him," Jez said. "One of them, Regis, hit him in the head while his back was turned."

"So he was defending himself."

Lina shook her head, and Lord Varin looked like he was going to explode with anger. Before he could say anything, Osmund's quiet voice cut in.

"No."

Villia looked at him. "I'm sorry?"

"No, I wasn't defending myself. I lost control of Ziary, and he would've killed them."

"You see!" Lina cried. "He's admitted it. Throw him in the dungeon. Throw him in and beat him until he can't stand. It's better than he deserves."

"Lady Lina," Villia said in a level voice. "You will control yourself, or I will have you removed."

Again, Varin shot to his feet. "You would dare?"

"The same goes for you, Lord Varin. I have all I need from the two of you. Be quiet or leave."

Lord Varin's eyes bulged, and Lina looked like she was getting ready to scream, but Villia was already ignoring them and addressing Osmund. After a few seconds, Varin and Lina sat down.

"Then, you are a limaph," Villia said. Osmund nodded. "Can you transform at will?"

"Yes."

"No," Jez cried out. Once again, everyone looked at him. "I mean he can now, but he couldn't then."

"Is that true?" Villia asked. Osmund nodded.

"It's also irrelevant," Lord Varin said.

"No, I don't think it is. You don't understand what the limaph are, Lord Varin. Osmund couldn't have done what he did if it weren't at least a little justified."

"He was justified in attacking my daughter? He could have killed her!"

Villia sighed. "A poor choice of words. Regardless, a scion will rarely manifest unless it is provoked. That may be a mitigating factor."

"What do you mean 'may be'?" the king asked.

"I'm sorry, Your Majesty. I just don't know. I'll need to see if there is a precedent for a scion committing a crime like this one. I recommend we break until tomorrow."

"What about him?" Varin asked waving his hand to the dejected Osmund sitting silently in the middle of the room.

Villia inclined her head. "Osmund, will you swear not to leave the city, and to return to this room tomorrow at noon?"

"What? You can't just take his word."

Villia glared at him. "You forget yourself. Whatever else he may be, Osmund is an Academy trained mage, or at least he will be once his training is complete. That gives him certain rights. Among those are the right to have his sworn word believed by another mage." That set the nobles to talking, but Villia silence them with a wave of her hand. She turned to Osmund. "Well?"

Osmund only hesitated for a second before nodding. Villia glanced at the guards. They gave each other nervous looks, but when the king cleared his throat, they rushed to obey. Their commander, a tall woman with red hair, pulled a heavy iron key ring from a belt pouch and fiddled with the chains. Osmund rubbed his wrists as the manacles fell away. Lord Varin stormed out with Lina right beside him. Neither looked at Osmund as they passed. The king was speaking to Villia and waved for Jez to go. He and Osmund walked out together. He hoped Villia would stay true to her word, but he had a feeling it wouldn't be so easy.

CHAPTER 8

There was a knock at Jez's door. He looked up from a chart of the nobility Sileon was explaining to him. Osmund nodded and went to open the door. The large boy just stared, his massive form obscuring the doorway.

"Osmund, who is it?" Jez asked.

Osmund looked over his shoulder and stepped out of the way. Lord Varin stood in the doorway. He glowered at Osmund before turning to meet Jez's eyes. Jez's jaw dropped. The nobleman cleared his throat and Jez looked at Osmund, unsure of what to do. Sileon stood up and bowed.

"Lord Varin. Please come in."

Varin inclined his head and entered. Sileon glared at Jez, silently demanding that he call Varin to task for his lack of respect, but Jez ignored him. Varin strode to the table Jez was at, but Jez didn't invite him to sit.

"What do you want, Lord Varin?"

"I wonder if I could speak to you." He gave Sileon a pointed look before turning to Osmund and back to Jez. "Alone."

Jez narrowed his eyes. "I can't really think of a reason I should do that."

He returned his attention to the chart until Varin put a hand on the parchment. Jez looked up and could tell Varin was trying to hide a scowl. He wasn't doing a very good job, though.

"Consider it a favor." Varin glanced at Osmund. "One that might be valuable enough that I would feel obligated to repay it with something equally valuable."

Jez met Osmund's eyes. Villia had said she would help Osmund in the trial, but she hadn't succeeded in doing anything but delaying it. If Varin agreed to drop the charges, all their problems could go away. Osmund's brow wrinkled, and he nodded, indicating he realized the same thing. The larger boy let out a breath and turned to leave.

"But my lord," Sileon said, "I really should stay and—"

"Go Sileon," Jez said.

"But—"

"Go. Wait outside." He waved at the chart. "We'll finish this after I'm done with Lord Varin. It won't take long."

Varin nodded. Sileon's face reddened slightly, but he managed to regain his composure before it became too obvious. He bowed, first to Varin and then to Jez before leaving the room. Almost imperceptibly, the edges of Varin's lips tightened in the faintest hint of a smile. Jez glared at him.

"What do you want?"

Varin looked down at the chair, but Jez still didn't invite him to sit. After a minute of silence, Varin shrugged and sat down anyway.

"I knew Dusan, you know. Before he became Baron of Korand."

A lump formed in Jez's throat, and he tried not to let his nervousness show. He shook his head.

"I didn't know that."

"I would've been surprised if you did. Dusan always was a secretive man, but we did speak of certain things. Tell me, how did he die?"

Varin raised an eyebrow, and Jez realized he'd slouched into his chair. He forced himself to sit up straight and look Varin in the eye. The small man didn't even flinch, and Jez resisted the urge to bow his head.

"I don't really know any more than anyone else, my lord." Varin smiled and Jez silently cursed himself. By calling Varin 'my lord', Jez had acknowledged Varin as a superior. Jez had had too many slips of the tongue since he'd arrived at court. He could recover from this one, but it was still happening far too often.

"Come now," Varin said. He reached into his doublet and pulled out a sheet of paper. Jez forced himself not to gasp. The paper had several of the runes Jez recognized from Dusan's summoning chamber. "I don't recognize all of them, but I understand enough to recognize this as the kind of working Dusan was best at. The rumors I've heard say he died due to a flawed working and that his magic backfired. Frankly, Baron," he said the title so it almost sounded like a curse. "I don't believe it. Dusan wouldn't make that kind of mistake."

"Evil deeds always come back to haunt you," Jez said. "Maybe he'd done so much evil that it fell in upon itself."

Varin rolled his eyes. "Don't tell me you're one of these idealists. When I was at the Academy, they made sure to drum all of that foolishness out of us."

Jez almost snorted. He'd known a few people at the Academy who thought that way, but almost everyone else thought they were fools. Instead, he shrugged. "Dusan is dead, isn't he? How else do you explain it?"

Varin nodded. "So he is." He examined Jez for several seconds before nodding. "Let me put this in a way you can understand. Tell me about Dusan's death. Tell me what he was doing, and why he really failed." He tapped the images on the nobility chart. "Tell me of any other runes he used. Tell me if anyone interfered and any other details you can think of. If I judge it enough, I will go to Haziel and drop all charges. Your friend is being charged for one crime, attacking six nobles. Only Lina is here, and I can still legally speak for her. If I declare that we will not pursue this matter, your friend will be exonerated not only of attacking her, but of assaulting all the rest."

"Why do you want to know?"

Too late, Jez realized his mistake. Jez stopped talking, but Varin was already smiling. A hungry look appeared in his eyes, much like a child eager from a new toy. After a second, Jez let out a long breath and straightened. "I'm sorry. The mages who found Dusan's ritual chamber destroyed it precisely to prevent others from learning what he'd done. I can't tell you any more than that."

Lord Varin glared. He got up to leave but stopped in the doorway. "I would advise you to reconsider. You would do well to have me as an ally."

Jez glared at him and remembered when Dusan had tried to make an alliance with him at the end. Jez had been tempted then, but he'd learned his lesson.

"I've had offers like that before."

Varin inclined his head. This time it did bother Jez, and he was on the verge of saying something when Varin turned his back. As soon as he'd left the room, Sileon walked in. He stared after Lord Varin.

"Sileon," Varin said without turning around. "Have you made your decision?"

Sileon looked over his shoulder and nodded, though Varin didn't turn to see it. The advisor bowed once to Jez.

"My lord, I regret to inform you I will be leaving your employ and taking up service with Lord Varin."

"What?"

"An excellent decision. I will have you knighted before the end of the day. Then we can move you into accommodations more suited for someone of your station." This time Varin did turn and met Jez's gaze.

"Think very carefully before you decide to make me an enemy. There is much I can take from you."

Then, he walked away, with Sileon following on his heels. As soon as they had turned a corner, Osmund poked his head in the doorway. He looked at the departing pair over his shoulder before turning back to Jez.

"What was that about?"

"Varin hired Sileon."

"Hired him to do what?"

Jez blinked at him. "I have no idea. I think it was to get him away from me so he couldn't help."

Osmund rolled his eyes. "It's not like he did much anyway."

"He talked to people," Jez said. "He knew who to talk to. I don't even know who to see if I want to speak to the king. We need to see Villia."

"Why?"

"Sileon knew Villia was helping us. When he tells Varin, I have no idea what he'll do."

"I'll go tell her you want to see her."

"We'll both go," Jez said.

Osmund shook his head. "I don't know much about court politics, but it's pretty obvious you shouldn't be setting up your own meetings. I'll go."

"How's that any better than me going? You're supposed to be my bodyguard not my messenger."

"Do you want to send one of those people Sileon hired?"

Jez snorted. "Only if we wanted Varin to find out about it."

Osmund spread his arms. "It's not like we have very many options."

Jez thought for a second before nodding. "All right. Go. Tell her I need to see her as soon as possible."

CHAPTER 9

Jez was looking over some the charts Sileon had left when Sharim burst into the room. His face was flushed, and he was breathing heavily. Sweat gleamed on his brow.

"Sharim, what is it?"

He held up his hand as he caught his breath. Then, as if realizing what he was doing, his eyes widened, and he bowed.

"Forgive me for the intrusion, Baron. Your bodyguard came to me looking for Mage Villia."

"Yes. You didn't have to run. Is she ready to see me?"

"No, that's just it," Sharim said between heavy breaths. "She's not in the keep. She went into town to get supplies. I told him he could wait, but he insisted on finding her. He was assaulted in the streets. He's with the healers now."

Jez shot to his feet. "What? Is he okay? What happened?"

"I don't know. The healers say he'll be all right. They were taking care of the worst of his wounds when I left."

"Show me the way."

He hadn't been to the sick chambers so Sharim led him through a maze of corridors. Jez tried to keep track of the way, but he couldn't focus and kept prodding Sharim to go faster. Finally, they entered a long room lined with beds along each wall. It smelled clean, and the faint scent of soap still hung in the air. Tall windows illuminated the room. Only a single bed was occupied, and Osmund's long legs hung over the end of the bed. A bruise covered half his face. He smiled when he saw Jez, and he had a gap in his teeth. A woman in a brown robe with an orange sash stood over him, her hands emitting a soft light that reminded Jez of the sun. The bruise started to fade, but when the healer stopped a portion of it remained.

"There," she said. "I don't want to send anymore magic through you." She turned to Jez. "Don't give him undue stress. He still needs rest."

Jez nodded.

"Thank you Mage…"

"Paleel," she said as she brushed an auburn strand of hair away from her face. "Though you're generous to label me a mage. I'm a simple healer."

Jez inclined his head. "Thank you all the same, Paleel."

She blushed. "I'll be in the next room if you need me."

She scurried away, and Jez went to stand by his friend. Osmund gave him a weak smile and took a cup of water sitting near his bed. He drank before sitting up.

"What happened?" Jez asked.

"They came at me from behind. There were only three at first. Then, half a dozen more appeared out of nowhere."

"Why didn't you transform?"

Osmund smirked. "Transform to fight off half a dozen common footpads? As if I needed that." He looked down at a bandage wrapping his hand and grimaced. "At least I thought I didn't need it. I was afraid to use magic too. I thought that would only make things worse for us."

Jez nodded once and leaned in closer to the bed, trying to ignore the shivers running down his back. Whatever else Osmund might be, he was still a skilled battlemage, and it would've taken far more than a handful of common thugs to do him any lasting harm.

"Who did this?" Jez pitched his voice low as his eyes darted around, making sure no one was close enough to hear.

"I don't know," Osmund said. "My attacks kept on missing. It's like they weren't there. I think some of them might've been illusions. Their fists were real, though, and I did manage to blacken one's eye.

"Illusion," Jez said under his breath.

"Lina's specialty," Osmund said. "She certainly has a reason to hire men to attack me."

Osmund tried to sit up straighter, but after a few seconds, he slouched back into his bed. Jez moved closer and took the cup from his hand and put it on a nearby table.

"Don't strain yourself. I'll take this before the king."

"We don't know anything for sure."

"We know someone who was good with illusion attacked you."

Osmund let out a long breath. "I don't think that's enough, Jez. You might be out of your league here. Lord Varin—"

"I still outrank Varin."

"Rank isn't everything."

Jez shook his head. "I only need political maneuvering if I'm planning on being subtle."

CHAPTER 10

Jez strode up to the door of the throne room with his head held high and glared at the guard who stepped in front of him. Rather than move, the stony faced man lifted a hand and held it to Jez's chest. Jez wondered if he could feel his heart racing. He scowled.

"Let me through."

The guard brought his free hand to the hilt of his sword and cleared his throat. "I'm sorry, sir. I can't do that."

"I am the Baron of Korand, and you will let me through."

"The king is in conference with Lord Varin."

"Good. That stops me from having to summon him." Jez looked into the guards eyes, and emphasized every word. "Now. Let. Me. Through."

It was almost laughable. The man was at least a foot taller than Jez and built like an ox. Faded scars ran down his arms, and his hands had the callouses that only came from years of working with the sword. He didn't even flinch. In a straight fight, Jez wouldn't stand a chance, but he had never intended to fight fairly. The guard wore a mail shirt, and though Jez hadn't studied terra magic in depth, it was an area he was naturally gifted in, especially in the application of brute force. He raised a hand and caught the guard's armor in his power. With a grunt, the man fell to the ground, held down by his own mail shirt. Jez stepped over him and pushed open the door.

Jez stepped inside to find the king, Lord Varin, and Lina glaring at him. Sharim and Villia, both of whom stood nearby, looked surprised, but Varin's face was red with anger. The bearded man Jez recognized as one of Lina's guard took a step forward to intercept him, and Jez saw his blackened eye. Instantly, rage filled Jez, and blue light shone from his hands. Propelled by his armor, the guard flew back and slammed against the wall. The impact of metal on stone sent sparks flying.

"Villia," the king said in a steady voice.

Jez felt a barrier forming between him and his power. His eyes widened. He'd learned how to do that at the Academy. Forming a barrier required countering the magic that was being worked. Only then could they be cut off. It couldn't be done otherwise, but yet he could feel the barrier forming while he held the guard against the wall. His eyes locked on Villia who had her hand raised toward him. Sharim stood behind her with eyes wide. Jez could sense the energy welling up in her. He formed a barrier of his own. The guard slid down the wall as Jez tried to separate Villia from her power. His barrier fizzled as Villia's settled into place.

"His power is bound, Your Majesty," Villia said.

"Good," Haziel said. "Now, Baron Jezreel, would you care to tell me why you charged into my throne room and assaulted those under my protection?"

The man who'd been guarding the door came in with his sword drawn. Haziel lifted a hand but didn't order him to put away his weapon. Jez suddenly found himself feeling less sure of himself. The king's steely gaze felt like it put the weight of a mountain on him. Jez clenched his teeth and glared at Varin.

"I only did what he already did."

"What he already did?" the king asked. "Even if that were the case, that is a child's excuse."

"It's not unexpected, Your Majesty," Varin said. "After all, he is a child."

Jez's face heat up, and he tensed his muscles. Sweat formed on Villia's brow, and she raised her other hand, but Jez didn't reach for his power. It would've been pointless with the barrier in place. Instead, he pointed at Varin.

"He sent men to attack my bodyguard." He looked at the bruised guard. "That one was one of them."

Varin chuckled. "Ah, I see. Forgive me, Your Majesty. It would seem this was my fault. I hired away his advisor. It was no more than I would do to any potential rival. I forgot to take his youth into account. No doubt Sir Sileon helped him keep his temper in check."

"What?" Jez said, his anger defusing.

"Brallion," Varin indicated his guard, "is guilty of nothing more than being clumsy going down stairs."

Brallion inclined his head. A smile formed on the king's face. "Perhaps you're right. I may have summoned him to court too soon. Perhaps another year or two at the Academy will properly season him."

"No," Jez said, "that's not—"

The king's sharp voice cut him off. "You were not given leave to speak, Baron Jezreel."

"But he attacked Osmund. Lina used her illusions—"

"That's enough," Varin said as he came to his feet. "Accuse me if you wish, but leave my daughter out of it. She has nothing to do with this."

"Who else would have a reason to do it?"

"Practically anyone."

"What?"

Varin rolled his eyes. "It's no great secret that your bodyguard is a monster."

"Osmund isn't a monster."

"No, he just transforms into a creature who attacks innocent children."

Jez bit back a reply about how Lina was anything but innocent. Instead, he turned to the king, but Haziel looked on him as if he was a child. Villia kept her arms raised, and she was shaking her head slightly. Jez let out a breath. He'd blundered badly. He hadn't even lost control of the situation. He'd never had it. The smile on Varin's face told him the lord hadn't even been worried. Jez turned to go, but the sound of the king clearing his throat stopped him. The man who had been guarding the door tightened his grip on his sword. Jez looked over his shoulder. Haziel was glaring at him. Jez realized what he was doing and turned and bowed.

"With your permission, Your Majesty."

"I believe you owe Lord Varin an apology for the slanderous accusations you brought against him and his family."

Jez flinched, but there was nothing to be gained by further argument. He nodded.

"Lord Varin," he said through clenched teeth. "Please accept my apologies. I spoke without thinking."

Varin gave him a patronizing smile. "Don't give it a second thought. After all, I'm not so old that I don't remember what it's like being young. I'm sure given time, you'll learn wisdom."

With those words, Lord Varin neatly painted him as a child in the eyes of the king, and any political power Jez had started to gather had been destroyed. He inclined his head and strode out of the throne room, feeling completely defeated.

CHAPTER 11

With no idea of what else to do, Jez climbed the stairs to Villia's tower to wait for her. Once at her door, he closed his eyes and extended his hand, intending to sense wards or other workings, but the door swung open at his touch. The workshop felt cold without Villia in it. Jez's eyes wandered upward. The stillness of the ceiling was unnerving after seeing the stars dance across it. He sat at her table and started flipping through a book of astronomy. He'd only been there a few minutes when a shadow appeared in the doorway. Jez rose, but it was Sharim. The apprentice nodded at Jez before taking a seat across from him.

"You shouldn't have done that," Sharim said.

"I know," Jez said. "I expected Varin to deny the accusation, but I didn't think he'd just dismiss me."

"Do you really think he's responsible?"

"He said he could take anything from me less than an hour before it happened. His daughter focused on the dominion of shadows at the Academy. She's obviously good with illusions."

"That's hardly proof."

"I think that's what he was counting on. I can't really get proof if he has that much influence with the king. He'll just keep standing in my way. I was hoping Mage Villia could help."

"Lord Varin is an expert at subtle manipulations. Have you thought about a more brute force approach?"

Jez lifted an eyebrow. "How do you think I got into this situation?"

Sharim's face reddened, and he brushed at a nonexistent spot on his robe. "Right. I meant have you tried a purely magical solution?"

"Like what?"

"Did you ever study the dominion of secrets?"

"Theology."

"But not divination?"

Jez shook his head. "It was never an area that interested me. Can you use it to prove Varin sent men to attack Osmund?"

"Maybe. It isn't as precise as other schools of magic, but I think it would point us in the right direction."

He opened a drawer in the desk and pulled out a silver saucer. Runes had been etched in the metal, though the only one Jez recognized was the one for water. Sharim dipped it into a nearby barrel and brought it back to the desk. The water shimmered in ways that didn't quite match with the light of the room. Sharim drew a crystal hanging from a chain out of a drawer. He closed his eyes and murmured a few words as he dragged the crystal through the water.

"He was attacked two hours ago in the alley near Bakers Street, right?"

"I don't know," Jez said. "I never found out."

Sharim flinched but nodded. "I think I heard someone say that."

"Why are you helping me?"

"You're a limaph," he said with smile, "and I've heard stories."

Jez resisted the urge to turn away. "Those are just stories."

Sharim's grin said he saw through the lie. "Maybe. Give me a few seconds."

Though the water in the saucer was less than half an inch deep, it grew murky until Jez couldn't see the bottom. Vague shapes moved around inside, there one moment and gone the next. They never resolved enough for him to get a clear picture though. He wasn't sure how long he stared at the images before Sharim let out a breath and stopped chanting. Instantly, the water cleared.

"It's not working."

"Well, you did say it wasn't precise."

"You don't understand. I've had divinations give me obscure answers, sometimes to the point of being completely useless. This time, I got nothing."

"What does that mean?"

Sharim shrugged and examined the saucer. "I'm not sure. All the runes look intact, so it's probably not the scrying bowl. It could be that whoever attacked Osmund took steps to protect themselves from scrying. Still, to stop me from getting even a hint means someone of extraordinary skill and power."

"Lord Varin attended the Academy, didn't he?"

Sharim nodded. "After his father was raised to the rank of Lord, he had the funds and prestige to attend as a member of the upper tier."

Jez paused for a second, trying to puzzle out what he would need to shield himself from divinations. "Protection and secrets."

Sharim inclined his head. "They say he was very good at them."

Jez raised an eyebrow. "Those aren't exactly noble areas of study."

"Don't you study protection?"

"I'm not your average noble."

"Neither was Lord Durn," Sharim said. "He didn't insist that his son study only proper fields."

"So he could've shielded himself against scrying?"

"It's still not proof. It could be anyone."

"Who else has the power?"

Sharim let out a breath. "I'm not sure. I don't know for certain Lord

Varin does."

"But you think he does."

Sharim paused and looked away. Jez cleared his throat, and the apprentice met his eyes. He looked scared, but he nodded.

"Well, you were right about one thing."

"What's that?" Sharim asked.

"It pointed me in the right direction. I just have to find some way to prove Varin is responsible."

"There's something you're not considering, Baron."

"Oh?"

"What if no one is treating your accusations of Lord Varin seriously because the king already knows?"

Jez's mouth went dry. He considered not answering, but Sharim was already risking himself by helping. Jez nodded.

"Then, the king is my enemy."

CHAPTER 12

Sharim paled. He glanced at the door as if expecting guards to burst through and arrest them. Jez waited for him to turn back. He was sweating, and his eyes darted around the workshop.

"You know about Dusan?" Jez asked.

"Your father?"

Jez tensed. "My adopted father."

Sharim's head bobbed. "Oh yes. I'm sorry. I forgot."

"There were…things Dusan needed in Korand. Villia says Dusan manipulated the king into giving him the barony, but I'm not so sure."

"Dusan gave up his lands north of Rumar for that assignment."

"I know."

"It wasn't exactly a good deal. The timber industry alone was worth almost as much as the gem mines of Korand. The gold mines are worth more."

Jez cocked his head. "You seem to know a lot about it."

Sharim shrugged. "I grew up in Ebon. It was the center of Dusan's lands before he surrendered them to the crown."

"I don't suppose you know anything about his relationship with the king."

Sharim shook his head. "I was already Mage Villia's apprentice when

Dusan got the appointment, but they didn't exactly discuss it with me."

Jez got up and paced back and forth through the workshop.

He stopped in front of the half-carved statue of the dog. Villia hadn't done much work on it, but now the dog's body was emerging from the stone. It almost looked like it was trying to climb out of the rock and come into the open.

"Maybe if I expose Lord Varin, I can convince Villia to support me openly."

"How do you intend to do that?"

"What would it take to block a divination like that?"

"It's not something that can be done easily. Varin would've had to do a major ritual, maybe even with a focusing stone." Sharim's eyes wandered up to the ceiling while he thought. "He couldn't have had much time to put it together. No one knew Osmund was going to be alone and in the city where he could be easily attacked. Varin almost certainly has a greater circle somewhere. We could try finding it. I'm not sure there's anything else Mage Villia would accept as proof."

"But that would be a little obvious, wouldn't it? It's not like greater circles are easy to hide. I mean wouldn't he destroy the evidence?"

Sharim shook his head. "If he did, he wouldn't be protected."

"So then, I have to find this circle. Where could he put it?"

"Somewhere out of the way, obviously," Sharim said. "He'd have to go there regularly to pour power into it."

"His quarters, then."

"Don't you think that would be a little obvious?"

"If, as you say, he didn't have a lot of time to set up this ritual, he wouldn't have had very many options."

"That's true, I guess."

"Let's go then. Where are his quarters?"

Sharim raised his hands and started shaking his head. "Now, just a second. I didn't say I would help you."

Jez stood up. "Fine. I'll find out myself. Thank you for the information."

Jez turned, but he hadn't made it to the door before he heard the chair scraping across the ground. He turned and saw Sharim walking toward him.

"I didn't say I wouldn't help you either." Sharim paused and took a deep breath. "Villia told me about the runes they found in Dusan's lair." Jez's jaw dropped, but Sharim shook his head. "Nothing specific, but she said that from what she could tell, he was trying to summon a great evil. She was scared. I've never seen her like that. If Varin is trying to do the same thing, he has to be stopped."

CHAPTER 13

Varin's chambers were in the north wing of the keep. Sharim put illusions on them to hide but as soon as they neared, the illusion fell. They exchanged glances, but Jez shrugged. Certain parts of the Academy were warded against illusions as well. There was probably some way to get around that or else Lina would never be able to maintain her disguise. Such a thing was normally done with a command word or talisman, but figuring that out was more trouble than it was worth. A pair of guards in the livery of Lord Varin stood at the door to the chambers. They stiffened as Jez and Sharim approached.

"I have a message from Mage Villia for Lord Varin," Jez said.

One of the guards snorted. "Is the baron reduced to being a messenger boy now?"

Jez tried to look embarrassed. "Look, just let me in."

The other guard let out a nervous laugh. He brought his hand up and absently ran his fingers across his mail shirt. No doubt he'd heard about the incident in the throne room. Jez briefly considered moving them out of the way but decided against it. The second guard cleared his throat.

"Lord Varin is still in conference with the king."

Jez pulled a folded sheet of paper out of his doublet. "I need to leave this for him." The guard reached for it, but Jez pulled back. "Mage Villia put a ward on it to guard against any hand but Varin's. I'm not sure what will happen if you touch it."

The guard pulled back as if he'd touched a flame. His gaze was locked on the sheet of paper with wide eyes. The other took a step back and didn't seem to realize it until he backed up against the wall.

"Just let me in," Jez said. "You can watch me leave it."

The guards exchanged glances. One gave a slight nod, and the other pushed open the door. Varin's sitting room was even bigger than Jez's. It looked like it could hold a hundred people. A long table sat in the middle of the room with a dozen chairs on each side. A massive window was covered by velvet curtains, and a map of Ashtar hung from one wall. Jez's eyes instinctively sought out the Barony of Korand and his own hometown of Randak. A massive picture of Lord Varin himself stared down at Jez as he walked in. Jez extended his senses, trying to find any signs of a ward, but there was nothing.

"Do you sense anything?"

"I think so," Sharim said. "There's something hidden by an illusion. Give me a second and I can take it down." Suddenly, he spun and stared into a corner.

"What is it?" Jez asked.

"Sorry, I thought there was someone there. It's nothing. Give me a second."

Jez walked to the table slowly and placed the paper on it. There was nothing written on it, and Varin would probably be upset when he found out Jez had been in his quarters, but as low as Jez's status already was at court, he doubted anything worse could happen. He felt a hum in the air and glanced at Sharim. The other boy had his eyes closed and was saying something under his breath.

"Well?" the guard said from the doorway.

"We're coming," Jez said, but he didn't move.

Sharim let out a breath, and Jez's sense of protection magic flared to life. There was powerful ward in this room, one of a complexity he could scarcely imagine. A circle of yellow light came into being and runes appeared in the air. They only lasted a second before fading. The guards said something, but Jez wasn't listening. He grabbed Sharim by the wrist and tugged him out of the room. They had left the hall and were nearing Jez's room before Sharim managed to pull his arm free.

"What's going on?"

"Didn't you see the runes in the air?"

"Yes, but I didn't recognize them."

"I did," Jez said. "They were the same kind Dusan used when he was trying to summon a nightmare demon."

CHAPTER 14

Jez spent a few minutes telling Osmund what had happened. The other boy was doing much better, and the healers said his strength should return by morning. He was still having trouble staying awake, but he made Jez promise to be careful before leaving. As soon as he stood to leave, Paleel went to Osmund's side to see if he needed anything. Jez nodded to her and walked out. Villia was waiting for him when he came out of the sick chambers.

"Do you have any idea how dangerous that was?"

Jez looked over his shoulder at the door to the sick chambers. He turned back to Villia and cocked his head.

"Talking to Osmund? He's not contagious or anything."

Villia narrowed her eyes. "That stunt you pulled in Lord Varin's room."

"He didn't see us."

"No, but his guards did. More than that, by leaving a blank paper, you ensured he would come looking for me wanting to know what it was about."

"Did he?"

"Yes. He was quite angry I had sent you into his rooms."

Jez tried to force down the lump that had formed in his throat. "I guess we didn't think that all the way through."

"No, you didn't."

"What did you tell him?"

"I told him it was a test for my apprentice and apologized for not letting him know ahead of time."

"He believed that?"

Villia shrugged. "Probably not, but he won't call me a liar to my face. My position is too secure. Now, tell me what you saw."

Jez turned away. "Nothing."

"Don't give me that, boy." Villia's voice came from everywhere at once, and it echoed in the long corridor. Even an empty suit of armor seemed to be speaking. Jez jumped and looked back at her. "Sharim told me about the circle, but he didn't know what he was looking at. He said you mentioned Dusan."

Jez hesitated for a second before nodding. "I saw some of the same symbols Dusan used."

"Then you did see his lair before the king's mages got to it?"

"Yes."

"What was he doing?"

Jez looked around. Villia pursed her lips but nodded after a few seconds. She motioned for him to follow, and they went to her workshop. She waved a hand, and when she spoke, her voice came out sounding flat. The sounds drifting in from outside became a muted buzz.

"I'm shielding us from sound. Even if anyone would dare to try to listen in, they wouldn't be able to hear us. Now, tell me about Dusan."

Jez nodded and briefly related how Dusan had eventually summoned the demon lord Marrowit, only to have it destroy him. Jez had followed the demon into the dream world and defeated it in its place of power and thus utterly destroying it. The only thing he left out was the truth about his own past, letting Villia believe he was a limaph.

"The runes that appeared in the air in Varin's quarters," Jez said. "They were the same ones Dusan used."

"You think he's trying to summon this Marrowit?"

"Maybe. He would have no way of knowing Marrowit was destroyed."

Villia looked at him for several seconds before nodding. "All right. I believe you. We'll need to gather proof before we can move against Varin, though."

"What do you mean proof? There's proof in his quarters."

Villia shook her head. "And I can take the king to see that, but Varin is still an influential noble, who is extremely skilled at the politics of the court. He'll likely have plans in place in case he's discovered. He may even be implementing them now, with the stunt you pulled."

Before Jez could say anything, a boy wearing purple livery burst into the room. His face was flushed, and he was sweating from the effort of running up the stairs.

"Mage Villia. Murder. The king. Immediately."

He spoke between breaths and leaned heavily on Villia's table. Villia and Jez exchanged glances. Villia walked to the boy and gripped his shoulders.

"Calm down. Say it again, but this time slowly."

The boy nodded and took a minute to catch his breath. "Mage Villia, the king requires your presence immediately. There's been a murder."

CHAPTER 15

Jez stayed by Villia's side as she pushed past the guards in the north wing of the keep. They turned down the hall leading to Lord Varin's chambers, and Jez stopped in his tracks. The coppery scent of blood filled the air, and he almost gagged. Two still forms sprawled across the floor. The first was a bearded man with a black eye and a crooked nose. Jez recognized him as one of Lina's bodyguards. The second dead man was Sileon.

Each body had a slash across its stomach. Jez started to examine them, but his stomach churned as his lunch threatened to come up. He turned away for a few seconds. When he looked again, he focused on their faces. They were pale in death. The guard's mouth was open, and his eyes were wide. He'd had green eyes. Jez didn't think he'd ever seen anyone with green eyes. He thought about that for several seconds before shaking his head to clear his thoughts. This was no time to lose his wits. He examined the other corpse. Sileon looked like he was trying to scream. His eyes were closed and his arms were outstretched as if trying to push someone away. The one commonality was that their expressions were frozen in terror.

"What happened?" Villia asked.

For the first time, Jez realized there were others in the area. Three guards stood near the bodies. The king was a little ways away, flanked by two others. Lina stood next to her father. Her face looked a little green, but she didn't turn away.

"Lord Varin sent me to summon Lady Lina," one of the guards said. "When I returned with her, we saw..." His face drained of color, and he reached up and tugged his collar. "They were already dead."

Lina looked up and her eyes locked on Jez. She pointed at him and screamed. Jez could almost hear the hatred in her cry.

"It was him! He accused Brallion of attacking his beast, and he was upset that my father hired away Sir Sileon."

"What?" Jez said. He glanced at Villia and she put a hand on his shoulder.

"It wasn't," she said.

"Are you sure?" Haziel asked as his eyes flickered to the sword Jez wore at his hip. "Lady Lina makes a good point, and we've already seen his ability against armored men."

Villia inclined her head. "That may be, Your Majesty, but the boy has been with me for the past half hour, and these men haven't been dead nearly that long." She looked from Lina to Jez and frowned. "I don't think they should be here, though. This isn't a sight for young eyes."

Varin started to protest but stopped when he saw the king nodding. His face reddened slightly, but Jez didn't think anyone but him had seen.

"Take my daughter back to her room," he said to Lina's guard.

The lean woman nodded and took Lina by the hand and led her away. Lina gave Jez a hard look, but other than that, she seemed listless, almost as if she were in a trance. One of the king's men motioned for Jez to follow, and Jez fell into step behind him, and they walked away from the hall Lina had gone down. Just before they turned a corner, Jez took one last look over his shoulder. Villia was speaking to the king, and she kept glancing at the bodies. Jez started to turn away when he caught a faint hint of sulfur in the air. He gasped, and the hairs on the back of his neck stood on end. He took a deep breath, hoping he'd been wrong, but the smell was there, not quite hidden by the scent of blood. These men had been killed by a demon.

CHAPTER 16

Jez practically ran to the sick chambers. One of the healers was leaving as he approached, and she scowled at him. It was an older woman, the one who was the head of the sick chambers. Her silver hair was tied in a bun, and she wore the orange robe of someone who had been trained at the Academy.

"I suppose he's with you," Mage Rana said.

Jez stared at her. "What?"

She narrowed her eyes. "Your bodyguard."

"Osmund? Isn't he here?" His eyes sought out the bed Osmund had been in last time, but it was empty, the blanket having been thrown off.

"No. He kept insisting he didn't need to be in bed. As soon as I turned my back, he was gone. He hasn't been gone half an hour."

"Where did he go?"

She raised an eyebrow. "I haven't the slightest idea."

He nodded, trying not to look too worried. He started walking out of the sick chambers. Rana called out to him, but he ignored her. Osmund would've probably tried to get to Jez's quarters. He couldn't have had worse timing. Jez had an alibi during the murders, but if Osmund didn't have that same protection, it was only a matter of time before he was accused too. Jez doubted Villia would be able to help him then. That was assuming the demons hadn't attacked Osmund already.

He was only halfway to his quarters when he found Osmund leaning against a wall breathing heavily. His eyes were sunken and looked a little red. He still wore the sick robes, and when he saw Jez, he gave him a weak smile.

"Maybe I should've listened to the healers." Jez grunted and Osmund raised an eyebrow. "What happened?"

Jez lowered his voice. As quickly as possible, he told Osmund about the murders and how Lina had accused him. Osmund nodded. He scanned the hall as if looking for guards. A young man and woman of the nobility came around the corner, arm in arm. Jez didn't recognize them, but when they saw Jez and Osmund, the lady whispered to her companion, and the pair turned to go, leaving Jez and Osmund alone.

"What do we do now?"

"You should find somewhere to hide. It has to be Varin summoning the demons, and he doesn't like you very much. Once I tell Villia what I detected, she'll have to convince the king to move against him. There's no way Varin will get out of this one. I'll come find you once this is all taken care of.

Osmund nodded. "Be careful. Last time you thought you had an advantage over Varin, it didn't turn out well."

"Last time, he wasn't summoning demons. Do you need help finding a place to hide?"

Osmund forced himself to stand up straight. "I'll manage."

Jez nodded but helped Osmund down the hall. They found an empty room, and he left Osmund there to rest. He went back to Villia's workshop to wait for her. She didn't take long to arrive and seemed surprised to see him.

"I didn't expect you so soon."

"What did you find?"

Her eyes hardened. "I may respect you, limaph, but do not presume to make demands of me. You're in enough trouble as it is."

"Those men were killed by demons," Jez said through clenched teeth. "Tell me what you learned."

"How…" she looked Jez in the eye. "Oh, I see." She sat at her table, and Jez took a seat across from her. Absently, she fingered the crystal Sharim had used in his attempt at scrying. "I didn't learn much. They were killed quickly, too quickly to cry out. The cuts came from a sword, or at least from something as sharp. It wasn't the stomach wounds that killed them, though, at least not directly. They just served as a conduit to their bodies. They were cooked from the inside out. I told the king they were killed by an expert in pyro magic. Are you sure it was a demon?" Jez nodded. "Do you know what kind?"

Jez searched his mind, looking for some the knowledge he'd been able to access during the ordeal with Marrowit, but Sariel had bound those memories away, leaving him with only mundane knowledge. He'd done research into demons in his study of how to bind the creatures, but even that was limited to lower level demons whose knowledge wasn't considered too dangerous by Master Besis. He shook his head.

"Not exactly. I mean there aren't many demons that can kill and not have it obvious it was a demon who did it. Most don't use swords, but a couple have claws that can make wounds that look like swords. Almost all of them can use at least some level of pyro magic. I just don't have enough information."

Villia nodded. "Can you find them?"

Jez shook his head. "I've been learning how to bind them, not how to track them. Can't you use divination?"

"No. Divination touches on another world. That's not exactly right. It's difficult to explain. It's not really a world."

"Between," Jez said before he could stop himself.

Villia's eyes widened slightly, but she nodded. "Yes." Her voice cracked on the word, and she cleared her throat. "That's as good a name as any. Where did you hear it?"

Jez waved off the question. "What does that have to do with divination?"

She narrowed her eyes but continued. "Rumar seems to be cut off from this…Between. No magic that touches it is functioning. I've never seen anything like it."

A chill ran down Jez's back. "I have. Dusan could do it."

Villia raised an eyebrow. "Could he? That's not a small working."

"Varin has been after me to give him specifics of what Dusan was doing. First the circle in his room and now this? He's trying to do the same thing. Marrowit is destroyed, but that's not stopping him from summoning other demons."

"I need more time."

Jez shook his head. "Dusan could've destroyed the kingdom, if not the world. There's no time for subtlety. We have to move against Varin now."

Villia pursed her lips but nodded. She looked up, and the stars in the ceiling began to dance. "You're right. By the seven, you're right. I hate moving so openly, but if Varin is summoning demons into the keep, we don't have much of a choice."

"So what do we do now?" Jez asked.

"Let's go speak to the king."

CHAPTER 17

As soon as they stepped out of the tower, they were surrounded by guards, all with swords bared. On instinct, Jez reached for his power. The three swords closest to him clattered to the ground, but in the next instant, he felt a point pressed against his throat. He froze. It might have been his imagination, but he thought he felt a trickle of blood running down his neck.

"We were warned about your ability," the guard holding the weapon said. He had a gold sun pinned to his chest, an indication of his rank as captain. "Lord Varin instructed us to avoid hurting you if possible but to take no chances."

"What is the meaning of this?" Villia asked. None of the guards were holding weapons at her, and a few backed up at the tone in her voice.

"Forgive the inconvenience, Mage Villia. By your own admission, the men who were killed died by pyro magic. His bodyguard is a known battlemage. One who specializes in pyro magic. He is one of the few who would have the power to do that, and he's missing." The guard glared at Jez. "He had reason to hate Lord Varin."

"Even if that were true," Villia said, "and I don't believe for a second that it is, why would you come after Baron Jezreel?"

"Lord Varin expressed concern that it was done on the Baron's orders."

"That is utterly ridiculous."

"We are here on Lord Varin's orders to take him into custody."

"Well, I am giving you new orders. Put down your weapons."

The guards exchanged glances. The pressure of the sword at Jez's throat lessened slightly, but the guard didn't lower it. Jez looked down without moving his head. He glanced at Villia and took a step back. The guard didn't follow. After another second, he lowered his weapon. Jez touched his neck looking for blood, but his fingers came away dry.

"You will convey us to the king." Once again, Villia's voice took on that strange resonance that made it seem like it was coming from everywhere at once.

The captain eyed Jez. "But Mage Villia…"

Villia raised a hand, and the corridor dimmed. She stood up straight, and somehow, she'd gained two feet of height. Her eyes glowed an angry violet, and the guards backed away. One man's hand was shaking so violently he dropped his sword. Villia's voice seemed to come from the stones themselves. The air hummed with power.

"I am a master mage in the service of King Haziel himself. My commands supersede those of any lordling. You will do as I say, or you will suffer the consequences."

The last word seemed to hang in the air for several seconds. As it faded, the lights returned. Villia was back to normal size, though Jez hadn't seen her change. The guard who'd dropped his weapon scooped up his sword and shoved it in its sheath as if afraid for Villia to see him with a weapon drawn. The captain nodded.

"Please," he said in a shaky voice. "Follow me."

The other guards fell into step behind him. Jez and Villia followed a few steps behind.

"That wasn't exactly subtle," Jez said, pitching his voice low.

She smiled. "When you have weapons pointed at you, the time for subtly has passed. I may not like to work overtly, but I can if I have to."

Jez's heart was pounding as they made their way through the keep. Some of the servants and nobles whispered as they passed, though no one tried to stop them. Whenever Jez tried to meet anyone's eyes, they turned away. The guards led them to the same dining room Osmund had originally been arrested in. They walked in, and Jez froze.

There, on the floor with chains around his legs and wrists, was Osmund. A brown robed woman with a blue sash stood near him, holding her arm toward him. Power flowed out and held Osmund's power in check. A guard held a sword to his back. For a second, Jez just stared. It was only when someone pushed past him that he blinked and gathered his thoughts. Varin and Lina, who had come in after Jez, walked to the other side of the room and stood next to the king. Lina refused to look at either Osmund or Jez, but Varin's face was twisted in a scowl.

"I ordered Jezreel taken."

Villia stepped forward. "And I ordered them to bring him here." She narrowed her eyes. "And it is Baron Jezreel, Lord Varin, not simply Jezreel. You are not so highly regarded that you can ignore the rules of the court, and you don't have the authority to order the arrest of a baron."

A cold grin formed on Varin's face. "Well, it seems the boy has managed to form an alliance after all. Too bad it's too late." He turned to the king who had been impassively observing the conversation. "Your Majesty, the evidence is clear. The boy's bodyguard attacked and killed my men, almost certainly under his instruction. Once he is arrested, the threat to your throne will be ended."

Almost immediately, the gathered nobles went silent. A few stared at Varin, and Jez resisted the urge to smile. Varin had made a mistake. If he could order the guards to arrest him, he could do the same to any noble in the room, and they knew it. Haziel wouldn't be able to allow this. From the grin on Varin's face, he hadn't realized his blunder. The king raised a hand and those few who were still speaking quieted.

"No," Haziel said in a quiet voice.

There was a collective sigh of relief. Some of the nobles started murmuring to each other. Jez wasn't close enough to hear any details, but the general tone was angry, and more than one gave Varin a piercing glare. Color had drained from Varin's face.

"Your Majesty?"

"I said no, Varin. Mage Villia is right. I will not permit you to ignore the forms when you're right in front of me. If you have an accusation against a baron of Ashtar, I will hear proof." Varin sputtered for a second, but said nothing. The king turned to Jez. "There is ample evidence against your bodyguard, I'm afraid."

"It wasn't me," Osmund said, but one of the guards slapped him.

"What evidence?" Jez asked as he glared at the guard. The man turned away and started muttering to a companion, as if afraid to meet Jez's gaze.

"He carries a sword." Varin practically spat the words.

"He's my *bodyguard*," Jez said. "He's supposed to carry a sword. Anyway, he hasn't even had one since he got hurt."

"Maybe not," Varin said, "but Brallion's sword wasn't found with his body."

That caught Jez by surprise. Most demons didn't have weapons, but there were plenty that could pick one up and use it.

"I saw Osmund after the men were killed. He could barely stand. There was no way he could overpower a guard and take his weapon."

"You saw him?" the king asked. "You didn't report him? This is not looking well for you, Baron."

"I didn't know you were looking for him until I came out of the south tower. I didn't think it was the best idea to be walking around in his condition, but he wasn't on the run as far as I knew."

Villia raised a hand. "There is evidence enough to hold Osmund."

"But…"

She looked Jez in the eye. "We cannot ignore the facts, Baron Jezreel, however, once your new information comes to light, I'm sure he will be released."

"What new information?" Haziel asked.

Jez looked at Villia, and she nodded. Jez took a deep breath. "Those men were killed by demons."

"Demons?"

Varin laughed, but the other nobles exchanged glances. For once Jez was happy about the rumors that had been circulated about him. They should lend his words more weight.

Villia raised a hand and the room went silent again. "There's more."

Varin paled a little, and Jez suddenly found his mouth going dry. The thing he was about to accuse Varin of was worse than murder. Summoning creatures from the abyss to take a mortal life was one of the most perverse acts a person could do with magic. Every eye was on him. He swallowed and forced himself to speak.

"We found the summoning circle in your quarters, Lord Varin. The demons were summoned by you."

CHAPTER 18

The room went completely silent. Varin stared at Jez with his jaw practically on the floor. The illusion on Lina's face wavered for a second before solidifying. The king's expression shifted between shock and rage. Osmund looked up, and the men standing over him were too distracted to stop him. He glared at Varin, and for a moment Jez thought he saw the other boy's eyes glowing, but if they had changed, they returned to normal after barely a heartbeat.

"You would dare accuse me of that?" Varin's voice shattered the silence.

Lina's face twisted in a scowl. She might have said something, but her words were swallowed in the commotion as everyone in the room started to shout. It went on for several seconds before the king cleared his throat. Those nearest to him went silent, but some of the other nobles were still crying out at Jez. Haziel rose, and as people saw him, silence spread out from the throne like a wave. When the entire room had quieted, he sat down. His eyes locked onto Jez.

"I presume you have evidence of this?"

"Your Majesty," Varin said with barely controlled outrange. "Surely, you can't believe him."

"Lord Varin, you have been accused of a high crime by a noble of this court before witnesses." He let the last word hang for a second as he glared at Jez, and Jez wondered if he should've addressed this quietly. "I cannot ignore that. Baron, this is a serious accusation. What proof do you offer?"

Jez hesitated. "I smelled it, Your Majesty."

Some of the gather nobles snickered, but the king raised a hand, silencing them. "You smelled it?"

"When I saw Sileon and the dead guard. I smelled sulfur in the air. It happens sometimes when I run into demon magic."

Varin sneered. "You expect us to believe you can smell demons?"

"It's not an unheard of ability," Villia said. "I'm told the baron has a natural skill at binding. That would lend itself to such an ability. I would think you'd know that. Dusan had unusual abilities of his own, and the two of you were friends once."

"Ridiculous." Varin waved at the bound Osmund. "He's just trying to throw suspicion off of that thing."

"Mage Villia is a higher authority than you in this matter, Varin. If she says such an ability can exist, I have no reason to doubt." Haziel returned his gaze to Jez. "I still haven't heard any reason to accuse Lord Varin."

"Like I said, Sharim and I saw the summoning circle in his quarters. It was hidden, but Sharim was able to take down the illusion hiding it for a few seconds. I recognized the symbols. Something like that is only used to summon powerful demons."

"When Villia sent you to deliver a message," Varin said in a flat tone.

Jez met Varin's stare without flinching. It was the king who eventually spoke, and Jez realized the entire room was staring at the two of them.

"I was not aware you had advanced so far in your studies," Haziel said.

Jez looked away for a second. "I haven't. Not exactly, Your Majesty."

"Explain."

Jez looked around at the gathered nobles. He was about to ask the king to speak in private, but the look on Haziel's face told him the king had little patience left. He tried to swallow the lump in his throat, but it did no good.

"It had the same symbols Dusan used in his lair in Kunashi."

"I knew you had seen it," Varin cried out. He turned to the king. "Your Majesty, I know you think Dusan did terrible things, but he was also a genius in multiple schools of magic. Even the Academy masters had never seen his equal. I've been trying to reconstruct his research. If this child has information…"

"Dusan got his knowledge from demons." Jez's voice was practically a shout.

"You don't know that," Varin said. "You weren't with him long enough for him to reveal his secrets to you."

"He didn't need to reveal anything to me," Jez said. "If you'd seen what he did—"

"Enough." The king's voice cut through the conversation. "Varin, I know Dusan was your ally, but what he did bordered on treason. I will not permit you to do the same. That being said, Jezreel, the knowledge Dusan had is not for you to hide or dispense."

"Actually, it is, Your Majesty," Villia said. "What any mage learns in his own research is his alone, and with respect, matters of magic are under the domain of the masters of the Carceri Academy, not yours."

"But it wasn't his research," Varin said. "It was Dusan's."

"It was research he should've never done," Jez said. "It's research you shouldn't be doing."

"I will research whatever I choose." Varin banged his fist on the table.

"He makes a good point," the king said. "If Dusan's knowledge is for Jez to keep, then any research Varin does is his alone."

"That's technically correct, Your Majesty," Villia said, "but as you pointed out, what Dusan did was very nearly treason. If Varin is duplicating his efforts, he must be stopped."

The king pursed his lips but nodded. "But is he doing it?"

"I'm not," Varin said.

"I saw it," Jez replied and the lord narrowed his eyes.

"This is easily resolved," Villia said. "We need only go to Varin's quarters. If my apprentice was able to find the circle, I can do so as well." He turned to Varin. "Provided you have no objections, of course."

"I most certainly do," Varin said. "I will not stand here and be accused."

"You will permit us to look." Varin's eyes practically bulged at the king's words but Haziel continued. "From what I've been told, what Dusan did was foolish and dangerous. We both know you aren't half the mage he was, and I won't have you taking such a risk in my keep." The king motioned to Villia. "Let's go."

CHAPTER 19

"That went better than expected," Jez said.

He was walking alongside Villia. Haziel, Varin, Lina, and half a dozen guards followed a few steps behind. The other nobles had tried to follow, but a curt command from the king dissuaded them. Once again, Villia had formed a barrier so they could speak without being overheard.

"Only because it was before the other nobles," Villia said. "We forced the king's hand, and he won't soon forget that."

"But once we show him the circle, he'll have to forgive us, right?"

Villia sighed. "You still don't understand, do you? Officially, there's nothing for him to forgive us of, but this will severely damage our influence at court, though yours more than mine."

"You know, I really don't care about that anymore. Once I get Osmund out of trouble, we're going back to the Academy. If I have my way, I'll never come back here again."

Villia snorted. "Well, I can't say that I blame you, but it's not wise to dispense with court politics entirely. If you're not careful, you might find pieces of Korand taken from you and given to your rivals."

Jez grumbled under his breath that they were welcome to it. His rank had brought him nothing but trouble. Then again, he might not be able to get back into the Academy without it. He sighed and shook his head. He just couldn't win.

They made their way through the keep until they came to Varin's quarters. A pair of guards stood watch, but a gesture from the king dismissed them. Villia turned to Varin and motioned for him to let them in. He scowled but pushed open the door. He stepped inside and spread his arms.

"There. You see? There's no summoning circle. Can we get back to dealing with the actual murderer?"

"It was hidden by an illusion when we were here before," Jez said.

Haziel nodded at Villia. "Mage Villia, if you please."

Villia inclined her head and closed her eyes. Jez did the same, trying to find some sign of the working hiding the circle. He had tried to learn illusion at the Academy, but he was hopelessly inept at it, and he had no sense of it. He opened his eyes, giving the effort up as pointless. Villia spoke after a few seconds of tense silence.

"There are a few illusions here," she said without opening her eyes. "I'm going to start taking them down. I would recommend Lady Lina leave."

"You will not give me commands in my own quarters, mage," Varin said.

"I was not intending to be rude nor was it a command. It's the nature of illusions to be difficult to tell apart, and I wouldn't want to take hers down by mistake."

Lina paled a little, and her fingers went to her cheek. She removed them a second later and clenched her teeth. The scar appeared, though almost instantly, she returned her hand to face to cover the mark.

"You may continue, Mage Villia. I have removed my illusion."

Jez and Osmund exchanged glances, and Lina grew red when she saw the expressions on their faces but didn't say anything. Villia nodded. She splayed her fingers and violet motes appeared around her hands. The gold frames of the paintings dimmed, and the sunlight streaming through the window suddenly didn't seem so bright. The entire room faded. All the changes had been subtle, and the chamber was still ostentatious, but it lacked the radiance it had held a second ago.

Varin frowned. "Are you satisfied now?"

"Villia?" Jez asked.

Villia opened her eyes and shook her head. "That's it. There are no other illusions in the room."

"But the circle," Jez said.

"If there was a circle here, it is gone."

"Now that we're done wasting everyone's time, perhaps we can get back to the sentencing," Varin said.

"But…"

The king's voice cut Jez off. "Lord Varin is right, Baron. You've wasted quite enough of our time with this baseless accusation."

"I saw the circle," Jez said.

"Did you smell anything?" Villia asked.

"What?"

"You said you can smell demonic energy. The circle in Dusan's lair required an enormous amount of power. If the one you saw was anything like that one, it would be extremely difficult to hide it from your senses. Do you smell anything?"

"No."

"What about before. If Sharim really took down an illusion hiding it, you would've smelled something then. Did you?"

Jez thought back and shook his head. "No, but I know what I saw."

"Your Majesty, I've had quite enough of this," Varin said as he scowled at Jez.

Lina was standing next to him. The illusion over her scar had been reapplied. She wore an expression similar to that of her father, though if anything, she looked even angrier.

"As have I," the king said. "Baron Jezreel, this was a clumsy attempt to divert attention, and I see no option but to take it as proof that your man is guilty and that you were trying to hide it. You are hereby forbidden from leaving the keep until we've determined whether or not you gave the order for your bodyguard to commit those murders. As for Osmund himself, out of deference to your position, I will not execute him. He is hereby sentenced to life in prison."

CHAPTER 20

Sharim ran the crystal through the water in the silver saucer. Once again, it clouded, and Jez thought he could see images inside. After a few minutes, the clouds vanished. Sharim let out a breath.

"I'm sorry. I still don't get anything."

"Can you try scrying for something else? Something simple." Jez put his hand behind his back. "How many fingers am I holding up?"

Sharim smiled and walked over to the water barrel to empty the saucer. "It doesn't really work that way."

"I was hoping that with the circle gone divination would work again."

"Maybe he made another one."

Jez nodded. "Maybe." He looked at the large blue crystal sitting on a nearby table, almost a perfect match for the one at the Academy. The speaking stone had been in the workshop when they'd gotten here. "I think I should contact Master Besis. This is getting too complicated."

"It won't work," Sharim said. "That's why Villia had it brought here. I tried to contact my parents earlier today, and it failed to establish contact. It makes sense since the speaking stones use a form of divination."

"They do?"

Sharim nodded. "You're basically scrying each other. The crystals do all the work, but the magic is the same."

Jez let out a breath in frustration. "I don't know what to do. I was sure we had him. You saw the circle too right? I wasn't imagining that."

"I saw it," Sharim said. "I didn't know what the runes meant, but I saw it."

"Could Varin have hidden it from Villia somehow?"

Sharim shook his head and motioned to the ceiling. Jez could imagine the stars dancing there. When Sharim saw the expression on Jez's face, he nodded. "Villia is one of the most skilled illusionists in the kingdom. Certainly, there's no one within a hundred miles that can match her."

"What about Lina?"

Sharim let out a bark of laughter, but it only lasted a few seconds. "I'm sorry. Lina is good. There's no doubt about that, but Villia is something else entirely. I heard she turned down the position of Shadow Master at the Academy. There's no way Lina could fool her."

An idea struck Jez. "Could she fool you?"

"What?"

"Could she fool you? You said you thought someone was there. Could she have been in the room when we were there, hidden by some illusion."

"It's possible," Sharim said slowly.

"What if she made the illusion of the circle?"

Sharim looked up at him. "You mean it might not have really been there?"

Jez shrugged. "Villia was right. If it was there, I should've been able to smell it, but we both saw it."

Sharim bit his lower lip and considered that for a second. His eyes wandered to the ceiling, no doubt envisioning Villia's stars instead of the plain brown stone.

"It makes sense," he said finally. "Why would she do it though?"

Jez stood up, certain he was on to something. "So I would do exactly what I did. She knew Villia wouldn't find a circle because there was nothing to find. By making it so the king won't listen to me, she's made sure he won't believe me if I accuse her."

"Accuse her of what?"

"Of trying to summon a demon lord."

Sharim stared at him for a second. "Don't you think you're jumping to conclusions?"

Jez shook his head. "You don't understand. Even if it was just an illusion, those were real runes. She has to have seen them somewhere and studied them at least well enough to duplicate them." He started walking toward the door. He pulled it open and turned around. "Come on. What are you waiting for?"

"Where are we going?"

"We're going to search Lina's room for proof."

Sharim blinked. "How do you suggest we get in? I don't think we're going to talk our way through the guards this time."

Jez ran his fingers along the wall and closed his eyes. He sent his power flowing through the stone until it became like putty to his mind. He concentrated and the wall rippled, forming a hole no larger than Jez's fist. Sharim gasped and Jez opened his eyes.

"The room next to hers won't be so well guarded."

CHAPTER 21

As it turned out, the room next to Lina's quarters was well guarded. It belonged to one of her personal attendants and had direct access to her chamber. The room above, however, was an empty storage chamber filled with boxes and covered in dust. Jez pried one open, kicking up a cloud of dust that set him coughing for several seconds. Inside the crate, he found a faded tapestry with the ends frayed. He put the cover back on and returned his attention to the floor. He knelt and ran his fingers across it, leaving a trail in the dust. He closed his eyes and concentrated.

He sensed the ward just before it slapped him in the face.

The next thing Jez knew, he was on the ground three feet away from where he'd been. A low chime rang in the air, but it faded after a second. Sharim rushed to his side.

"What happened?"

Jez shook his head. "I should've realized this way wouldn't be unprotected. That chime was supposed to be an alarm, but it looks like no one's bothered to maintain it."

"Does that mean you can't get through?"

"Give me a second."

Once again, Jez extended his senses into the stone, but this time, he did so slowly. He found himself clucking his tongue. The ward was terrible. Thick cords of power ran through the stone, ready to lash out at any energy that tried to cross. They were strong, but strong like diamonds were strong. One hit delivered in the proper manner could shatter them. He could probably do it. It wouldn't even be that difficult. He considered it for a second before rejecting the idea. The ward itself may have fallen into disrepair, but if he were to break it entirely, his efforts might well be noticed. He would do no one any good if he ended up in a cell next to Osmund.

Gingerly, he touched one of the chords of power without trying to move past it. It quivered but didn't attack. Slowly, he wrapped his consciousness around it and pulled, trying to get it out of his way, but it was like trying to move a house. It moved, but only a fraction of an inch before snapping back into place. Briefly, he considered using Luntayary's power, but that was risky in the best of times. Fortunately, there was another source of power nearby. His eyes locked on Sharim.

"Have you ever formed a contingent?"

"Once. Mage Villia showed me."

"I think we need one."

"It took us an hour to form it."

Jez shrugged. "Do you have anything better to do?"

"I'm not sure we should be doing this."

"It's this or go back," Jez said.

Sharim sighed. "What do we use for the joining thought?"

Jez pointed to the box containing the tapestry. "Let's try that."

They both concentrated. In order to form a contingent to combine a portion of their power, they needed to have the exact same thought while attempting to interweave their magical senses. The more complicated the thought, the more completely they could join their power. It was difficult even with a simple image, but all they needed to set it off was one instant of shared thought.

The moment their powers touched, Jez cried out. His mind felt like it was on fire. He realized he had fallen and picked himself off the ground. He looked at the other boy who was rubbing his head, though he seemed to have kept his feet.

"What happened?"

"We didn't match up. What were you thinking of?"

Sharim pointed. "That box."

Jez's vision swam, and it was several seconds before he could maintain his balance. He let out a breath. "We were looking at it from different angles."

Sharim blinked several times before nodding. "How about just a black background?"

"Maybe," Jez said. "I'm just not sure that would provide enough power."

"We have to start somewhere."

Jez shrugged. "I guess so."

He formed the background in his mind. Even with such a simple image, it was difficult. There was the black of coal and the black of night, and Master Balud had several figures carved of a black wood. In the end, Jez focused on the obsidian of the Academy tower. As long as he could get close to Sharim's thought, they should be able to establish a link, though it may not be very effective. Again, he tried to join his senses with Sharim's. This time, they formed a tenuous link. Images were superimposed onto Jez's sight. It was like he could see himself, though it was only a dim outline.

"What?"

His voice seemed to come from two places at once, though one was much fainter. Sharim tried to take a step, but fell. Jez's vision shifted, and he felt a faint tingling on his elbow. Sharim was rubbing his own elbow, and a bruise had started to form.

"Let's get this over with," Jez said, trying to ignore the peculiar doubling of his own voice.

Sharim nodded, and the movement made Jez feel dizzy, and he had to grab onto the crate to keep his balance. When Besis had shown him this technique, it hadn't been nearly this disorienting. Of course that link had taken a full hour to establish, and Jez wondered if there was something he was missing, but he had neither the time nor the means to figure that out.

He closed his eyes. It helped, but he was left with a faint afterimage. He could see himself, and he guessed the image was coming from Sharim's eyes. Before he could ask the other boy to close his eyes, the vision vanished. Jez drew power from Sharim and joined it with his own. A wave of nausea washed over him, and he resisted the urge to double over and throw up. Sharim's power felt like an oily slime going down his throat. It felt so alien, and he had to fight the instinct to pull away. Instead, he extended their combined senses, wrapping them around one of the ward's chords.

Jez grunted as he pulled. For a second, it seemed like nothing would happen. Then, the darkness flowing in from Sharim swelled. The chord moved an inch. Then another. Sweat formed on Jez's brow, and he pulled with everything he had. Slowly, the chord moved, opening the way to the stone itself. The ground rippled, and a circular hole appeared in the floor between them. It expanded slowly until it was wide enough for them to fit through. Jez let out a breath and released Sharim's power. The other boy slumped to the floor, but Jez peered down the hole and into Lina's quarters.

CHAPTER 22

Lina's room was surprisingly empty. The bed looked wide enough to sleep ten and had a golden frame that was probably worth more than most people see in a lifetime. There was a cabinet of rose wood in one corner, but those were the only pieces of furniture. Even the walls were bare. He looked up at Sharim. The other boy was rummaging around in the storage crates. He pulled out a rope and passed it to Jez.

"Lower me down," he said. "I'll look around and you can raise me back up."

"Don't you think it should be me?"

Sharim shook his head. "You're no good with illusions. If there's something hidden there, I should be the one to look for it."

"You don't know what you're looking for," Jez said.

Sharim rolled his eyes. "A book with a lot of runes, right?"

"There are a lot of different kinds of runes."

"But Lina supposedly only knows illusions. That's not a school that uses very many runes, and I know all of those. Besides, it's not likely she'll have a book of demon summoning out in the open. So I'll just bring back any hidden book filled with runes I don't recognize."

Jez didn't like it, but Sharim had a point. He nodded, and the other boy tied the rope around his waist. Sharim was plump and a little taller than Jez. Jez grunted as he held Sharim's weight. It was easier than he expected. In addition to studying magic and a variety of other subjects at the Academy, Jez had spent time learning the sword, and hours of practice had hardened his muscles. He lowered Sharim to the ground in a few seconds and peaked into the hole to watch as Sharim examined the room.

Sharim opened the cabinet. It was mostly gowns and other clothes, but half a dozen books lined a shelf at the top. Sharim ran his fingers along the spines and pulled one out. He thumbed through the pages before shaking his head and returning it to the shelf. He lowered his head and concentrated. A few seconds later, he looked to one side. He glanced up and smiled before walking to the other side of the room, outside of Jez's sight. There was a flash of violet and Sharim came back with a leather-bound book that had cracks on the cover.

"I think this is it. It was hidden behind a loose stone in the wall. There was an illusion over it to make it look smooth."

"Did you put the illusion back?"

"Oh right."

Sharim looked to where he'd gotten the book for a second. "There. Pull me back up."

Jez grunted and braced himself. He pulled, and Sharim inched up. The rope was old and it hurt Jez's hands. His muscles ached by the time he'd brought the other boy high enough for him to climb out. Restoring stone in the floor proved no great challenge, though it didn't exactly match the rest of the floor. Jez hoped the other side was at least close enough not to be noticed right away, but there was nothing more he could do. He took the book from Sharim and opened it. It was so old that the spine cracked. The book was written in a language Jez didn't know, though he recognized it as one he'd known once, before Sariel had locked his memories away. His eyes locked onto a symbol of a closed eye cut in half.

"Marrowit."

The word escaped his lips before he realized he'd spoken. Sharim was staring at him. His jaw had dropped, and his eyes were so wide it was almost funny. He opened and closed his mouth a few times before he was able to speak.

"We…" The word came out as a squeak. Sharim took a deep breath and cleared his throat. "We were right? She's really trying to summon a demon lord?"

Jez nodded. "Yes." He flipped through the pages, but aside from an occasional rune, he had no idea what any of it meant. "This must be how Dusan learned to summon Marrowit. Who knows what else it says."

"How did Lina get it?"

"I have no idea." He lifted the book. "Will this be enough to convince the king?"

Sharim started to nod, but let out a breath and shook his head. "We have no way to prove where we got it. We could put it back, but then we'd have to convince the king to have her room searched."

"He wouldn't do that," Jez said, "not after finding nothing in Varin's room"

"Maybe we can manipulate her into incriminating herself. If she accuses us openly of taking the book…"

Jez started pacing. The rope got tangled in his legs and he kicked it away. "Again with the subtly. We don't have time."

Sharim put a hand on Jez's shoulder. "We have the book, and from what you're telling me, she couldn't summon Marrowit even if she had it."

"She might be able to adapt it."

"But not without the book. We may have, at least, bought a little time."

“Fine,” Jez said as he forced himself to calm down, “but I’m going to warn Osmund.”

“Maybe it would be better if you didn’t.” Jez glared at him, but Sharim only shrugged. “I only mean that he’s accused of murder. If you’re seen as being too close to him, it could damage your reputation even more. You don’t want to give Lina anything else she can use against you.”

Jez shook his head. “You don’t understand. She doesn’t like me, but she hates him. She got that scar six months ago, and she still keeps that illusion over it. If she actually summons an upper level demon, who do you think she’ll send it after first?”

CHAPTER 23

Osmund was pacing back and forth in his cell. The small room only allowed him to take three steps before he had to turn around and go the other way. His anger was almost tangible, and there seemed to be a faint glow around him. Jez thought he could smell something burning, but he told himself it was only his imagination. When Osmund saw Jez, his expressions softened, but Jez could still see the anger just beneath the surface.

"Well, this is new," Jez said.

"What is?"

"You. Normally, when you get thrown in the dungeon, you're so depressed you'll barely look up. I don't think you stood up even once last time."

"This is different," Osmund said in a voice that wasn't quite a shout.

"How so?"

"This time, I'm innocent. Do you know how you're going to get me out of here?"

"Not yet. We know it was Lina who actually killed those men, or at least she summoned the demons who did."

"Really?"

"You seem surprised."

Osmund shrugged. "Jez, I don't know. She's a spoiled brat, but I don't think she'd summon demons to kill someone, and why would she send them against her own people instead of me?"

Jez shrugged. "I've given up trying to understand politics."

"This isn't politics. It's common sense. Besides, do you really think she could? She didn't go the Academy for that long, and I don't think she's ever studied summoning."

"That was six months ago," Jez said, "and there places besides the Academy where things like that can be learned."

Osmund rolled his eyes. "Jez, be serious. She's not going to learn to summon a demon of the third order in six months."

"Maybe not, but that's obviously not stopping her from summoning lesser demons."

"I don't know."

"Why are you defending her?"

"Because if we're wrong, I don't want the real summoner to get away."

"Look, I just came down here to warn you. Lina might send demons after you. Can you defend yourself?"

Osmund lifted a hand and wrinkled his brow in concentration. His hand took on a cherry red glow, and a curl of smoke rose from his fingers, but the light faded after a second.

"The wards around this place keep me from using any ordinary magic, but I think I can still transform."

"Be careful," Jez said. "I still don't know what kind of demons these are. We're doing what we can to get you out."

"All right. Remember, court politics can be almost as dangerous as battle. You be careful yourself."

"I will."

Jez walked toward the stairs up, somewhat surprised that he didn't see guards anywhere. He was halfway across the dungeon when his nose wrinkled at the smell of sulfur. He turned just in time to see three demons emerge from the shadows.

CHAPTER 24

The demons were covered in red scales and stood nearly as tall as Osmund himself. Their legs ended in cloven hooves, and their knees bent backward. Each hand had six bronze claws that almost seemed to glow with their own inner fire. Sinuous tongues flickered out of long faces, and curved horns rested atop their heads. Red hot flames burned in their eyes. Jez had studied these creatures at the Academy. They were chezamuts, the foot soldiers of the abyss.

Instantly, Jez's hands started weaving patterns in the air. He forced power into them, and a silver beam of light shot forward toward the nearest demon. It should have impaled the beast and sent it back to the abyss, but though the wards on the dungeon were concentrated in the prison cells, they didn't stop at the bars, and they weakened any magic used in the prison. The light splashed against the demon's chest, driving it back a few inches. The demon snarled, the fire in its eyes intensifying. It took a step toward Jez, and he started weaving the binding again, intending to pour even more power into it.

Before he could release, there was a flash of light from Osmund's cell. When it faded, Osmund was gone. In his place was a winged creature even taller than Osmund himself. Though his wings didn't move, he floated several inches above the ground. He wore scarlet robes that reminded Jez of blood. He had pale skin and eyes that burned even hotter than those of the demons. He closed his fist and a sword appeared in his hand, its blade shrouded in red flame: the same sword that had given Lina her scar.

Ziary took a step forward and slashed. The bars melted before his blow, and Jez was left with a streak of light in his vision. Ziary looked at the demons, and his eyes brightened. He spread his wings, shedding a light almost too bright to look at. Jez had seen that light blister the skin of people Ziary perceived as evil, but the demons just roared. Two lunged at Ziary while the third ran at Jez.

If not for his training with the sword, Jez would've been cut down in the space of a few heartbeats. The demon slashed with its claws, but Jez jumped back. His hand fell to his belt, but Dusan's sword wasn't there. He cursed himself for leaving it in the room and instead, he wove a quick binding, pouring three times as much power as such a working would normally require. A sphere of darkness shot forward, splashing against the demon's face. Its eyes went dark, and the creature let out a bellow that shook the room.

Jez danced several steps back as his fingers crafted the silver binding again. This time, he put everything he had into it. It crashed into the demon, making the air vibrate with silent thunder. The demon showed its teeth, jagged things that looked like dancing flames. It took a step forward, and for a moment, Jez thought it would kill him in spite of the binding, but as it took another step, its skin cracked. Scales flaked off revealing pure white light underneath. It tried to roar, but music drifted out of its open mouth. White lines that looked almost like tears appeared on its cheek. It looked at Jez and for a second, he wondered if it would speak, but instead, the light inside burst, enveloping the creature. When it faded, the demon was gone, and Jez fell to his knees, completely drained.

Ziary was holding his own against the demons. Every slash of the claws was met with burning blade, and their teeth never found his flesh, but the demons evaded most of his attacks outright and managed to deflect the rest on their claws. It looked more like a dance than a battle; all three combatants moved with a liquid grace far beyond what any human could achieve. Neither side could gain an advantage over the other. Jez tried to summon his power. Anything he could do, any distraction, even a temporary one, should allow Ziary to take out his foes, but pushing his binding through the prison wards had taken everything he had.

The demons struck from two different directions. Ziary caught one attack on his blade. Without even looking, he batted the other away by hitting the demon's hand with his fist. He didn't, however, see the kick that went into his side. There was a sound like cracking bone as the kick tore through cloth and flesh alike. He cried out as motes of orange light bled from the wound. A demon lunged at him. He tried to react but was too slow, and its teeth latched onto his shoulder. Ziary screamed.

Jez forced himself to his feet and leapt at the demon closest to him. He crashed into it with all the force of a butterfly running into a stone wall, and the demon reacted no more than the wall would have. Pain lanced down Jez's arm. The demon looked down at him and showed Jez its teeth. It opened its mouth.

It was all the opening Ziary needed.

Heedless of the one clamped onto his shoulder, the scion lashed out with his sword, taking the head of the one going for Jez. It screamed, its body transmuting to fire before becoming a pillar of smoke that reeked so badly of sulfur that Jez gagged. The eyes of the one biting Osmund brightened as it tried to ram its claws into him, but with only one foe, Ziary turned his full attention on his attacker. He caught the demon's arm by the wrist and drove his sword into the creature's chest. The chezamut screamed before it too puffed out of existence. Ziary turned his burning eyes to Jez.

"Osmund?" Jez asked trying his best to keep his voice steady.

Ziary could be an unforgiving enemy, descended from those pharim tasked with destroying evil, and if he perceived the slightest wrong in Jez, he would attack without hesitation. Jez didn't have the strength to stop him right now. Ziary nodded.

"He still hasn't woken up from whatever working Marrowit put on him." The voice speaking was Osmund's, not the peculiar double voice of Ziary. "I'm still in control."

"Maybe you should change back. It would probably be bad if anyone saw you free."

Ziary nodded and his form seemed to melt away leaving Osmund in his place. The wounds he'd suffered in the fight were gone, though Jez noticed that he clutched the side where the demon had kicked him. Osmund looked at the remnants of the bars to his cell.

"How are we going to explain this?"

"We were attacked," Jez said. "You defended yourself."

"Assuming they believe us."

Jez pointed to the ground. The imprint of clawed feet had been burned into the stone.

"That should be proof enough for anyone."

CHAPTER 25

A full minute after the demons had been banished, the guards rushed into the dungeon. The first one, a man who looked like he enjoyed pastries a little too much, saw Osmund and cried out. Those behind him drew swords so quickly one almost dropped her weapon. Osmund smirked at them but made no threatening move. The captain opened another cell and gestured to Osmund. The boy was obviously trying not to laugh as he stepped inside. The guards started calming once he was safely put away, but that changed when Jez showed them the charred footprint in the stone.

"What could do that?"

"A demon being banished," Jez said. "We were attacked."

"You can't be…"

The guard stopped when Jez narrowed his eyes. He took a step back, keeping his eyes locked on the footprint. He uttered a few terse words, and one of the other soldiers ran up the stairs to get a binder to confirm Jez's story. Jez clasped Osmund's hand and left the guards to their work. Apparently, the guard that went up ahead of him didn't keep his mouth shut because everyone was talking about the demon footprint, though Jez supposed it was better to have it widely known so Varin or Lina couldn't sweep it under the rug. He considered going straight to Haziel to bring his accusation against Lina, but he thought better of it. Varin had shown how easily he could manipulate a situation like that. Instead, he made his way to the top of the south tower to Villia's workshop. He pulled the door open to find Villia on the other side reaching for the handle. She had a pack slung over her shoulder. The desk in the room behind her had been cleared and the rest of the room was empty. Even the floor had been wiped clean. He looked from her to the empty workshop.

"What are you doing?"

"I'm leaving."

"I can see that. Why? I need your help."

She tried to push past him, but he held his ground and gave her a hard stare. She shook her head.

"The kind of help you need, I can't give."

She waved her hand and faded from view. Footsteps came from behind him, and he turned to see her walking away. He reached for her, but realized his mistake and brought his arm to the side just in time to catch the invisible woman trying to walk past him. He pulled water from the air and doused her, leaving an outline floating next to him.

"Let me pass, boy," she said. "You have no authority over me."

"Please," Jez said. "I don't know how to deal with the king."

The watery outline took a step back into the room. Jez followed, but before he could say anything, the room went dark. Stars appeared above them and swirled across the ceiling. The sun rose in the east, though it did nothing to banish the darkness. In the west, the full moon appeared and began its slow ascent through the illusionary sky. Spheres came into being and began circling him. Some had thin rings around them, and Jez had the impression that they were huge, larger than the entire world.

"The king?" Villia's voice came from everywhere at once. Jez tried to reach for his power, but a barrier appeared cutting him off. "You would try to force me to help you with the king? To aid in your petty squabbles? Insolent child. You cannot begin to understand my concerns. I have done things you cannot comprehend."

"Lina is summoning demons!"

"What is one more mortal summoning demons?"

"Mortal? Are you something else?"

"I will leave now. You will not interfere."

Jez moved to where he remembered the door being. Pain blossomed in his chest, and he had to put a hand against a wall he couldn't see to support himself. He used his power to claw at the barrier shielding him, but it might as well have been a mountain for all it reacted.

"How are you doing this?"

"You have no idea what I can do."

One of the spheres passed through him, and he felt nothing.

They're illusions.

"I have seen more than you can imagine."

Pain filled him, but Jez forced himself to ignore it.

It's all illusions.

He remembered his first illusion class. Master Kerag had said that a master illusionist could deceive all twelve senses. The five standard ones and the seven relating to the seven dominions.

Including protection.

The barrier was still there, but Jez reached for his power anyway. A being appeared in front of him, clothed in robes of violet light. Its face looked vaguely human, but it wore a hood that shrouded its features in shadows, all except for twin points of purple light. Bird-like wings emerged from its back, translucent and almost seeming to be made of shadows, though like the ceiling, stars moved across the feathers.

"I am older than you can imagine."

Jez didn't feel his power, but his hands wove a ward against illusion. It snapped into place, and the starry background shattered, leaving a room made of gray stone with a brown ceiling. The being before him, however, was no illusion, and it remained. Jez knew what it was, and he could think of only one thing to do, a thing he'd hoped he'd never have to do again. He closed his eyes and touched the terrible power within him, the power he'd used when battling Dusan and the demon lord Marrowit. He didn't draw fully, though. Mortal flesh couldn't contain that power, and he wasn't willing to risk the damage that drawing too deeply would do, but he did draw enough to change.

Jez's robes became brilliant blue, and a crystal sword appeared on his belt, its weight comfortable on his hip. Pure white wings emerged from his back, and he floated off the ground.

"No, you aren't."

Surprise flashed across the shadow's face, evident in spite of its concealment. The form began to evaporate until Villia stood before him, her eyes wide. Jez returned to his normal form as well and met Villia's gaze. She shuddered and looked away.

"You're no limaph," she said.

"No."

"You're a pharim."

"So are you."

Sharim looked at the ground and her shoulders slumped. "I was."

"Was?"

She lifted her head and Jez found himself searching her eyes for some sign of the ancient knowledge he knew had to reside in her mind, but they just seemed to be ordinary eyes. Tears welled up, but she managed to keep from crying.

"Before I rebelled." Her voice was barely above a whisper.

Jez stared at her, shocked by what he'd heard. The pharim rebellion had happened so long ago it was more myth than history. Some of the pharim had rebelled against the Creator, and as punishment, they had been cursed to wander the earth searching for a purpose forever denied to them. The limaph, like Osmund, were descendants of these outcasts, but they had vanished from history so long ago many didn't believe in them. It was almost too impossible to believe.

"You're an afur."

"Have you come to destroy me?"

"I didn't even know you were here."

She barked out a laugh and a single tear ran down her cheek. "You are a pharim."

Jez bit his lower lip but only hesitated for a second. "You should probably sit. This is about Dusan."

Jez spent the next several minutes explaining to Villia everything that had happened since he first went to the Academy. Her eyes widened at times, but she never interrupted. Once he was done, she gingerly poked his arm as if making sure he was really made of flesh. Apparently unsatisfied, she did it again. When she tried a third time, he caught her finger, and she looked up at him. She smiled, and Jez released her finger.

"I've never heard of anything like this."

"What about you?" Jez asked. "How did you end up here?"

She shrugged. "I am a Veilspeaker." She coughed. "At least I was once. Where else would I be but influencing the politics of a kingdom?"

Jez waved his hand at the ceiling. The stars weren't there, but he could see them in his mind.

"And this?"

The stars appeared and started a slow movement. Villia didn't look away from them as she spoke. "I do what I can to remember the time before I rebelled, when I could walk among the stars."

"Why were you leaving?"

"I heard the rumors. There were battle demons summoned into the keep, and I want no part in that. My abilities are limited in direct conflict. My power was distilled when I was banished from the Keep of the Hosts, and my essence was bound to this world."

Jez nodded in understanding. "You can be destroyed."

"Please, let me go."

"Dusan summoned a demon that threatened the whole world. If Lina is trying to do something similar…" A thought struck him, and he pulled the book from Lina's quarters out of his robes and handed it to Villia. "Can you read this?"

Villia flipped through the pages and nodded. "It's written in the language of the Knitos who died off thousands of years before the first king of Ashtar was born. They were demon worshipers. Where did you get it?"

"It was in Lina's room, hidden behind an illusion."

"She doesn't know this language."

"Are you sure?"

"Not entirely, but it would take years to learn. She's not old enough."

"Does it talk about how to summon Marrowit?"

"That and more." She turned the page and shook her head. "There are summoning rituals for at least a dozen major demons and a host of minor ones. This book should be destroyed."

"We can't," Jez said. "Not yet. We don't know what Lina is trying to do. This might have a way to stop her."

Suddenly, Jez's nostrils flared with the scent of sulfur. It came on so strong Jez felt dizzy and he had to hold onto the table to avoid falling. A crystal fell to the ground, and it was only then that Jez realized the ground had been shaking. Villia scooped the crystals off the ground and returned them to the desk. She met his gaze.

"Assuming we're not too late already."

Jez looked from the door to Villia. She shifted the pack on her shoulder, but she was obviously ready to leave.

"You are needed, Shadowguard," she said.

"Promise me you won't leave."

She shook her head. "No. I will be gone within an hour. If you did not come to the city because of me, then I will not submit to your authority."

Again, the ground shook, and his nostrils flared. "But you're a pharim. You're supposed to protect people from demons."

She smirked. "I was a pharim, and even then, I was a manipulator, not a warrior. You and your kind were the defenders. I don't believe it is in you to stay and keep me here."

"I could bind you."

"You won't. If what I suspect is true, you'll need your strength."

"But…" the smell of sulfur surged. Jez looked back to the door and moved to leave. Just before he started down the stairs, he looked over his shoulder. "You're right. You are not a pharim."

CHAPTER 26

Jez practically flew down the stairs. He heard screaming before he reached the bottom. The crystal sword appeared in his hand, and he barely gave a thought to his skin crawling in response to the power pulsing inside of him. He burst into the corridor and ran right into a group of chezamuts surrounding a pair of cowering servants. Their surprise lasted only a second, but by then, Jez's sword had cut shallow gashes in two of them, and blue fire erupted from their wounds. Though it was only a shadow of a true pharim's weapon, the crystal sword had been created with the purpose of fighting demons, and even seemingly insignificant wounds dealt to such creatures could be devastating.

The demons howled and vanished. The other two came at him, but without the dampening effects of the prison, he was well prepared for them. The silver binding shot out of his hand, entering one demon through the mouth and exploding out of the back of its head. Before it even had a chance to cry out, Jez swung his arm, pulling the light along with it. The beam split the final demon in two. The entire engagement had happened over the space of half a dozen heartbeats, and the servants hadn't even had a chance to cry out.

"Are you all right?"

A golden haired woman nodded, though she couldn't seem to form words.

"Go into Villia's tower," he said. "You should be safe there."

He didn't wait to see if she went. Sulfur wafted from every direction. Down one hall, he saw a group of soldiers holding their own against an eight foot tall creature that stood on two legs and had the head of a raven. It was a kantu, a scout demon that was deadly in its own right. With a flick of his hands, Jez shot a glowing ball of water at it which enveloped the demon in a bubble. It howled for a second, trying to claw its way out, but though the skin of the bubble seemed thin, it resisted the demon's efforts. It slashed, and its hand got stuck. It tried to pull out, but the skin absorbed it, pulling the demon into the bubble. The kantu floated across the surface, banging in an effort to break out. It floated up to the ceiling, and when the bubble popped the demon was gone. Jez didn't stop to speak to the guards. Odds were good not every foe would be so easy to defeat. He needed help. He turned down a hall and pushed open the door to the stairs leading to the dungeon.

A familiar orange light flickered beneath. Jez rushed down the stairs, emerging in the dungeon just as a demon flared and disappeared. Ziary had once again burned through his bars and was fighting a dozen demons of all shapes and sizes. His sword moved so fast it looked like a fiery blur. He was keeping them at bay, but there were so many of them, and he couldn't spare any attention to attack without opening himself up to reprisal. Orange motes bleeding from wounds on his chest and arms said he had already made that sacrifice more than once. His right wing had been broken, and orange liquid bled out, but he used the other to push away attackers. He was like a living weapon, but he couldn't last long.

Jez didn't bother to try a binding. The wards on the prison were still intact and would dampen any working he tried. Instead, he lunged forward, severing the spine of a creature that looked like a wolf that stood on two legs. It stiffened before disappearing in a cloud of smoke. Ziary met his eyes for a second before refocusing his efforts on attack.

Jez's sword cut down two more, and Ziary destroyed one of his own. They met in the middle of the horde and turned away from each other so they could fight back to back. The demons surged forward, but none got close. They all fell to crystal sword or to flaming one. In mere seconds, the demons were gone. Ziary winced as he turned back to Jez.

"Thanks. What's going on?"

"The keep is under attack. Come on. I need your help." Ziary turned to look at his cell, but Jez shook his head. "We'll take care of that later. I don't know how many there are, and I'll need all the help I can get. Let's go."

Ziary nodded. His broken wing twitched, and he gestured with his sword for Jez to lead the way.

CHAPTER 27

They headed toward the throne room, moving as quickly as they could without risking an ambush. A few times, they encountered people fleeing, and Jez directed them to Villia's tower. Half a dozen times, they ran into groups of demons battling soldiers. Most of the time, the humans were losing, and only the arrival of Jez and Ziary turned the tide. Once, though, they found a dozen men fighting half as many demons, and the men were winning. Steel wasn't as effective as the flame or crystal blades Jez and Ziary bore, but it was enough. At each encounter, more soldiers joined Jez. By the time they reached the throne room, thirty men had gathered around them. Most were wounded, and one had an arm that hung limply by his side, but they all carried looks of steely determination. The demons had invaded their home, and they would be repelled.

The door to the throne room had been torn away, its splintered remains lying just inside. A demon, at least ten feet tall and resembling nothing so much as a statue of molten gold, clasped its hands together and slammed them down at the throne where King Haziel huddled in utter terror. A dozen other creatures, smaller but otherwise identical to the larger beast, leapt at the king. Haziel screamed. As their attacks neared, however, a sphere of violet energy appeared around the throne.

With a flash of light, the demons were driven back several feet. Bits of gold splashed to the ground and burned holes into the stone. One of the smaller demons turned toward Jez and his companions. It was no more than three feet tall. Its head was human-shaped and bald. Its face had no features whatsoever, seeming to be only a flat plane of molten metal.

"What are those things?" Ziary asked.

"I don't know," Jez said.

The demon pointed and cried out in a language Jez couldn't understand. He had no idea how the creature spoke without a mouth, but the sound made the hairs on his arm stand on end. The other demons turned, and though it had no eyes, Jez knew the largest one was focused on him.

"Keep the smaller ones off my back," he said without taking his eyes from his foe.

"Are you sure?" Ziary asked, but Jez was already halfway across the room.

He lifted his sword and struck at the demon, but the creature's body parted, flowing like water, and Jez's blade sliced through empty air. Behind him, the sounds of battle erupted. He slashed again, but his second strike was just as ineffectual as the first. The demon balled its fist and rammed it into Jez's side. The force of the impact sent pain shooting through his body. The next thing Jez knew, he was leaning against the wall, twenty feet away from the throne. A blackened circle had been burned into the side of his robe.

Ziary and the soldiers had engaged the smaller creatures, but they were having no more luck than Jez. The demon forms were too fluid, and they kept flowing out of the way. He needed to do something to help. The larger demon took a step toward him, but Jez was already weaving a binding. He threw his hands toward the head creature, and a wintery blast shot forward, enveloping the demon. In response to Jez's will, the wind circled the room catching all the others. It wasn't intended to banish them. Banishing a demon without knowing what it was could be a risky proposition, one that failed on the first attempt more often than not. Trying to banish over a dozen would've been suicide. He could, however, bind some of their power.

The demons stiffened for a second before continuing, and a layer of frost crept over their skin. One of the soldiers slammed his axe into a demon, and the blow shattered the creature. Man and demon alike stopped and stared at the pieces as they evaporated. The surprise lasted only a moment before the demons surged forward.

The lead demon brought its fist down, but Jez's crystal sword flicked forward, slicing off its hand. Its closed fist shattered when it hit the ground. The demon's skin rippled, but it was too strong to be destroyed by any incidental wound, and it shoved the remains of its arm into Jez's chest, sending him to the ground. He landed on his burned side and cried out in pain. He tried to lift his sword, but the demon brought its foot down on his arm. As the pressure increased, pain rushed up his arm. The world blurred as tears formed in his eyes. Just as he thought his arm would break, a flash of red crashed into the demon.

It was Ziary. His flaming sword bounced off the demon's skin and the scion slammed into it, causing the demon to rock back and forth. It was only a little bit, but it was enough. Jez ripped his arm free, clenching his teeth against the pain, and he got to his feet. The demon grabbed Ziary by the neck. Jez lunged, his sword moving in a blur. The demon's legs came off, though it held on to Ziary as it fell. Ziary grunted, but couldn't free himself. Jez stepped forward and drove his sword into the center of the demon's body. Sapphire cracks spread through the creature, and pieces of it flaked off, evaporating before they hit the ground. It let out another roar before collapsing into dust. Jez moved toward Ziary, wincing at the pain running up his side. He offered Ziary a hand up, and the other boy's form melted away leaving a tired looking Osmund. Jez looked around, but the demons were gone. Several of the soldiers lay unmoving on the ground, and even more were injured. The crystal sword dissolved as Jez and Osmund looked toward the king.

CHAPTER 28

"What happened?" Haziel's voice was unsteady, and he seemed on the verge of tears.

"It was Lina," Jez said. "I don't know if she had her father's help, but she's the one who summoned all these demons."

The king blinked at him. "Lina? That's not possible."

Anger surged through Jez. He stamped his foot on the ground sending a flow of terra magic into the stone floor. The room shook, and Haziel started to whimper and sank back into the throne. The sight of the king on his throne looking so terrified drained the anger from Jez.

"What will it take to convince you?" Jez asked in a quiet voice. "She tried to kill you."

"If she tried to kill me, why aren't I dead?"

"I actually don't know," Jez said.

"It was royal magic," a voice said from behind. Jez turned to see Villia with Sharim right behind her. She gave Haziel a bow, but the one she direct at Jez was even deeper, though if the king noticed the slight, he gave no sign. "Haziel is the rightful king of Ashtar. The rights of kings were established by Daziel, the Lord of the Veilspeakers himself, and there are certain magics protecting those rights. A demon can't easily overcome them."

"You mean they can't kill him," Jez said.

"They can kill him. It wouldn't be easy, but a strong enough demon could do it. So could the one who summoned them since the power won't stop a human."

"Lina."

Villia nodded. "She is human, and even the power of a pharim high lord won't interfere with a human exercising their free will."

"What are you two talking about?" the king asked as he stood on shaky legs.

Villia inclined her head. "It's not something many people know, Your Majesty. There is very real power in the throne of a kingdom, and the ability to overthrow that is denied to demons, at least to those without mortal help."

Haziel took a deep breath and nodded. His eyes locked on Osmund. He looked like he was trying to scowl but was too tired to manage it.

"What is he doing out?"

Jez resisted the urge to roll his eyes. "Your Majesty, he could've gotten out at any time. I told you it was demons that killed those men. I knew about them the same way I knew about the ones attacking you here. Osmund did nothing to deserve imprisonment."

"What about when he attacked the nobles at the Academy?" Haziel asked.

"Your Majesty?" Sharim spoke up and he almost shrank away as every eye turned to him. He looked like he wished he could call the words back, but instead he coughed. "It's like Mage Villia said in the trial. He wouldn't have been able to hurt her if it wasn't justified at least a little bit. If Lady Lina summoned demons to attack you…"

Sharim let the words hang, and after a few seconds, the king nodded and bowed to Osmund. "Osmund Jecklson, I thank you for coming to my aid and hereby absolve you of all guilt relating to the attack on Lina and her allies while you were at the Carceri Academy, and I release you from suspicion in the murder of the two men in Lord Varin's service." He turned to Jez. "Are you certain about Lady Lina?"

"Absolutely, Your Majesty."

"Very well. I'll send guards to apprehend her."

Jez took a step forward. "Actually, that may not be the best idea."

"Why not?"

"She's a powerful mage, and she can obviously summon demons. The guards might not be able to handle her. I'll go."

"But you're a child."

Jez glared at him, and the king glanced at his broken door. He paled a little and nodded. Jez motioned to Osmund, and they headed toward the south wing. Jez summoned his sword and Osmund once again took the form of Ziary. His wing was still bent at an odd angle, though he no longer bled orange light. Jez eyed him.

"Are you sure you're ready for this?"

Ziary cocked his head. "Are you sure you want to go without me?"

Jez inclined his head in concession. The guards formed a perimeter around the throne room, and Jez and Osmund began moving through the hall slowly. Jez kept his attention focused on the path before them, but they saw no demons as they made their way to the south wing.

The smell sulfur hung in the air, but it was more an echo of a scent than anything else. Demons had been here, though Jez couldn't tell how long ago that was. They could still be here, for that matter. Carefully, they pushed open the door to Lord Varin's chamber butfound it empty. Their footsteps echoed through the hall as they moved further down the corridor to the chambers assigned to Lina, and the smell of sulfur grew steadily stronger. They came to the door and stopped. Jez had to resist the urge to shiver. He had no idea what could be on the other side. If there was a demon lord, he needed all the power he could get, even if it destroyed him. He made his decision quickly and closed his eyes to reach for Luntayary's power. Wings emerged from his back and his robes transformed to sapphire blue. The amount of power coursing through him made his body ache. Ziary gave him a deep bow, and Jez pushed open the door.

No one was in the room. The bed had been pushed to one side to clear a space in the center of the floor where the blackened remnants of a summoning circle had been burned into the stone. Jez recognized some of the runes composing it. He bent down and ran his fingers along it, wincing at the thread of magic that remained. His hands closed on something hard, and he picked it up out of the ash. It was a crystal that looked like it had been singed badly. He held up to the light. It had been yellow once, and had been used to channel a great deal of summoning magic.

"Oh no."

"What is it?"

"She must've realized the book was gone and used what she knew to do this." He held up the focusing crystal. "This makes it even worse."

"But what is all this?"

"This is a circle used to summon a greater demon, and she used the power of this crystal to make the summoning permanent."

CHAPTER 29

Villia ran her fingers across the circle and clutched the burned out focusing crystal in her left hand. She turned back to the book and examined the image she'd been comparing the circle to. She let out a low whistle.

"What is it?" Jez asked.

She shook her head. "You have to understand, this has never been my area of expertise."

"You're the only one who can read the book."

"All the runes aren't here either," she said. "Some would've been in the air. It's not necessarily this summoning. What she was doing may not even be in this book."

"Villia what is it?" Jez asked.

She tapped a rune that looked like a broken crown. "Maries."

Jez looked at her blankly. "Who's Maries?"

"He's a battle demon."

"Like the chezamuts?"

She laughed. It was almost hysterical, and Jez and Osmund exchanged uncomfortable glances. "He's to the chezamuts what a master swordsman is to an unarmed farmer." She snorted. "An unarmed farmer with no arms and legs. He is one of the generals of the abyss."

Jez tried to swallow the lump in his throat, and when he spoke, his voice was pitched higher than usual. "Of what order is he?"

"Fourth."

Not as strong as Marrowit. Jez let out a breath of relief, but he realized he was being foolish. A demon of the fourth order was a deadly threat and could take on entire armies and decimate cities. It was only in comparison to a demon lord such as Marrowit, who had been of the third order, that the idea of facing such a being could be a relief.

"Still," Osmund said, "if he's just a battle demon, he can't be that great a threat. I mean he can only be in one place at a time, right? There are only so many he can kill even if he has access to some sort of magic."

"He can't kill many until he summons his army," Villia said. "He's a *general* of the abyss. If he's not stopped soon, we could have a thousand chezamuts on our hands, and that would only be the first wave." She looked from Jez to Osmund. "Not all of us have powers suited to battle. A thousand chezamuts could tear Rumar apart and not leave one stone atop another. Maries could overcome Haziel's protection with little effort."

"What do we do?" Jez asked.

Villia looked around and shuddered. "First, we get out of here. Lina may have left traps."

Jez nodded and followed Villia out of the door. Haziel was waiting outside and raised an eyebrow. Villia shook her head and motioned for him to follow. The fact that he offered no argument showed how worried he was.

"Stay on the lookout," Villia said. "We could be attacked at any time."

Jez nodded and kept his sword drawn. He was almost used to how the power made his skin crawl. Some of the guards escorting them eyed his sword with something very near reverence. Jez felt like he was being watched from the shadows, but no attack came. Villia led them to a small room Jez hadn't been in. The only furniture was a rectangular table in the center of the room. Rolled parchments sat on a shelf, and a map of the kingdom hung from one wall. Numbers had been written on it, though Jez had no idea what they meant. Villia motioned for them to sit. Jez sat but made sure he could easily get between the king and the door if the situation demanded.

"Your Majesty, you have to dispatch guards to find the demon Lina summoned. Send as many as you can spare without reducing the defenses of the keep."

Haziel nodded. "What does this demon look like?"

Villia glanced at the ceiling for a second as if searching her memory. "He looks like a man with blue skin and red eyes."

"What about Lord Varin and his daughter?"

"We should find them if they're alive, but our priority has to be the demon."

"What do you mean 'if they're alive'?" Haziel asked.

"A demon as powerful as Maries isn't easily controlled, particularly when his summoning was made permanent with a focusing crystal. It would take years of study to get it right, and if there's even the slightest error, he'd kill his summoner. Regardless of whether or not he's free, the result will be the same. He'll try to summon his army and attack the keep."

"How big?"

"Maries is one of the highest generals. He can command a thousand lesser demons, and each of those can command a thousand more. I doubt he can bring them all here at once, but he won't wait to attack."

There was silence for several long seconds before the king spoke.

"How could we possibly stand against an army of a million demons?"

Jez's mouth went dry. Even if every mage from all across the kingdom were a master binder, they still wouldn't be able to handle an army of that size. They wouldn't be able to handle one a tenth that size.

"We can't," he said, and the silence that followed felt like it would swallow the world.

CHAPTER 30

The door to the north tower creaked as Jez pushed it open. According to the king, this tower had been uninhabited for the last couple of years, and a layer of dust coated the stairs. It was a good indication that no one had been here, but still, he ran his fingers along the floor, checking to see if the dust was an illusion. It didn't seem to be, but he dashed up the stairs and checked every room. They were all empty, illuminated only by Jez's lantern. Osmund let out a breath when they had come out again.

"Do you really think they're still in the keep?"

"No," Jez said, "but I'm not always right."

Osmund rolled his eyes. "We haven't looked in the dungeon. Why don't we check there next?"

Jez glanced at him. "You were there when the demons attacked. We would've seen them if they had gone that way." Jez bit his lower lip. "I guess it's possible they could've snuck down while we were talking with Haziel. Good idea. We'll go there."

Osmund groaned. "I was joking about that."

Jez shrugged. "It won't take that long. After that, we can help search the city."

"That wasn't exactly what I meant either," Osmund said. "We've been going nonstop for hours. There are plenty of soldiers. Don't you think we should take a break?"

Jez's hand tightened around his sword. He knew it was hurting him, but the damage it was doing was minor, and he could barely feel it anymore. He shook his head as he led Osmund down the hall and to the stairs down to the prison. "It's a fourth order demon, Osmund. Soldiers won't be able to handle it. They probably couldn't even handle Lina."

"The king's mages are out looking too. Some of them are binders."

"You know this would be too much for an ordinary mage."

"It'll be too much for you if you're too tired to stand."

Jez held up his hand and sniffed at the air, but he didn't smell anything. He poked his head around the corner, but the hall was empty, and he motioned to Osmund that they should keep going.

"I'm fine."

"No you're not. You're losing yourself again."

Jez paused and looked at his friend. "That's not going to happen. Sariel shut away those memories."

Osmund looked pointedly at the crystal sword. "Sariel also has to respect mortal choice. You've been relying on that sword almost exclusively. You studied binding for a reason, after all"

"I don't know the best way to bind every demon," Jez lifted the sword. "I know this will work, though."

"You don't necessarily need the best way," Osmund pointed out. "Does it really matter if you use the second best way? Or the third, as long as the demon is gone?"

Jez let out a breath. "Not really."

"Maybe you should put the sword away, at least for now. It's not like it takes you a long time to bring it out."

"Am I really that different?"

"Since we've gotten here, practically all you've cared about is finding who was summoning demons."

"It is kind of important."

"Definitely," Osmund said. "But it shouldn't be all you're worried about. This is your first time in the capital, and you're a baron. You've ignored court politics. Did you even step out of the keep?"

"There wasn't really time."

"That's my point."

Jez pursed his lips and nodded. The sword dissolved, and Jez felt half dressed. The ache he'd gotten used to receded. He drew his physical sword, and though the weapon was light compared to other such blades, it felt heavy and clumsy, and Jez suppressed a shiver. Osmund was right. Jez had known drawing too deeply of his power might burn through his flesh, but he hadn't expected the trickle he'd been accessing to cause any lasting harm. He certainly hadn't thought it would affect his mind. He would have to be careful with how he used it.

His senses of mystical forces dimmed as they descended into the dungeon. Jez tried to make idle conversation, but he had trouble splitting his concentration away from their search. He looked down at his weapon, and his hand itched to hold his real sword. He told himself that was only because they were in the midst of danger. It was a reasonable enough explanation. He just wasn't sure if he believed it.

The first level of the dungeon was empty, though Jez couldn't help but glance at the two cells Osmund had broken out of. The melted bars still hadn't been repaired. Jez could almost feel ambient power emanating from them, though he was almost sure it was his imagination.

As they went into the lower level, the wards thinned, and he knew it wouldn't be nearly as difficult to access his power. No one had been down here in a long time, and the wards had been allowed to decay. None of the lanterns were lit, and Osmund summoned a ball of flame to float over his hand and light the way. They moved forward, but the floor here was uneven. Jez stumbled, and his foot splashed into a puddle. He groaned as a wave of stagnant stench rose from the water.

"Ugh," Osmund said. "That smells terrible. Can we just go back? They're obviously not here."

Jez started to nod, but paused. How had water gotten down here? He'd seen none on the floor above. Granted, it could've been here for a long time, but there was another possible explanation. After all, it had almost made them turn away.

He wove a ward against illusions of all types. It was an effort to push it past the wards, but as soon as he did, the smell vanished. Jez and Osmund exchanged glances, and Jez closed his eyes. He wove a larger ward, one that could encompass the entire floor. Someone cried out, and Jez and Osmund rushed forward. There, in one of the open cells wearing clothes that were more rag than formal attire sat Lina and her father.

CHAPTER 31

The two backed up when they saw Jez and Osmund. Lina's eyes were locked on Osmund. Their clothes were ripped, and Varin had a bruise on the left side of his face. He stood up straight and tried to appear confident, but his voice wavered.

"Baron, you will escort us to the king." He glanced at Osmund. "I will do you a favor and not report his escape, but he must leave now."

Osmund laughed, but he stopped when Jez glared at him. "Osmund has been declared innocent of any wrongdoing in attacking Lina as well as for the death of your men."

"What?" Lina's eyes widened and her voice was a shriek.

"You're right about one thing. The king wants to see you." Jez took a step forward and lifted his sword. "He wants an explanation for why you were summoning demons."

"What? That's ridiculous. Haven't we already dealt with this nonsense?"

"It was clever of you to hide the summoning circle in Lina's room." Osmund said. "We didn't find it until it was too late." He turned to Lina. "Or was it you that did the summoning? Is that why you're here? The demons got away from you, and you were looking for a place to hide?"

Varin took a step forward and moved to walk past them. "I will not stand here and be accused."

He grunted as a blast of wind knocked him back and held him against the wall. Lina stood on shaky legs and stepped forward, her hands moving. She froze when Osmund lifted his sword and held it to her neck.

"None of that," Osmund said, his voice dripping with rage. "We're not going to underestimate you."

"Why are you doing this?" Varin struggled to speak against the wind.

Jez waved at Osmund, and the lord slid to the ground as the wind died. He looked up, but all confidence had drained from his face. He tried to speak but couldn't seem to find his voice. Jez wove a ward, separating him from any power he may have. Varin's shoulders slumped, and Jez did the same to Lina immediately after. She glared at him, but he ignored it. His workings would fall in the level above them, where the wards were still strong, and he would have to redo them once they got back into the keep. For now, however, their power was bound, and it should easy enough to get them upstairs.

"We found more than enough proof," Jez said. "Will you come with us, or do we have to bring you by force?"

"How dare you!" Varin's face was twisted in anger. "You, a mere peasant…"

He stopped when Jez summoned a ball of water around his hand. The shifting liquid reflected the light of Osmund's flame, and it crawled up his arm giving it a wicked sheen.

"You can't be serious," Varin said, though he no longer sounded so sure. Jez glared at him, and Varin took a step back. "This has to be a misunderstanding." He looked at Lina. "We'll come with you, and clear up this matter."

Jez nodded and let the water around his arm splash to the ground, but he held his sword toward Varin. He motioned with the weapon for them to go first. At first Lina just stared at him, her eyes wide, but when Osmund cleared his throat, she scrambled to the stairs with her father right behind her. Jez's wards fell under the stronger working protecting the main level of the prison. They moved through it in silence and continued up to the keep. As soon as they were up, power flared in Lina, and she vanished. Jez was ready, and he wove a ward against illusion, counter her working. Before he'd even finished, he felt her power fizzle. She appeared, and immediately, he turned his power to weaving another ward of binding. He felt it slide into place between her and her power. Varin just stared at her as if unwilling to believe what she'd just attempted. He didn't even flinch when Jez's ward cut him off. Jez put his sword directly at Lina's back.

"Go," he said.

She let out a whimper but when she nodded, she wore a half smile that unnerved Jez. He marched them down the hall, drawing the eyes of servants and lesser nobles as they passed. They went to the where they had taken the king after rescuing him. Jez pushed open the door, and a breeze brushed past him. Papers had been taken from shelves and a map of the city had been rolled out. Haziel was speaking to the captain of his guard. Villia and Sharim stood behind the king. Sharim was weaving a working Jez didn't recognize, but the apprentice let it go when he saw Jez was looking. Haziel looked up when Jez stepped inside with the prisoners. Anger flashed in his eyes when he saw Varin and Lina, and for a second, Jez thought he might call for their execution then and there, but a quiet fury settled on his face.

"Varin."

Varin winced at the lack of title, and he bowed deeper than Jez had ever seen him. "Your Majesty, I don't know what this boy has told you but…"

"The *baron* saved my life, and he showed me proof of your treason. The only reason I haven't locked you up is your long years of service. If you're next words aren't an explanation of your acts, I'll have you thrown in prison."

"Your Majesty, I never summoned…"

"Guards!" The two men outside came in. "Throw these two in dungeon. I never want to see them again."

CHAPTER 32

"Your Majesty, I should go with them," Jez said. "We need to keep them cut off from their power until they get to the dungeon."

The king nodded and waved him off. Jez walked out of the room. Osmund started to follow, but Jez shook his head.

"We need someone here to protect the king."

Osmund nodded and went back in, and Jez followed the guards back toward the dungeon. Varin kept his head down. All signs of his previous defiance were gone. He seemed like a man defeated. Jez wondered if he really was innocent. Perhaps it had all been done by Lina. She still wore that same half smile she'd had since they'd come up into the keep. They were halfway to the dungeon when Villia caught up with them. She looked over her shoulder and seemed somewhat surprised.

"Sharim was right behind me." She was about to say something else when she turned to Lina. "What's going on here?"

"The king has commanded that they be thrown in prison," Jez said.

Villia rolled her eyes. "Yes, I gathered that. What's the purpose of the illusions?"

"What illusions?"

She raised an eyebrow and lifted a hand. Before she could do anything, however, Lina vanished as did his sense of a ward on her. Jez blinked but heard footsteps running down the hall. He turned to see Lina running through the passage.

"How…" Jez started but didn't bother to finish the question. He took off after Lina.

He'd only gone a few steps when his nostrils flared with the scent of sulfur. He skidded to a stop, dropping his metal sword and holding out his hand to summon his crystal one, but he hesitated, his mind going back to what Osmund had said. He took several steps back until he was right next to Villia. He motioned for the guards to get behind him. They glanced down the hall in the direction Lina had fled, but one by one, they complied. Light drained from the lanterns on the wall as the hall darkened.

"Baron, what's wrong?" one of the guards asked.

"Can you fight?" Jez asked, his eyes locked on the pair of shadowy figures that had appeared at the end of the corridor and that were slowly heading toward them.

"Of course we…"

Jez raised a hand and cut off the guard before turning to Villia. She looked him up and down.

"I'm not…Where is your sword?"

The figures came closer, never moving faster than a slow walk, but their images remained vague and indistinct. They were like living shadows walking down the hall, and where their hands should be, they had shadowy blades. Jez had no idea what they were, but he started weaving a ward meant to bind incorporeal beings and give them physical form.

"Do you have a sword?"

Villia sputtered for a second. "Well, yes."

"You should probably summon it."

Twin bands of light shot forward from Jez's hands, wrapping themselves around the creatures. They staggered for a step but kept coming, and the light continued to dim. For a second, Jez was seized by the irrational desire to run. He clenched his teeth just as the guards took off in the opposite direction. It was then that he recognized the supernatural fear emanating from the shadow demons. A smile crept onto his face. He'd experienced this before. It was one of the first bindings he'd ever done, when he'd faced the phobos on his first day at the Academy. He made two circles with his left hand and one with his right. Lights shot forward, splashing against the creature on the right. He sent another binding against the left one, and the desire to run vanished. Villia stepped next to him and held out a hand. A sword made of shadows materialized in her hand. She inclined her head to Jez and leaped forward just as the demons came into range.

CHAPTER 33

The demons moved faster than Jez would've believed possible after watching their slow advance. One blurred and impaled Villia through the wrist while she was still in the air. She barely had time to cry out before it slammed her into the wall. The stone cracked at the impact. Villia grunted, and her shadowy blade fell from her hand, dissolving before it hit the ground. She slid off the demon's arm, and slumped against the wall, unmoving. There was no blood though a faint violet glow shone from her wounds.

Hastily, Jez wove a ward, holding sunlight in his hands and crafting it into a pair of manacles. They shot forward and closed around the demons' legs. They stumbled, but a second later, darkness spread across the chains, and they exploded in a flash of light. Jez threw himself back, and when his vision cleared, the creatures were darker than they had been before and were standing in the spot he'd been in just a moment ago. He held out his hand, drawing of Luntayary's power and calling forth the crystal sword. It appeared just as one of the shadows brought a blade down on him. Jez batted it aside and tried to stab, but once again, it moved too quickly and danced out of the way with an almost casual ease. A chill ran down his spine as he realized these beings were masters of the blade.

Villia groaned and tried to get to her feet, but it was obviously a struggle, and she gave up, never having fully shaken off her daze. Jez rolled to his feet and tried to make it to her, but the demons blocked his way. She wasn't moving. Rock dust from the broken stone covered her. Jez caught the blade of one shadow, but the other stabbed him in the arm. Cold shot out from the wound, filling him from his fingers to his shoulder, and he lost all feeling in his arm as it fell limp to his side. He glanced at Villia, but the demons were ignoring her.

"Rock dust," he said under his breath.

He backed off several steps and started weaving another ward, this one drawing power from stone. One of the bricks in the floor exploded, completely covering the shadows in rock dust. Almost instantly, Jez was bathed in sweat. With anything other than the brute application of force, earth was difficult for him to deal with, but he couldn't think of anything else. Jez closed his fist, and the dust solidified, slowing the creatures. One of the demons slashed at him, but Jez caught it on his blade. Weakened by the earth binding, crystal sword cut through shadowy blade, and the tip of the demon's bladed arm fell to the ground. Jez lunged forward. The creature tried to move out of the way, but binding had removed its unnatural speed, and Jez's blade pierced the chest. He drew it out almost immediately and turned to face the other, not even watching as the first shadow died.

A blade came at him from his left, and he tried to back away, but the limp arm was awkward. He wasn't used to not having control over it, and the stone covered shadow cut a gash from his elbow to his hand before Jez moved out of the way. He didn't even feel the wound, which he suspected was a very bad thing. He tried to strike back, but either this demon hadn't been as strongly affected by the binding, or it was simply more skilled than its companion. Jez's sword missed it by inches as it backed away. The lack of resistance threw Jez off balance, and he recovered just as the demon thrust. The blade went into Jez's stomach, and cold ran over his entire body. He cried out, but his voice sounded weak. He tasted blood on his lips. The last thing he saw before he lost consciousness was Villia rising and slashing off the demon's head.

CHAPTER 34

Jez woke as an orange sashed healer was standing over him. The grandfatherly man held his hands clasped over Jez's stomach, and warmth flooded into his body. He took in a deep breath and the healer smiled.

"I'm glad to see you awake. We weren't sure you'd make it. The wound was bad enough but what that thing left inside…" The healer shivered. "No matter. It's gone now."

"What happened?" Jez asked.

"We were hoping you could tell us." Jez turned to see Osmund standing near him. "We found you unconscious in the hall. The guards said something about shadows, but they were so scared it was hard to get anything out of them."

Jez nodded, though the effort drained him. "It was some kind of demon. Lina got away and sent them to cover her retreat. Did you find her?"

Osmund shook his head. "We got Varin. He actually came running back to us, screaming. It's why we went looking for you. The king threw him in the dungeon."

"What about Villia?"

"What about her?"

"Is she all right?"

"I haven't seen her in the past couple of hours."

"She saved me," he said. "Maybe she went after Lina."

"Jez, her workshop is empty."

"What?"

"It looks like she left."

"No," Jez said as he tried and failed to sit up. "I convinced her to stay. She wouldn't just…"

Jez's words died out. He'd convinced her to fight, and she'd done it badly. She was lucky to be alive. She'd been hurt and should've been here. If she wasn't, and her body hadn't been found, Osmund was probably right. Of course, that was all assuming a dead afur would leave a body.

"What exactly happened?" Osmund asked. "How did Lina get away?"

"I'm not sure." Jez thought back to her capture. "When we came out of the dungeon, she tried to use her power, but I countered her and cut her off. Oh no."

"What?"

"I thought I cut her off. She turned invisible, remember? I thought I countered her, but it was too fast. She made an illusion of herself. That's why her expression never changed. She made me think I had warded her by fooling my protection sense." He remembered feeling the draft as they had gone in to see the king. "She even brushed by me in the map room, and I still didn't put it together."

Osmund let out a low whistle. "She's very good."

"That's enough for now," the healer said. "He needs his rest."

"The king will want to see him."

"The king will have to wait if he wants anything more than a few minutes with him."

"A few minutes will be fine," Haziel said as he came up next to Jez.

His eyes were hard, and his brow was creased in anger. "Baron, I was given to understand you were a skilled binder. Villia's apprentice has been trying to convince me of that, but I don't see any evidence. Would you care to explain how a mere child escaped your personal escort using only illusions?"

"Your Majesty?"

"I would not have entrusted her into your care if I'd known you were so incompetent."

"She tricked us," Jez said. "Even your guards didn't know."

"My guards are not mages. Give me one reason I shouldn't throw you in the dungeon alongside the traitor Varin."

Jez just stared at him for several seconds, unsure of what to say. Finally, he blurted the first thing that came into his mind. "It was all Lina. I don't think Varin actually did anything."

The king's face reddened, and he spoke through clenched teeth. "You're working with him."

"What? No." Jez started coughing, and the healer practically pushed Haziel out of the way. The king glared, but the healer didn't seem to notice. He put a hand on Jez's forehead, but Jez waved him off. "Your Majesty, I'm the one that accused him."

Haziel snorted. "A clever ploy."

"To do what?" Osmund asked.

The king rounded on him. "Don't take that tone with me, monster. You're lucky you're not already in prison. That can be remedied."

Osmund's eyes went wide, he looked at Jez, but Jez could only shrug. What could've happened to so completely change Haziel's attitude? Before he could say anything, however, the healer stepped forward. He flinched when he saw the expression on Haziel's face, but he stood firm.

"Your Majesty, I really must insist you continue this after Baron Jezreel has gotten some rest. It does no one any good to exhaust him further."

The king scowled but nodded. "Very well, but I want him under guard." He glared at Osmund. "I want both of them under guard with binders to keep their powers under control. If the baron does not provide a satisfactory explanation for this disaster, he and his attack dog will be thrown into the dungeon and suffer the same fate as Varin."

The king started to walk away, and Jez reached up and grabbed his sleeve. The king turned and gave him a look that could've burned stone. He pulled away. Jez tried to hold on, but he didn't have the strength, and the king's robes slipped away. Jez gasped, and Osmund moved forward. Jez shook his head, and Osmund backed up. The healer ushered the king out and Osmund went to Jez's side.

"What was that about?"

"He smelled like sulfur," Jez said. "I think Haziel is under the influence of a demon."

Osmund watched the departing king. "Are you sure?"

Jez shook his head. "Not really, but nothing else makes sense."

"He's controlled by Lina, then?"

"It looks like it." Jez's thoughts were fuzzy. "She's a summoner and a mentalist. Where did she learn it all?"

"But the king was mad that Lina got away. Why would she make him feel like that?"

The healer exchanged a few words with the king before shutting the door. He started to walk back to them, so Jez spoke quietly so the old man wouldn't here.

"I have no idea."

CHAPTER 35

Jez fell asleep shortly after the king left. For the next several hours, he slept in fits and spurts. Nightmares of his battles with Marrowit stopped him from slumbering too long. He kept worrying he wouldn't wake up. Every time he woke, Osmund was by his side though they never spoke for very long. Once, he dreamed the arm he'd been stabbed in was on fire. The pain was so intense his arm still tingled after he woke up. A few times, he woke screaming, his cries summoning whatever healer was on duty. Most of the time, they would only touch his forehead or give him a drink of water. Once, it was Paleel, and she clasped her hands over his chest. They glowed, and warmth spread through his body. His eyelids felt heavy, and he couldn't keep them open. He fell asleep a few seconds later.

The sun was shining when he awoke the last time. There was a bowl on a small table by his bed. Chunks of chicken were floating in a yellow broth. The soup was still steaming, and Jez's stomach growled at the scent. He grunted but managed to sit. Osmund, who was dozing in a nearby chair, stirred and woke. Almost instantly, he was at Jez's side, but Jez smiled at him, and Osmund relaxed a little. Jez took a few spoonfuls of soup while a healer, a young woman with dark hair, came to examine him. Her eyes glowed orange for a second, and she nodded before scurrying away. Osmund handed him a cup, and Jez drank deeply of the water. He hadn't realized how thirsty he was until he put the cup down and saw that he'd emptied it. Once he was done with the meal, he felt stronger, though the sight of the guards inside the sick chambers made his stomach churn.

"Have they been here all night?"

Osmund followed his gaze and nodded. "Haziel came in a little while ago, but Mage Rana turned him away." He shuddered. "That's one mean old woman."

Jez smiled. "Master Balud said some healers are like that when they're taking care of someone. You didn't have to stay here all night."

Osmund looked back at the guards. "Actually, I did."

Jez's mind was still foggy, and it took him a while to figure out what Osmund was talking about. "Oh right."

"Can you free the king from whatever is controlling him?"

Jez let out a breath. "I don't know. Without knowing if it's a full possession or just some kind of influence, I don't know what I can do. It's not like he's going to sit down and let me examine him." Jez shook his head. "I need more information. There's more going on here than we thought. Have we been declared prisoners?"

"No, not officially."

"Then, I'm still the Baron of Korand."

Osmund nodded. "As far as I know."

He called over the healer. She walked to him and inclined her head.

"Yes, do you need something?"

"Can you get me a canvas and some paints?"

Osmund smiled. Jez had used this technique to access hidden knowledge before, but the healer's brow wrinkled. "My lord?"

"A canvas and some paints." Jez smiled. "Don't worry, I promise it won't tire me too much. I'd very much like to paint right now. It helps relax my mind."

The healer looked uneasy. "I'm not sure. I should probably ask Mage Rana. I think she's still sleeping though. She was tending to you all night."

"I don't think you need to bother her. I don't even need to get out of bed. I just want to paint a little."

"Well, yes, I suppose that would be all right, as long as you didn't tire yourself."

Jez smiled. "I'll be careful."

Her head bobbed, and she scurried away to speak to the guards. A gruff faced man glared at him, but Jez didn't blink. Osmund stood next to him with his hand at his side. It could've been a coincidence, or he could've been preparing to summon his sword. The guard blanched but nodded. It took nearly a quarter hour for the supplies to be delivered. Servants who brought them in struggled to set up a small easel near the bed so Jez wouldn't have to get up. He always felt awkward when people were serving him like that, but this time, the image fit with what he was going for. An old man with ink stained fingers handed Jez a palette. It held half a dozen colors as well as three brushes. Jez took the biggest one and dismissed the servants. The healer was trying to look over Jez's shoulder, but she left at a wave of Jez's hand. He turned and stared at the canvas.

"Go ahead," Osmund said.

Jez rolled his eyes. "This isn't really something I can do on command. Talk to me."

"What do you want to talk about?"

Jez shrugged. "Anything. Is this your first time in Rumar?"

Osmund nodded. "I never made it this far inland before."

"Where else have you been?"

"Mostly the places you've been."

"But you come from the Narian Isles, right?"

"Yes."

"What were they like?"

"Hot," Osmund said, though the beginnings of a smile had formed on his face. "So hot, you thought you were sweating a gallon every day. There were animals of every kind you could imagine, and jungles so thick you couldn't walk through them. I used to hide there when the people got too hostile because of this." He waved his hand in front his of face and wrinkled a nose that was just a little too large. He smiled. "It was nice except for the people, and the water was so blue you wouldn't believe it."

"I did come from a coastal town," Jez pointed out. "I've seen blue water before."

"Not like this. It's almost like the water is made of sapphire. I think you would like it." Osmund blinked. "It's not working."

"What?"

Osmund pointed at the canvas. "You're not painting anything."

Jez blinked and let out a breath of frustration. The canvas was still blank, and the brush was dry in his hand. He was tempted to keep trying, but it wouldn't do any good. Sariel had locked away his memories too well, and even if he needed them, they were beyond his reach. He put down the brush. "What do we do now?"

Just then, the door opened, and Haziel stormed in, two blue sashed mages on his heels. The king's eyes looked as hard as diamonds, and he stalked over to Jez's bed and glared as if trying to drive Jez into bed with the weight of his stare alone. A second later, the binders cut Jez off from his power.

"Enough of your delays. You will tell me everything, or I'll lock you up for the rest of your days."

CHAPTER 36

Jez looked to Osmund, and the other boy nodded. He took a step toward the king, and the binding on Jez's power weakened as they focused on Osmund who had started blabbering something about how they were both innocent. Jez wasn't listening. He knew the binding to get rid of a possession, and he splayed his fingers. He stood up on shaky legs, and the healer ran to his side, but he waved her off. The king turned to him, and Jez pretended to stumble. He threw his hand forward, touching the king's head. He brought the hand down to Haziel's heart, forcing power through the barrier the binders had set and channeling it through his fingers.

The king scowled and shoved Jez back. Jez nearly tripped but managed to keep on his feet. The binding had been complete, and he hadn't felt any resistance. Almost instantly, he felt the binder's barrier slide back into place. Jez fell back onto the bed. Osmund moved toward him, but Jez shook his head and the other boy remained where he was.

"Well, boy?" the king said. "You don't honestly expect me to believe your monster of a bodyguard, do you? Did Lina escape through your incompetence or through your treason?"

"Have you seen her?" Jez asked. "Did she come to you?"

"If she had come to me, she'd be in the dungeon next to her father. Now, answer the question."

Jez sighed. "Your Majesty, she escaped because she's very good. She's one of the best illusionists I've ever seen."

"She's only a child."

"She's older than I am," Jez said.

The king snorted. "Is that your only excuse?"

"I don't know what else to say. She's practically a master. I have no idea what she's capable of."

"How convenient for you that one of the few people who could confirm that is missing. Would you care to tell me what you did to Mage Villia?"

"There were demons attacking your keep," Osmund broke in. "Half the people living here ran away. Why are you so surprised she's no different?"

"Muzzle your beast, Baron," the king said, "or I will have him thrown in the kennel with the rest of the dogs."

Osmund's eyes flashed orange. His sword flickered into existence only to vanish a second later as Osmund made a visible effort to calm down. The king never even looked at him, though the healer's eyes went wide. Jez searched his mind for how to ward against the indirect influence of demons, but it was a subtler part of binding, and while Luntayary might know how it was done, that knowledge was locked away, and he hadn't yet studied it at the Academy. The only thing he could think to do was tell the truth.

"Lina got to you," he said quietly, his eyes darting around to make sure none of the healers were close enough to hear. "She must've summoned a demon who could influence the mind. She's controlling you or at least influencing you."

The king balled his fist, and for a moment, Jez thought he would hit him, but Haziel took a deep breath. "First, you release the traitor. Then, you accuse me of working with her. You go too far. Guards, take him to the dungeon."

"Sire," the healer said as she stood between Jez and the king, "he's not strong enough to be moved."

The king's face went scarlet. "You do not command me in my own keep, little girl. The guards will take him."

The girl paled and backed up several steps, her head bobbing. She moved so fast, she almost tripped over her own feet. "Yes, of course, Your Majesty. Forgive me."

The guards came up to Jez and lifted him by the shoulders. Pain rushed down his arms, and he clenched his teeth to stop from crying out. They practically dragged him across the room before found his balance. Osmund walked in front of him with a sword at his back. Both had a blue sashed mage walking next to them, and the barrier separating Jez from his power felt stronger than ever. The king remained in the healing chambers as the guards led them away.

"This isn't really necessary," Osmund said as they led him across another corner.

"Sir, I'm afraid it is. The king has ordered you confined."

"I know that," Osmund said, his voice perfectly calm. "I only mean that if I wanted to escape," he let the words hang for a second, and Jez heard the unasked question, "you wouldn't be able to stop me."

A guard with a thick black beard let out a bark of laughter. Jez stopped, and the man escorting him gave him a harsh shove that almost pushed him off his feet. He stumbled into Osmund. Jez's voice was barely above a whisper.

"Don't hurt them."

The bearded guard heard him and laughed. "What do you expect him to do?"

The next second, the guard was knocked of his feet as wings emerged from Osmund's back. The others cried out, but before they could draw their weapons, Ziary stood in their midst. The light from his wings was almost blinding. A blast of wind rushed out from the scion, though it parted around Jez. Everyone else was pushed to the ground. Some grunted and tried to get up, but the wind was too strong. The ward between Jez and his magic wavered as the binder tried to split his power between Jez and Osmund, no doubt hoping the extra energy would help bind Ziary.

Jez reached for his power. The ward bent, and the mage's eyes widened, but Ziary swung his flaming sword at the man. The ward vanished entirely, and Jez cut off the two binders from their power. Ziary's sword stopped an inch from the man's face. He went pale, and abruptly, he fainted. Ziary offered Jez a hand, and Jez took it. There was a rush of wind that lifted them off the ground, and they flew down the hall, turning several corners faster than Jez could keep track. Before long, they stopped in the middle of a hall Jez didn't recognize.

"What do we do now?" Ziary asked.

"The guards will be looking for us," Jez said. "We can't stay in the keep."

"All the ways in and out will be guarded. Even if we did get out of the keep, we'd never get out of the grounds."

Jez glanced from a nearby window to Osmund. "We don't really have to go through the grounds. The wall is only so high, after all."

"What do you mean?"

Jez smiled. "How are your wings?"

Jez cried out, half in fear, half in sheer excitement as Ziary jumped toward the window. Strong hands gripped him, and for a moment, the ground rushed up toward them. They'd been on the third floor, and it only took a couple of heartbeats for them to reach the ground. They were mere inches away when Ziary's wings caught the wind. Jez laughed as an air current carried them higher than the height of the keep itself.

The grounds stretched out before them. The main building was made of pale gray stone that would seem to be gold in the light of the rising sun. It was bigger even than Jez's manor in Randak. A series of smaller buildings were scattered about the grounds-storage areas and stables. The walls surrounding the grounds were thick enough that three men could walk atop them side by side. Towers rose at regular intervals giving a good view of city beyond and providing an ideal place from which to launch arrows or other missiles. Rumar Keep had been built for war. People milled about, but no one looked up. Three men on armored horses rode out of a building that Jez assumed was a stable. They thundered toward the entrance to the grounds shouting for the drawbridge to be lowered.

"They're looking for us," Jez cried out.

"I can't keep this up," Ziary said. "My wing is still hurt."

"Can you get us over the wall?"

"We're about to find out."

Ziary spread his wings in a glide, but he leaned heavily to the right. Jez struggled to look up. Ziary's right wing was still crooked from his injury, and he was having trouble keeping aloft. A gust of wind caught them, and their course straightened as they lost altitude. They were heading east, directly into the rising sun. The wall rushed toward them and one of the guards patrolling it pointed. Jez cried out as they flew over the wall. They were too low. His foot slammed into the stone sending a jolt of pain up his leg. The impact threw off Ziary's balance, and they tumbled in the air. The world spun, and Jez could barely make out the building they were heading toward. There was a scream, though Jez couldn't tell if it had come from him or from Ziary. The scion tried to flap his good wing, but it did no good. Ziary slammed into the building, and they bounced off onto the ground. Jez groaned, and Ziary's form melted away to reveal Osmund. The larger boy rose, seemingly uninjured, and though it hurt Jez to move, he forced himself to stand up.

"We need to get out of here. They saw us at the end."

Osmund nodded and helped Jez walk as they headed into the streets of the city.

CHAPTER 37

Jez had spent most of his life in the city of Randak. As the main port of the barony of Korand, it had been a busy city, filled with people from all over the world. He thought he'd be prepared for any city, but Rumar was something else entirely.

People crowded the streets so tight it was difficult to move. More than once, he was jostled aside, though a few apologized to him when they saw he was injured. They kept an eye out for guards, but they never saw any. Osmund took him down streets seemingly at random before stopping in front of a large building with two candles painted on a sign in front. He pushed open the door and stepped inside.

Like the city, the inn was crowded. Every table was completely full, and a man played a lute in one corner while another man juggled colored balls. A fat man, presumably the innkeeper waddled over to them and looked Jez up and down. He raised an eyebrow. Jez blushed and pulled his sick robe tight around him.

"Greetings, young master," the man said. "I run a clean establishment. We can't have the sick here."

"I'm not sick." Jez pointed at a scrape along his arm that he'd gotten when Ziary crashed. "I was hurt."

"Is that so? Well, I don't want you in my common room."

"Do you have a room available?" Osmund asked.

The innkeeper cleared his throat, and his eyes wandered up to Osmund's face. He took a step back but sputtered for a second before nodding. "Yes sir. There's one left, but we cater to wealthy merchants and the like." He eyed Jez. "I don't think you could afford it."

Osmund scowled, and produced two heavy gold coins and pressed them into the innkeeper's palm. The man looked at the coins, and his demeanor instantly brightened. He led Jez and Osmund to a door in the back of the room, ignoring the looks the other patrons gave them. They went up a flight of stairs and to the end of a hall. The room he led them to was nearly as big as Jez's quarters in the keep, though it wasn't so opulently decorated. A wide bed dominated the room, and a tall window overlooked the city. The only other pieces of furniture were a pair of chairs and a small table carved to look like it had bird's legs. Jez sank into one of the chairs and let out a breath. The innkeeper bowed and handed Osmund a key. He turned to go, but Osmund grabbed his arm and handed him another coin.

"We weren't here," he said.

The innkeeper looked from Osmund to Jez. Suddenly, he looked less sure of himself, but nodded. He snatched his hand away and scurried back the way they had come.

"That won't work, you know." Jez said. "I'm in a sick robe, and you're a giant. Everybody saw us. It won't be long before Haziel hears about it."

"I know," Osmund said. "What do you want to do? The city gates are probably being watched by now, but I'm sure we could get out of the city if we had to. Lantian is only a few days away. We could find a speaking stone there, and contact the Academy. The chancellor could send help, or maybe the queen."

Jez thought about it for a second. By all accounts, Queen Istar was one of the most brilliant military minds alive, and he would give much to have her aid, but he shook his head. "I don't think there's time for that. If Maries is as bad as Villia says, he could have his entire army summoned by the time we got back. If that happens, I don't think even the queen would be able to stop him."

"I was afraid you'd say that. How do we find him, and how do we stop him when we do?"

Jez's mouth went dry, and he realized he was reaching for a sword that wasn't there. "I think I'll have to transform. I might even have to go all the way."

Osmund pursed his lips, but he didn't disagree. They were desperate, and a demon of the fourth order was so powerful, it was almost beyond imagining. Without transforming into Luntayary and fully embracing the pharim's power, Jez could think of no way to stand against Maries. The only problem was Luntayary's power couldn't be fully contained by human flesh. If he drew that power too deeply, the radiant energy would consume his body from the inside out.

CHAPTER 38

They stayed in the inn for a few hours. Osmund went out to get clothes and bandages for Jez's wounds while Jez kept a watch through the window. He placed a ward on the hall that would warn him anytime someone approached, but he took it down the fourth time one of the inn's patrons set it off. He never saw guards in the street, and as impossible as it seemed, he began to hope they had called off the search. Once Osmund returned, and Jez had dressed and bandaged his wounds, they went back out into the city.

Avoiding the guards turned out to be fairly simple. They never saw any, which was conspicuous in and of itself. The people just went about their day to day lives, oblivious to the events of the keep. Jez looked for any sign of demons, but the only smells were the normal scents of a city. People sweated under the sun. The scent of coal hung heavy near a blacksmith. Bakers displayed wares at their stands, and the smell made Jez's mouth water. It was only when he neared the gate that he finally caught the scent of sulfur. It was the only place he'd seen guards. A man and a woman stood in front of the gate, refusing to let anyone out. They reeked of sulfur, and as Jez neared, they turned toward him. Their movements mirrored each other so precisely, Jez doubted it was natural. He ducked his head and tried to fade back into the crowd.

"There are probably men armed with bows on the walls," Osmund said. "They don't want us to fly over them again."

"They're warded against illusions too," a woman said.

Jez turned to her, but before he could say anything, her wrinkled face smoothed and her silver hair became jet black. Her clothes flickered to violet for a second but returned to brown homespun after a moment.

"Villia," Jez said, remembering at the last minute to keep his voice down. "What are you doing here?"

"Trying to get out of the city," she said. "Do you have any ideas?"

"We weren't really planning on doing that," Jez said. "What happened to you? Why did you run?"

She narrowed her eyes. "You've been cast out of the keep, the king is your enemy, and there is a demon general of the abyss loose somewhere in the city. I was nearly killed fighting a battle I had no business fighting. Of course I'm going to run. What I'm wondering is why you're not running."

"There's a demon general loose somewhere in the city," Jez said in a level voice.

Villia let out a breath. She waved for them to follow and led them away from the crowded streets and into an alley.

"You're just a mortal," she said. "No one could expect you to stand up to Maries."

"No one expected me to stand up to Marrowit either," Jez pointed out. "We could use your help."

Villia laughed. "Help? You need more help than anything I can give. Call Sariel if you want. See what help he can give."

Jez scowled, but his expressions softened. "Can I do that?"

She shook her head. "Not even you can summon a pharim high lord."

"What about another Shadowguard?" Osmund asked.

Jez turned to him. "What?"

"Another Shadowguard. You guarded Marrowit. Shouldn't there be some other Shadowguard to watch over Maries?"

Jez looked at Villia and raised an eyebrow. "I don't know. Is there?"

Villia looked at him for several seconds. Then, her face twisted in anger. "By the seven, why didn't we think of that before? A demon as powerful as Maries would have to have a Shadowguard set to watch over him. They should've showed up the moment anyone tried to free him. I don't know why they didn't."

"Shadowguard can be bound," Jez pointed out. "Did Lina's book say anything about doing that?"

Villia shook her head. "It was all about demons, not pharim. Perhaps whoever that book belonged to had other resources."

"What you mean whoever the book belonged to? It was Lina's."

Villia shook her head. "No, it wasn't."

Jez stared at her. "Of course it was. We found it in her room. The summoning circle was burned into her floor."

"I know that," Villia said, "but it wasn't her."

"Who else would it be?"

"I'm not sure, but I found her wandering the streets in a half daze. She's terrified of the demons and of the guards. She's doing everything she can to leave the city."

"She probably has you fooled too." Jez practically spat the words out. "She's managed that with just about everyone."

Villia snorted. "Deceiving someone like you is easy. You have no talent for lies and misdirection. It's not such a simple matter to fool a Veilspeaker."

"But you're not a Veilspeaker."

"I'm close enough. Believe me, she wasn't lying. In any case, once I got the chance, I examined her more closely. She has great ability in shadow magic and a fair amount in secrets, but she doesn't have the ability to summon anything more than a minor imp. Even that would be a stretch."

"But if it wasn't her, then who?"

"I have no idea," Villia said. "Would you like to talk to her?"

"You know where she is?"

"Of course. I've been protecting her ever since I left the keep."

CHAPTER 39

Villia led them down another dark alley, though this one made the first one seem like a paradise. The emptiness felt odd after the overcrowded city streets. A man slept in a corner on a pile of rags. He stirred as they approached but didn't get up. The place reeked of cheap ale and unwashed flesh, and Jez resisted the urge to hold his nose. Villia reached for a wall, and her hand passed right through it. A short gasp escaped Jez's throat. Villia pulled, and a door appeared seemingly out of nowhere. She glanced at them and stepped through the wall. Jez and Osmund exchanged glances.

"I'll go first," Osmund said.

He stepped forward and gingerly put his hand on the spot Villia had walked through. His finger sank in, and he nodded. He moved forward, ducking slightly, and disappeared. Immediately, he cried out, and Jez reached for his power. The crystal sword flickered into existence, but it only lasted a second before disappearing.

"Sorry," Osmund said. "The ceiling is lower than I expected. I hit my head. It's safe. You can come in."

"Don't do that," Jez said before following through the illusionary wall.

The room on the other side was barely big enough to be called such.

The floor was nothing more than padded dirt, and black spots of mold grew on the walls. Lina sat huddled in one corner. Her dress had once been a fine gown of purple silk but was now covered in dirt, and the fabric was torn in several places. More than one spot had dried blood crusted on it. The illusion covering her scar was gone. Her face looked plain, and he realized he'd never seen her without her face decorated in powders. She was staring at Osmund, but seemed to lack the strength to be afraid. Her eyes, red from crying, flickered to Jez and then to Villia.

"Have you brought them to kill me?"

"I brought them to help you."

"Help her," Osmund's voice boomed in the small room. "She had me thrown out of the Academy. She put me on trial. She wanted to have me beaten or worse. She deserves whatever she gets."

"Consider your words carefully." There was the slightest hint of echo in Villia's voice, making it sound more ominous. "Do you really think she deserves to be hunted like an animal by demons and men alike?"

Some of the anger drained from Osmund's face, but he didn't respond. Villia looked at Jez who shook his head.

"Even if I believed she didn't summon the demon, we can't help her leave the city. There's too much we have to do here."

"What you want to do here will only get you killed," Villia said. "At least by helping this girl, you can do some good. Isn't that what you want?"

"I can't leave a powerful demon in control of the King of Ashtar."

"You can't do anything to stop him," Villia said. "You don't even know where he is."

"He has to be back in the keep," Jez said. "There are no other demons in the city except for maybe at the gates, and that wasn't nearly strong enough to be Maries."

"You want to get back into the keep?" Osmund asked. "That place we almost killed ourselves getting out of?"

"I know, but there's nowhere else Maries could be. We have to find a way back in."

"Can you save my father?" Lina asked. Jez looked at her. Her voice had been strong and had caught him by surprise. She met his gaze with steel in her eyes. "If you can rescue him, I'll help you."

Osmund snorted. "What do you think you can do to help us?"

"Why do you think my father and I were hiding in the dungeon? We certainly weren't going to lock ourselves up. There's a secret passage in the lower level of the dungeon that leads out."

"You can get us in?"

She sat up straight and returned his glare. For a second, she exuded the pride and haughtiness that he'd come to expect from all nobles, but then the light in her eyes faded, and she slumped her shoulders. "If you promise to help my father."

Jez glanced at Osmund. "It's not that simple. We all thought it was you that was summoning the demons. If it wasn't, it has to be your father."

"It was not my father," Lina said. "It was the king."

Jez and Osmund exchanged glances. "What?"

"He could've gotten into my room. No one would stop him from going anywhere he pleases in the keep."

"It does make sense, in an odd sort of way," Villia said. "If he summoned the wrong demon, it might have been able to control him. It would explain why he got so unreasonably angry when Lina got away."

"But can we be sure it's not Varin?"

"For all his flaws," Villia said, "I don't think Varin would allow this to happen to his daughter."

Jez considered for a second, trying to find a flaw in the logic. There were a couple, but none that measured up to the single unavoidable truth. He had no choice.

"Fine," Jez said. "Show me the way inside."

CHAPTER 40

"A graveyard?" Jez asked as Lina led them through the iron gate near the Creator's shrine.

They were near the northern edge of town. The graveyard took up an entire city block and was relatively empty. Lina led them between a row of markers and shrugged.

"It doesn't do much good to have a secret passage if everyone can see you coming in and out of it."

"Fine," Jez said. "Let's just get through here as fast as we can. This place makes my skin crawl."

She turned and raised an eyebrow. She wore a half smile on her face "You study binding."

"And?"

"You deal with monsters and demons every day, and a graveyard bothers you so much?"

"She does have a point," Osmund said.

Jez glared at him but addressed Lina. "You're telling me it doesn't bother you?"

She rolled her eyes. "I don't like it, but I also don't like riding in a stuffy coach. I'll do them both though, and I won't complain about it."

"Maybe you should just lead the way and not talk so much."

Lina snorted. "I would've thought Dusan would teach you better manners."

He narrowed his eyes. "He was too busy summoning demons."

"That really happened, then? I mean I'd heard what everyone said, but there's been no official word on what Dusan was doing other than dealing with forces best left alone." She grinned. "You know, the typical ambiguous statement from the crown when they don't want to confirm something."

Jez's mouth snapped shut, and he looked away. He needed to get a handle on himself, especially if he was distracted enough to let something like that slip. Lina cocked her head but didn't say anything else. She continued walking through the graveyard, finally coming to a stop in front of a large marble building. The flaming sword of the kings of Ashtar had been carved over the door.

"What is this?" Jez asked.

"The kings and queens of Ashtar are entombed here," Villia said. "If there's a secret passage into the keep, it makes sense that it would be here."

Lina nodded. "My father found it when he was a child at court." She looked away from Jez. "He was hiding from other children who made fun of him for being the son of someone raised to nobility rather than born into it."

Osmond started to say something, but Jez waved him off. Nothing good would come from bickering right now. Lina, seeming to sense this, moved forward. The metal bars of the door had been painted white, and Lina pulled it open. It squeaked so loudly that Jez thought it must've been heard a mile away. He looked around, half expecting the noise to draw guards or demons to them, but no one came. Lina stepped onto stairs going down. A thick carpet of dust covered them, but Jez could see the footsteps she had left in the dust when she'd gotten out. As Lina descended, she lifted a hand and a ball of light appeared.

The chamber below was basically a long hall. Alcoves lined the walls and statues stood atop stone crypts. A crown had been carved onto the head of each. The stones near the entrance were old and dust had been ground into the rocks, but as they moved farther away, the slabs in the alcoves became cleaner, the edges harder. About halfway down the hall, Lina stopped in front of the statue of a woman who almost seemed to look down at her and scoff.

"Queen Meeshan," Lina said. "Her ship was lost at sea four hundred years ago. Her body was never recovered." She started running her fingers over the wall and pressed in several places. "There has to be a release here somewhere."

"What do you mean? I thought you came through here?"

"I was leaving, not entering. The release for the door on the other side was easy to find. There should be one on this side too."

She had moved further along the wall and pressed a lighter stone for several seconds, but nothing happened. Jez walked up to her and put a hand on her shoulder. She jumped and looked back at him. He did his best to suppress a smile, but judging by the scowl on her face, he hadn't succeeded.

"We don't need to do that," Jez said. "Just show me where the door is."

She looked confused for a second before pointing the wall at the back of the alcove. Jez rested his hand on it and closed his eyes. It was different from the rest of the alcove. Magic had been woven into the stones themselves forming a web that stopped it from being moved. He tried to lift the door, but though the wards were older than the ones surrounding Lina's quarters, these were far more powerful, and they seemed not to have suffered the ravages of age. He drew back.

"Wow, that's impressive."

Villia walked up next to him and placed her hand on the wall. After a second, she nodded. "This is pharim work."

"Why would a pharim ward this place?"

"To protect the rightful ruler," Villia said.

Jez shook his head. "I can't open the door, at least not directly. Lina, where was the release on the other side?"

"About three feet off the ground. There's a stone that stands out from the others. I had to pull it down."

Jez nodded and closed his eyes again. This time, his touch was lighter and he wove his power through the strands of the ward. They pulsed when he got too close, and more than once, he pulled back. After nearly ten minutes, he found the release Villia had mentioned. He was sweating as he tugged the stone down. There was a click and the wall before him groaned and slid up. As the door moved, the wards brushed against his presence. He shouted, and there was a flash of light. He was thrown several feet back, but Osmund summoned wind to cushion his fall. By the time he got back to his feet, the door stood open. Everyone was staring at him.

"It's nothing. I just got caught by the wards. I'm fine."

"We should hurry," Lina said. "It'll be up for less than a minute."

Jez nodded and stumbled into the passage. Osmund helped him walk, and Villia came in right behind him. Shortly after, the door slid down, leaving them in a long hall, not quite wide enough for two of them to walk side by side. Osmund cried out, causing Jez to jump.

"Sorry," Osmund said. "I ran into a spider web."

"They're all around here," Lina said. "I lost count of how many I ran into on the way out." She grinned, and it looked odd in the light of her glowing sphere. "I didn't quite catch the ones that high up though." Osmund laughed, and she joined him. Then, as if realizing what she was doing, she turned away, her hand going to the scar on her cheek. "Let's go. It's this way."

The corridor wound back and forth, and they walked for almost a half hour, Osmund constantly complaining about spider webs, before they came to a staircase up. They found another raised stone, and Lina pulled it. The wall near them slid aside and they found themselves looking into a cell in the lower level of the dungeon. Jez couldn't be sure, but he thought it was the same one he'd found Lina and Varin in. They stepped into it and the door slid closed behind them.

"Okay, we're inside," Osmund said. "What do we do now?"

"We save my father," Lina said.

"That's not the most important thing here," Osmund said.

"No, but it is the easiest," Jez said. "He'll be in the level above us. We'll free him, and you can escape through the passage."

Lina nodded. Osmund looked like he was going to say something, but instead only shrugged. They went up, careful to watch for any guards, but the prison seemed empty. They found Varin without too much trouble, though he looked little like the man who'd so often stood against Jez in the political arena. His features were gaunt, and he groaned as they approached. When Lina saw him, she gasped and ran forward, tugging on the bars.

"Oh father, what have they done to you?"

"Lina?" His voice came out in a rasp almost too soft to be heard.

"I'm here, Father," she said through tears. "I'm sorry I left you. I'm here now." She turned to the others. "What are you waiting for? He needs help. Get him out of here."

Jez turned to Osmund and nodded. The other boy mumbled something under his breath. Ziary shimmered into existence just long enough for him to cut through the bars to Varin's cell. The man still barely seemed to notice until Lina went into his cell and embraced him. Osmund helped him to his feet and back down to the lower level. This time Lina found the entrance with no difficulty and smuggled her father inside. Osmund summoned a ball of fire as she stepped into the passage, taking her light with her.

"I won't be able to help you anymore," Jez said. "You're on your own."

Lina nodded. "Thank you," she said as she disappeared down the corridor.

CHAPTER 41

We should go to my tower first," Villia said. "I left certain supplies in my quarters that may be of some use, not to mention my personal library. I started looking through it when this whole thing started, but more eyes will certainly help."

"Can we get there without being seen?"

"I can craft an illusion that would keep us hidden," Villia said. "The king might have wards up against that sort of thing, though."

"We'll have to try it anyway. Lead the way."

Villia nodded and raised her hand. The room darkened, though the ball of fire above Osmund's hand seemed brighter. They climbed the stairs into the keep. To Jez's surprise, no one stood guard over the door to the prison. In fact, the entire keep was unnervingly empty. There were a few guards patrolling, but none came near them. There were no servants at all and only once did Jez see one of the nobility, a tall man who had long ago lost his hair. Even he was constantly looking over his shoulder until he entered a room. A couple of times, Villia felt wards woven around a particular area, and they had to find a way around it.

Finally, they reached the base of the southern tower and started up. They were two floors up before Villia let the illusion fall, though they still moved quietly. They had just passed the fifth floor when Villia paused and cocked her head. She went down a few steps to the door that led to the main hall on the floor and placed her hand on it

"Well, that's unexpected," she said.

"What is it?" Jez asked

"There's an illusion here. A good one."

Jez rolled his eyes. "This is your tower. I'm sure there are a lot of illusions here."

Villia shook her head. "I've been wandering the earth for longer than you can imagine. When I leave a place, I leave no sign than an afur was ever there. I took down all my illusions, but this feels like mine. It's probably why I never noticed it before."

"So you missed one."

Villia snorted. "Don't be foolish. Even rushed, I would never make such a mistake."

She moved a few steps back down to the door. Jez let out a breath. "Do we really have time for this?"

Villia turned to look at him. "Someone has been crafting major workings. You've twice been wrong about who that was. Don't you think it's important to investigate who is crafting illusions good enough to nearly fool a pharim who specializes in them?"

"But you're not a pharim," Osmund said.

She let out a slow breath. "Not in any way that matters, but I do still know illusions. This one is no insignificant working."

"What's on this floor?"

"A few supply rooms, nothing of any importance. Spare quarters to house any of my guests." She went silent for a second and met Jez's eyes. "And Sharim's room."

Jez's opened his mouth to speak, but he couldn't think of what to say. Osmund was shaking his head. Villia ignored them and pushed open the door and strode in, forcing the two of them to hurry to catch up.

"You don't really think it might be Sharim, do you?" Jez asked. "I mean he's so…" he fumbled for words.

She nodded. "We don't know who made this illusion. For all we know, it could've been the king intending to throw people off his trail."

"Is he skilled in illusions?"

"Not as far as I know, but it's possible."

They walked down the hall before stopping before a plain wooden door. Villia extended her hand and nodded but didn't open the door.

"Sharim's room?" Jez asked.

Villia nodded. Jez took a deep breath and pushed open the door. The room beyond looked ordinary. The only piece of furniture was a bed that seemed barely wide enough for the apprentice to sleep in. The blankets were scrunched up at one end, and a book Jez recognized from his time at the Academy rested in the center of the bed. He picked it up and showed it to the others. It was a beginner's guide to illusions.

"Why would he have this?" Jez asked. "I've seen him. He's no beginner."

"Perhaps to throw off suspicion. Things here are not what they seem."

Villia lifted her arms and her eyes glowed violet. For a second it looked like nothing would happen. Then, the room shimmered. The smell of sulfur flooded in, and the ceiling shed blue light. Jez looked up and gasped.

A circle of runes glowed in the ceiling. Jez recognized the combination as a binding circle, one more powerful than any working he had ever crafted without tapping into Luntayary's power. A being clothed in sapphire robes sat chained in bands of light. He was kneeling on the ceiling as if it were the floor.

"Jez," Osmund said in a quiet voice. "Look at his sword."

The blade hanging from the beings hip was made of crystal. Jez stared at it, not able to believe what it meant, but with the illusion dispelled, he could feel the power emanating from the blade. There was only one type of being in all of creation that had one of those.

"That's a Shadowguard."

CHAPTER 42

The circle holding the Shadowguard was immensely complicated, weaving runes in combinations Jez could scarcely imagine. It even seemed to draw power from the stone itself, a thing Jez had no idea how to achieve. He was still years away from being able to craft a working even remotely close to this, but fortunately for him, destroying was far easier than creating. He gathered his power and threw it into the circle. A triangle with a horizontal line through it sputtered and went dark as cracks spread through the stone. The pharim raised its head and looked down at them. He extended his wings. The runes glowed, but the one nearest him brightened briefly and went out. One by one, the light coming from the other runes flared before dying until the circle had gone dark. The pharim extended his wings and launched himself from the ceiling, turning in the air to land on his feet between Jez and the bed. He stood up straight, showing signs of neither injury nor fatigue, but of course, he wasn't human. Even his body was more a reflection of his will than an actual physical form.

The Shadowguard's deep blue eyes focused on Jez. "Thank you."

"You're the one set over Maries?"

"I am Shamarion, and you are Luntayary."

Jez blinked. "You know about that?"

Shamarion inclined his head. "Sariel told us of your fate. We are to treat you as a mortal, and not involve ourselves in your affairs unless you involve yourself in ours." A smile crept across the pharim's face. "I take it that by your presence here that you know of Maries and have decided to oppose him." Jez nodded and Shamarion spread his wings. "I look forward to fighting by your side again, Luntayary."

"You mean we've fought together before?"

"Of course. When the foundations of the world were being laid, we worked to banish the demons from this realm."

Osmund gaped at him. Villia smiled, but the expression faded when Shamarion glared at her. Jez cleared his throat. "Yeah, I don't really remember that."

"Ah yes, Sariel said he'd locked away your memories. Well, it's only a temporary matter, and you'll be back among us soon."

Jez blinked. Sariel had promised he would be allowed to live his life. "I will?"

"Of course. Surely no more than sixty or seventy years. Perhaps eighty at the most." He smirked, and Jez let out a sigh of relief. "I suspect it will be considerably less if you continue to involve yourself in matters like this. They are, after all, quite dangerous, but then I can't really blame you. It must be so tedious to go about in mortal form."

"Um, that's not really the point."

"No, of course not. My charge has been loosed upon the world. I need to bind him again." He turned to Jez's companions. "The mongrel can be useful, but I see no reason to take the traitor with us."

Osmund stiffened. "Mongrel?"

Shamarion turned to him with a raised eyebrow. "It is an accurate term, is it not? You are neither fully human nor fully pharim. I meant no offense by it."

"The more polite term is limaph," Jez supplied.

"Half-breed?" Shamarion wrinkled his nose as if smelling something unpleasant. "That's not accurate at all. He is far less than half pharim."

The response caught Jez off guard. "You mean limaph is a word in some other language? Which one?"

"Tirantian," Villia said. "It's been perhaps three thousand years since anyone spoke it."

"No one asked you, traitor," Shamarion said.

"Actually, I did," Jez said. "Or at least I asked anyone who knew. Look, can you just call him a limaph? It can't be wrong if no one even speaks the language anymore. Better yet, call him Osmund."

Shamarion thought about that for a second, and inclined his head to the limaph. "Forgive me for my careless words, Osmund."

Osmund looked at Jez who only shrugged. The larger boy looked unsure of himself. "Okay. I forgive you."

"Excellent. Shall we go deal with this mage and banish Maries?"

"Just one second," Jez said. "Who was the mage?"

"A boy, though he seemed to have much more power than one of his age should. I underestimated him. I only hope we can stop him from enacting his plan."

"It was Sharim, then, but he already enacted his plan. Maries is free."

Shamarion shook his head. "Maries was only the beginning of the plan, and he can only call so much of his army at one time. Unless he wants to spend a year summoning them, he'll need help. The mage wants to create gateways throughout the city and use those to summon the whole of Maries's army. With enough, he can bring them through in a single day."

"Is he strong enough to do that?" Jez asked.

"Not alone, but I do not know if he has allies."

"Do you know where he would be?"

"Such a circle would require a place of power."

"The throne room," Villia said. Shamarion sneered at her, but she continued. “If Sharim has taken control of the king, he may be able to use the power of the royal magic.”

“The traitor may be right.”

“Can you stop calling me that? I’m trying to help.”

“Will your help make it so you never turned away from your duties and rebelled? You are what you are.”

“She’s coming with us,” Jez said.

“Luntayary, I don’t know.”

“If Sharim was able to bind you, we’ll need all the help we can get.”

“I think it’s a bad idea, but as always, I will submit to the will of those set above me. It will be as you command, Luntayary. With your permission?”

Jez nodded and Shamarion drew his sword and walked out the door. Jez started to follow, but Osmund grabbed his arm.

“Did you know you outranked him?”

Jez shrugged. “I had no idea.”

CHAPTER 43

Shamarion didn't bother to go around the wards. He walked straight through them, disabling them as he entered. Before long, a group of soldiers ran at the party. Shamarion waved a hand and azure sparks flew forward. One hit each soldier, and they stopped in their tracks and looked around. One asked where he was, but Shamarion just continued past them.

"What was that about?" Osmund asked.

"They were controlled," Jez said. "He released them."

It happened a few more times, but each encounter had the same result. On occasion Shamarion would wave a hand, and the wall or floor would ripple revealing a glowing rune which he burned out. Jez recognized one as the broken crown of Maries.

"Will that hurt him in some way?" Jez asked.

"Probably not," Shamarion said, "but it's possible. Come, I can feel him gathering power."

Jez nodded and realized he could feel the same thing. The air felt wrong, and it wasn't just the ever present scent of sulfur. He held out his hand and summoned his sword. A second later, Villia did the same. Shamarion glared at her but she gave no response. Osmund looked at the three pharim weapons and sighed. He closed his eyes, and when he opened them again, they were the burning eyes of Ziary. The scion's form replaced his a second later, and he drew his own weapon. The guards at the door to the throne room barely had time to bring their hands to their hilts before they were hit by Shamarion's sparks. They looked at each other in confusion, though one drew his sword and held it up. Whether it was due to actual loyalty or out of a realization that he probably shouldn't let just anyone into the throne room, Jez had no idea. Still, before the unearthly forms of Ziary and Shamarion, his blade shook in his hands. Ziary didn't even resort to his own weapon. His hand darted forward and struck the guard on the wrist, sending the sword clattering to the ground. The others moved to draw their swords, but Ziary glared at them, his eyes glowing even brighter, and they took a step back. Shamarion actually looked disappointed.

"Disgraceful."

"Did you actually want them to fight?" Jez asked.

"They are *guardians*. They should not abandon their duty."

Jez shook his head but didn't reply, and they moved past the terrified guards. Shamarion flicked a finger, and the metal-framed doors swung inward. Sharim stood near one wall of the throne room with his hands raised. He was at the edge of a circle of glowing runes. In the center, Haziel sat on his throne. The king stared blankly in front of him, and he seemed to be having trouble keeping his eyes open. The purple barrier periodically flashed around him, but each time, it was a little fainter. As it faded, the king slumped a little more. Strands of power emanating from the circle latched to the barrier and drained its power, feeding it to the being standing next to Haziel.

The demon was the same size and shape as a human but with red eyes and blue skin. His hair, a darker shade of blue, had been cut short. His body was lean but with the same whipcord strength that many of the truly dangerous swordsmen had, those who relied on skill rather than brute strength. Unlike every other demon Jez had seen, this one wore clothes. His uniform was the white cloth that Jez had so often seen on officers at formal functions. A diving eagle token had been pinned to the right side of his chest, the sign of the supreme commander of the forces of Ashtar, a position that should have been held by the queen. He had other metals pinned beneath it. Jez didn't recognize most, but one was in the shape of the broken crown of Maries.

Sharim lowered his hands and laughed. All the uncertainty was gone from his voice. "You took longer than I expected, though I admit, I didn't expect you to free the Shadowguard."

"You came from Dusan's lands. You were his apprentice," Jez said.

Sharim grinned, and the expression on his face looked like it belonged to someone far older. "Something like that."

"It was you all along. You made the illusion of the circle in Varin's room. You searched Lina's room. You didn't really find the book. You had it with you all along. You've been with the king every time he's gotten angry."

"I was surprised you fell for it so easily. I didn't have to manipulate your mind at all, but then Shadowguards have never been the most subtle of creatures."

The blood drained from Jez's face. "Dusan told you about that."

There was flash of purple, and Haziel screamed. The light around him flared, and the strands connecting it to the demon pulsed with power. Shamarion let out a battle cry and launched himself at Sharim. An instant before his sword would've split Sharim in two, a blade made seemingly of bone darted in front of him and caught his weapon. Maries had moved across the room faster than Jez's eyes could follow. The circle continued to feed him power, he smiled revealing teeth of pure darkness. His dry voice made the hairs on Jez's arm stand on end.

"The last time we fought, you had the advantage. Let's see how you react when the roles are reversed."

"You're still outnumbered, Maries."

Shamarion drew back his sword and thrust with one fluid motion, but Maries deflected the attack with casual indifference. He rebuffed three more strikes in the time it took Jez to take a breath.

"Am I?"

A dozen pillars of flame appeared around the throne room. When they faded, each left behind a chezamut. The creatures growled, and as one, they attacked.

CHAPTER 44

Five of the beasts rushed at Jez. A quick slash dispatched one of them, but the others attacked so furiously he had to turn all his efforts toward defense. There wasn't time to think. There was only the instinctive reactions drilled into him by countless hours of sword practice. Blade met tooth and claw in movements almost too quick to be seen, but there were too many. It wasn't enough, and after a few seconds, gashes ran down his arms, and a claw had sliced across his stomach. He batted aside one claw but another sank into his leg, and he stumbled.

He looked up, and time slowed down as the trio of claws descended toward him. His own blood gleamed on them. Even if he could raise his sword in time, he'd never deflect all three of them, and he wasn't sure he could survive even one. With nothing more to lose, he drew deeply on Luntayary's power. Wings emerged from his back and strength flowed into his limbs. His wounds closed, and his robes shifted to a shimmering blue. One of his wings knocked a demon aside as his sword opened the stomach of another. The third scored a hit against his shoulder and dragged its claw down his chest. Jez barely even felt it. The power coursing through him was too much. It threatened to consume him. A flick of his sword decapitated the one that had wounded him, and he lunged at the one he'd knocked aside, impaling it. He threw his hand toward the last creature. The silver binding shot forward, crashing into the demon's chest. It cried out once before vanishing into the abyss.

The power inside of him was too great to be contained by his mortal form. He could feel it burning his flesh away. He released it, and his wings disappeared. He sank to the ground feeling utterly drained. His sword vanished, and it was several seconds before he could gather his wits enough to take in the situation. Ziary battled four of the creatures while Villia fought two. The others, presumably, had already been banished. Shamarion and Maries moved in a blur of light and power. The room pulsed every time they came together. Sharim was still at the edge of the circle with his arms raised as he chanted.

With an effort, Jez got to his feet. He tried to summon his crystal sword, but it refused to come, and the effort nearly sent him to his knees again. Instead, he drew his metal blade and started moving across the room. He was halfway to Sharim before he was seen. Sharim uttered a word Jez didn't recognize and one of the demons fighting Ziary disengaged and moved toward Jez, but that was all the opening Ziary needed. He batted aside a claw and immediately counterattacked, splitting open the demon's head. The other two fell in quick succession before the one moving toward Jez had made it halfway there. It didn't stand a chance when Ziary reached it.

"Now!"

The dry voice rang through the throne room like a hurricane. Jez turned and his blood went cold. Maries had driven his sword through Shamarion's stomach. Its end came out of his back. His wings twitched and liquid blue light bled from his mouth. Harsh syllables rang out of Sharim's mouth. The strands that had been draining power from Haziel lashed on to Shamarion. The pharim screamed as a hole of darkness appeared beneath him, and Jez gagged on the sulfuric smell. Maries lowered his sword, and Shamarion slid off of it. His limp form fell into the hole. The entire castle shook as the abyss consumed the Shadowguard. Jez's senses exploded as the boundary between the physical world and the abyss became paper thin. He could sense them. Maries's army was coming.

CHAPTER 45

Sharim staggered and fell to one knee. Jez summoned what strength he could muster and launched himself forward, but Sharim rolled out of the way. Maries darted in, and his bone blade flicked Jez's sword out of his hand. Before he could cut Jez down, however, Ziary interposed himself. Maries sneered, and spoke in a voice like crackling ice.

"I've just defeated a pharim warrior, little scion. What chance do you think you have?"

Ziary flicked his sword at Maries's leg. There was a rent in the demon's pants that Jez hadn't noticed. Red motes flaked out. "You weren't wounded then."

Villia stepped up next to Ziary, her shadow blade casting odd shades of its own. "And you only faced a single opponent."

"By the end of the day, my hoard will pour through that hole. What will you do against so many?"

Villia grinned. "By the end of the day, you'll be banished. Shamarion will be retrieved and the hole will be closed, that is, if you're not too much of a coward to face us."

Maries's eyes flared and he raised his blade. "Come at me, then!"

He hadn't finished speaking when Ziary charged. Maries flicked the weapon away as if it were held by a child. Villia was on him a second later, but the demon effortlessly warded off her attacks. Even when Ziary recovered and joined the battle, Maries barely seemed inconvenienced. Jez, however, kept his attention focused on Sharim.

The false apprentice was chanting, and the hole seemed to rumble with every word. Everything smelled like sulfur now. Every once in a while, Sharim would cry out, and the hole would spew forth a great column of smoke, and the smell intensified. He was trying to hasten the army's arrival. Jez raised his sword and charged.

Sharim moved aside, but Jez's blade followed him, slashing across the left side of his chest. Sharim cried out, and the circle dimmed a little. Jez's eyes went wide. It was dependent on Sharim's power. Without that to feed it, the circle might be disrupted. Jez threw himself at his foe, drawing on a reserve of strength he hadn't known he'd had. He even tried to call on Luntayary's power, willing to risk his life if would end this threat, but transforming was a strain at the best of times. As exhausted as he was, he couldn't get a grip on the pharim's power. Sharim reached toward Haziel and drew the smaller sword from the king's scabbard. Like Jez's own blade, it was a light weapon more suited to personal dueling than true battle. If Jez had been fully rested, he would've taken Sharim apart, but as it was, his movements were slow and sluggish. Equally tired from his ritual, Sharim barely avoided his attacks.

The room rumbled and a gout of sulfur billowed from the hole. Sharim stumbled and Jez thrust his sword forward. Sharim fell back to avoid the blow.

"Maries!"

The demon howled as Ziary's sword slashed across its arm, but in the next instant, it was by Sharim's side. Ziary and Villia joined Jez. Ziary bled fiery motes from half a dozen wounds, and Villia was favoring her left leg.

"The circle depends on Sharim," Jez said.

Ziary nodded, but Maries sneered. "You'll have to get past me to get to him, and I don't think you're up to that. Run, and I just might let you live."

"He's right," Ziary said. "A few more seconds, and he would've killed us both. You wouldn't be much help right now. If we survive today, we can come back stronger."

Jez shook his head. An army of demons would take over Ashtar and very likely the world after that. It wouldn't matter how much stronger they were when they came back, it wouldn't be enough. He couldn't let that happen, no matter the cost. He raised his sword and stepped forward. Ziary's arm shot out in front of him.

"He'll kill you."

Jez met his friend's gaze. "I know."

Ziary's eyes blazed, but he withdrew his hand. If Jez died, Luntayary would be unleashed in the fullness of his power. He wasn't sure if his pharim self was strong enough to defeat Maries or if he'd be allowed to fight even if he was. Pharim had unusual rules about that sort of thing, but he suspected Maries didn't know the answer either. It was probably why he'd told them to run.

"If this doesn't work," Jez said. "Do whatever it takes to stop him."

"I will," Ziary said.

"I will," the image of Ziary standing behind Maries said.

"I will," the one near the throne said.

One by one, a dozen doubles appeared all over the room. Maries reached for the one nearest him, and it shimmered as his hand passed through it.

"Illusions."

The images started moving around the room, though their steps were jerky. One darted forward and slashed at the demon, but his sword passed right through Maries. Maries laughed, but then the real

Ziary started moving in a circle, mimicking the movements of the illusions. After a second, Jez had lost track of him completely.

"How will you tell which one is real," Lina said from the door. She was leaning heavily on the doorway. "How will you know which to block?"

One of the Ziarys darted forward, and Maries's sword rose to meet the attack, but his weapon passed right through it. Another image lashed at his throat. This time, the sword left a wide gash.

Sharim threw his hands toward Lina. The images of Ziary vanished as she reached up and grasped at her neck. She screamed. Maries slashed at Ziary, his blade missing the scion by inches. Without the illusions, Ziary didn't stand a chance. Jez raised his blade and charged at Sharim. He was only a few feet away when Sharim saw him. Sharim redirected his working, focusing it on Jez, and the throne room vanished.

He was in the middle of a courtyard, chained to a wooden block. The manacles cut into his wrists, and the block left splinters on his face. He turned his head just enough to see the ax gleaming in the sun. He screamed as it came down toward his head

"I've sealed the circle," Sharim's voice shattered the illusion. "Get us out of here."

The images of Ziary were back and Maries was struggling to find the right one. He snarled. "The army."

"The army will come even if we're not here. They can't stop that now."

Three Ziarys rushed forward. Maries tried to block one, but they were all illusions. He grabbed Sharim in one hand and growled at the images before leaping into the air. He went almost to the ceiling and crashed through the window bearing the image of Sariel. The images of Ziary vanished, and Lina let out a long breath before turning her eyes to the hole.

"What is that thing?"

Villia looked like she was about to be sick. "It's a portal to the abyss."

CHAPTER 46

We need a rope," Jez said, "as long as we can get."

"Why?" Villia asked.

"So you can pull me out of the abyss when I'm done," Jez said as he stepped toward the hole.

"What?" Villia's voice was almost a shriek.

"We need to get Shamarion out. We don't stand a chance against Maries without his help."

"Jezreel, you can't go into the abyss." Villia grabbed Jez's shoulder before he could take another step. "Even we can't go into the abyss. Not and come out again."

"Maries came."

"Maries was summoned into this world," Villia said. "The focusing crystal made his form permanent, but I doubt he'd be willing to come into this world fully. The risk would be too great. He's still a creature of the abyss, and when his form is destroyed, he'll return there."

"You mean if Shamarion is destroyed there, he'll return here?"

"He wasn't summoned. He was sent. I don't think this has ever happened before. I have no idea where his power is. If it's still in the Keep of the Hosts, he's safe. If it's not…" She let out a breath. "It's different if you go by choice. You won't be able to come back, much less bring anyone with you."

"How do we get him back, then?"

Villia glanced at the hole. "I'm not sure we can, not without a focusing crystal and another greater summoning."

"We can't just leave him there. He's a Shadowguard."

"The Shadowguards are warriors. They have been lost before." The ground rumbled, and Villia gave the hole an uneasy glance. "We need to get out of here."

"But it's only one hole," Ziary said. "If we stay here, we can hold it against the army. They can't possibly come at us more than two or three at a time."

"Can't you feel it? Energy is building in that hole. As soon as it's enough, they'll come through, at least a thousand of them, and these aren't mortal beings. They won't care if their form is destroyed. They will throw themselves on your sword so that the ones behind them can get a little closer. We'll be overwhelmed."

"But…"

Jez glanced at the hole and took a step toward it. Maybe if he could summon his wings, he could get back out. Villia touched him on the shoulder, and he jumped. He hadn't seen her approach.

"If it was that easy, Shamarion would've already done it." Jez's mouth dropped open, but she waved away his concern. "I didn't read your mind. You were tensing, like you were ready to jump in. It's not really a hole though. It's a conduit of energy, and it can only function in certain ways. Sharim was right. There's nothing we can do to prevent those things from coming through. We have to do what we can to minimize the damage."

Jez looked from the hole to Villia. Finally, he nodded, but he pointed to the king.

"Fine, but we're taking him with us. He has a lot of questions to answer."

Ziary nodded and slung the king over his shoulder. Between one step and another, he returned to Osmund's form, and the four of them rushed out of the throne room.

CHAPTER 47

The keep was in an uproar. The shaking caused by the opening of the portal had sent everyone into a panic. The guards were nowhere in sight. Servants and the rest of those who had retreated to their quarters when the demons had attacked ran toward the exits. There was so much commotion that no one noticed the limp form of the king on Osmund's shoulder. Rather than going through the secret passage in the dungeon, they just left through the main door. The grounds were unguarded, and a few people thought to go to the stables to procure horses. Jez and his companions, however, just stayed with the main body of people. The drawbridge was down, and they crossed the moat without incident. Once they were on the streets, the crowd thinned.

"It doesn't look like the panic has spread to the city yet," Jez said.

"It will. I suspect Sharim had some sort of mental working over the keep so that the people would remain calm. Otherwise the fear would already be out here. A lot of people saw the demons though, and it's difficult to keep something like that hidden, even with mental magic."

"If there's that kind of working, why didn't you detect it?"

"Sharim is very good," Villia said. "Better than he should be at his age. Even instinctual magic can only take one so far."

"Do you think someone could be controlling him? Or maybe he's an afur."

Villia pursed her lips. "He's not controlled. It's not possible to force someone to complete a ritual. They're too complicated and the control offered by mental magic is too clumsy. As for being an afur, it's possible. I've seen him age, but we're not bound to one form, and growing up can be managed, but why would he want to summon demons?"

"Maybe he resents being forced to wander for so long."

Villia shook her head. "You don't know what you're talking about."

"All I'm saying is that it's possible not all afur regret rebelling."

Villia sneered. "No, you're wrong. We were all created with a purpose, and you can't imagine what it's like to have that purpose denied to you. You who left the Keep of the Hosts a mere dozen years ago and who will return within a century. We were banished millennia ago and are doomed to wander until our final judgment, never knowing peace or rest. We all regret what we did. Some of us have nothing left but the regret."

Lina stepped between them. "This is all rather fascinating, but maybe the middle of the street isn't the best place to discuss this."

Jez glanced around. Nobody seemed to be paying attention to them, but that could easily be an act. He could see the same thought reflected on Villia's face, and the afur nodded to Lina.

"You took your father back to the house?"

"I couldn't think of anywhere else to go."

Villia nodded. "It will be cramped with all of us in there, but it's a start."

"Can you hide the king?" Jez asked.

Lina eyed Haziel's limp form. She started to nod but shook her head instead. "The illusions in the throne room took all I had."

"I can do it," Villia said.

She waved a hand, and the king vanished. That drew startled glances from those around them, but just then, the ground rumbled, and red smoke billowed from the keep. Villia went pale as a wave of sulfuric scent washed over Jez. His blood went cold.

"Does that mean what I think it means?"

Villia nodded. "The army has started coming through the hole."

CHAPTER 48

The room had been tight with only four people in it. With six, they could barely fit. Varin huddled in a corner, hugging his knees and shaking back and forth. Lina knelt by his side, trying to comfort him. The king did nothing on his own. He would walk if led by the hand. If not, he would just stand still with a blank expression on his face. He alone seemed not to be bothered by the heat of so many people crammed into such a small room.

"Do we really have to hide in here?" Jez asked. "With their army arriving, they wouldn't bother looking for us."

"We're the only thing that's a threat to them," Villia said. "If they're not looking for us, they soon will be."

"A threat?" Osmund asked. "Last time we outnumbered them and we had a pharim with us." He glanced from Jez to Villia. "We had at least one, and we barely made it out of there alive. What kind of threat could we possibly be to them?"

Villia gave Osmund a level look before gesturing toward Jez. "What kind of threat could an untrained boy pose to the demon lord of nightmares?"

"That was different," Jez said. "I fought Marrowit in the dream world. I wasn't limited by human flesh."

"What are you talking about?" Lina asked. "That demon was destroyed by a contingent of pyromages when Mount Carcer was about to erupt."

Jez, Osmund, and Villia looked at each other, but no one said anything. Lina's expression went from confused to angry. She glared at Jez. "What's going on? Who are you?"

Villia put a hand on her shoulder, but she drew away. "No, there's more happening here." Lina turned her gaze to Osmund. "I thought you were the freak, but neither of you are ordinary mages, are you?"

"Lina."

Villia's voice was gentle, and a warmth blossomed in Jez's chest. He could feel himself calming, but Lina's face twisted in a scowl. "Don't try that manipulation with me."

Villia nodded, and when she spoke again, her voice was back to normal. "Forgive me. You have been thrust into a situation greater than most people ever experience. You've done remarkably well thus far, but perhaps you should take your father and go. Whatever danger follows us is unlikely to come after you once we're separated." She looked to Jez and Osmund, both of whom nodded. "I think we can get you out if we work together. You'll be safe."

"Until a demon army takes over Ashtar, you mean."

Villia inclined her head. "It's possible the army will still be stopped."

She pointed at Jez. She was nearly screeching. "You want me to go, but him to stay? He's just a peasant who was raised to the nobility by a traitor baron."

Jez tense his muscles but calmed at Villia's look. "He is a mage, and as you pointed out, he's no ordinary one."

She closed her eyes and took several deep breaths. Her skin cleared of the dirt smudges, and her clothes straightened and looked freshly washed. The scar faded from her face. She opened her eyes, but shook her head, and her illusions faded. She let out a soft laugh.

"It's a little silly, isn't it? Taking comfort in looking like that."

Villia smiled. "We find peace where we can."

She shook her head. "I'm a mage too. What can I do to help?"

"Nothing," Osmund said before anyone else could respond.

"I did save your life less than an hour ago."

Osmund glowered but didn't say anything. Villia shook her head. "You're not exactly a battlemage."

"Neither is Sharim."

Villia and Lina looked at each other for a long time before Villia turned to Jez. "Well?"

"Well what?"

"It's up to you. Do we bring her with us?"

"Him?" Lina cried out.

"Me?" Jez said at almost the same instant.

"You are…" Villia's eyes flickered to Lina. "What you are, and I am what I am. If anyone makes this decision, it makes sense that it should be you."

"But that's not fair. He hates me."

Villia turned her gaze to Lina. "Perhaps that is more a statement against you than it is against him."

"But…"

She lifted her hand and Lina went silent. She turned to Jez, pleading with her eyes.

"Why do you want to come?"

Her lips quivered, and she looked at her father, still huddled in a corner. She let out a long breath. "They have no right."

Jez's mind flashed back to the time he'd been standing over his father as he withered away under the sleeping sickness. Jez had managed to bring him out of it, but it had been too late. The greater part of Bartin's soul had already been consumed by Marrowit. That event, more than anything else, had set him on his path to battle against, and ultimately destroy, the demon. He gave a slow nod. Osmund gasped, but Villia smiled. She turned to Lina.

"Welcome to the team."

CHAPTER 49

"What do we do now?" Osmund asked.

"They've probably opened other portals by now," Villia said.

"Other portals?" Jez asked.

Villia nodded. "He'll use them to bring demons here more quickly. They won't be nearly as powerful as the main one in the throne room, but they'll all be linked to it. We need to find a way to close the main one." He glanced at the king. "It would help if we had access to the royal magic Sharim used in his ritual."

"Don't we need the throne for that?" Jez asked.

"Both the throne and the king, yes, but as long as whatever is affecting the king has a hold over him, we don't have either. Can you free him?"

"Maybe," Jez said as he walked over to the king. "I saw what Shamarion did to the soldiers, but I need a better understanding of it before I try it myself."

Jez put his hand on the king's forehead and closed his eyes as he searched for a sign of what was influencing him. It didn't take him long to find the web around Haziel. Thousands of strands latched on to both the king's mind and his heart, and Jez knew that so long as even one remained, the king would be under the influence of whoever put the working on him. Any one strand would be so thin it would be practically impossible to see. It was only when they were together that he could see them. It was unimaginably complex, and tearing this away wouldn't be as simple as taking down the circle around Shamarion. That time, his efforts had cracked the ceiling, and he couldn't risk that here. If he didn't do it right, he'd leave the king's mind damaged and vulnerable to Sharim's control.

It took him ten minutes of examination to find what he was looking for. He took several steps back and threw his hands toward the king, sending power into his fingers. A single spark, much like the ones Shamarion had used, floated forward and landed on the king's chest, right where all the strands came together. For a second, to Jez's mystical awareness, Haziel flared up as the strands were consumed by his binding.

The king looked up, his eyes widening slightly. Then, he doubled over and started to cough directly onto Lina. She squirmed, but there was nowhere to go in the tight room. After a few seconds, the king got a grip on himself and stood up straight, though he looked a little pale. When he saw Jez, he took a step back.

"What's going on? Why am I here? I warn you, Baron, if you have captured me to get some sort of ransom, it won't end well for you."

Jez gaped at him, but a after few seconds, he started to laugh. The king's face grew red, but his companions started laughing as well. After all they'd been through, the king's threat was ridiculous. Haziel looked like he was going to explode with anger before Jez stopped.

"I'm sorry, Your Majesty," he said. "We didn't kidnap you. We saved you from Sharim."

"Sharim?" The king looked confused for a second. "Villia's apprentice? What does he have to do with anything?"

"I think you better sit down," Jez said. Then, looking around at the crowded room which lacked any furniture, he shrugged. "Maybe just find a comfortable piece of wall to lean on. This is going to take a while."

"Wait," Lina said. They all looked at her, and she glanced at her father. "Can you do anything to help him?"

Jez nodded and walked over to Varin. He repeated his examination but shook his head. "Sharim didn't do anything to him."

"What do you mean?" Lina asked. "Look at him."

Villia walked to Lina and put a hard on the girl's shoulder. "He means Sharim doesn't have any sort of magical control on him. What people see can have a profound influence on them. Given time, an illusionist can do terrible things to a person, and Sharim had him for hours."

"But why would he do that?"

Villia shrugged. "Your father was looking for information about Dusan. Maybe Sharim saw him as a rival."

"A contingent." Varin's voice was barely a squeak.

"You formed a contingent with him?" Jez shivered, remembering his own joining with Sharim. He'd thought it had been because they'd done it wrong, but now he wasn't so sure.

Varin's head moved slightly and Jez thought he was shaking his head. "He forced me."

Jez blinked at him. "He forced you?" He turned to Villia. "Is that even possible?"

Villia closed her eyes but nodded. "It's a vile thing. Through a mixture of illusion and mental magic, an image can be burned into a person's mind so that they could think of nothing else." She gave Lina a sad look. "It normally destroys a person's mind. Your father must have an extraordinary strength of will to be able to communicate at all. It's actually a good sign that he's spoken."

For a moment, Jez saw the ax descending toward his neck. The manacles felt cold against his wrists, and the blade gleamed in the sunlight. It hissed as it cut through the air. He forced the image out of his mind. Lina was rubbing her neck, an indication that she'd experienced the same thing. Villia eyed each of them.

"The image will fade in time."

Jez wasn't sure if she was talking about Varin or him, but he nodded all the same. Haziel was looking from one person to another, obviously confused, and it took Jez a few minutes to explain what had happened over the past couple of days. The king's memories since being rescued by Jez and Osmund were fuzzy, and he had no memories at all after Lina had escaped. As they told the story, Jez found himself hesitating. He thought he'd seen Haziel angry before, but the red-face scowl that the king's face had so often taken on under Sharim's influence was nothing compared to this. Haziel's face was completely still, but Jez could practically see the rage boiling beneath the surface. When the story was done, the king spoke slowly.

"They think to take Ashtar from me?" His fists were clenched so tight Jez wondered if Haziel's nails were biting into his hand, and he half expected to see blood well up from beneath his fingers. "I won't allow it."

"Your Majesty," Villia said, "there's little you can do. I recommend finding someplace to hide. If we manage to take the throne room, we can send for you. If not, you should find a way out of the city."

"No."

Villia started. "What?"

"No, I will not run."

"But Your Majesty—"

"I am the King of Ashtar," Haziel snapped. He sounded strong, nothing like the shadow of a man he'd been only moments ago. "I will not surrender my kingdom to a boy who stumbled into too much power. Rumar still stands, and so long as it does, I am its king. That boy may have taken my keep, but I will take it back."

Without waiting for anyone to respond, the king forced his way through them as he headed for the door. The movement so shocked Jez that he just stared for a second. Haziel pulled at the latch, and it clicked, but Villia put a hand on the door. Though they were the same height, Haziel seemed to be looking down at her.

"Remove your hand."

"If you're captured again, they'd regain access to the royal magic. I don't think you understand the danger."

"The danger doesn't matter. Ashtar is mine. I am charged to defend her, whether that be against mage or demon."

"But what can you do?" Villia asked.

"The four of you can't stop this demon alone," Haziel said.

"Do you know what happened to your mages?"

Haziel's hand went to his forehead, but he shook his head. "I don't remember. I fear they may be dead, but that's not what I was talking about. You need an army. I happen to have one."

"An army that's under the influence of Maries," Jez said.

"When they see me standing before them, we'll see where their loyalty lies."

"Loyalty doesn't enter into it," Jez said. "They're controlled by magic."

"Actually, he may have a point," Villia said.

"What do you mean?"

Villia shrugged. "It's the royal magic. If the rightful king goes out to his men and calls them into service, it may well overcome whatever working Sharim put on them."

"Really?"

"The magic of kings is the magic of command."

"How sure are you that this will work?"

"There are no certainties, but it's no greater risk than the one we take by opposing Sharim."

"Still," Jez said. "He's the king. We can't risk him."

Villia smirked and inclined her head to the king. "How exactly do you intend to stop him? He's no demon for you to bind."

The king grinned. "You'd have to tie me up to stop me."

Jez looked from one to the other before letting out a breath and nodding. The king looked moderately surprised at the gesture, and Jez realized no one had actually asked for his permission on this. He felt his face heat up but didn't say anything. Haziel looked at Villia, and she removed her hand. He opened the door just as the screaming started.

CHAPTER 50

Jez followed Villia and Haziel out. Osmund came right behind him, and to his surprise, Lina was only a few steps behind. People ran past their alley, screaming. A chezamut leapt through the air and landed on one woman. Jez didn't think. He just threw his hand forward, and the silver binding shot out, running the creature through. The woman scrambled to her feet and kept fleeing, never even glancing in Jez's direction. He was out of the alley before he even realized he'd started running. Demons were mowing through the screaming people. Most were chezamuts, but there were at least a half dozen other kinds that Jez couldn't identify. He gripped the empty air and slashed, his sword appearing in mid-swing. His blade banished two more of the creatures before his friends reached him. Osmund, once again, had taken the form of Ziary, but Villia's sword was conspicuous by its absence.

"You've seen me fight," Villia said when she caught him looking at her hands. "I'm not good at it. I can do more if I use my power to hide people from the demons."

Jez nodded and moved to engage a trio of demons surrounding a family. The man was wielding a heavy wooden stick, probably a piece of firewood. It wouldn't do him any good. The skin of a chezamut was almost as strong as steel, and there was simply no way the man could hurt them. Jez's sword, on the other hand, was a different matter altogether. The creatures never saw him coming, and he gutted them like they were fish. The family looked at him, shaking. Villia grabbed his wrist.

"We don't have time for this."

Jez tore his arm away. "What do you mean we don't have time?" He gestured at the family. "What do have that's more important?"

"You're only one person. You can't fight an entire army."

Jez rushed forward and cut down a pair of wolf-headed demons. Villia ran to his side, but Jez didn't bother to look at her.

"I can't just stand by while people are dying."

"Haziel was right. We need an army. Our efforts would be best spent helping him gather one rather than engaging these creatures one at a time. None of these are so powerful that they can't be killed by an ordinary sword."

"Where are we supposed to find an army?"

"We're not far from a guard station. There should be a dozen men there."

"That's not an army."

"It's a start, and they can do more than you can alone."

A little ways down the street, Jez saw one of the large shadows that had attacked him in the keep. A group of men were shooting arrows at it. Most passed through the creature, but a few stuck, and the creature was starting to slow. Jez tried to summon his power, but his energy reserves were depleted. Though he hated to do it, he turned away and nodded at Villia. Together, they headed toward the king, who was already on his way to the guardhouse with Ziary by his side.

The guardhouse was two stories high with barred windows. Haziel pulled on the handle to the door, but it didn't move. He looked over his shoulder at Ziary and nodded once. The scion slashed with his sword, reducing the door to ash. Half a dozen soldiers stood inside, their eyes wide with shock. The surprise only lasted a second before two of them stepped into the doorway and drew weapons. Jez lifted his own sword, but the king stepped in front of him.

"Put your weapons down."

He spoke in the voice of absolute command. The soldiers had their weapons halfway lowered before they realized what they were doing, and they raised their weapons again. Haziel scowled and a violet aura shimmered around him so faint Jez wasn't sure it was actually there.

"Now!"

The word cracked like a whip, and the soldiers fell to one knee, their swords clattering to the ground. They went down so quickly that they sent up a cloud of ash from the remains of the door. The smell of sulfur hanging about them was so subtle Jez didn't notice until it was gone, but a second later the soldiers looked up. One had tears in his eyes.

"My king. I'm sorry. I don't know what happened."

"Pick up your sword. The people of Rumar need you."

As one, the men rose and drew their weapons. They charged out into the street. Six other men ran down the stairs, following their companions. They wore expressions of horror mixed with rage as they saw the demons in their city. They surrounded a nearby chezamut and cut it down without taking a wound. Then, they rushed down a street looking for more enemies. The king looked over his shoulder at Jez and smiled.

"Shall we see who else we can find?"

CHAPTER 51

The soldiers seemed braver and stronger than they should be. While none of them could stand up to a demon in single combat, two or three proved more than a match. The dozen men from the guardhouse formed a core of resistance, but others began to join them. At first, it was other soldiers, but after a few minutes, ordinary men and women were fighting by their side. They wielded knives or sticks or rocks. Jez even saw one washwoman pummel an ape-like demon until it went up in gout of flame. The woman seemed unharmed and continued to fight with a ferocity equal to any soldier.

"How are they doing this?" Jez asked.

Villia pointed at Haziel who seemed to be growing steadily stronger. Their impromptu army had grown to nearly a hundred, and more people joined them every few minutes.

"A king does more than rule, and he has called on them to fight. Did you think the title, 'Defender of the Land' was ceremonial? So long as he is with them, they are empowered to do battle with exactly this kind of foe."

Jez stared at Haziel with wide-eyed amazement. "Maybe this isn't a hopeless battle after all."

"Don't be foolish," Villia said. "These are only the lowest of Maries's demons. Once he unleashes his lieutenants, it won't be nearly so easy."

A pair of chezamuts rushed at them. Jez cut them down and leapt toward a bird demon. He sliced into it. It squawked, and there was an explosion of feathers that were caught up in a gust of wind before puffing out of existence. Jez went back to Villia's side.

"Are you saying he can't win?"

"I have no idea. Royal magic has never been used on this level. I don't know what its limits are."

They turned a corner, and the keep came into view. The drawbridge was still down. The king raised a sword he'd gotten from one of the soldiers, and the impromptu army thundered forward. Demons of every shape and size materialized, seemingly out of nowhere. The army fell upon them like a tide. The sound of men screaming was drowned out by demon roars. There were more of the demons than the people, though, and it didn't take long for the battle to turn against them. Jez and Ziary waded into the sea of the monsters of the abyss, swords flashing. With every strike, a demon died, but it was mere seconds before the creatures recognized the threat and started concentrating their attacks on the two warriors.

Jez and Ziary stood back to back, a circle of death in the middle of an army of demons. For Jez, there was no thought, no strategy. There was only the blade and whatever demon he was engaged with. He was dimly aware of his sword blurring. Demons who tried to parry his strikes missed his blade. It had to be Villia or Lina using their abilities to give him an edge, but his sword only looked a little distorted. They probably didn't want to twist the sight of his weapon too much and risk distracting him. If only he could tell them not to bother. He didn't need to see his blade to fight.

Without realizing he was doing it, he began to draw of Luntayary's power, but there was something else too, something he didn't recognize. His flesh was burning, but another power was holding the damage at bay, and strength welled up inside of him. His sword arm moved faster, cutting through the demons like a scythe cutting down wheat. Moments melted together, and he lost all track of time. After an hour or a day, the tide of demons stopped. Jez released his power and fell to his knees, breathing heavily. Ziary offered him a hand up. For the first time Jez had seen, the scion's scarlet robes were in tatters. Jez looked around. Many of the people with them had fallen. Only a few on the ground were still moving, but there were no signs of Maries's army. Everyone, Villia included, was staring at Jez in utter shock.

"By the seven," Villia said in a half whisper. "It's been…" Her eyes flickered to Haziel, and she caught herself, "ages since I've seen anything like that."

The king nodded, and there was something very close to reverence in his voice. "If only I had a hundred more like you, or even a dozen."

People peaked out of doors and windows, looking for demons and relieved when they didn't find any. Slowly, they began coming out. Some eyed the dead bodies on the ground, but rather than being repulsed by corpses, the people seemed to draw strength from them. More than one face showed a determination that said they would not allow these creatures to claim their home. In a few minutes, their army had grown to twice its previous size. The air around Haziel practically shimmered with power, and as soon as the king approached, Jez's fatigue vanished. He stood up, still a little weak. Whatever power shrouded Haziel had kept Jez's own power from consuming him, but it didn't stop the damage entirely. Neither could it reverse what had been done, but Jez could fight again. He looked from the keep to their army. This wouldn't be easy. Rumar Keep had been built for war, and they had no siege engines and only a few real soldiers. Then again, he would've never suspected a group of townspeople could beat back an army of demons.

He stood up straight, conscious that every eye was on him. He looked to Haziel who nodded, and Jez lifted his crystal sword in the direction of the keep. It glowed so bright most had to look away, and Jez wasn't sure if the power had come from him or Haziel. When the light faded, everyone began to cheer. He took a step toward the keep and the wall around the doorway exploded outward. The people cried out as shards of rock flew over them, though few were large enough to cause any damage. Jez looked up and paled.

In what once had been the entrance to the grounds stood a demon twenty feet tall. Its face was pasty white and rows of sharp teeth showed in a mouth that looked too big for its head. It was covered in plates of black metal, though Jez couldn't tell if it wore armor or if that was just its skin. It had four arms, each carrying a long curved blade, and its jet black eyes focused on the army.

"Oh no," Villia said.

"One of Maries's lieutenants?" Jez asked

Villia nodded. "Flinas, demon of violence, and one of the deadliest fighters in the abyss. I had hoped he would be last to be summoned. He could tear us apart."

The king snorted. His sword actually seemed to glow, and his face took on the stony expression of pure rage.

"Let him come."

CHAPTER 52

A cloth appeared over the demon's head. It drew back, and for a second, his head passed through it, but the blindfold followed a heartbeat later.

"That won't hold him for long," Villia cried out. "Your Majesty, we must flee!"

"Not while my breath remains!"

Haziel rushed forward, ready to swing his sword, but an image of Villia appeared in front of him, and the king skidded to a stop.

"This isn't a fight we can win," the image said.

Haziel looked over his shoulder to the actual Villia to her image and scowled.

"I won't…"

"Not in a head to head conflict. You'll only lead your people to death."

Jez thought he was going to order his men to attack anyway, but he nodded and the image of Villia vanished. Haziel waved his sword, and his people retreated to the city, though Flinas's roars never abated. They turned a corner and stopped in the middle of a large street. Their army was still growing by trickles, but other than that, the street was empty. The people had either fled the city or were hiding. Jez's grip tightened on his sword, but the demon didn't come.

"Sharim will need to guard his center of power until the army has finished coming through," Villia said. She pulled the book they'd gotten from Sharim out of her robe.

"The throne room?"

"Yes. He won't risk us taking a freed king there for fear that we'd close the gateway, so he'll keep Flinas guarding the way in."

"We can go through the passage in the graveyard."

Villia shook her head. "He had Varin for hours. He'll know about it and have that way guarded."

"But Varin didn't know where the passage was."

"He knew it existed, and Sharim is no fool. Now that we've come through once, he'll have the dungeon guarded. Only one or two can come through the passage at a time. He could hold off an army, and even if you were able to get in, you'd still have to pass through the dungeon, where its wards would block your magic. If you're attacked there, you wouldn't have a chance."

"We'll assault the keep then," Haziel said.

Villia shook her head. "Your Majesty…"

Haziel waved off her objection. "If what you said is true, I have no intention of trying to fight that thing, but if we attack, we might open the way for the baron."

"Me?" Jez asked.

The king smiled. "You're the best chance we have."

"We'll need you though, Your Majesty."

"No, I don't think you will," the king said. He touched his sword to Jez's shoulder, and though it was normal steel, power rushed down the blade and flowed into Jez, filling him with energy. "I name you Sir Jezreel, Knight of the Realm and defender of Korand."

Jez blinked and looked at Villia. "Will that work?"

"It will," Haziel said without waiting for Villia to answer.

Jez glanced at Villia, and the former pharim shrugged. "All schools of magic have those who are naturally gifted at them. Royal magic is no different. He's endowed you with a portion of his power. It's a powerful working, though I doubt he can do it many times." She looked at Haziel, and the king shook his head. "It should be just like you're fighting by his side."

Jez's mouth dropped slightly. He closed it and inclined his head. With royal magic, he could draw on Luntayary's power without it consuming him. He could fight, and just maybe, he could win.

CHAPTER 53

Everyone who had ever held a bow was given one. A few were armed with slings. It made Jez feel sick to see many who, under ordinary circumstances, would've been considered children.

"So are you," Villia said when he pointed it out.

"I know how to protect myself."

"You didn't when you faced Marrowit, and they're doing much less than you did then."

Jez watched as one let a stone fly with his sling. It smashed a clay pot, and the boy, no older than ten, smiled at the old soldier directing a group of boys and girls of a similar age. "Still, I wish they didn't have to do this."

"We won't be engaging Flinas, just drawing him away from the gate."

"Are you sure there won't be some other demon watching the way in?"

"Not really."

"I'll go with you," Lina said.

"No," Osmund said, but went silent when Jez glanced at him.

"I can help. At least I can hide you while you get inside."

Haziel came over and started speaking to Villia about the distribution of the weapons. Jez pretended to listen while he mulled over his thoughts.

"She does have a point," he said eventually.

"Do you really think we can trust her?"

Lina sniffed. "No one cares what you think."

Jez raised an eyebrow. "Actually, I care what he thinks."

Lina's face flushed, but eventually, it gave way to a scowl. "Do you want to fight all the way to the throne room? You'd never make it."

"We might," Jez said, "but you're right. We'd stand a much better chance if we could go unseen."

"Jez, are you sure about this?"

"She's not going to betray us to Sharim. That's all that really matters."

"If the three of you are done arguing," Villia said as she finished her conversation with the king, "we're ready to begin the assault."

The silent movement of the army was a sharp contrast to the sounds of battle that had accompanied them last time. The plan was simple. They would shoot Flinas until he grew angry enough to run after them. Then, they would scatter. If the demon stopped chasing, they would shoot him again. The only problem was that Flinas was faster than they were. They would run as soon as the demon started chasing them. Villia would try to use her illusions to distract the demon. Jez doubted they'd all make it, though. He felt like he had the weight of the world on his shoulders. They were resting their hopes on him.

As soon as they rounded the last corner, Flinas's eyes fell on them. It might've been his imagination, but Jez thought he felt a chill running down his spine every time the demon took a breath.

"Do it," Jez said.

Lina nodded, and everything darkened slightly. The whispers from those near him told him he'd vanished from their sight. He could still see Osmund and Lina, though they seemed hazy. He nodded at them, and the three started forward. Haziel's gaze lingered on the spot Jez been standing before motioning for the army to follow him. At a hundred paces, they stopped. Flinas glared at them, and a few people turned away, but most kept their eyes on the king.

Haziel raised his sword, and the bowmen took aim. He brought his sword down, and a volley of arrows flew toward the keep accompanied by dozens of stones flung from slings. Most of the missiles fell short, and a few clanked against Flinas's armor. A handful embedded themselves in the demon's face. Flinas just stared at them, apparently unaffected by the arrows. Jez found himself holding his breath. Haziel paled and moved closer. A rumble escaped Flinas's throat as the bowmen raised the weapons again. They loosed, and more found their mark, but still, Flinas didn't move. The king took another step forward, but before his foot touched the ground, the pale demon surged forward in a white blur. The people didn't even have time to cry out as he fell upon them, seizing a person in each of its four arms, having discarded his weapons in favor of his bare hands. Jez took a step toward them, but Osmund put a hand on his shoulder.

"The way is open."

Jez glared at him and looked back at the army. They had multiplied tenfold. Flinas tried to grab a woman, but his hand passed through her. Jez smiled as he sought out Villia. There were at least a dozen of her, each with arms raised and glowing violet eyes. The demon recognized what was happening and tried to grab one, but his hand passed uselessly through her image. Lina was staring, her mouth open in surprise.

"By the seven, how can she do so much?"

Her voice echoed strangely, and Jez realized she wasn't just keeping them invisible. She was keeping any sound from escaping. He grinned at her amazed expression. "You wouldn't believe me if I told you. Let's go."

She nodded and they started for the broken door of the keep. She threw one more glance over her shoulder before they entered the place that had become a demon stronghold.

CHAPTER 54

"You're a pharim, aren't you?" Lina asked as they walked through the grounds of the keep.

"What?"

"When you were arguing about the fight with Sharim, Osmund said we had at least one pharim with us. At least. He was looking at you when he said it."

Jez glared at Osmund, but the other boy pretended not to notice. He sighed. "It's a long story. The short version is that I have a pharim's soul. It makes me stronger, but I can't use its power all the time."

"How—"

"Not now," Jez said. "If we survive, I'll tell you."

"Jez…" Osmund started.

"I think by then, I'll know I can trust her."

Osmund nodded. Lina looked from him to Jez but didn't press the point further. Like the entrance to the grounds, the main door to the keep had been torn away, and they passed through it without raising an alarm.

The keep was curiously empty. Most of the doors had been torn off their hinges, and in a few places a particularly heavy demon had left a clawed footprint in the stone. The smell of sulfur permeated the air and stone, and Jez wondered if it was possible to become used to it. They passed one of the dining rooms, and Jez peered inside. Three demons with the heads of dogs but that stood upright paced the room. A yellow summoning circle dominated the center. It flared, and a fourth demon appeared and moved to join the others.

"It's one of the other portals," Jez said. "Who knows how many he's crafted."

"We could take them out," Osmund said. "It would be four less we'd have to deal with later."

Jez considered for a second before shaking his head. "We'd only let Sharim know we're here. That circle is linked to the one in the throne room. Once we deal with that one, this one should go away too."

"And them?" Osmund asked, pointing at the demons.

"I'm not really sure," Jez said. "Our first priority needs to be closing the main portal, though."

Osmund nodded, and they continued toward the throne room. A few seconds later, the dog demons padded out of the room. They looked right at Jez, and their noses twitched. Jez's breath caught in his throat, and he looked at Lina.

"Are you disguising our smell?"

She uttered something under her breath and shook her head. "I didn't think of it. Did they notice us?"

Jez was about to say he didn't know when one of the creatures howled and bounded toward them. The others followed a second later. Instantly, Ziary rushed forward to meet them. The demons' arms were so long they dragged on the floor as they ran. When Ziary got close, one of them threw itself onto his sword. The gesture so surprised him that he paused. It was only for an instant, but it was enough, and the other three barreled into him, two sinking their teeth into his legs and one biting down on his sword arm. His sword went skittering and vanished when it got a few feet away. Jez ran forward and brought his blade down on the one biting Ziary's arm. It collapsed to ash, leaving blackened tooth marks in Ziary's arm. The scion held out his hand, and his sword reappeared. He drove it down in a two-handed strike at the demon biting his left leg while Jez took the one on his right, and both of the demons dissolved. Ziary examined his wounds and took a shaky step forward.

"These won't heal quickly. I wasn't expecting one to sacrifice itself."

"Some demons have pack instincts," Jez said. "They care more for the group than the individual, and remember, we didn't really kill them. We just sent them back to the abyss, and right now, the way his open for them to come back as soon as the portal has recharged."

"So it's not really sacrifice," Ziary sniffed. "You know, that doesn't seem terribly fair."

Jez shrugged. "They're demons." He glanced around. "Someone would've heard that howl. Lina, can you make some sort of illusion that we went in another direction?"

She shook her head. "There are wards on the keep that make standing illusions difficult. Maybe if I had an hour."

"We don't have minutes," Jez said. "Hide us again. Let's go."

They moved through the hall quickly, keeping alert for other creatures that might be able to pierce their illusion. The few demons they saw wandering the hall, however, didn't notice them, and it wasn't long before they came to the door to the throne room.

A pair of creatures that looked like miniature versions of Flinas guarded the door, though they could only be called miniature in comparison to the larger demon. They stood eight feet tall, and their black armor almost seemed to suck in the light. Their eyes looked like empty pits. As Jez and his companions neared, the demons' eyes snapped to them. The rumble in their throat made the air vibrate against his skin.

Lina paled. "There was a ward against illusions. They can see us."

As if unleashed by Lina's words, the demons charged. Jez struck at one, but an ax made of pure shadow materialized in one of its hands and knocked his weapon aside. Another hand lashed forward and left a gash across his chest. There was a flicker of fire as Ziary's sword surged forward, and the hand holding the ax came free. The other demon, however, sank all four of its claws into the scion's chest and its teeth tore a chunk of flesh from his shoulder. Ziary cried out, but at the same time, he gripped the demon's head in his hands. The other moved to attack, but Jez intercepted it, his sword flashing. Fire burst to life between Osmund's hands. The demon roared, but it only lasted for an instant before its head was reduced to ash. Jez couldn't do much more than hold his own against the demon, but with Ziary free to help, injured though he was, some of the pressure came off of Jez. One of the demon's arms moved to stop Ziary's attack, but Jez's sword darted forward and stabbed it in the chest. The demon screamed before sliding off his blade and vanishing.

Ziary sank to the ground. He was in bad shape and bled motes of red light. His form shimmered into Osmund's for a second before solidifying itself as the scion.

"Stay here," Jez said.

Ziary shook his head. "You need all the help you can get."

"Right now, you can't give it. I'd have to protect you. You'll only get me killed."

"Jez, you know Maries is on the other side of that door. Sharim wouldn't have anyone else guarding his circle."

"I know."

"You could barely stand against one of the door guardians. How are you going to fight against their general?"

Jez closed his eyes and touched the power that had been so frightening to him. His fatigue vanished and all the aches and pains he'd gathered recently faded away. His wounds closed as power spread through him. The crystal sword in his hand didn't change weight, but it somehow seemed more solid. He could already feel the power consuming his body, but it was a slow thing, like a spark that was slowly burning a piece of parchment. As he opened his eyes, wings emerged from his back, and his robes shimmered to deep blue. When he spoke, his voice came out deep and resonating with power.

"Any way I can. Watch him, Lina. You can't do any good in there."

She looked like she was about to argue, but her lips pursed, and she nodded. Jez threw forward his hand, and the doorway twisted until the wood splintered. There was a flash of magic as the trap that had been laid on the door fizzled. Jez stepped over the remnants of the door and walked into the throne room.

CHAPTER 55

Sharim sat on the throne of Ashtar as if he'd been born to it. Rich purple robes draped down his back, and the golden band of Haziel's crown sat on his head. Maries stood by his side, and when Jez came in, the demon took a step toward him. Jez's hand shot forward as he drew on Luntayary's power, and bands of blue light appeared around the demon's wrists. Chains materialized and pulled him to the ground. Maries's groan shook the throne room. It wouldn't hold the demon for more than a few minutes, but that should be more than enough. Jez moved toward the bound creature, though he never took his eyes from Sharim.

Sharim stepped down off the throne and held his hand out. The weapon that appeared in his hand seemed to be made of liquid flame. Sharim smiled and raised his sword to Jez in a mock salute. As he stepped into the circle, the runes glowed brightly, and the portal snapped shut as Sharim redirected the power into himself. His face elongated and curved horns grew from his head, knocking the crown off. Bat-like wings emerged from his back and fire burned in his nostrils.

"You can't beat me," Jez said.

"Are you so sure? Unlike you, my memories were never bound."

"Your memories?"

Sharim launched himself into the air. He went up to the ceiling before tucking in his wings and diving at Jez. Jez cried out and barely jumped out of the way in time. The sword left a melted gash steaming in the stone floor. Sharim landed next to Jez, his sword moving in a blur, and Jez brought his own weapon to bear. There was thunder as the two swords met. Each blow shook the room, and after a few seconds, his arms throbbed. The heat from Sharim's blade was almost overwhelming, and it burned Jez's lungs to breathe.

"Who are you?" he asked as their swords clashed.

A wicked grin appeared on Sharim face. "Binding a pharim to human flesh is no simple magic. Even one as talented as Dusan couldn't improvise that. Did you really think you were the first?"

"You're a demon."

"Bound to human flesh to do things normally forbidden to my kind."

"You're like me."

"Except that I'll still be alive at the end of the day."

Sharim surged forward, and again the swords thundered. They moved like lightning. Had Jez been in his mortal form, his eyes wouldn't have been able to follow it. As it was, he could barely keep up. On top of his skill with the blade, Sharim had the power of illusion, and too often, Jez tried to block an attack that wasn't real. As the seconds ticked by, Sharim's blade left small burns where it scorched his flesh, but Jez's weapon never touched his enemy. He realized with a cold certainty that Sharim was better than he was. He needed to find a way to turn the tide.

The burning blade rushed at him. Jez's sword darted forward, trying to push it aside, but he underestimated the strength of the blow, and he only succeeded at moving it aside slightly. It stabbed into his arm, and he cried out. He sank his power into the stones of the ground. Like the ones above Lina's room, these were warded, but he was drawing on Luntayary's power, and the wards placed by the Veilspeakers recognized the power of another pharim. They melted away, and he seized the stone. The floor beneath Sharim opened, swallowing him. The ground closed around his neck, leaving only his head above the surface. Jez took a deep breath and gripped his sword, pointing it at the trapped human with a demon's soul. For the first time, he saw fear in Sharim's eyes, but then, Sharim focused on something behind Jez. Jez turned around just in time to see Maries shatter the binding holding him to the floor. The demon drew his bone blade, and charged. Jez raised his own weapon. Even drawing on Luntayary's power, he'd nearly been outclassed by Sharim, and Maries was a demon of battle. There was no way he could win.

The demon slashed downward, and Jez prepared himself to die.

CHAPTER 56

Jez caught the demon's blade on his own. It felt like he was trying to hold back a mountain, and his arms shivered with the force of the blow. Again and again, the demon rained down blows, and Jez kept expecting his sword to snap. Maries didn't have to employ any skill. The sheer strength of his blows was staggering. Jez could feel his grip loosening on his sword. The next blow would knock it free, but just before it connected, another sword lashed toward the demon. Maries twisted his blade to catch the new attack, but his sword passed through the illusionary weapon. Lina stood in the doorway, her eyes glowing violet. Jez didn't bother to acknowledge her help, not with such a powerful demon crossing blades with him. He lunged, driving his blade right at the demon's chest.

It felt like he was trying to stab through stone, and he barely managed to cut through the demon's coat. Maries snarled and turned. Jez lifted his sword and saw the blurring of his weapon that he'd noticed before. Maries's sword twisted and slammed against Jez's weapon, though not as hard as it had been before. Jez tried to strike, but Maries blocked his blow easily and, with a flick of his wrist, tore Jez's blade from his hands in the process. The weapon vanished in midair. Jez threw himself to one side but not before Maries's sword cut a gash in his arm.

Fire burned in Jez's veins as he crashed into the ground. As soon as he hit, three other images of him scattered from the point of impact. One rose and charged Maries, but the demon impaled it on his sword. He didn't even slow as he walked through it and drove his sword down into one of the other images. Jez gritted his teeth against the pain and threw his hand forward, shooting another one of the blue bands. Maries was ready for it though and caught the binding on his sword. The blade glowed blue for a second before the energy dissipated, and Maries's eyes locked on to the real Jez.

A cloth appeared over the demon's eyes just like the one that had blinded Flinas, but Maries kept on walking, and the cloth shimmered and vanished. Lina cried out and threw her hands forward. Balls of light erupted from her fingertips and circled Maries's head. The demon slashed at them, and they exploded so brightly that it hurt Jez's eyes. He scrambled to his feet and held his sword in front of him. When his vision cleared, Maries was stalking toward him, though he was moving slowly. Swords appeared in the air and flew at him, but he ignored them, and they passed harmlessly through him.

"Osmund," Lina's voice said. "He needs your help."

Ziary burst forward, flying over the room and landing between Jez and Maries. He was taller than he had been, and his sword glowed brighter. His arms were thicker and his fingers ended in sharp claws. Jez couldn't see his face, but he could imagine a snarl. All of his wounds were gone. Jez glanced at Lina, and she was frantically motioning for him to come to her. Maries looked at her and lifted a finger. The circle encompassing most of the throne room glowed. A chezamut appeared and, in response to Maries's silent command, it dashed toward Lina. She screamed and vanished, but the chezamut spread its arms wide and kept running. Lina cried out as its left arm crashed into her, causing her to reappear.

Jez was moving across the room before he realized it. His sword moved in a blur that had nothing to do with illusion. A few quick slashes removed the demon's arms before Jez rammed his sword into its head. When he looked up, Maries was walking toward them, his red eyes giving off an evil glow.

"We need a contingent," Jez said.

"What?"

"You can do illusions here, right?"

She nodded. "Once I stepped inside, the wards against them vanished."

"I need to be able to control the illusions while I'm fighting. You don't know enough about swordplay to be much help there."

"There's no time. We haven't practiced."

"Think of the chopping block."

"What?"

"The image Sharim put in our minds. He put the same one in each of us."

Maries was almost to them. Jez closed his eyes. He could feel the shackles around his arms, and his face pressed against the wood. The ax gleamed in the sunlight. It was almost impossibly complex for a contingent image. If Sharim hadn't burned it into their minds, he would've never even attempted this. Jez reached out for Lina's power, and they melded into one. This time, there was no oily darkness. He was aware of her senses, but he didn't get the disorienting double image. Her power flowed into him. He opened his eyes to see Maries's blade coming for his head. He caught the attack, grunting under the power of the blow. He drew back and lunged towards the demon's head. The bone blade lashed out, attempting to catch the image of the sword heading for Maries's stomach. He never even saw the invisible blade that bit into his neck.

His throat was so thickly muscled that Jez couldn't force the blade all the way through. The demon looked up. Brilliant red beams shot from his eyes, burning a pair of holes in the ceiling. When Maries looked back down, his eyes had gone black. The circle sputtered. Color drained from Maries's face until the skin was the same white as the uniform he wore. The medals fell off his chest and crumbled to dust when they hit the ground. The demon slid off his blade. For a moment, he stood upright, but then, like the wax of a candle that had grown just a little too hot, Maries began to melt. He seemed to say something at the last moment, but it came out as a gurgle, and he was gone.

The ground rumbled, and the portal opened for a second and spat out the battered form of Shamarion. The pharim's robes were ripped and his sword looked tarnished, but he stood up and saluted Jez. With the throne reclaimed, the royal magic withdrew. Jez screamed as his own power began to consume him. He let it go, returning to his mortal form and falling to the ground. The last thing he saw before he lost consciousness was the cracks in the stone where he'd trapped Sharim.

The demon in human flesh was gone.

CHAPTER 57

Jez woke to see the healer Paleel standing over him, her hands glowing orange. When she saw he was awake, she yelped and ran out of the room before he could say anything. Haziel came in a few minutes later. He wore new robes and had obviously bathed recently. To Jez's surprise, he bowed.

"Baron Jezreel, I owe you a great deal. Ashtar may well have fallen if not for you."

Jez glanced at Paleel. "You found the mages."

Haziel nodded. "Once Maries was free, he summoned demons that could bind their powers and imprisoned them in their own rooms."

"Flinas?"

"The demon we were fighting disappeared when we saw that red light in the sky. As far as we can tell, the rest of the demons did that too."

Jez tried to sit up, but he didn't have the strength. Haziel put a hand on his shoulder and pushed him down. "I wouldn't. The healers say you're weak. It's like you've gone days without eating. You had burns too, but the healers have taken care of those."

"Osmund? Lina?"

"They're both fine. They want to see you if you're feeling up to it. I insisted on coming in first." He smiled. "Being king does have its privileges."

Jez was feeling tired, but he managed a nod, and the king walked out into the hall. Osmund and Lina came in a second later. Osmund's arm was in a sling, and he had a bandage on his face, but otherwise he looked fine. Lina wore one of her gowns, though she no longer used an illusion to hide her scar. When she noticed him looking, she turned away, and her fingers went to her cheek.

"Sorry," he said.

She turned back and inclined her head, and her hand dropped back to her side. "No, it's nothing. After all I've seen, it seems ridiculous to spend my power hiding this, doesn't it?"

Jez grinned. "Just a little bit." He glanced at Osmund. "We never did apologize for accusing you of summoning the demon, did we?"

She shook her head. "No, but I understand why you did. Sharim fooled us all."

"All the same, I apologize. We had no right."

Jez glared at Osmund, but he only shrugged. "Technically, I never accused her. That was you."

Jez's eyes were heavy, and he wanted to rest, but this was important. "Osmund."

Osmund let out a breath, and his shoulders sagged. "Sorry Lina."

"I suppose I should apologize to you as well, for bringing you to trial." She reddened a little. "And for before, when Regis and I attacked you."

Osmund gaped at her for a few seconds, unable to speak until Lina was obviously uncomfortable under his stare.

"How is your father?" Jez asked.

Osmund blinked and, as if realizing he'd been staring, he turned back to Jez. Lina shrugged. "They say he'll be fine. There's nothing physically wrong with him. He's going back home. Mother will hire someone to care for him while she sees to the affairs of our lands." She grinned. "She's been doing that for years anyway."

"You're not going with him?"

"I think I'll go back to the Academy. I was hoping you'd permit me to ride with you."

"You're coming back?"

She glanced at Osmund. "I left because I was afraid of what he would do to me. I don't think I need to be afraid anymore." She smiled. "You know, you never apologized for that either."

"I'm sorry," Osmund said without hesitation. If Jez hadn't known Osmund as well as he did, he might've missed the sorrow in his friend's voice.

Osmund didn't meet her eyes. Lina seemed confused, but Jez understood. Nothing weighed down on Osmund's conscience so much as the actions he'd take while Ziary was out of control. He cleared his throat, and they both looked at him.

"Of course you can come with us. You've earned our trust and respect."

"What about…" she let the words hang.

"I'll tell you on the way back to the Academy. Like I said, it's a long story."

"Thank you."

"Did Shamarion say anything?"

"The pharim?"

"Yes."

She nodded. "He said to thank you. Maries's power was holding him in the abyss. When you banished Maries, you allowed him to find his own way back."

"What about Sharim?"

She shook her head. "He was gone. He must've gotten free and fled. Haziel sent men looking for him."

"They'll never find him."

"I think he knows that. He just doesn't know what else to do."

"The speaking stones are working again," Osmund said. "I contacted the masters. They'll spread the word. If he shows his face anywhere in Ashtar, we'll know."

Jez nodded, but he doubted even they would find Sharim. He'd hidden in the keep for years under the eye of an afur. He wouldn't be found unless he chose to. Jez had no doubt he would see Sharim again, though. He tried to say as much, but his words came out in a mumble. Dimly, he was aware of a healer ushering his friends out. The pillow felt wonderfully soft, and for the first time in a long time, Jez allowed himself to truly rest.

ABOUT THE AUTHOR

Gama Ray Martinez lives near Salt Lake City, Utah. He moved there solely because he likes mountains. He collects weapons in case he ever needs to supply a medieval battalion, and he greatly resents when work or other real life things get in the way of writing. He secretly hopes to one day slay a dragon in single combat and doesn't believe in letting pesky things like reality get in the way of his dreams.

Find him at http://gamarayburst.com/ as well as http://www.facebook.com/gamarayburst

www.ingramcontent.com/pod-product-compliance
Lightning Source LLC
Chambersburg PA
CBHW020304030826
48979CB00027B/2119/J

* 9 7 8 1 9 4 4 0 9 1 1 2 5 *